The W
Who Knew

Debbie Viggiano

Foreword

The subject of clairvoyance and the whole *trying-to-peek-into-the-future* thing, is fascinating! Research was fun, not least because it included a visit to charming psychic, Anne Sharman. Unlike the character Madam Rosa, Anne does not claim to be a woman who knows everything. However, she certainly knows a lot! My tarot reading revealed much, including an impending trauma. Shortly afterwards, my computer not only crashed, but was lost by UPS Couriers somewhere between PC World's warehouse and the contracted repairer – and with it the manuscript for *The Woman Who Knew Everything*. At the time of writing, I still await news of my computer's whereabouts. Investigation has been met with the same urgency as a tortoise racing in the Grand National.

My fabulous writer friend, Madalyn Morgan, came to the rescue with an earlier draft copy which I'd emailed over before techie disaster struck. Thank you, Maddie, for reading the manuscript and pointing out bloopers, which included a passion for repeating words like *clearly, immediately, so-called, instantly* and *actually*. I'm clearly blind to them, but I immediately removed these so-called words so that instantly the MS was actually stronger!

A big thank you also goes to the gorgeous Joanne Fleming for the loan of her eagle eyes regarding spelling and grammar.

Thank you to my patient son, Robert Coveney, for designing the mock-up cover after trawling through hundreds of images for the fortune-teller and her glowing crystal ball. Special thanks to the brilliant Cathy Helms at Avalon Graphics, who waved her magic wand and turned it into a book jacket.

A massive thank you to the wonderful Rebecca Emin at Gingersnap Books for meeting a horribly tight deadline, and turning the manuscript into both an e-book and paperback.

And finally, my sincere thanks to you, my lovely reader. I hope you enjoy this tale, that it makes you smile, and root for the three best friends looking for love and what the future holds.

Debbie xx

To Maddie with love

Chapter One

'Well I don't know about your Christmas,' huffed Amber, thumping her handbag down on her desk, 'but mine was decidedly second-rate.' She shrugged off her coat and slung it over the back of her typing chair. With little enthusiasm, she leant forward and flicked on her dusty monitor. 'Please tell me at least one of us had a marriage proposal before Big Ben bonged the midnight hour?' Amber raised her eyebrows at work colleagues Chrissie and Dee.

Chrissie, sitting at the desk opposite Amber's, shook her head. 'There was definitely no engagement ring in any of the Christmas crackers I pulled.'

Dee, sitting side-on to Amber and Chrissie, waved her ring-less fingers in the air. 'I'm still a single lady.'

'Never mind,' said Chrissie sympathetically. 'Perhaps the three of us will have Valentine proposals instead. The fourteenth of February is only six weeks away.'

'Girls,' said Amber, 'the three of us have been living with our men for ages. If they haven't proposed by now, maybe they never will.'

'Perhaps *we* should propose to *them*?' Chrissie suggested.

'That's a good idea,' said Dee. 'Is it a leap year?' For her, the idea of going down on one knee to her boyfriend seemed full of possibility. Although Dee could imagine Josh looking faintly horrified as he pointed out that weddings cost money. A *lot* of money. Dee had secretly been squirrelling away some of her wages every month for the last three years, in case Josh ever had a funny turn and suddenly wanted her to be Mrs Dee Coventry. Her savings wouldn't pay for anything lavish, but she'd

1

happily settle for a second-hand gown off e-Bay, and say "I do" in the local registry office with only immediate family and close friends. Afterwards they could all go to the local pub's function room for a slap-up meal. A wedding didn't have to cost thousands of pounds. The important thing was *who* you married, not *how* you married.

'Well I'm not proposing,' said Amber grumpily. Her fingers tapped at the keyboard and she logged in. 'It's a man's job. I want Matthew whisking me off for a weekend somewhere staggeringly beautiful, preferably where it's warm and sunny.' A misty picture formed in her mind. There would be emerald green fields carpeted with golden buttercups. Overhead a lemon sun would beam down on her and Matthew as they walked – naturally in slow motion – their hands linked as they laughed at some private joke. Then Matthew would pull her towards him, tenderly cup her face with his hands, all the while admiring the way golden sunlight haloed his girlfriend's fair hair. He would lower his head to her upturned cherry lips, and kiss her lovingly. Then, like the ultimate conjurer, Matthew would produce a Tiffany ring from thin air – ta da! In a sexy, husky voice he would declare his undying love, and beg Amber to be his lawfully wedded wife.

The picture faded and Amber grimaced. Tiffany rings might not be on the agenda if Matthew's Christmas present had been anything to go by. She'd been stunned for all the wrong reasons when he'd presented her with a tantalising little box. Her heart rate had tripled as she'd taken the proffered gift, checking Matthew's expression for clues. He'd been smiling. Good sign. With increasing excitement, she'd tugged off the ribbon and gift wrap. Her hands had trembled as, giddy with anticipation, she'd lifted the lid on the box...to find a £9.99 pair of hoop earrings from Argos. She knew how much they'd cost because she'd checked their website. After that Amber's Christmas had no more sparkle than a can of flat cola. Hell, she'd be thirty next birthday. Chrissie and Dee, both two years younger than herself, had the luxury of time on their side. If Matthew didn't hurry up and get on with it, she'd be creaking up the aisle on a walking stick en-route to the post office for her pension.

Chrissie was inclined to agree with Amber when it came to proposals. At heart she was an old-fashioned girl and wanted an old-fashioned proposal. She and Andrew had been together for five-and-a-half years. In the beginning their relationship had been full of passion, laughter and impulsive romantic gestures. Granted, things changed when you got down to the nuts and bolts of living together. She couldn't remember the last time they'd stared at each other with dewy eyes over the cornflakes, or when they'd last tumbled into bed and bonked like spring bunnies, but they loved each other. Didn't they? Although these days the dewy eyes seemed to have turned into scowling on Andrew's part, and the bunny rabbit bonking had become an infrequent coupling that was more perfunctory than passionate. On the rare occasions it happened, it had left Chrissie totally unsatisfied. She pushed those thoughts away. She didn't like to admit it to herself, never mind to Dee and Amber, but her relationship with Andrew was in the doldrums.

'So what's wrong with us, girls?' Amber demanded. 'Why haven't our men proposed?'

'I suspect,' said Dee, 'they're perfectly happy in their current comfort zones. Anyway, you know how that saying goes. "If it ain't broke, don't fix it." Look at Angelina Jolie and Brad Pitt. Lived together for eons, but were barely married for five minutes.

Some wedding rings become a circle of doom.'

'Rubbish!' Amber scoffed.

'Talking of wedding rings,' said Dee conspiratorially, 'over the Christmas break I spotted a certain person at Bluewater shopping mall peering into the window of a wedding ring shop. She was on the arm of a much younger man.'

'Are you by any chance talking about Cougar Kate?' asked Chrissie.

'The very one and same,' said Dee, with a nod.

Cougar Kate, whose real name was Katherine Colgan, was the office siren at Hood, Mann & Derek Solicitors. Amber, Chrissie and Dee had worked for the Gravesend law firm ever since leaving college with their secretarial qualifications. They'd seen staff come and go. They'd also witnessed Katherine Colgan's arrival after she'd sailed through the interview with the senior partner, Clive Derek. Nobody had been surprised at Katherine being a hit with the smarmy Clive. He was the office wolf. He was such a Lothario that if someone had draped a short skirt around his executive chair, he'd have waggled his eyebrows at its metal legs. Katherine Colgan had wowed Clive with her low-cut blouse, brightly lipsticked mouth, and enormous false eyelashes that she'd fluttered so quickly Amber had made a snide comment about tipping Katherine upside-down and using her to sweep the floor. Rumours were always circulating about Katherine. There were tales of her having had an affair with Clive Derek. The gossip was further fuelled by whispers that his wife had caught Katherine in a restaurant with Clive, and made free with several glasses of wine. Katherine always defended herself insisting men misread the signals she gave off.

'What did the guy on her arm look like?' asked Amber curiously.

'Not sure,' said Dee. 'I only saw the back of him.'

'Then how do you know he was younger than her?' asked Chrissie.

Dee tilted her head in the manner of one considering. 'Well, for starters he wasn't bald. In fact, he had a lovely head of thick hair. It reminded me of your Matthew,' Dee said to Amber. 'And he was slim – no love handles like most middle-aged men. Oh, and he had a very pert bum,' she added.

'Perhaps,' said Chrissie, 'Katherine has finally found the man of her dreams.'

'Yeah,' said Amber cynically, 'but we all know that where Cougar Kate is concerned, her boyfriend usually belongs to another woman.'

'Or,' added Dee, 'another woman's fiancé...or even another woman's husband.'

'As long as she keeps her cougar paws off my Matthew,' said Amber with a sniff, 'peace shall remain within the walls of this building.'

The three women briefly fell silent as they cast their minds back to the Christmas before last. Hood, Mann & Derek had announced there would be an office party and that members of staff were welcome to bring their other halves. Everybody had piled into the boardroom at half past five on the dot, devouring the buffet and hoovering up champagne. Then somebody had produced speakers and suddenly there was music. Everybody, partners included, had danced around the boardroom wearing paper crowns and singing off-key. It had descended into a massive piss-up with the young office clerk drunkenly jumping onto the photocopier. He'd printed off two-hundred copies of his bare bum captioned with "World's Biggest Arsehole" before stapling them all over Clive Derek's office walls. And young Jessica, from Accounts, had grabbed nerdy junior partner Alan Mann by the tie and pulled him into the stationery cupboard, just as someone else was vomiting into

5

Reception's feature potted plant. To top it all off, Katherine Colgan had undone another two buttons on her blouse and made a direct play for Amber's boyfriend. When Matthew had protested he wasn't into "older women", Katherine had turned an unfetching shade of magenta and spat, 'I'm a cougar, *darling*,' coining her nickname.

Amber had been incensed and shoved the remains of a salmon quiche into Katherine's face whereupon Amber's boss, Steve Hood – who'd been the least drunk of them all – had flicked on the overhead fluorescent lights and called time.

'At least Katherine apologised to you the following morning,' said Chrissie.

'Chuffing right too,' Amber growled.

There had been no Christmas party this year on the grounds of cutbacks and a need to tighten financial belts. In reality, the partners had decided to boycott it. There had been a nasty episode on the morning after the party with an elderly female client. Mrs Fosberry had arrived early at Hood, Mann & Derek for an appointment with Clive Derek. She'd been directed to Clive's office to wait. Upon seeing the clerk's captioned backside plastered all over the walls, Mrs Fosberry had suffered a mild coronary. The paramedics had barely finished strapping the pensioner on a stretcher, when the junior partner's wife had turned up in a rage. Mrs Mann had cannoned into a paramedic, tripped over the stretcher and landed on the gasping Mrs Fosberry. Hauling herself up, Mrs Mann had demanded to know who "sodding Jessica" was and why "sodding Jessica's" telephone number had been tucked into her "sodding husband's" suit jacket that she was taking to the dry cleaner. Fortunately, the client had lived and Alan Mann's marriage had survived. However, the partners had mutually agreed the rumpus hadn't been good publicity for the firm. There would be no more Christmas parties.

At that moment the door to the girls' shared office opened and Cougar Kate walked in. 'Morning,' trilled Katherine. 'Happy New Year to you all! I trust everyone had a good Christmas?' She beamed at them one by one. 'Just thought I'd pop by while things are relatively quiet, and invite you all to my birthday celebration this Saturday evening.'

Three sets of eyebrows shot up into three hairlines. Since when had Cougar Kate ever been Kate the Mate?

'Oh, er, I'm not sure if I'm already doing someth–' began Chrissie.

'Cancel it,' Katherine ordered. 'I won't hear any of you say no. Firstly, it's my fortieth. Secondly, instead of having a big bash, I'm doing something really alternative. I'm having a psychic evening!'

'A what?' asked Dee.

'You know...a fortune teller... a clairvoyant,' Katherine explained. '"Madam Rosa" will be reading auras, palms and tarot cards in my very own front room. One-hundred per-cent accuracy guaranteed.'

The girls exchanged looks before Amber answered for them all. 'Count us in. We want to know if our other halves will ever propose.'

'Don't we all, sweetie,' said Katherine with a big smile. She had large teeth that reminded Amber of Bruce the shark in *Finding Nemo*. Hungry... predatory. 'Good, that's settled then. I'll ping you all an email with my home address. See you!' And with that she turned on her heel, shutting the door quietly after her.

'Did you hear that?' asked Dee. '*She* wants to know if *she's* going to get proposed to as well. So that guy I saw on her arm outside the wedding ring

7

shop must be her beau after all.'

'Bully for her,' said Amber sourly. 'On the plus side, if Cougar Kate is loved-up she'll leave our men alone.'

'Surely you don't believe all that clairvoyant nonsense.' Chrissie rolled her eyes.

'Who knows,' said Dee, wistfully thinking of her secret wedding savings. 'But I would certainly like to believe it. Roll on Saturday night.'

Chapter Two

Amber slotted her key into the front door of her neat terraced house. The place was in darkness. Matthew wasn't home. Again. He seemed to be coming in later and later. Not that it was *late* late, but at quarter-past six in the evening he used to beat Amber home by half an hour. Up until a few months ago she'd come home to a smiling boyfriend who'd already started cooking their dinner. They would eat together whilst snuggled up in front of the telly. Afterwards, Amber would make her contribution by clearing up the kitchen and doing some ironing. Then she would go upstairs and run a deep bubble bath which they'd share together. Matthew's long legs would stick out at right-angles to her shoulders. She'd always been given the luxury of lying back, because Matthew had insisted on taking the end with the taps.

Amber wondered how late Matthew would be tonight. Unlike her employers, who always closed from Christmas Eve right the way through to the third day of January, Matthew had returned to work the day after Boxing Day. Between then and New Year's Eve he'd arrived home at eight, half past eight, nine o'clock, half past nine, and then not at all. Amber hadn't told anybody that she'd spent the last night of the year on her own. She'd hugged Mr Tomkin, her cat, and sobbed into his ginger fur. Matthew's excuses were always the same. Work, work, work. Busy, busy, busy.

Like Amber, Matthew worked locally. His career in digital marketing had its moments of stress, as did all jobs. But Amber wasn't sure if she believed Matthew's recent excuses. There was the one about Matthew's boss demanding the team stay longer at the office to reach their end-of-year targets. Okay, that sounded plausible. But then there had been the rather far-fetched one about going for a few drinks with workmates on New Year's Eve, completely forgetting what day it was, accidentally getting blotto, and crashing on a mate's couch. Matthew's justification had been fluently delivered, and Amber had desperately wanted to believe it, even though she suspected Matthew was lying. On New Year's Eve, she'd rung his mobile more than thirty times. At first her calls had been hesitant and apologetic. But, as worry kicked in, her voicemails had become tearful and frantic.

Stifling a yawn, she walked into the kitchen and rummaged through the freezer. Thanks to the Christmas break and bank holidays, the first week of the New Year at Hood, Mann & Derek had been only three days. It had felt like three months. And now, on the cusp of the weekend, Amber couldn't wait to have a long luxurious sleep-in. Her fingers hovered over a couple of steak-and-kidney pies. Should she cook one or two? Matthew used to order a takeaway for them both on a Friday night. Recently he'd stopped doing that. Amber was instantly reminded of another reason Matthew had given for lateness. On the Friday before Christmas he'd arrived home with his breath reeking of onion bhajis. He'd blamed his boss yet again for making him and the team work late. Matthew had explained away the smell of spices by saying a colleague had volunteered to get a take-out from the Star of India. The restaurant was right next to their offices. Matthew said he'd been grateful to his colleague because no-one had gone hungry whilst toiling away at their desk. Amber had made suitable noises about being glad Matthew wasn't famished, and how thoughtful Matthew's colleague was, and how awful his boss was starting to be. Matthew had arranged his features into one of weary acceptance

10

and said, 'It will all be worth it in the long run. The next promotion is bound to be mine.'

Amber's thoughts fragmented as Mr Tomkin shot through the cat flap. He yowled a greeting and began to weave around her ankles, head-butting her legs.

'Hello,' she cooed, stooping to stroke his soft head. 'At least one of the men in my life has turned up for some dinner.'

She removed two steak-and-kidney pies from the freezer. She'd cook both anyway. So what if one wasn't eaten? Matthew could always re-heat it tomorrow when she went out with Chrissie and Dee to Cougar Kate's psychic evening. Amber peered in the cupboard under the sink where Mr Tomkin's cat food was kept. She withdrew a sachet of rather stinky flaked fish.

'Someone's a lucky boy having a trout treat this evening,' she said to the purring cat, and set the dish down for him. Her mind wandered to another trout, and most definitely an old one. Cougar Kate. Amber couldn't stand her. From the moment Katherine Colgan had arrived at Hood, Mann & Derek, Amber's "people radar" had gone haywire. Amber was someone who could suss a person in five seconds flat, but she'd figured out Katherine Colgan in half a heartbeat. The woman had "devious" stamped all over her, from her heavily made-up face to her pumped-up silicon breasts. When Katherine Colgan had arrived for her interview with Clive Derek, Amber had been in Reception collecting a "by hand" courier delivery. Amber had watched with interest as Clive had greeted Katherine, his eyes lighting up like Harrod's at Christmastime. Katherine had simpered a greeting and extended one hand. For one ridiculous moment Clive had looked like he was going to press Katherine's hand to his lips. The stupid idiot. Amber hadn't been remotely surprised at Katherine and Clive's rumoured fling, and Katherine had made no secret of the fact that she was looking for a hubby – even if he did belong to somebody else.

Amber turned the oven on and began chopping veg. Thankfully her own boss wasn't a letch. Her mind wandered to Steve Hood. He'd joined the firm a couple of years ago when Amber's old boss, Bernard Blake, retired. Amber had heaved a sigh of relief when she'd been informed by Human Resources that her new boss would be Mr Stephen Hood. She'd been a bit twitchy about old Bernard retiring in case she'd been made redundant. Steve was everything dear old Bernard wasn't – thirty years younger, a whole foot taller, and extremely good-looking. Steve had opted to leave the rat-race of London and work closer to his home in the picturesque village of Culverstone Green. Within a year he'd been made a partner. Amber would not have passed a Jeremy Kyle lie-detector test if the presenter himself had stuck a microphone under her nose and asked whether she had a crush on Steve Hood. *All* the secretaries had a crush on Steve Hood. What was there not to like, especially as he was so eligible. Despite having now worked for Steve these last two years, she still didn't know much about him. She smiled as she remembered the last day of their first week working together.

'See you on Monday,' Amber had trilled, pulling on her coat.

'Sure. Have a nice weekend,' Steve had replied.

'Up to anything nice?'

'Yes, chilling out.'

'Doing what?'

'Absolutely nothing if I can help it.'

'Nice. But won't Mrs Hood expect you to mow the lawn and wash the cars?'

He'd grinned. 'No. There isn't a Mrs Hood, and I

pay a man to mow the lawn, and I take my car to the car wash.'

Amber had secretly been thrilled to hear there was no Mrs Hood, although she didn't know why she'd felt that way. After all, she had her own boyfriend thank you very much, and one she was hoping to eventually marry. But she'd persisted in her nosiness with Steve Hood.

'So, doing anything nice with your girlfriend on Saturday night?'

'I have plans, but not with the girlfriend.'

Amber had pulled a face. 'Aw, that's not very nice. I hope she's not annoyed that you're not spending time with her.'

'No,' he'd smiled at Amber's dogged questioning. 'The girlfriend definitely won't be put out because there is no girlfriend.'

'Oh, right,' Amber had said casually as she'd zipped up her coat. There had been something about Steve's tone that had been friendly but firmly polite in letting her know he wasn't answering any more questions. She'd deduced there and then that Steve Hood must be gay, which was probably just as well. Amber hadn't told anybody about how her heart had bounced about when Steve strode past her desk and said, 'Good morning, Amber,' in his deep sexy voice. She'd even been a little bit fanciful thinking that perhaps his accompanying smile had been just for her. It had certainly made her knees wobble when she'd gone off to the staff kitchen to make his morning coffee. She truly hadn't liked Steve playing havoc with her emotions. It had made her feel disloyal to Matthew. Since then, whenever she'd enquired on a Monday morning if Steve had had a nice weekend, she'd not been surprised to hear he'd had a great time cycling with a mate, or fishing *with a mate*, or hitting golf balls *with a mate*, or playing football *with a mate*. She'd heaved a sigh as she'd organised a Land Registry search, privately lamenting that it was always the good-looking guys who were gay. Two years later her heart still leapt with joy at the sight of Steve every morning, but knowing he was gay meant she no longer became flustered.

As she scraped carrots, the landline rang, bringing her back to the present. She quickly wiped her hands before snatching up the phone.

'Hello?'

'It's me,' said Matthew.

'Hi.' Amber felt her tummy start to knot. Interesting. Since when had her boyfriend's lateness affected her so much that butterflies took off in her stomach for all the wrong reasons?

'Don't bother cooking for me. I have to work late.'

'Again?' Amber's shoulders sagged. She'd allowed herself to get carried away with the vegetable peeling. She'd never eat all this. 'Why?'

When Matthew spoke again he sounded impatient. 'Because I'm trying to further my career, Amber. Surely you realise that? I'm doing this for us. It would be helpful if you were supportive instead of sounding like a nag.'

Stunned, Amber opened her mouth to say something but then shut it again. The last thing she wanted was Matthew thinking she didn't support him. After all, if he achieved promotion he'd receive a salary increase. And hadn't he said he was "doing this for us"? A beam of hope flickered through her. If Matthew was promoted and received a salary increase, maybe he'd think about putting a ring on her finger – instead of two rings through her earlobes.

'Sorry,' Amber apologised. 'I didn't mean to sound annoyed, darling. I'm a little disappointed. I haven't spent a proper evening with you for, well, it seems like ages.'

'Sometimes these things can't be helped,' Matthew huffed. 'And before you ask, I'll be going to the office tomorrow as well.'

'But tomorrow is Saturday!'

'Yes, Amber, I do know what day comes after Friday, and there you go again. Whining.'

'N-no, I'm not,' said Amber quickly. 'I'm just surprised, sweetie.' Her voice was placating, and she hated herself for it. Shouldn't Matthew be the one placating her?

'There's a big account up for grabs. I want to make sure I'm the one who gets it. I probably won't be home until early evening. I know you like us to go out on a Saturday night, but I'll be too tired. Sorry.'

'That's fine,' said Amber, deciding to play it cool. 'I'd suspected you might be doing something like that, so don't worry. I wouldn't have been able to go out with you on Saturday evening anyway. I have my own arrangements.' Amber felt a smidgen of satisfaction that she was turning the tables for one night. This time it would be Matthew alone at home with only Mr Tomkin for company.

'Oh?' Matthew sounded surprised. 'Where are you going?'

Amber felt a burst of happiness. *Matthew does care about what I'm up to after all*! 'I'm out with Chrissie and Dee. We're going to Cougar Kate's.'

From the other end of the phone came silence. When Matthew eventually spoke, he sounded puzzled. 'Who?'

'You must remember her! She was at the office Christmas party. Don't tell me you can't recall the woman who launched herself at you?' When Matthew didn't speak, Amber prodded his memory. 'She had a trout pout and plastic bosoms like a life-size Barbie doll.' Amber couldn't help being

15

derogatory where that woman was concerned. At the other end of the phone the silence continued. Clearly Matthew was having trouble recalling who Amber was sniping about. 'Her proper name is Katherine Col–'

'Yes, I remember now,' Matthew interrupted. 'What on earth are you doing spending Saturday night with her? I thought you couldn't stand her?'

'I can't,' Amber confessed. 'But she absolutely insisted we all attend her fortieth birthday celebration.'

'Fortieth?' Matthew made a harrumphing sound. 'Surely she means *fiftieth*.'

Amber grinned. 'I thought it was only women who had the monopoly on being bitchy!' This was more like it. The two of them were having a joke at Cougar Kate's expense.

'What exactly will you all be doing when you get together?' asked Matthew curiously.

'She's having a psychic evening. Some woman in a head-scarf and gypsy earrings is going to tell everyone their fortune. Cougar Kate has a secret lover. She made some comment about wanting to know if he was ever going to–' Amber ground to a halt. She didn't want to mention the words "propose marriage". Otherwise Matthew might put two and two together and realise that she, too, was hoping for a bit of information about whether or not her near future would be full of wedding bells. Getting your boyfriend to put a ring on your finger, especially a boyfriend like Matthew, required the softly-softly approach. 'Er, she wants to know if...her lover will leave his wife.'

Matthew snorted. 'What a load of tosh. You don't honestly believe all that twaddle, do you?'

'No, of course not,' said Amber hastily. Even if this Madam Rosa did tell Amber that Matthew would eventually want to whisk her down the

16

nearest aisle, the fact was Amber wouldn't really believe it until it happened. She wasn't that gullible.

'Well have fun at your psychic evening tomorrow with...whatever-she's-called...Clapped Out Kate,' said Matthew, suddenly brisk. 'Meanwhile, I'll see you later tonight.'

'Bye, darling,' said Amber. 'I love y–'

But she was talking to herself. Matthew had already rung off. Amber's buoyed-up emotions popped like a soap bubble. For a couple of minutes there she'd kidded herself everything between them was okay.

Returning the handset to its cradle, she stared at the pile of veg on the chopping board. Since when had her relationship changed from love and fun to, well, indifference? She didn't know. These days Matthew was more like a brother, and an irritable one at that. It had happened so slowly she'd not even noticed. Never had she felt so miserable.

Filling the steamer with water, she tipped the veg into the top pan and put the lid on. Suddenly she was glad she was seeing this acclaimed psychic. Maybe, just maybe, Madam Rosa would be totally brilliant, read Amber's palm and say, 'Your boyfriend is a gem. He's hard-working and saving every penny for a secret wedding you know nothing about. One day very soon you're going to get the surprise of your life. Hang in there!'

Amber didn't really believe in all that nonsense. However, she was so desperate for crumbs of information about her relationship, she was prepared to give Madam Rosa the benefit of the doubt. Roll on tomorrow night.

Chapter Three

Chrissie slotted her key into the front door of the crumbling maisonette she shared with Andrew. Their home was on a sprawling council estate on the outskirts of Gravesend. She was desperate to move. She'd love a house like Amber's – a dear little two-up-two-down in New Ash Green, complete with chocolate-box sized garden filled with flowering tubs. Amber's home was surrounded by woodland pathways and restful fields. By contrast, Chrissie's estate was bounded by a network of roads punctuated with industrial parks and chimneys that constantly belched smoke.

The estate, no matter what hour of the day or night, was never quiet. Many of its residents were unemployed. There was always somebody playing music at three in the morning, or hanging out on a street corner doing a dodgy deal, or having a domestic indoors, or screaming at their kids – like Fran on the other side of the maisonette's dividing wall. At least twice a week a police siren wailed through the meandering roads that criss-crossed like scars on a convict's face. The Old Bill's flickering light would flash against Chrissie's bedroom curtains, like a blue spaceship coming in to land.

For Chrissie, the only plus for living here was the bus stop directly outside the estate. Monday to Friday the local transport service rumbled all the way into town dropping her outside the front door of Hood, Mann & Derek. Fortunately, the fares weren't too pricey. Which was just as well, because Andrew was always asking Chrissie to bail him out of financial trouble. He had a credit card that delivered a regular statement full of spiralling figures. More often than not he couldn't meet its monthly minimum payment. Chrissie couldn't remember the last time Andrew had paid his share of the rent. His contribution to the grocery bill was getting smaller by the week. She couldn't understand what he did with his money. After all, he worked. He kept telling her that electricians didn't make very much, but she was sure they earned a lot more than a secretary working for Gravesend solicitors. Sometimes Andrew did the odd private job, but where the money went she didn't know. Once she'd dared to ask, and Andrew had got very stroppy. He'd irritably countered that he didn't ask how she spent her wages, so to quit nagging how he spent his. She'd answered him back and said, 'It's quite obvious how I spend my wages – I pay for your share of things.' He'd punished her bluntness by ignoring her for an entire week. In the end Chrissie had been the one to deliver a grovelling apology to smooth things over.

Chrissie loved Amber and Dee like sisters. It went without saying they were both her best friends. However, she hadn't confided in them about how Andrew really was. Why? Because she was ashamed. Instead she painted a picture of him being a hard-working guy, one who didn't take her out because he was always busy with private weekend jobs to supplement their income. She also made out they were saving up to get on the property ladder, which legitimately excused her from Amber and Dee's occasional trips to Bluewater shopping mall. Her besties thought nothing of blowing twenty quid on a lipstick they didn't need, but had to have because they liked the colour.

Chrissie spent her wages on essentials, never frivolity. Her wardrobe for work was a supermarket clothing brand. It was more affordable than the garments hanging on the mannequins of Bluewater's brightly lit shops. To Chrissie, the enormous mall was a slice of heaven. She'd love nothing more than to join Amber and Dee as they went into shoe shop after shoe shop and deliberated whether to buy Ugg boots in tan or black. She couldn't imagine spending over a hundred pounds on such an item. Instead Chrissie had bought herself cheap imitations from e-Bay at ninety-nine pence.

As Chrissie entered the maisonette's narrow, cramped hallway, the television blared from the lounge. She stuck her head around the door to greet Andrew. He was sprawled in an armchair, a can of lager in one hand. On the floor, by his feet, were two empty tins.

'Hi,' she smiled.

'Hello,' he replied, and belched loudly. 'What's for dinner? I'm starving.'

Chrissie lived in hope that one day she'd walk in and find the table laid and a hot meal awaiting her. That was what Amber said her boyfriend did for her. Lucky Amber. How she'd love a boyfriend like Matthew. No wonder Amber was desperate to wed him. He was so hard working. So caring. Chrissie wanted to marry simply because that was how she'd been brought up. Her parents had expounded the virtues of keeping her head down at school in order to bag a decent job. They'd also suggested it was through the work place one met a like-minded person with similar values. Their lessons to Chrissie had been simple: study, date, become engaged, marry, have children, then bring your own children up to do exactly the same thing you'd done. But somehow the game plan with Andrew had gone wrong.

They'd met at college when he'd been studying to be a spark and she'd been on her secretarial course. Chrissie had been instantly attracted to the good-looking lad with the floppy fringe, and he'd made a bee-line for her. So far, so good. They'd moved into the maisonette together not long after they'd both started work. Previously, Andrew's divorced aunt had lived in it, but she'd met and subsequently married a much older man with an enormous pension pot. She'd moved into her new husband's house but, rather than relinquish the maisonette, she'd opted to illegally sub-let the council property to Andrew and Chrissie at a discounted rate. The maisonette was meant to be a stop-gap home while they saved up for their own property. But somewhere along the way Andrew had settled into a routine of going to the pub for darts nights, or PlayStation games on a rota with other beer-swilling buddies.

Chrissie absolutely hated it when it was Andrew's turn to 'host' a games evening. The lounge would be filled with burly men stabbing at consoles, carrying on like they were Darth Vader taking over new universes. Invariably, on those nights, Chrissie would absent herself. She'd climb into bed with an old paperback that Dee had finished with, only to nod off but then be awoken in the early hours by the stink of weed creeping through the gap under the bedroom door. Last time around she'd caused a bit of a rumpus. How dare Andrew let these men outstay their welcome *and* stink her home out with illegal substances!

Throwing back the thin duvet she'd marched, bug-eyed and sporting bed-hair, towards the lounge. The door had crashed back on its hinges startling everybody.

'That's IT!' she'd bellowed. 'Some of us have work in the morning. Get your feet off my chairs and shift your backsides out of my house, NOW. And take your funny fags with you – do you HEAR?'

Andrew had been appalled. He'd squinted at her through the fug, his eyes glassy from dope, as one of

21

his mates had rounded furiously on Chrissie.

'Fuck me, Andy. Is this yer missus? I'd give 'er a right pasting for speaking to yer like that. It's fuckin' humiliating. What a cow.'

'GET OUT,' Chrissie had screamed. On the other side of the maisonette's wall, Fran's kids had woken up and started bawling. Seconds later Fran could be heard shrieking at them to shut up and go back to sleep.

After everyone had left, Andrew had been so disgusted he'd spat at her. Chrissie had been stunned. In the morning he'd grudgingly apologised, but remained livid that she'd laid down the law in front of his mates. The ridiculous thing was, Chrissie had ended up feeling the guilty one. Just because she didn't do recreational drugs, did that make her a prude for not allowing Andrew and his mates to "relax" with a bit of wacky-baccy? Had she really been bang out of order? Was she a harridan?

Occasionally, and it really was very occasionally, Chrissie would fantasise about being swept off her feet by some gorgeous hunk who didn't run up credit cards, didn't drink gallons of lager, didn't break wind to order, and actually gave her some attention. But another part of Chrissie pushed such thoughts away. She had no self-esteem or confidence. She didn't believe herself to be attractive, like Amber or Dee. Her long brown hair was never styled. She wore it every day in a ponytail that trailed the length of her back. She didn't have money to waste on hairdressers and highlights, and she rarely wore make-up.

'Any chance of eggs and chips?' asked Andrew, jolting her back to the present. 'I'm off to the pub in half an hour with the boys, and need something to mop up the booze.' He patted his stomach by way of explanation. 'Oh, and before I forget, the lads will be here tomorrow night. It's my turn to be host, so no barging in and kicking off.'

'That's fine,' she said stiffly. 'I'll be out.'

Andrew's eyes widened with surprise. 'Oh? I was counting on you making us all chip butties.'

'Sorry,' she shrugged.

'Do you have to go?' asked Andrew irritably.

'Yes. It's a work thing,' said Chrissie, bending the truth. 'It would be bad form not to.'

'Right,' Andrew huffed. 'Well don't let me hold you up with the egg and chips.'

Chrissie shut the door. On her way to the kitchen, she hung her coat on one of the pegs in the hall. She was twenty-seven years old, but right now felt older than Cougar Kate, although nothing like as glamorous. Ha, and she was hoping some unknown clairvoyant would have her grinning with pleasure at news of Andrew proposing!

Chrissie sighed as she set about pulling the frying pan from the cupboard and shaking oven chips on a baking tray. She couldn't leave Andrew unless she moved back home with her parents – and who wanted to go home to Mummy and Daddy at the age of twenty-seven?

This wasn't the life she wanted, but she didn't know how to extricate herself. Maybe this Madam Rosa could give her a few pointers. Roll on tomorrow night.

Chapter Four

Dee slotted her key into the front door of her Northfleet apartment. It was a pleasant low-rise block set back from the main road. She and Josh had bought it off-plan when they'd first started living together. By coincidence, it was the same block that Chrissie's brother lived in. Sometimes Chrissie would pop in on Dee after visiting her six-month-old nephew. Chrissie was besotted with the baby boy.

'I reckon it's the closest I'll ever get to having children,' Chrissie had said.

'Why? Aren't you and Andrew planning on having a little'un one day?' Dee had asked.

'Oh, yes, of course.' Chrissie had looked flustered for a moment. She'd spoken without thinking. 'But I suspect it won't be for a long time. Not until we've managed to buy our own place. I wouldn't want to raise a family where we currently live. The kids are more street-wise than sewer rats. By the time my son reached two, he'd probably be mugging other toddlers for their toys. Where I live, any child over ten is too scary for words.'

'How's the saving-up coming along?' Dee had asked.

'Nicely, thanks,' Chrissie had replied, and then swiftly changed the subject.

Dee had thought Chrissie to be very twitchy on the whole subject, so hadn't asked her friend any more personal questions.

She walked into the flat's inner hallway and slipped off her coat. Dee wouldn't mind moving. Perhaps Chrissie might be interested in buying this flat? It was light and airy with a big balcony. It afforded a pleasant view of the communal landscaped area to the rear. However, it was crammed with hers and Josh's belongings. The longer they lived here, the longer starting a family would be a non-event. Such plans required a second or even third bedroom, and preferably a little garden. Dee loved Amber's green postage-stamp lawn bordered by shrubs and blooms. It was perfect for a child to play in. Some time ago she'd broached the subject of moving to Josh, but he'd shaken his head.

'Not yet, Dee. We can't afford it.'

His reply was at odds to what he grandly liked to tell people. Josh liked nothing more than showing off and telling anybody who'd listen that he was managing director of his own company. High Fliers Limited oversaw cleaning contracts. However, when you stripped away the fancy words, the reality was that Josh was a window cleaner. Even so, his earnings were good. He'd secured work with the management companies of several blocks of flats and offices in the area, which had given him the idea of the company name. Putting on a safety harness and leaping, like Spiderman, down the walls of a high-rise block to clean external windows didn't daunt him. What did scare Josh, however, was spending money. And Dee knew it. Josh was meticulous about finances. He made sure all their bills were split fifty-fifty. Josh never indulged Dee. Even if they went out, she always paid for her share of a chicken korma and glass of wine.

Dee loved working for Alan Mann in the matrimonial department at Hood, Mann & Derek, but her wage was only in line with local businesses in that part of the country. If she'd worked in London she could have doubled her salary, but she'd held off doing that until her CV could show loyalty and experience. Apart from anything else, she was now twenty-seven years old. She was very keen for Josh to make an honest woman of her before knuckling down to the business of making babies. These days it wasn't important whether babies came first and the wedding second, but either way both subjects were close to her heart. Unfortunately, as yet they weren't close to Josh's. She knew that if they went down the road of starting a family first, they'd need a bigger home. With her biological clock starting to stir, Dee thought it might be better to move first, have a family second, and finally get married. She had all the time in the world to walk down the aisle in a big white dress, but ovaries had a shelf life. Her mother had taken years to get pregnant. If Dee experienced the same problem, she wanted to ensure she was young enough to have time for tests and all the rigmarole that came with it.

She folded her coat in half and, seeing the bedroom door open, leant through the doorway and aimed the garment at the bed. It sailed through the air and landed with a gentle whoosh. The wardrobe space in their one-bedroomed apartment was at a premium. Coats took up a lot of room. These days Dee and Josh increasingly seemed to be using the top of their bed as a place to dump coats, which wasn't practical. Also, it looked messy. Josh hated untidiness. Come bedtime they'd be fighting their way through a layer of coats, jackets, and waterproofs just to get to the duvet. She decided to tackle the subject of space – as in the lack of it – with Josh later this evening. Hopefully the idea of moving would register in his brain.

Dee went into the kitchen. She hung her handbag over the corner of one of the tall stools next to the breakfast island. Now then, what to cook for dinner? She didn't want to mess about preparing from scratch. It was Friday night, and Dee wanted something quick and easy so she could later relax. Peering into the fridge, she selected a quiche, some slices of ham, and a pot of fresh potato salad. Dee was preparing a salad when she heard Josh come in.

'Wotcha,' he called.

'Hiya. I'm in the kitchen. Tea's ready.'

'Really? That's quick.' Josh appeared in the kitchen doorway.

'That's because it's a cold meal tonight,' Dee explained.

'Oh,' said Josh. The one word was loaded with annoyance. 'I was expecting something hot. In case you'd forgotten, Dee, it's January. Outside it's colder than Mr Frosty the snowman's bum. I've been working out there. All day. *Some* of us don't have the luxury of warm offices to sashay off to, or drink endless cups of coffee while we gossip with our mates.'

Dee felt peeved, but held her tongue. She supposed Josh had a point. It *was* cold outside. However, his snide words that she did nothing at work other than put the kettle on and have a tête-à-tête with Chrissie or Amber had infuriated her. She worked damned hard for Alan Mann, churning out Petitions and Statements and Affidavits and piles and piles of correspondence – not forgetting fielding calls from distraught clients. Sometimes it was a stressful job. Of *course* she enjoyed a bit of chit-chat with Chrissie and Amber, but it was hardly all day. If that were ever the case the three of them would be sacked.

Two angry blotches began to mottle her otherwise pale face. Not for the first time Dee realised that, lately, Josh tried to provoke arguments. She wondered why? Yesterday he'd complained about the heating being on, and turned it off. Josh had pursed his lips and told her to wear a fleece if she was cold – which hardly made sense after professing to be frozen due to being outside all

27

day long. The day before that Josh had asked if she'd put on weight because her face looked fat. Dee had felt incredibly hurt. There were other little digs that had occurred over the last several weeks. Her clothes were frumpy. Her short hair was unfashionable. Her conversation was boring. And no, he didn't want sex with somebody who only ever lay in the missionary position. Embarrassment whipped up the two red marks on her cheeks until her whole face felt like it was on fire. Her self-esteem was unravelling faster than dropped knitting. She gave herself a mental slap.

Come on, Dee. Buck up. Take a trip to Bluewater this weekend. Buy a ramped-up bra so your boobs are bigger than Cougar Kate's. Then push Josh backwards onto the bed, tug down his trousers and straddle him like a cello.

She picked up the plate of quiche and moved towards the microwave. 'This won't take a second to warm up.' She pressed a button and the microwave's door sprang open.

'Don't heat it up in there,' Josh warned, 'it will make the pastry soggy. I can't bear microwaved pastry.'

Dee tried not to show her frustration. It seemed she couldn't do right for wrong. 'I can put it in the oven, if you'd prefer. It will only take half an hour.'

'No, Dee. I'm hungry. I don't want to wait half an hour. Just forget it,' said Josh moodily. He turned on his heels.

'Where are you going?' Dee called after him.

'Out. I'll get myself a takeaway. Preferably one that's piping hot to warm me up.'

'Don't be silly,' she said, trotting after her boyfriend's rigid back. 'By the time you've driven to the restaurant, waited your turn in the queue, and then got back home again, the quiche would long be hot from the oven.'

'No thanks,' Josh growled. 'I don't want bloody quiche.' He stomped past the open bedroom door and saw Dee's coat lying on top of all the other coats. 'And put that little lot away,' he snapped. 'The flat looks a tip. You've turned into such a slob, Dee.'

Dee's mouth dropped open, but she hastily closed it again. Now was as good a time as any to mention the lack of space in their apartment. 'I'm sorry,' she apologised, 'but there's no room in the wardrobes. Perhaps, darling, we could spend this weekend looking on-line at some properties? It's about time we took the next step up the property ladder.'

'Absolutely not,' Josh roared. 'If space is such an issue we'll buy another wardrobe. There's plenty of room for one in the hall. Oh, and before I forget, I'm out tomorrow night.'

'Oh, that's good,' said Dee with a conciliatory tone. 'I forgot to tell you that I'm out too.' She watched as her boyfriend shoved his feet back into his work boots, and bent down to do up the laces. 'It's a girlie evening. What about you?' she gabbled, desperate to diffuse Josh's anger and get everything back to some level of calm.

'I'm schmoozing a potential client. There's several blocks of flats in Thamesmead that are run by the local council. I'm wining and dining the contracts guy and his wife.'

'That's brilliant, Josh. Well done. Don't you need me there?' Dee's brain whirred. She'd happily forego her evening at Cougar Kate's if it meant helping Josh.

Her boyfriend suddenly stopped lacing his boots. He glanced up at her in bemusement. 'Why would I need you there?'

'Well...to...to...support you. Maybe I can keep the gentleman's wife company while you talk business.'

'My mistake,' said Josh, finishing his lacing. 'His wife isn't coming.' He straightened up. 'But even if she was, I wouldn't want you there. You'd bore the pants off her.' He opened the apartment door. 'See you later.'

And then he was gone. As the door shut behind him, Dee stood in the hallway shocked to the core. Had Josh *really* said that? Her lovely, good-natured, sunny Josh? Surely, she'd imagined it? The words reverberated round and round in her brain like a merry-go-round, until she swayed with dizziness. And she wanted to marry this man and be mother to his children? As two fat tears ran down her cheeks Dee decided not to forego Cougar Kate's psychic night, even if Josh came back and kissed her feet by way of apology. She hoped this Madam Rosa was as good as Cougar Kate proclaimed, because Dee wanted to know what the hell was going on in her relationship. Roll on tomorrow night.

Chapter Five

Chrissie didn't have a car, so Dee had offered to be taxi on Saturday night and pick Chrissie up enroute to Cougar Kate's house. As Dee approached the outskirts of the council estate where her friend lived, she felt as though she'd parachuted into a scene from *Taken*. Gangs of watchful hoodies stood on every corner. Dee swung a left and then a right, sensing narrowed eyes following her vehicle. Progressing into the depths of the estate, the only thing that changed about each gang was their age. As she took another left, a mob of five stared after her. They couldn't have been more than nine years old. Since when did a group of primary school kids become so intimidating?

Dee drove past a burnt-out car. It was wrapped like a Christmas present in blue and white ribbon – except it was police tape. A few yards on, she cruised past another car that had fallen victim to prey. It was jacked-up on bricks because its wheels had been stolen. Dee continued to take various lefts and rights through the estate's maze of inner streets, before arriving at Chrissie's maisonette. Dee was most reluctant to get out of her car and ring the doorbell. She felt that if she left her vehicle for more than thirty seconds, all the gangs would converge as one and strip her car to a metal shell before she could say, 'Hoodies 'R' Us'.

Scuffing her tyres against the kerb, she opted to toot her horn. Every visible curtain in the street began twitching like a Tourette's sufferer. Dee sucked on her teeth. How the hell did Chrissie stomach living here? It was a wonder her friend had never been mugged on her own doorstep. Seconds later the maisonette's tatty front door opened. Her friend stood haloed in light from the inner hall, checking the contents of her handbag. Suddenly Chrissie blinked out of sight as two burley guys walked past Dee's car window. A second later Chrissie was back in view, but the men were walking menacingly towards her. Dee squeaked with anguish as she watched them move closer to her friend. What were they doing? Dee clenched her car's steering wheel in anguish. They looked like they were going to shove their way inside Chrissie's house, no doubt grabbing her handbag at the same time. Bloody hell. This estate was the pits. Dee was witnessing robbers oh-so-casually committing a crime. She didn't know what to do. Chrissie had spotted the approaching men. She was looking at them with a mixture of loathing and apprehension. Now they were speaking to her. Chrissie's entire body had tensed. Her face showed anguish. Dee couldn't stand it for a moment longer. Sod the car. The gangs could strip it. This was an emergency. She had to help her friend.

Dee threw open the driver's door ready to rush to the rescue, but was nearly garrotted by the seat belt. Fighting her way out of the belt's constraints, she picked up the bottle of wine she'd bought for Cougar Kate and waved it about.

'Oy. You two. Bill and Ben. Stop right there!'

The men paused. Turning, they stared unblinkingly at Dee. 'Are you talkin' to us?' said one with a growl.

Dee swaggered over to the men looking, she hoped, a lot braver than she felt. She brandished the bottle of red like a weapon of mass destruction. 'I know your game.'

'Do yer play then?'

'How dare you,' hissed Dee. 'I'm a respectable woman. Now step away from my friend.'

'Er, Dee—' said Chrissie.

'Shut up, Chrissie,' Dee snarled. 'Close your front

32

door. Slowly. No sudden movements. Don't worry about these two bozos. I have them covered. One false move and I'll bottle them.'

'Yer wot?'

'I said step away from her,' snarled Dee, waggling the bottle about. 'DO IT. NOW!'

'Fuckin' hell. Have yer got...wot does me missus call it?...oh yeah...TMP.'

'I suppose that's code for drugs, eh? No, I don't have any TMP. Do I look like somebody who carries TMP about her person?' Dee raised the bottle menacingly. Keeping her eyes on the two men, she addressed Chrissie. 'Get in the car.'

'Um, Dee—'

'JUST DO IT, CHRISSIE,' Dee roared. For the last thirty seconds, adrenalin had been whooshing around her body. The short burst of hormone had empowered her, making her feel like she could take on anyone – even these two thugs – but it was fast diminishing and could sputter out at any second. The last thing she wanted was for her legs to buckle, and her backside to thump down on this dog-shit covered pavement with these two heavies towering over her.

Chrissie obediently scuttled over to the car. Dee waited until she'd heard the sound of the passenger door open and close. Good. Her friend was safe. She gave one final shake of the bottle, eyes not leaving the brutes' scowling faces.

'If my friend returns home to find her house has been burgled, I'll seek you two out. I have a very particular set of skills,' she dared to prod one of the men with the neck of the wine bottle, 'skills I have acquired over a very long career. Skills that make me a nightmare for people like you. If you leave my friend alone,' Dee seemed to have morphed into Liam Neeson, 'I will not look for you. I will not pursue you. But if you don't, I *will* look for you, I *will* find you, and I will–'

'Oh piss off, you silly tart.'

At that moment the door to the maisonette flew open and Andrew stood there. He saw Dee and gave a polite wave before addressing the two men.

'Are you two coming in or what?' he asked them. 'Everyone else is here and waiting.'

Dee blanched. Oh dear God. 'I-I'm so terribly sorry,' she stuttered to the men. 'You're right. I had some TMP after all. It's a bastard. Here,' she proffered the wine bottle to the man nearest to her. He flinched away. 'Peace offering.'

'Ta,' said the other man, snatching the wine. 'If Chrissie hangs out with nutters like you, no wonder she has attitude problems. Thank fuck yer not my wife.'

'Yes,' said Dee, her voice wobbling. 'Thank...fuck.'

She yanked open the driver's door, practically threw herself inside, then hit the central locking button. 'Sorry about that,' she gasped.

Chrissie was looking po-faced. 'I kept trying to tell you, but you wouldn't let me speak. They're Andrew's friends.'

'Yes,' Dee gulped. 'I've since gathered.'

'When he finds out you were threatening to put two of his mates in hospital, he'll probably ban me from ever speaking to you again.'

'Then let's hope Bill and Ben don't tell him.'

Chrissie's shoulders began to shake. She was laughing. 'Can we get out of here? And make it quick. Before Andrew comes roaring out and hauls me back inside on the grounds of me fraternising with a lunatic.'

'Done,' said Dee, as the car engine burst into life. Her tyres squealed away from the kerb as she wrestled with the steering wheel. 'Bloody hell, Chrissie. What sort of blokes does Andrew hang out

34

with?'

'Oh, they're not so bad,' Chrissie lied. She wasn't about to give anything away regarding Andrew's friends, even though they were more undesirable than pet cockroaches. Chrissie didn't like any of the men her partner hung out with. She felt they were a bad lot and an even worse influence.

'What are they all doing in your place? Discussing drug deals?'

Chrissie looked out of the window so Dee couldn't see her face. 'They play games.'

'What...you mean...cards?'

'No. Computer games.'

Dee gulped. Talk about reading a situation wrong. 'I need to stop at an off-licence and buy Cougar Kate another bottle of wine.'

'Whatever for?'

'It's her fortieth, remember? We can't turn up empty-handed.'

'Hell, I'd forgotten it was her birthday. I'd better buy some chocolates. Have you bought her a birthday card?'

'Steady,' said Dee, 'she'll be thinking she's one of our besties if we overdo it. Wine and chocolates are fine.'

Dee exited the estate and zoomed towards New Ash Green. She'd offered to pick up Amber too, even though Amber did have her own car. At least her friends wouldn't have to worry about drinking and driving. As luck would have it – or bad luck in Amber's case – Cougar Kate lived in Redhill Wood. This was the posh side of New Ash Green with detached houses in a woodland setting. It was also less than a quarter of a mile from Amber's two-up-two-down.

By the time Chrissie and Dee had bought more wine and some chocolates, they were running ten minutes late. Amber was waiting for them, standing on the pavement of the ring road that circumnavigated New Ash Green.

'At last,' she said, getting into the back of Dee's car. 'I've been freezing my Victoria's Secret tits off waiting for you two.'

'Ooooh, hark at you!' said Dee. 'Wearing a new bra?'

'Yes,' said Amber. In the back seat, and in the dark, the girls couldn't see the grimace that crossed her face. The bra had cost an absolute fortune. She hoped Matthew appreciated it when she put her seduction plans to the test later on. Come hell or high water, she was going to inject some va-va-voom in their relationship. Her plan was to woo her partner from total indifference to non-stop lust. She'd have the contents of Matthew's M&S underpants permanently standing to attention. Come Monday morning he'd have no choice but to ring his office and throw a sickie. Or a *stiffy* in this case.

Two minutes later, Dee pulled up outside Cougar Kate's house. There were several cars outside indicating the party girl had a full house.

'Ready, girls?' asked Amber, as Dee locked the car after them. 'I, for one, can't wait to meet this Madam Rosa and find out what my future holds.'

Chapter Six

'Come in, come in!' Katherine Colgan greeted Dee, Chrissie and Amber as if they were long lost relatives who'd travelled to Redhill Wood from the other side of the world. 'You must be gasping for a drinkie-poo. Oh, Dee, thank you *sooo* much,' she said, accepting the bottle of red, 'that's one of my favourites. Ooh chocolates, Chrissie. You're *too* kind.' She looked expectantly at Amber.

'They're from all of us,' said Amber with a sniff. Buying this particular woman a birthday gift, even a two quid supermarket spray of carnations, was not something she'd ever planned to do. The fact that Amber was even in this house was purely because she'd been steamrollered into coming along. Her grudge for Katherine Colgan was as fresh as the day she'd made a play for Matthew. Amber checked out Cougar Kate's outfit. She was wearing a fitted dress with a big gold zip that went from bottom to top. Naturally the zip hadn't been done up to the neck. It stopped short of Cougar Kate's jostling bosoms which looked like two puppies trying to make a break for freedom. Amber slid her coat off and handed it to Cougar Kate, taking satisfaction in seeing the woman check out Amber's figure as she did so.

Yes, cop a load of my cleavage, Amber silently sneered, *and not a molecule of silicon in sight*! Amber couldn't wait to get home and see Matthew's reaction to her newly-upholstered breasts. She'd drive him insane. He wouldn't know whether he was coming, or coming and coming and coming.

'Thank you all so much for being here to celebrate my birthday,' said Cougar Kate graciously. 'Go and join everybody else,' she indicated a door leading off the hallway, 'and eat, drink and be very merry.'

Everybody had congregated in the open plan kitchen-come-dining-room. A flat-screen on the wall was tuned to a radio station playing club anthems. There was quite a crowd in the room, some already tipsy from drinking on empty tums. Others were grouping around a table heaped with food. Amber's stomach let out a growl of hunger. She had to concede that Cougar Kate had put on a lovely spread. The three women wandered over to another table loaded with different bottles of spirits and ice-buckets full of champagne bottles. Opting for champers, they took their glasses and huddled in a corner of the room, assessing the crowd while they sipped.

'You have to hand it to her,' said Chrissie, 'Cougar Kate has done a lovely job.' She nodded at the mini banquet everyone was enjoying, then gazed around the room. How she'd love to have a birthday bash like this, and in such a glorious house too.

'It's all right, I suppose,' Amber shrugged. She was looking increasingly like someone with a bad smell under her nose.

Dee laughed. 'Put the face away, Amber. Cougar Kate isn't interested in Matthew. Accept her hospitality and leave the past where it belongs.'

'Easier said than done,' said Amber, her lip curling like Elvis Presley. 'Just look at her. She's in her element playing the hostess with the mostess.'

'You have to admit she looks pretty good for forty,' said Chrissie. 'I'd settle for looking like that now, never mind in thirteen years' time.'

'Anyone can look like that,' Amber rolled her eyes. 'All that's required is two hours in front of the mirror every morning, preferably with the contents of Boots' beauty counter at their disposal, not forgetting a spare five thou for the Dolly Partons.'

'Ooh, ouch,' said Dee with a laugh. 'Did you get out of the wrong side of bed this morning? What's up with you?'

'Nothing,' said Amber quickly. She mentally shook herself. She must stop bitching. The girls were right. Cougar Kate's flirting with Matthew was water under the bridge. Even so, Amber would never forgive her.

Suddenly the music's volume dimmed and Cougar Kate clapped her hands. 'I want to let you all know that the wonderful, internationally-acclaimed Madam Rosa, has arrived!'

'Gawd, she's carrying on like she's a presenter for the Royal Variety Performance,' tutted Amber.

'Madam Rosa will start receiving you, one by one, in my lounge as soon as she's cleaned the room from negative energy...'

'I'll bet there's plenty of that,' said Amber nastily.

'...and lit her candles and incense sticks to invoke peace, harmony and contact with the spirits.'

'Madam Rosa could easily do that if she did her readings by that table full of booze,' Amber snorted.

'Give it a rest, Amber,' muttered Dee.

'There's quite a few of us here tonight,' said Cougar Kate, 'and consequently time constraints are in place. Each of you will be granted an audience of ten minutes precisely, so make sure you have any questions you want to ask at the ready. Further in-depth consultations with Madam Rosa can be booked at a later date for the very affordable fee of forty-five pounds for forty-five minutes.

'That's a pound a minute,' gasped Chrissie.

'Nice little earner if you can get it,' Dee pointed out.

'Oh for heaven's sake,' said Amber, rolling her eyes. 'This evening is a marketing ploy for Madam Rosa. It's like any product party. The hostess gets a free gift for drumming up business for the franchise member. Cougar Kate has safely bagged a free forty-five-minute reading for herself, and all she had to do was invite a few friends round.'

'I don't think so,' said Chrissie, 'after all, Katherine's gone to a lot of trouble and expense here.'

'It's her birthday,' said Amber. 'She's simply combined something she'd have done anyway with a freebie for herself.'

'Does it matter?' asked Dee. 'The main thing is we're going to have a whole ten minutes to ask Madam Rosa if our partners will ever pop the question. That's the purpose of us being here, so let's make the most of it. One question, one answer. By my calculations we'll still have eight minutes left to ask a second question. Sounds fair to me.'

'Well I think it's obscene,' said Amber moodily. 'There must be thirty people here. If they all go ahead and book a further appointment with Madam Rosa, that's well over a thousand pounds she'll be pocketing. And I'll bet she doesn't pay tax either, unlike the rest of us.'

Dee and Chrissie exchanged looks. Amber seemed more wound up than a clockwork mouse.

'I wonder who will go in first,' said Chrissie. 'I'm feeling a bit apprehensive, even though I don't really believe in fortune-telling.'

'It's a load of old rubbish,' said Amber scornfully. She drained her glass and smacked her lips appreciatively. 'I'm going to have at least three glasses of fizz before I go in. And something to eat. I might as well freeload while I'm here before listening to Madam Rosa's twaddle.'

'Oh for goodness sake, Amber,' said Dee rolling her eyes. 'Get another drink down you and shut up. I've never known you moan so much.'

Amber's eyes flashed. That was all very well for Dee to say, but then Dee didn't have a boyfriend absenting himself all hours. Amber was starting to feel like Matthew's mum rather than a girlfriend. Her role had become one of housekeeper - cooking his dinner and doing his washing. She wanted a boyfriend who kissed his way down her neck while expertly undressing her, and to hear her clothes drop to the floor in a rustle of silk – not a boyfriend who chucked his own clothes everywhere and left them there for *her* to pick up.

'C'mon,' said Chrissie. 'I'm starving. Let's enjoy some of this lovely food, and have a few more drinks to get us in the mood. And while we're chomping our way through that delicious looking poached salmon, we'll think up more questions to ask Madam Rosa for the remaining eight minutes you reckon we're going to have, Amber.

Cougar Kate once again clapped her hands. 'I'm delighted to say that Madam Rosa is ready. Now, who would like to go first?'

Chapter Seven

Two hours later, Amber was feeling quite drunk. So far, the guests who'd seen Madam Rosa had returned to the kitchen-come-dining-room with wide eyes. They'd been excited to share what they'd been told.

'She's amazing,' one woman gushed. 'She told me I'm going to get a new job, and guess what? Yesterday I went for an interview!'

'She told me my daughter-in-law is pregnant and going to have a little girl. That must be why my Simon and his Jessica rang me earlier. They said they want to see me tomorrow with some exciting news, and that it's a surprise!'

'She told me we're moving home. Quite by chance, earlier this week, I saw a *For Sale* board outside a house I've liked for ages. Me and my hubby are viewing it tomorrow!'

Amber didn't like to admit it, but her stomach was starting to churn with nervous anticipation. Everything she'd eaten was mixing unhappily with an overload of booze. She should have stuck to champagne instead of starting on the gin. She knew she was more than tipsy. The chip she'd had on her shoulder for the last year about Cougar Kate suddenly felt like a humungous boulder. Amber put down the bowl of half-eaten sherry trifle she'd been tucking into. It was delicious but she was too stuffed for even a teaspoonful, and there was no chance of fitting in a black coffee for sobering up.

'Amber, it's now your turn!'

Amber looked up to see Cougar Kate smiling at her. Amber's fingers itched to squash her leftover trifle into the woman's heavily made-up face. Either that, or tip it down her cleavage. Amber had a vision of custard blobs and bits of cream spread over

Cougar Kate's breasts, and some dickhead like Clive Derek going into meltdown wanting to lick it all off. Amber frowned. Perhaps Matthew might like to do something like that? Not with Cougar Kate, but with her? Amber put her head on one side as she considered. Perhaps, when she was home, she'd have a rummage in the fridge and then greet Matthew with two olives impaled on her nipples. It would have been a whole lot cheaper than splurging on this wretched bra which was now digging into her.

'Are you all right, Amber?' Cougar Kate tried to frown, but her botoxed forehead wouldn't let her.

'Ne'er better,' Amber assured. Spotting Chrissie and Dee helping themselves to enormous slices of Black Forest Gateau, Amber lurched over to them. She tugged on their sleeves. 'S'my turn to see Madam Raspberry.'

'Are you drunk?' asked Dee.

'Don' be rid-clous.' Amber belched, engulfing her friends in trifle and gin fumes.

'Good luck,' said Chrissie, gently taking Amber's unfinished dessert from her. 'Don't forget to have all your questions at the ready.'

''kay. Back inna bit.'

Chrissie and Dee watched Amber stagger off to Cougar Kate's lounge.

'She's not a happy bunny,' Dee murmured.

'No. I wonder why.'

'Let's hope Madam Rosa cheers Amber up.'

***

Amber swayed towards Cougar Kate's lounge door, which was shut. For a second, Amber felt like she was visiting the headmistress at her old secondary school. She was always getting into trouble with teachers and being sent off to Mrs Thomas's office.

'Talking in class again, Amber?' Mrs Thomas would tut as she shook her head. Her hair had been snow-white which had been a source of fascination for Amber. At the time Amber thought she'd never seen anybody so old. Even Amber's grandma hadn't had snow-white hair. As each term rolled by, Amber had found herself in Mrs Thomas's office more and more often.

'Flicking paper at the English teacher again, Amber?'

'Yes, Mrs Thomas.'

'Yet another whoopee cushion on the English teacher's chair, Amber?'

'Yes, Mrs Thomas.'

'Frightening the English teacher by putting a jack-in-the-box under her desk, Amber?'

'Yes, Mrs Thomas.'

'Why? Don't you like English?'

'Yes. I just don't like the English teacher.'

Amber wondered if Mrs Thomas was still alive. She'd been a nice old girl and Amber felt bad that she'd been such a bored and rebellious pupil. She hoped there wasn't such a thing as karma. If so Amber would have to brace herself for balled-up paper being flicked at her, being scared by clowns popping out of boxes, and embarrassing moments of breaking wind.

She knocked on the door.

'Come in,' said the voice within.

Amber pushed down the handle and walked into Cougar Kate's lounge. She blinked as her eyes adjusted to the gloom. Tea lights in storm lanterns were dotted about, giving the room an ambient glow. In each corner of the room, fragrant incense sticks burned. Thick curls of smoke twisted their way up to the ceiling. The smell reminded Amber of church. Her eyes focussed on the small woman sitting in Cougar Kate's armchair. Whatever Amber had been expecting, it wasn't a female who looked as ordinary as this. Where was Madam Rosa's colourful scarf wound around her head? Or the big chandelier earrings? Or wrists full of jangling bangles? Madam Rosa was more like Amber's mum. Ordinary.

Madam Rosa beckoned to the nearby sofa. 'Sit down, love.'

Amber inwardly groaned. The woman even *sounded* like her mum. Amber felt befuddled from booze. Her brain was struggling to connect with her mouth. She'd have to take great care to hide her drunkenness and not slur her words.

'You're a beautiful young lady,' Madam Rosa began, 'but I can see you're not a happy one.'

'Yers,' Amber said, sounding like a pissed Margaret Thatcher.

'You haven't told a soul how unhappy you are because a part of you feels that if you don't tell anybody, the problem might magically disappear.'

'Yers.'

'But there *is* a problem. That is very clear to see.'

'Howww can yooo tell?'

'Because your heart is heavy. You are carrying a burden. It was obvious from the way you walked into the room. You are weighted down with sadness.'

'Bart can yooo tell me wart this sadness is?' Amber crossed one leg, leant her elbows on her knee, and steepled her fingers together in an attempt to look both sober and intelligent.

'But of course. It's your boyfriend. He's giving you a run for your money.'

Amber frowned. Matthew hated running. And what did money have to do with it?

'Ay don't think ay understand.'

'Your boyfriend is messing you about.'

'Wart?' Amber was so confused her elbows slid

45

off her knees and one of her steepled fingers shot painfully up her left nostril.

'All this nonsense about working extra hours at the office, then coming home late, not to mention treating you like his personal housekeeper-come-cleaning lady—'

'Haw do yoo know awl this?' Amber's eyebrows were so knitted together she looked like she was sporting a monobrow.

'Because I'm Madam Rosa. I know everything.'

'My Math-yoo is warking very haard,' Amber protested.

'Your Matthew is having an affair. Time's up, love.'

'B-but,' Amber stuttered. 'Ay haven't even asked yoo my kwes-tune!'

'Here, take this,' said Madam Rosa. She leant towards Amber and pressed a plain white card into her hand. 'If you want to know anything else you'll have to book a full consultation. Send the next person in, please.'

Amber stood up, her face a picture of bewilderment. Matthew was having an affair? What a load of rubbish! As she lurched out of Cougar Kate's lounge, Amber suddenly felt sick. And it was nothing to do with her booze overload.

Chapter Eight

'I'm next,' Dee squealed with excitement. She'd been listening to the growing buzz in the air all evening. Everybody was talking about Madam Rosa's accurate chit-chat and wait-and-see predictions. The fortune teller was going down a storm. Cougar Kate was giving triumphant smiles to everybody. Dee noted that their hostess had yet to take her turn. Dee suspected Cougar Kate was waiting right until everybody had left and then Madam Rosa would stump up the birthday girl's "commission" with the full forty-five-minute reading.

'Good luck, Dee,' said Chrissie with a smile. 'Ooh, look. Here comes Amber. She's looking very out-of-sorts. She's had far too much gin.'

Amber's face was chalk-white, and her eyes conveyed distress.

'I must dash,' said Dee, 'or I'll miss my slot. Hey, Amber,' she greeted her friend, 'keep schtum until I'm back. In fact, let's all keep schtum until the three of us have been seen. Then we'll compare notes.'

Amber nodded like a zombie.

'Are you okay?' Chrissie asked with concern.

'Drink,' said Amber, her voice quavering. 'I need a very big drink.'

'Don't you think you've had enough?'

'Nowhere near,' said Amber darkly.

While Chrissie was wrestling a gin bottle off Amber, Dee hurried over to Cougar Kate's lounge. She knocked eagerly on the door.

'Come in,' said the voice within.

Dee entered the room like a whirling tornado, shifting the sofa back a couple of inches as she thumped her backside down on its upholstery. She gave Madam Rosa a smile that stretched from one ear to the other.

'Now I know we only have ten minutes,' said Dee, 'so I'll get straight to the point. All I want to know is–'

'I'm afraid not.'

Dee's smile slipped. 'I hadn't finished my sentence.'

'You didn't need to.'

'But how do you know what I was going to ask?'

'I know everything.'

'What? How?'

'Where do you want me to start? With the word of God? The gifts He gave? The distortion by mankind, and the burning of supposed witches at the stake?'

'Er, no...just,' Dee scratched her head, 'back to the beginning of my sentence. What was I going to ask?'

'You were going to ask if your boyfriend was ever likely to propose marriage.'

Dee gasped. Hearing Madam Rosa speak aloud the very words that had been going around in her head, was both exhilarating and shocking. And then Dee collected herself. Every young woman dreamt about finding her prince, falling in love, getting married and living happily ever after. Well, most of them anyway. Dee reasoned that probably eighty per-cent of the women here tonight had wanted to know the very same thing. Wasn't that the exact question Cougar Kate would also be asking Madam Rosa too? Of course!

Ha, Madam Rosa! Nice try, but I'm three steps ahead of you!

'Actually, my boyfriend has already proposed,' Dee lied.

Madam Rosa raised an eyebrow in surprise. 'Sorry, but there will be no wedding.'

'Well maybe not this year,' Dee bluffed, 'after all,

48

we're saving very hard. Weddings aren't cheap.'

'No, they're not. But if I were you I'd keep quiet about that bit of money you have squirrelled away. Save it for the next young man you're going to meet. He'll be coming along soon enough, and he's a smasher.'

'W-what?' Dee stuttered. She felt as if Madam Rosa had thrown cold water in her face. 'Okay, I'll level with you. He hasn't really asked me to marry him. Not yet, anyway. But please, tell me why you're so sure there won't be a wedding?'

'He's seeing someone else, love. He's having an affair.'

Dee nearly hooted aloud at such a ridiculous prediction. This Madam Rosa was an absolute charlatan. She was playing guessing games, and trying to scramble Dee's brain cells. Anger rippled through her. Not only was Madam Rosa a fraud, she was also a nasty piece of work. She stared at the mild looking woman sitting in the armchair opposite her. 'How dare you!'

'Sorry to cause you pain. But it's better to know the truth. It will save you greater heartache later. Send in the next person, love.'

Dee sprang to her feet. Rage was pumping through her veins, turning her blood to molten lava. 'Yes, I'll send the next person in. But before I go, I'd like to question what sort of fortune teller you are to inflict such distress?'

'I believe in honesty. Apart from anything else, you were in distress before you even came to me. And that's all down to your boyfriend. Josh.'

Dee gasped. How did Madam Rosa know her partner's name?

'I told you,' said Madam Rosa. 'I know everything. Now please send in the next person.'

Dee stared at Madam Rosa with a mixture of fury and indignation. She realised she was on the verge of tears. Without another word, she stormed out of the room almost knocking into Chrissie who was waiting outside.

'I'm warning you now,' Dee growled under her breath, 'don't believe one word that woman says. She's bang out of order. She'll try and wreck your life.'

'Oh?' said Chrissie, looking alarmed. 'Surely ten minutes can't cause any harm? Whatever's happ–'

'Come in,' said Madam Rosa, her voice filtering through the still open doorway.

'I'll see you in a few minutes,' whispered Chrissie. 'Please go and look after Amber. She seems intent on going from drunk to paralytic.'

'Yeah, and I'll bet I know why,' said Dee, before stalking off to Amber.

Chrissie shut the door after her. 'Sorry about that,' she apologised to Madam Rosa. 'My friend seems a bit, er, fired up about something.'

'Ah, yes, I see now. You're here with the two ladies who have just left. Like them, you would like to know if your boyfriend is going to propose marriage in the near future.'

'Er, yes. That's right.' Chrissie assumed either Amber or Dee had mentioned this to Madam Rosa.

'You didn't need to see me to have that question answered, young lady. Your heart already knows the answer.'

'Does it?' asked Chrissie uncertainly.

'Indeed.' Madam Rosa put her head on one side, as if considering. 'You haven't been happy for a long time. Years. You're wasting your life with the man you're living with. He is more interested in his fake friends – men who bring negative energy into your home. It's a darkness that, like glue, sticks to every cell of your body, and causes misery. If you're not careful, you could end up with full-blown depression.'

Chrissie gulped. This was a bit too honest for her liking. Madam Rosa was staring at her as if she was nothing more than an open book from which she was reading. A sudden feeling ambushed Chrissie. It was one of realisation. She felt as if she was seeing herself in the weeks, months, then years ahead, looking harassed and worn down. Chrissie grasped all this in a nano-second. But she knew there was no way out.

'Oh yes there is,' said Madam Rosa.

'Sorry?' said Chrissie looking startled. Was this woman also reading her mind?

'A way out will become apparent sooner than you think. Meanwhile don't make yourself a financial slave to this man. He's using you. And he's having an affair. Time's up, love. Send the next one in.'

'An affair?' said Chrissie stupidly. The only affair Chrissie knew about was Andrew's love affair with his mates and their stupid computer games.

Ashen-faced, she stood up and made her way to the door. No wonder Amber and Dee had looked shell-shocked after their readings. As Chrissie left the room she spotted Amber, who was still knocking back the gin. Dee, who had to drive, appeared to be sniffing the contents of a whisky bottle in an effort to calm her angst. Chrissie decided she might have to do the same. It was quite obvious the three of them had been given disastrous news.

Chapter Nine

The girls made leaving excuses to Cougar Kate soon after their "readings".

'Good news?' enquired their hostess, trying and failing to look concerned about their downcast faces.

'Yesh,' slurred Amber. Her expression was one of belligerence. 'Absholutely the besht newsh,' she took a deep breath and put all her effort into adding, '*everrr*.'

'It's been, um, an interesting evening,' said Chrissie.

'You can say that again,' mumbled Dee.

'Excellent,' said Cougar Kate with delight. 'See you all at the office on Monday. Hopefully I'll shortly have good news too, and we can celebrate over an instant coffee in our employer's manky kitchenette.' She gave a gurgle of laughter at her stab of wit.

The three friends drooped out of Cougar Kate's house to Dee's car.

'Right,' said Dee, starting up the engine. 'Who's going first in sharing the "wonderful" news delivered by Madam chuffing Know-It-All?'

'I feel shick,' said Amber.

'Don't you dare throw up in my car,' warned Dee. She reversed off Cougar Kate's driveway and headed in the direction of Amber's house. The sooner she got there, the better. The last thing she wanted was Amber regurgitating champagne and gin all over the back seat.

'You don' unnershtand,' Amber mumbled. 'I feel shick at what that 'orrible woman tol' me.'

'Go on then,' said Chrissie, 'you go first, Amber. Tell us what Madam Rosa said to you.'

'She shed my hearth was,' Amber waved her

hands extensively, 'ever'where, an' Math-yoo wash bein' a ver' naughty boy.'

'Eh?' asked Dee.

Chrissie translated. 'I think Amber said her heart is everywhere and Matthew is being a very naughty boy.'

'How naughty?' demanded Dee.

'Havin' an affair.'

'Huh,' said Dee. 'Right, Chrissie. Your turn.'

'Madam Rosa said pretty much the same thing to me.'

'I knew it,' Dee crowed. 'The woman is a fraud. For sure. She told me Josh is having an affair.'

'Why would she tell us such things?' cried Chrissie, distress apparent.

'Don't you see?' said Dee, swerving around a fox that was dithering, about dashing in front of the car.

'Don' do that,' Amber warned, 'or I'll be shick.'

'Sorry,' said Dee. 'Listen to me. We've sussed Madam Rosa's marketing ploy. That's as obvious as the noses on our faces. Madam Rosa is telling us something so shocking we'll ring her up and make a forty-five-minute appointment and spend a fortune in the process. Then she'll probably tell us not to worry, our men have seen the error of their ways, all is well in Romance Land, and we'll be married by Christmas. You mark my words. The woman is a swindler. A money-making charlatan.' Dee clutched the steering wheel in anger. To hell with Madam Rosa. She hoped the wretched woman's head rotated one-hundred-and-eighty degrees at midnight and she had to rush off to the local church to get exorcised.

'The only thing ish,' said Amber unhappily, 'she tol' me some other shtuff. And that was accurate.'

'Oh?' Chrissie raised her eyebrows enquiringly, and looked over her shoulder at Amber sitting on the back seat.

'I haven't tol' either of you. It's embarrashing.'

'Told us what?' asked Dee, glancing at Amber in the rear-view mirror.

'Math-yoo an' me have not been,' Amber paused to think how to phrase her words in her befuddled state, 'you know, "right" together. For a while. Something ish wrong. He says he's busy at work. He comes home late, every night. He's even working weekends. He said it was for us. But I don't believe him. Do you know how much he shpent on me at Chrissmush? Well I'll tell yoo,' said Amber, not bothering to wait for Chrissie and Dee to prompt her. 'Ten squid.'

'Ten pounds?' asked Dee incredulously.

'Yesh. An' I can't remember the last time we had shax.'

'I think that's a cross between "shag" and "sex",' muttered Chrissie to Dee. She cleared her throat. 'Okay, girls. Confession time for me too. I haven't confided in either of you before now, but Andrew and I haven't been getting along for a while.' She stared out of the passenger window, her eyes momentarily blurring with tears. 'Madam Rosa said Andrew is using me. That I was nothing more than a financial purse for him. And the awful thing is,' Chrissie gulped, 'she's right.'

'What?' Dee knew Chrissie never splashed her cash, but had assumed it was because of saving for a house deposit.

'Andrew never has any money. I don't know what he does with it. He works. But he disappears off to the pub every five minutes with those...those...*horrible* men that he calls friends. The reality is they're nothing but losers. I don't think they work – or can even be bothered to find work. I suspect Andrew is funding their booze and,' she swallowed unhappily, 'other stuff.'

'What other stuff?' Dee prompted.

54

'Drugs.'

'Drugsh?' gasped Amber.

'You're kidding?' said Dee.

'Sadly not. The place stinks of pot, and the other day there was white stuff all over the kitchen work top. Andrew denied all knowledge of it and blamed Mick – one of the guys you tackled earlier on this evening, Dee.' She took a deep breath. 'And the little bit of money I'd saved was spent ages ago when Andrew couldn't stump up his half of the rent and bills. He's not been paying his way properly for months. And as for sex,' she shook her head, 'I can't remember the last time we were intimate.'

'Chrissie, you poor love,' said Dee. She reached across the gearstick to squeeze her friend's hand. 'Why don't you leave him?'

'I have nowhere to go.'

Dee and Amber were silent. Both of them momentarily considered offering Chrissie a bed so she could escape her depressing relationship. But no sooner had the thought entered their heads, another thought replaced it – neither Matthew nor Josh would want a guest sofa-surfing until alternative digs were found.

'I keep hoping,' said Chrissie wistfully, 'that he'll change back into the Andrew I fell in love with. *That* Andrew was sweet and kind and thoughtful. *This* Andrew is a stranger.'

'You need to talk to him,' said Dee. 'A frank *sit-down-and-listen-to-me-you-moron* sort of chat.'

'Yes,' Chrissie sighed. 'You're right. I'll do that tomorrow. And what about you, Dee? Is everything all right with you and Josh?'

Dee took a deep breath. 'No.' Now that she was admitting it to her friends, it somehow hit home harder. 'I'd like us to move from our flat and buy something a bit bigger. An extra bedroom, for when a baby comes along. And a garden. I'd love a place like yours, Amber.' Dee slowed the car, put the indicator on and pulled up outside Amber's house. She looked across at the little property. It stood in the warm glow of footpath courtesy lights. To Dee, it was perfect. 'But whenever I mention moving, Josh blanks it. And lately he seems to pick an argument over everything and anything. He's also shredding my self-esteem to pieces.'

'Never!' Chrissie gasped. Dee had to be the most poised, self-assured and confident person she'd ever met.

Dee gave a bark of mirthless laughter. 'Apparently I'm fat, frumpy, unfashionable and have no conversation skills.'

'He shed that?' Amber slurred in outrage.

'And like you two,' Dee continued, feeling her face flame, 'we haven't made love in ages. He said,' she hesitated for a moment, 'that I was boring in bed.'

Amber and Chrissie were gobsmacked. There was a resounding silence interrupted only by the tick-ticking of Dee's blinking indicator, as they sat in the stationary vehicle outside Amber's house.

'I hate to say this, said Chrissie tentatively, 'but maybe we *should* make an appointment to see Madam Rosa again.' She didn't really have a spare forty-five quid to give to someone who professed to know everything. The woman could be playing a very clever game of hoodwinking. But doubt had set in. It would be nice to see Madam Rosa one more time if only to be reassured, and dismiss her earlier revelations as utter tripe. 'I don't have her number though.'

'I do,' said Amber. She rummaged in her handbag and pulled out the stiff white business card. 'I agree with Chrishie. We should see the old bat again.'

Dee sighed and stared blankly at the windscreen.

She didn't know what to think. Right now, she was fed up and tired. This had not been a happy evening. 'I'm not sure,' she shook her head. 'Maybe we should sit down with our men tomorrow, and calmly ask them what's going on – whether they still want to be with us? We should tell them we feel anxious, and want to put things right.'

'Good idea,' Chrissie nodded.

'Yesh,' Amber agreed. 'I already have a plan of action, starting tonight.'

'Oh?' said Chrissie and Dee together.

'I'm going to roger him senseless,' Amber declared. 'Shtarting right now.' She blew kisses to Chrissie and Dee, and wrestled with the rear door. It flew open, nearly whacking an oncoming car. A blaring horn made them all jump. 'Shee you both on Mon'ay,' Amber said, falling out of the car, 'an' let ush hope we all have good newsh.'

Chapter Ten

As Amber breathed in the cold night air, she experienced a wave of nausea. It made her realise how drunk she was. She teetered on her stilettos, delicately picking her way along the semi-dark footpath towards her house. Ice glittered underfoot, and a chill wind lifted the hem of her short skirt. Her body prickled with a spray of goose-bumps. Flipping heck. She needed to get indoors before her private parts suffered frostbite.

Fumbling with her keys, she stabbed several times at the lock. Suddenly the door was yanked open. Matthew stood before her. He was glaring.

'Drunk?' His chilly tone matched the weather.

'Don' be shilly,' said Amber indignantly. As she stepped over the threshold into the warm hallway, she shivered. The sudden change of temperature brought on another moment of nausea. She gulped uneasily, and bestowed Matthew with her brightest smile.

'*Dah*-ling Math-yoo!' she gushed.

'Great, you're definitely drunk.'

Amber waved a hand dismissively as she shook off her jacket, but her arm hadn't left the sleeve. She ended up looking like a large demented bird as she flapped the garment about in the small hallway. Matthew wrestled it off her and tossed it over the bannister.

'Thanksh.' Released from her coat prison, she staggered slightly. A moment of dizziness engulfed her.

'Nice evening?' Matthew enquired tersely.

'Would've bin nicer if yewd bin wish me.' Amber blinked owlishly at Matthew. 'Why're we shtanding in the hallway? Letsh go into the lounge an' 'ave a nice chatty-poo.'

'No thanks. I'm tired.'

'Tired?' Amber frowned. 'But it's only...,' she squinted at her watch, 'five to four.'

'It's twenty past eleven,' said Matthew irritably. 'Remember, one of us here went to work earlier.' He made it sound like Amber was lazy for not going to the office on a Saturday. 'My eyes are burning after going over all those figures.'

'Look at my figure inshtead,' said Amber coquettishly. She tried giving a seductive Mae West wink, but instead looked like she was trying to blink grit out of her eye.

'I'm going to bed,' said Matthew briskly. He turned and marched up the staircase.

Oh goody, thought Amber, *he's dead keen to get to the bedroom*. 'Yeah, letsh go to beddy-byes.'

She followed Matthew, gripping the bannister rail tightly. Good heavens. Had Matthew ripped out the staircase while she'd been out, and installed an escalator? Amber's head momentarily spun. Steadying herself, she stepped off the moving stairs and trailed Matthew into the larger of the two upstairs bedrooms. He was shedding clothes at the speed of light, letting them drop in the usual untidy pile on the floor. Amber bit back words of complaint about her boyfriend's slovenliness, and instead concentrated on being the most seductive woman on the planet. This was it! She was going to reclaim Matthew's love and lust.

'Oh Math-*yoooooo*,' she cooed. Amber began wiggling her mid-riff, as if rotating an invisible hoop around it. 'Wanna see me dance, babe?' She moved away from the bed so he could watch the whole of her gyrating body, from the top of her jiggling breasts down to her sexy high heels. She lifted one side of her dress teasingly, revealing the lacy top of a hold-up stocking. When they'd first started dating, Matthew had always told Amber what lovely legs she had. She reached down with her other hand and tugged the hem upwards so both stocking tops were revealed, all the while constantly twirling her body. She threw her head back as if in ecstasy, and made what she imagined to be a sound of arousal.

Matthew grimaced. 'Are you in pain, Amber?'

'Oh yeah, yeah, gimme some pain, hunny-bunny.' She stuck her bottom out, in all its cheeky glory. Earlier, she'd put on her best thong with a diamanté heart where the string joined the top. 'C'mon, Math-yoo. Get yourself over here and gimme some wanky.' She shook her head. That didn't sound right. It made it sound like she wanted Matthew to, well, *wank*. And she definitely didn't want that. She wanted him to stride over, sweep her into his strong arms, then fling her down on the bed in a masterful manner. If he could do a bit of chest bashing like Tarzan, even better. Then he would look at her with intense desire and murmur, 'Amber, darling. What a fool I've been for ignoring you. Part those beautiful stockinged thighs, and let me plunge into you before my balls burst.' And if he could do that sooner, rather than later, even better. All this blasted gyrating was making her tummy feel like it had turned into a washing machine – and one that was revving up for a final spin. 'C'mon, Math-yoo,' Amber urged, 'gimme some spanky. Oooh, yeah, baby. Spanky-spanky-spanky.'

'Amber–'

'Yes...say my name...say my name,' Amber gasped, as a Destiny's Child soundtrack began playing in her head. How annoying. She didn't want to think about the lyrics – which might be dangerously close to the truth.

She pulled the dress up her body, ready to discard it. She would toss it on top of Matthew's pile of clothes. This would prove she wasn't a nagging girlfriend, and instead just like him – slovenly. A slut! That's what men liked in the bedroom, right? Her head briefly jammed in the dress's narrow neck hole. Lipstick smeared across both the fabric and her face as she fought to free herself.

'Look, Amber–'

'Yeah, yeah, look all you like,' panted Amber as she immerged, pink-faced, from the dress. She balled it up and chucked it across the bedroom. It sailed through the air and hooked itself on the ceiling lampshade. No matter, because now her Victoria's Secret upholstered breasts were revealed in all their glory. She cupped the underwired fabric and wobbled her boobs about as she resumed gyrating. 'Do you like what you see, Matty boy?'

Matty boy? She'd never called her boyfriend "Matty boy" in all their time together.

'Amber, I really wish you'd stop and–'

At last! He finally wanted her to stop all this twirling about and get down to basics – good old-fashioned bonking. She giggled naughtily.

'Are you ready, Matty man?'

Matty man? The booze had done strange things to her vocabulary.

'Truly, Amber, can we–'

'Oh my darling Matalan.'

Matalan? Wasn't that a shop?

Amber opened her mouth and attempted running her tongue sexily across her lips. She was so dehydrated from all the booze, her top lip chose that moment to adhere to her front teeth. She stabbed at it with her parched tongue. She looked like someone doing an impression of a hissing snake.

'Oh for fuck's sake –'

'Yes,' Amber squealed with delight, 'fuckity-fuckity-fuck!' At last, the green light! And boy did she need to get this over with. Sod her own sexual gratification. She wanted to impale herself on Matthew, salvage their relationship in the most natural way a man and a woman did these things, then lie down and sleep for a million years. Her head was whirling and, thanks to the continued gyrating, her stomach was rolling like a cement mixer. She mustered all her wherewithal and concentrated on the task in hand.

'Are you ready to COME?' Amber bellowed. 'Because I AMMM!' She took a running jump at Matthew, and belly-flopped onto his private parts. Matthew convulsed with pain. His head came up as his hands flew down to clutch throbbing testicles, causing him to nut his forehead on Amber's jaw.

'Jesus H Christ,' he screamed.

It was too much for Amber. As she opened her aching mouth to scold Matthew for blasphemy, she vomited all over his bare chest. A waterfall of regurgitated trifle and gin splattered over his skin, splashing outwards across the bedding. Amber's last coherent thought, before she passed out, was that she still had some way to go before she won Matthew over.

Chapter Eleven

At about the time of Amber passing out, Dee was pulling up outside Chrissie's crumbling maisonette.

'Thanks for the lift,' said Chrissie gratefully.

'You're welcome,' Dee replied. 'I'll watch you walk to the door.'

'I'll be fine,' Chrissie assured. 'This place isn't quite as bad you think.' Both women knew that wasn't true. 'Catch you later.' As Chrissie pushed open the passenger door, Dee's nostrils twitched at the stink of weed. Goodness knows what it was like inside Chrissie's home. Dee saw her friend's soft mouth change into a hard line.

Buzzing down the driver's window, Dee kept her eyes on Chrissie. She could hear the men inside the maisonette effing and jeffing, followed by raucous cheers. Their bulky shapes were silhouetted behind the net curtains. Someone punched the air in triumph and let out a primeval roar. From next door came the sound of Chrissie's neighbour, who Dee knew to be called Fran, yelling at her kids to go to sleep. This was followed by Fran screaming at the men to shut their gobs or she'd come around and do it for them. Chrissie's body was visibly stiff with tension as she turned to wave to Dee. Seconds later she'd disappeared into the hallway. As the car window whirred shut, Dee thanked God and all the angels in Heaven that she didn't live on an estate like this one.

Inside, Chrissie took a deep breath. She told herself to count to three before she went into the lounge. It was important to stay calm and reasonable. After all, it *was* Saturday night. After a hard week of doing sod all, it was only natural Andrew's friends should want to unwind and enjoy a few funny fags. She just wished they didn't do it in her home. The place stunk. She checked the time. Half past eleven. Would it be mean asking Andrew's "guests" to leave at this hour? She dithered. Most working people, like herself, would think it late but not extraordinarily so. Midnight would probably be more appropriate for ending in-house entertainment. She sighed, trying to muster up some energy. If her body had been a car, the petrol tank's gauge would be reading almost empty.

For goodness sake, Chrissie. Get a grip. You've now been standing in this hallway for several minutes. Do something!

Making a decision, she pushed down on the door handle to the lounge. Chrissie immediately bumped into Big Mick, one of the men Dee had harassed earlier, who was coming the other way.

'Oh, h-hello,' Chrissie stuttered. 'Are you going?' Her heart leapt with joy. With a bit of luck, the rest of them would follow. She could reclaim her home, tidy up, and be in bed a little after midnight.

'Nah,' Mick said, enveloping Chrissie in beer fumes. 'I'm off to use yer bog. I need a crap.'

Chrissie tried not to look disgusted. After all, it was a bodily function that all humans did. She just wished Mick kept such information to himself, and preferably went home to use his own toilet rather than ponging out hers. As he squeezed his bulk past her, one of his hands landed on her left breast. She froze.

'Nice tits,' he murmured. 'Yer wasted on him.' He jerked his head at Andrew in the gloom behind him. 'Any time yer fancy a bit of rough, look me up. I'll show yer a good time, darlin'.'

Chrissie was so shocked she couldn't move. Mick's hand lingered for a moment longer, fingering her nipple through her worn-out bra before his bowels got the better of him. As he hastened off to the bathroom, Andrew appeared in the doorway.

'Ah, good. You're home. All right?' he enquired. He didn't bother waiting for a reply. 'We're starving. As it's still early, can you make everyone some chip butties? That all right with you, lads?' Andrew bellowed over his shoulder. From behind him came various grunts of approval. Chrissie could see at least ten men in there. Eleven if you included Mick who was currently enthroned on her toilet.

'Andrew,' said Chrissie, in a low voice, 'even if I wanted to make chip butties at twenty-to-midnight – which I don't – I would need half a dozen bags of frozen chips and several loaves of bread. Neither of which we have.'

Andrew's lip curled. When he next spoke his voice matched Chrissie's in quietness, but not in tone. 'You're not going to show me up, are you?' he hissed. His face was full of contempt. 'There's an Asda around the corner. It's open twenty-four-seven. Get your backside over there, buy what's necessary, and do it pronto. You need to learn some basic hospitality skills. Calum's missus is a diamond. She waits on us hand, foot and finger, all night long, with never a cross word and a big smile on her face. In fact, all the lads have respectful wives. It's just me who doesn't.'

'You're forgetting something, Andrew,' Chrissie growled.

'Oh?'

'I'm not your wife.'

'For fuck's sake,' Andrew rolled his eyes. 'Is that what this is about? Hey, if the difference between you being obstructive or pleasant boils down to a ring on your finger, then let's get married.' Chrissie stared at Andrew in disbelief. In the space of two minutes she'd been groped by Andrew's mate, had an invitation to have an affair, received an obscure marriage proposal, and been ordered to make umpteen chip butties at nearly midnight. What the hell was going on in her life? She desperately needed to claw back some control. 'So can you hurry up and chuff off to Asda,' said Andrew through clenched teeth. He gave her a push towards the front door. 'Oh, and before you ask, no I don't have any money for the shopping. I'll reimburse you when I'm paid. Tonight's been a bit expensive. In addition to all the booze for everyone, there were certain...er...things I had to buy for the lads. At the weekend they like their...you know... *luxuries.*'

'I understand,' Chrissie nodded.

Andrew's face lit up. This was more like it. A compliant Chrissie. It was amazing what the promise of marriage achieved. 'Off you go then.' He gave her another prod, but Chrissie stood her ground.

'I too like certain *luxuries* at the weekend, Andrew,' Chrissie murmured.

Andrew sighed. It was becoming crystal clear. She wanted a bonk. 'Sure, sure,' he said, once again jostling Chrissie towards the door. 'I'll sort you out later.'

Chrissie laughed, but there was no joy in the sound. She put up her hands to stop Andrew propelling her out into the night. 'The luxuries *I'm* talking about, are coming home to a house that doesn't resemble a cross between a pub and a drug den, being able to get into my own bathroom without the stench of Mick's bowels polluting the atmosphere, sleeping in a fragrant bedroom without everything – including the contents of my clothes hanging in the wardrobe – reeking of weed, and not being groped by one of your hideous mates–'

Andrew's face darkened. 'You dirty liar.'

'–and finally, to have a boyfriend who behaves like a boyfriend and not some *prat* who–'

There was the sound of a flushing toilet struggling to cope with the contents of its bowl. The bathroom door sprang open revealing Mick doing up his flies. It was evident no hand washing would be taking place. He squirted a lavender aerosol into the poisonous air, and waved one hand at the loo. 'Sorry, darlin',' he said, addressing Chrissie. 'Think yer loo's blocked. Be a good girl an' sort' it out fer us. One big bucket of water should shift it.'

'She'll be right there,' Andrew assured Mick, 'and then my lovely *fiancé*,' he said mockingly, 'is going to do us all proud with a feast to make your eyes pop.'

'Is that right?' said Mick with a leer. He was standing slightly behind Andrew who couldn't see Mick staring lasciviously at Chrissie's breasts.

Chrissie had had enough. She realised she wasn't going to get any sleep until these cretins had left. It would be best to do Andrew's bidding. She didn't want an argument. She'd sort out the loo, go to Asda, make the damn butties, and then at least everyone would finally go home. Tomorrow she'd properly clear the place up and then insist she and Andrew sit down and talk. If there was any chance of salvaging this relationship and rediscovering the sweet man she'd first fallen in love with, then she would pull out all the stops. But Andrew would have to do likewise. Firstly, these revolting "friends" had to go, also this awful maisonette on this unpleasant estate. They both earned a fair wage. If it meant paying a little more rent to live in a nicer street surrounded by pleasanter people, then so be it. But one thing was for sure, she was not going to carry on living like this.

Chapter Twelve

At about the time of Chrissie returning from Asda with enough chip butty fodder to feed a small army, Dee was back home in her cosy one-bedroomed apartment with not a chav to be seen or a whiff of weed to be smelled. Walking into the hallway, the only thing lingering in the air was a trace of Josh's signature aftershave and...she sniffed...an unknown perfume. Dee inhaled again, but the smell had disappeared and only Josh's scent remained. She must have imagined it. Madam Rosa's words whispered in her ear.

'He's seeing someone else, love. He's having an affair.'

Anxiety fluttered through Dee's stomach.

You're being paranoid, she told herself. *That blasted fortune teller has shaken you like an upside-down snow dome. Your boyfriend has been out this evening schmoozing a client, remember? He's securing a cleaning contract for several blocks of flats in Thamesmead, so stop imagining things.*

She slipped off her shoes and went to leave them in the hallway, then remembered Josh accusing her of being a slob because she didn't put things away. Dee picked up the footwear and padded over to the hallway's small cupboard. It was already overstuffed with the Christmas tree, ironing board and a mountain of Josh's work boots and paraphernalia, but she jostled things about and put the shoes away. Then she added her handbag for good measure. The less clutter about, the better. Soft music was coming from the lounge. Josh had beaten her home.

'Yoohoo,' she called.

'In here,' Josh replied.

Dee moved down the hall and paused in the lounge doorway.

'Hi,' she smiled hesitantly at her boyfriend. Josh was sitting on one of the sofas. The television was off, and he appeared to be relaxing. Hopefully he'd had a successful evening, and they could get some rapport going again. Since Friday night, things had been very strained with Josh. Earlier this evening, when she'd left him to go to Cougar Kate's, Josh had been up to his neck in a bubble bath "de-stressing" and planning his pitch to the potential client. Even so, Dee was now taken aback at how much effort Josh had made with his appearance for some fusty old guy who worked for the council. His daily stubble had gone. Currently her boyfriend's skin looked as soft as a peach and twice as glowing. Josh's hair, normally untidy, was now stylishly tousled. Her boyfriend didn't usually care about clothes, especially as his wallet was fitted with invisible padlocks, but he was wearing a shirt she didn't recognise and...Dee's eyes widened...new jeans?

'You look nice,' she let her tentative smile widen. Flattery was always a good starting point in restoring relationship harmony. 'That colour really suits you.'

'Thanks.'

Dee moved across the room and sat down next to Josh, snuggling into him. She feigned a sigh of deep contentment, and pretended to let the gentle music wash over her.

'Isn't this lovely?' she murmured, leaning her head against his shoulder. So far, so good.

'What's lovely? Our front room?'

'Well, yes, darling. Of course. But what I actually meant was how lovely it is to be sitting here next to my equally lovely boyfriend, chilling and listening to love songs.' It could only mean one thing. Josh was sending out romantic signals.

'Love songs?' Josh shifted his body, forcing Dee to sit up straight. She glanced at him, making sure her features were arranged into one of adoration, and was disappointed to see him frowning. 'I wasn't aware I was listening to love songs. I came in, exhausted, and simply put the radio on to wind down. To be honest, I can't stand this sort of music.'

Dee chewed her lip. The first lie. The radio had previously been set to a pop station. She knew, because she'd programmed it herself. However, *this* station was renowned for its smooth melodies without DJ chatter, especially at this late hour.

'Shame,' said Dee lightly. 'I think it's nice. Very…soothing.' She had hoped to lean against Josh again, but he was now sitting at a different angle and had crossed one leg. Even if she shifted her own position, she'd have a kneecap in her side. Instead, Dee slung one arm along the sofa's back. Her fingers were now within touching distance to her boyfriend's shoulders. She inclined her head towards him, trying to re-establish body language that conveyed intimacy. 'Well don't keep me guessing,' she grinned. 'Tell me all about it.'

'About what?' asked Josh.

'The client.'

Josh looked blank. 'What client?'

Dee's smile wavered. 'The client you were practising your pitch to when I left you earlier this evening.'

'Oh, *that* client.'

'Yes, *that* client,' Dee echoed, a slight edge to her voice.

'What is this? Twenty questions?'

'Sorry?'

'I feel like you're cross-examining me.'

'Darling, I'm asking how your evening went. You said it was a really important contract. I'm

70

interested in your work, that's all. I know how much effort you've put into High Fliers and I'm really proud of your success.'

'Why?' asked Josh belligerently, 'so you can nag me about moving again?'

'Not at all,' said Dee calmly. She didn't know why Josh was so on the defensive, but she was absolutely determined not to get into an argument. 'I always like hearing about your work. It sounds exciting. I'd much rather be leaping off building parapets wearing a hard hat, than wearing earphones and listening to my boss's voice droning on and on.'

Josh regarded Dee for a moment. 'Are you making fun of my work?'

Dee pushed down a rising sense of exasperation. Why on earth was Josh behaving like this? It was almost as if he was spoiling for a quarrel. 'Sweetheart, you must be very tired, because I can't think why you'd suggest me making fun of your work. What you do is amazing.' She leant forward and gently touched Josh's hand. He tensed under her touch, and made no effort to fold her fingers into his palm. Perhaps things had gone wrong for Josh this evening, and that was why he was being so irritable. 'Is the wretched man making you wait before he gives an answer?'

Josh shook off Dee's hand and made a deal of rubbing his face, as if pushing away frustration. 'Yeah,' he said wearily. Dee didn't know if his tired tone was genuine or affected. 'The guy is a pain in the proverbial. He said he'd let me know about the Sevenoaks contract on Monday.'

Dee caught her breath. The second lie. Josh had definitely said the contract was for blocks of flats in Thamesmead. However, she didn't correct him. She wasn't going to be accused of cross-examination again. Instead she made a mental note about his slip. 'Poor Josh,' she soothed, 'the blasted man

71

sounds like a nightmare.'

'Yes,' Josh agreed. 'And I don't mind telling you, he ordered the best of everything off the menu as well. I hope he's not wasted my money.'

'At least it's tax deductible.'

'That's not the point, Dee. There are only so many expenses I can present on my annual accounts without raising the hackles of the mighty Inland Revenue.'

'Where did you take him?'

'For goodness sake. There you go again.'

'Eh?'

'You heard. You're like the Gestapo, Dee.'

Dee shook her head slowly. 'I'm...simply making conversation with you, Josh. To be perfectly honest I haven't the faintest idea why you're behaving like this.'

'Oh, so I'm behaving in a way that doesn't please you now, eh? My God, Dee. Other men are supported by their partners. But you keep giving me the third degree over everything.'

Dee stared at Josh incredulously. 'Why are you being so argumentative with me?'

'Try asking yourself the same question,' Josh spat. 'And for what it's worth, I took Roger Brown to the steak house in the High Street. Happy? Now stop questioning my every move.' Josh jumped to his feet. 'I'm going to bed.'

Dee watched in astonishment as her boyfriend stalked off. Seconds later the bedroom door slammed. She sat for a few moments, stunned and not a little upset, unsure what to do next. The clock on the wall told her it wasn't quite midnight. And then she spotted Josh's wallet on the coffee table. She snatched it up, released the popper clasp and flicked deftly through bank notes and receipts. Her fingers hovered over a bill for Serafino's Cucina. She'd heard of it. One of Cougar Kate's conquests had regularly taken her there. It was a posh Italian restaurant in Sevenoaks. Was that why Josh had slipped up and said "Sevenoaks" instead of "Thamesmead"? She checked the date at the top. It was for tonight. The third lie. He definitely hadn't taken this Roger Brown person to any steak house on the High Street. She pushed the receipt back into the folds of the wallet, and replaced it in the exact position Josh had left it. Slipping off the sofa, she went out to the hallway and quietly retrieved her handbag from the cupboard. Reaching inside for her mobile phone, she tapped into the search engine "Serafino's Cucina". One second later she had the restaurant's number. Dee stood silently outside the closed bedroom door. From within came the sound of soft snoring. Good, because she didn't want to risk Josh overhearing her. As an extra precaution, she released the catch on the front door and stepped out onto the landing of the communal hallway. With a trembling hand, she hit the "call" icon on the mobile's screen.

'Serafino's, good evening?'

'Hello,' Dee whispered. 'I'm sorry to ring so late.'

'No problem, signorina. How can I help?'

'My...er...boss was in earlier, entertaining a client. He wondered if...um...his companion left a scarf behind?'

'I don't think anything has been left behind by anyone tonight, signorina.'

'Are you certain? I'm not sure what table they were sitting at, but maybe you could check underneath? Just in case it fell on the floor. I can give you his bill details to trace the correct table.'

'That would be helpful, signorina.'

'My boss spent one-hundred-and-forty-five pounds including service charge, and the payment was processed at ten o' clock this evening.' Dee gulped down the realisation that such a time had afforded Josh to come back to the flat with his companion for coffee. Or rumpy-pumpy. The brief smell of perfume gnawed at her memory.

'Ah, here we are. Table twenty-eight. I remember the couple now. I will check myself to see if any scarf has fallen under the table.'

'Oh...er...I'm so sorry...would you believe the scarf has been found.'

'Not a problem, signorina. I'm glad the item has turned up.'

'Um...one more thing...my boss is very secretive,' Dee attempted a casual laugh, 'and he told me he was entertaining a gentleman client. But I rather suspect his client was female. Would you remember who he was dining with, by any chance?' There was a telling pause at the other end of the line. Dee realised she'd been rumbled. Personal Assistants didn't ring up restaurants enquiring about their boss's dining companions late on a Saturday night. 'I'd be ever so grateful,' she said in a small voice, 'if you would tell me.'

'Signorina,' the man sighed, 'your "boss" was dining with a young lady. And I did not give you this information.'

'Thank you,' Dee replied. 'And I didn't ask.'

She hung up. The fourth lie. There was no Roger Brown. When Dee slipped back inside her flat, she was shaking.

Chapter Thirteen

Amber's Sunday...

Amber was awoken on Sunday morning by somebody knocking on her head.

'Gerroff,' she grumbled.

The rapping continued. Annoyed, she stuck one arm out of the duvet and swiped blindly through the air.

'I *said*...,' she tried hitting the culprit again, 'pack it in.'

Whoever was bashing her bonce had a hygiene issue. She wrinkled her nose in disgust. Phew, they stank to high heaven!

'You are seriously beginning to annoy me,' she said to the head knocker. But the head knocker took no notice. Amber could feel her temper fraying. It was no good. She'd have to punch the head knocker's lights out. She cracked open one eye. The bedroom was in gloom. Bright January sunshine peeked through gaps in the curtains, indicating the day was well underway. With monumental effort, she managed to open the other eye. Where was the head knocker? She rolled onto her back and squinted up at the ceiling. There was nobody here. So where was the insufferable smell coming from? And then a jumble of memories collided. Clarity was restored in a second. She'd attended Cougar Kate's psychic night, been told Matthew was having an affair, and got monumentally drunk. Once home, she'd tried to seduce Matthew and...she groaned...puked all over him. Oh dear Lord, she'd spent the night sleeping in a stinking bed.

Carefully she eased herself upright. The head knocking went into overdrive. A combination of immense hangover and pongy bedding caused her to retch. She needed to hit the shower.

Shoving the disgusting bedding to one side Amber clutched her head like a football, as if holding it tightly would stop it from rolling off her shoulders. Feeling more fragile than Kate Middleton suffering hyperemesis gravidarum, Amber tottered off to the bathroom. She couldn't hear Matthew up and about. But then again, she couldn't really hear anything with all this head knocking going on. Amber had a sudden desire for a bucket of water. She dithered between quenching her thirst, or drenching the horrific body odour. The latter won. *Sod it*, she told herself, *I'll drink from the shower nozzle while washing myself.*

Ten minutes later she was clean and a little more hydrated. However, a hangover wasn't going to be magicked away simply by gulping down half the hot water tank. Winding a towel turban around her head, she pulled on her bathrobe and inspected her face in the mirror over the basin. A grey-complexioned creature with bloodshot eyes stared back. Sighing, she cleaned her teeth and slapped on some moisturiser. She added an extra layer around her eye sockets which, according to the pot, guaranteed reducing puffiness.

Returning to the bedroom, she cupped the palm of one hand over her nostrils. How the heck had she slept in *this*? She whisked back the curtains, wincing at the sudden light infiltration. Pushing open the window to let in fresh air, she set about stripping the bed. Balling everything up and holding it at arm's length, she went downstairs to the kitchen and shoved the disgusting bed linen into the washing machine. She placed two soap capsules into the dispenser hoping it would doubly do its stuff, then headed for the kettle. It was only then that she saw the kitchen clock. Half past one in the afternoon? She'd been asleep for hours and hours.

76

She filled the kettle, wincing at the noise the water made as it splashed in, and then went off to find Matthew.

She peered around the door to the lounge. No boyfriend. She went back upstairs and checked the spare bedroom. The bed was unmade and empty, apart from Mr Tomkin nestled between folds of the quilt. The cat stood up, stretched, then re-curled himself into a tight ball. Matthew hadn't bothered to draw the spare room's curtains. Wet towels left in a heap on the floor told Amber he had showered. She stared at them in annoyance. Why did Matthew always presume she'd tidy up after him? She wouldn't dream of treating him like a servant, expecting him to pick up her knickers complete with – she grimaced as she retrieved Matthew's inside-out boxers – brown skid marks. Ewww! Well that certainly cancelled out her shame of sleeping in a vomit-covered bed.

Two hours later, Amber was still feeling fragile. Only her pale complexion gave away the fact that she wasn't yet her old self. The house was shining after being blitzed, and also fragrant after liberal squirts from a floral-scented aerosol. She'd just collapsed into a squashy arm chair with a mug of tea when Matthew came through the front door.

From her position in the lounge, Amber was able to see her boyfriend before he spotted her. In the five seconds that Matthew was oblivious to being watched, Amber noted that her boyfriend's face was lit up brighter than Rudolph the reindeer's nose. He was also exuding more happiness than Father Christmas putting his feet up after a record night of delivering presents. Her eyes swept over Matthew, from his freshly washed shiny hair to his highly polished shoes. He was wearing a particularly fetching shirt under a – was that new? – Designer jacket and looked more styled than David Beckham.

Her nose twitched as a whiff of aftershave wafted on an updraft of cold air. The scent overrode the floral aerosol squirts. Since when had Matthew started wearing aftershave on a Sunday? Amber took a sip of her tea and, over the china rim, regarded her boyfriend as he removed his shoes and slipped off the posh jacket.

Matthew turned to hang his coat on the stand in the hall, and caught sight of Amber watching him through the open lounge doorway. His face clouded, and the warm glow he'd been emitting notched down several degrees. Suddenly the atmosphere was chilly.

'Hi,' said Amber.

'Hello,' said Matthew tersely. He wandered over and flopped down on the other armchair.

Amber decided it was best to get her apology over and done with. 'Sorry I chucked up on you last night.'

Matthew shrugged. 'I'd like to say that's okay, but it's not. It was pretty revolting.'

'Obviously. Sorry again,' said Amber. 'Where have you been?' She had meant for her question to have a conversational tone. Instead, because she was still feeling fragile, the words unfortunately came out like a pistol-shot accusation.

'While you've been sitting there drinking tea and nursing a hangover,' said Matthew indignantly, 'I've been to work.'

Amber recalled chatting with Dee and Chrissie about making today one for no-nonsense talks with their partners. The three friends had all agreed they wanted to salvage their relationships.

'I *have* been working,' said Amber.

'Really?' asked Matthew. 'I'm astonished you've been to Hood, Mann & Derek on a Sunday when you not only look like crap, but must feel like it too.

Amber nearly choked on her tea. Matthew was

78

being deliberately obtuse. 'I have two jobs, actually.'

Mathew looked puzzled. 'Since when?'

'Since you moved into my house,' said Amber. Ah, that had rattled him. Matthew didn't like Amber reminding him the house was hers. It was her name on the deeds, and she was the one who paid the mortgage. She'd bought the property before she'd met Matthew. The deposit had been paid with money bequeathed by her deceased granny. Matthew didn't contribute anything other than "keep", which was only right and fair. He had a voracious appetite and practically ate her out of house and home. 'My *first* job,' said Amber matter-of-factly, 'is working as a legal PA. My *second* job is looking after you.'

'Me?' Matthew laughed humourlessly.

'Yes. You. While you've been out at,' she posted quotation marks in the air, '"the office", I've been busy. I made the bed you slept in–'

'–because you threw up in the bed I usually sleep in,' Matthew pointed out.

Amber ignored him and ploughed on. She began ticking off on her fingers everything she did for Matthew. 'I pick up after you, do your washing, ironing, do the housework, clean the windows, shop for you, and cook. You rarely mow the lawn–'

'–well it's *your* bloody lawn, as you've now reminded me. Why the hell should I mow the sodding thing?'

'It's called "pulling your weight",' Amber retorted. 'I do loads for you, so it wouldn't hurt you to help occasionally.'

'I am helping,' said Matthew, his eyes narrowing.

'How?' Amber demanded.

'I've been working my socks off, Amber, as you well know. How many men go into the office at weekends, eh?'

'And what exactly are you achieving there,

Matthew?' asked Amber boldly.

'Stacks of money, if all my number crunching and go-getting pays off.'

'I see.' Amber took another sip of her tea. 'And who is benefitting from this financial increase *if* it comes off?'

'Us, of course,' Matthew harrumphed.

'You think?'

'What's that remark supposed to mean?'

'You earn good money anyway. Three times as much as me. What exactly do you do with it?'

'I resent the line of questioning you're taking,' said Matthew in annoyance.

'Really? I don't,' said Amber flippantly.

'I give you plenty of housekeeping every month.'

Amber shook her head. 'That's not housekeeping, Matthew. It's meant to be grocery money, but it barely covers the cost of what you eat, never mind the expensive wines you drink. You're doing very well out of me. You must have a bank balance to rival Donald Trump.'

'Oh don't be ridiculous,' Matthew scoffed. 'You always did have the ability to talk out of your backside.'

'Not this time, Matthew. In fact, do please explain why you spent the paltry sum of ten pounds on me last Christmas?'

'Ten pounds?' Matthew blustered. 'Try putting a zero on that!'

'I checked the Argos website. I know exactly how much you spent.'

'I've had enough of this,' said Matthew, standing up.

'Where have you *really* been today, Matthew?' A part of Amber was appalled that her mouth had spat the question out. It had certainly failed to consult her brain before going down an accusatory route.'

'Fuck you, Amber.'

'And fuck you too,' Amber spat. Oh no. She hadn't meant for the two of them to argue like this. She'd wanted things to be put right – for Matthew to see the funny side of his drunken girlfriend endearingly attempting lap-dancing in order to please him, even if she had puked up. She'd hoped he'd laugh it off and say, 'It's a good thing you have charms in other areas so I can overlook what happened. Come here, you ravishing creature. Let me kiss all your tiredness away, and then we're going to sit down and talk about all the money I've saved up. I want us to start sharing the cost of things properly – not forgetting planning a wedding that will put more roses in your cheeks than a bride's bouquet.'

Instead they spent the rest of the day not talking to each other. Amber felt too tired and upset to eat anything. She punished Matthew by not cooking any dinner, but he didn't seem particularly bothered. She wondered if he'd eaten earlier. Perhaps he'd had a pizza on the go.

At bedtime Matthew took himself off to the spare bedroom for the second night. Five minutes later, Amber crawled into the double bed she usually shared with her boyfriend. The sheets were beautifully fragrant but so cold without Matthew next to her. What a horrible weekend it had been. Reaching out to the bedside table, she plugged her mobile phone into its charger, and set the alarm for seven the following morning. Thirty seconds later the mobile buzzed. Her heart leapt. Perhaps it was Matthew texting from the other side of the bedroom wall. She grabbed it, desperately hoping to read: *Amber, I'm feeling so lonely without you. Fancy showing me those dance moves again*? She'd fall into his arms in a flash. Instead it was a WhatsApp message from Dee. She'd set up a group chat for the three of them under the name "Secs in the City".

Amber gave the smallest of smiles. She clicked on Dee's message.

Sorry to text late, girls, but I'm beyond miserable. I hope the two of you had a better evening than mine. Will catch up with you both tomorrow. But be warned, I might slump over my keyboard in a flood of tears! xx

Amber immediately texted back.

Your evening cannot have been any worse than mine. Matthew is sleeping in the spare room. Even Mr Tomkin has abandoned me xx

Seconds later, the mobile pinged with a message from Chrissie.

I'm in bed and crying my eyes out. Have had the worst weekend ever xx

Dee was the next to reply.

Okay, girls. Sounds like Plan A – straight talking with our men – has been a bigger flop than my tits without a bra. Hugs to you both. We'll fully update each other tomorrow at the office and discuss Plan B. Sleep tight xx

Thanks, Dee. This from Chrissie. *Don't know what I'd do without my besties* xx

Amber's fingers flew across the screen's keypad.

I'll second that. See you both tomorrow xx

Feeling a smidgen happier she wasn't alone in her misery, Amber curled into the foetal position. Closing her eyes, she wondered what Dee would come up with for Plan B.

Chapter Fourteen

Dee's Sunday...

At the time of Amber still slumbering in her puke-whiffy bed, Dee had set about making Josh a top-notch Sunday morning breakfast.

There was an old saying Dee's mum had sworn by. "The way to a man's heart is through his stomach." Dee had decided to put it to the test. She'd made Josh the full works. Egg, bacon, sausage, beans, fried tomatoes, mushrooms and giant slabs of toast smothered in real butter, not margarine.

'Brekkie, darling,' she trilled as she set his plate down on the breakfast bar.

Josh came into the kitchen, pulled out a tall stool, and stared at the heaped plate in disdain. 'I can't eat all this.'

'Oh.' Dee was visibly crestfallen.

'I'm still full from last night's meal with Roger Brown.'

Dee resisted the temptation to ask why Josh's female dinner companion had a man's name and innocently said, 'Poor Josh. It must have been a huge steak.'

'Yes, it was.'

Dee busied herself loading up her own plate, all the while appearing cheerful and upbeat, even though her brain was whirling. She'd given Josh the perfect opportunity to correct himself and say, 'Steak? What am I talking about! I took Roger Brown to Serafino's Cucina in Sevenoaks. I had a bowl of spaghetti. It was the size of a coffee table. I don't think I'll want anything to eat until next week. And by the way, Roger is a transvestite. He always wears a dress and full make-up on a Saturday night.

83

He completely fooled the head waiter.' But Josh said nothing. Instead he picked up his knife and fork and began toying with a sausage.

'Nice?' Dee asked. She sat down opposite, her own plate before her.

'S'okay,' Josh shrugged.

'Excellent!' Her tone was jolly, belying any anxiety. 'I do love a bit of sausage,' she chirruped. Dee hadn't meant for her banter to sound smutty, but it had.

Josh put down his knife and fork, and regarded her coolly. 'Are you being sarcastic because we haven't had sex recently?'

Dee's eyes widened. 'No. I'm simply saying I like a nice big sausage.' Oh heck. Josh would think she was winding him up. 'And...and egg,' she added. She speared a virgin yolk which oozed over a sausage. 'Mmmm,' she said, sounding like she was orgasming.

'Okay, I get it,' said Josh, looking peeved. 'You're definitely being facetious about the lack of sex.'

Dee continued to smile, but her mouth was suddenly very dry. She ran her tongue across her lips. 'No, Josh, I'm not. Really.'

'Then what's with all the oohing and aahing and lip licking? I presume you're dropping hints.'

Dee put down her own knife and fork. 'Would it be so bad if I *was* dropping hints?'

'I knew it,' Josh crowed. 'You want sex.'

'Is that an invitation?'

'No.'

'Can I ask why?'

'I'm not up for it.'

'And what about Willy? Do you think Willy might be up for it if I smear egg yolk all over him and lick it off?'

Josh regarded Dee as if she'd spoken in tongues. 'Are you feeling all right?'

'Never better. You?' Now the subject of sex had come up she was determined to pursue the subject to the bitter end.

'I'm tired,' Josh snapped.

'At eleven o'clock in the morning?'

'I have a very physical job,' Josh countered.

'Then perhaps you need to go back to bed. With me,' Dee added seductively. 'I'll massage all the kinks out of you and,' she waggled her eyebrows, 'kiss your tired bits better.'

'I'd like to relax, thanks. Not embark on a sexual marathon.'

'I'm not asking for one. I'm suggesting we have sex. You can lay back and think of England while I climb on board. In fact, forget the bedroom. Let's do it in the kitchen!' She whipped off her sweatshirt revealing a jacked-up bosom. Dee was a busty girl and proud of her assets. When she'd first got together with Josh, he'd joyfully caressed her breasts and called them "Dee's Delights". Well now they could work their magic on her boyfriend all over again. She leant back on the tall stool, thrusting out her "delights" for Josh to admire. 'You'd better tell the soldier in your trousers to start standing to attention,' she purred.

'Dee, I said I don't want a sexual mara–'

'I'll do all the work,' she said dismissively, and began shaking her shoulders so her breasts jiggled in their lacy hammock. 'All you have to do,' she said, her voice breathy as she tangled her fingers in her hair and parted her lips wantonly, 'is sit there, you...you hunky..,' she tried to quickly think of something sexy to call Josh, but the lie he'd told invaded her brain, '...steak.' Bugger. She ploughed on. 'I want to jump off this stool, leap on your lap and grind like...,' oh God, like what? She was so badly out of practice. '...like a salt mill all over your pepper pot and–'

'Dee, I really think you should put your top back on and–'

'Oooooooh,' Dee gasped, sounding like the soundtrack to a porn movie. She unhooked her bra and released her boobs. They bounced forth in fulsome glory, until gravity took over. Josh watched, unmoved, as her breasts landed with a faint squelch on her plate.

Dee decided to style it out, and gave a naughty giggle. 'Bet you weren't expecting bosoms with your bacon, eh?' She shoved her hands into her breakfast and began smearing brown sauce and egg yolk across her nipples. 'Ahhhhh,' she gasped, shuddering with apparent pleasure. 'Get your tongue out, babe,' she panted, 'and start licking this lot off.'

Josh jumped off his stool. But instead of roaring towards her in a blaze of hot breath and bulging trousers, he headed toward the kitchen door. Dee's gung-ho shrivelled and died.

'W-where are you going?' she asked in a panicky voice.

'Out,' snapped Josh.'

'B-but why? Please, stay. Let's have some fun.'

'Fun?' Josh barked. 'Look at you, Dee. Are you deranged? And since when did "hunky steak" become a term of endearment? What the hell's got into you?'

'Not you, that's for sure,' Dee shouted. She felt completely humiliated, but also angry. Josh had made her feel smaller than the condiments on the breakfast bar. Only the other day he had told her she was boring and unimaginative in bed. Here she was, pulling out all the stops and making Nigella Lawson look like Theresa May in a soup kitchen, but Josh wasn't having any of it. 'What's wrong with initiating sex with my boyfriend?' she asked in a small voice. 'I can't remember the last time you made love to me.' Tears threatened. She tried to blink them back into their tear ducts. She knew Josh wasn't swayed by blubbing. But the more she tried to stop it from happening, the harder it became. A small river seemed to be rushing down her face, dripping off her chin, and splashing across her food-covered breasts. Her nose was filling up with snot and threatening to dribble. When she spoke, her voice was choked with emotion. 'Don't you f-fancy me anymore?'

There. She'd asked the question. It was out. She'd meant to spend today taking a softly-softly approach with Josh, gently cajoling him to get to the bottom of what was wrong between them. But now, after weeks of wondering, she'd ended up throwing a very dangerous question at him. It hung in the air like an unexploded hand grenade, and from the expression on Josh's face he was contemplating whether to pull out the pin. Dee didn't have long to wait.

'No, Dee,' Josh murmured. 'I don't fancy you anymore.'

And Dee felt the explosion of his answer boom through her heart, ripping it into a million tiny pieces.

Chapter Fifteen

Chrissie's Sunday...

At the time of Dee sitting at her breakfast bar with her bare breasts covered in fry-up, Chrissie had been scrubbing the maisonette.

She'd slept fitfully. It had been after two in the morning before everybody had left. She'd got as far as washing up the glasses and plates before tiredness had overwhelmed her. By the time she'd crawled under the duvet it was nearly three in the morning. Andrew had been fast asleep, on his back, mouth open. Full of booze, he'd been snoring like ten farrowing pigs. It seemed as though Chrissie had barely fallen asleep when she'd been awoken by Andrew. He'd rolled onto his side, lifted one buttock and loudly farted. It had sounded like a firework going off, and she'd nearly choked on the smell.

The neon figures of the alarm clock read just before seven in the morning. So much for a Sunday lie-in. Slipping out of bed, Chrissie pulled her night t-shirt across her nose in an attempt at making a gasmask. She pulled on some old jogging bottoms and left Andrew slumbering.

Outside, not even the January sun was awake. Chrissie made herself a strong coffee hoping a caffeine hit would pin back her eyelids. Downing the scalding liquid, she began deep-cleaning the maisonette. She suspected there was a psychological reason for her voracious scrubbing. It was as if the harder she scoured, the more she removed the essence of those men who'd been in her home. There was something about them that made her skin crawl.

Chrissie squirted the furniture with anti-bacterial liquid, rubbing away grubby fingerprints, and marks that had also been left on the walls. Her polishing cloth whirled over the coffee table until it shone. She even cleaned the door handle and light switch. A forensics team would have been hard pushed to prove a crowd of men had been in her lounge a few hours ago. She decided to leave the bedroom until Andrew was awake. At least none of the men had been in there. Chrissie then turned her attention to the small kitchen, before tackling the tiniest room – the disgusting bathroom.

She had no idea whether it was just Mick who'd used the loo, or all eleven men, but aim had been awful. The stink of urine was like that of a public urinal. Holding her breath, she went in armed with soapy water, disinfectant, an old-fashioned scrubbing brush, and a roll of kitchen towel to dry off the lino. She hoped pee hadn't seeped into the many cracks within the old flooring, otherwise the smell would be difficult to shift.

Finishing off, she patted the floor dry. She emptied a bottle of bleach down the loo. Chrissie was just shuddering at the memory of Mick's bowel motion winking up at her, when Andrew appeared in the bathroom doorway. He was dressed, albeit scruffily.

'Hurry up, Chrissie. I need a pee.'

'One second.' She straightened up, easing kinks out of her body, then picked up her bucket of cleaning paraphernalia. 'Could you watch your aim, please.'

'I'm not a two-year-old,' said Andrew crossly. 'I do know how to pee in a straight line.'

'Good. In that case perhaps you could show your mates.'

'Leave my friends out of it, Chrissie. I don't know why you get so worked up about them. They're nice enough.'

Chrissie snorted. The memory of Mick's hand on

her breast was still fresh. 'Odd friends you keep. I reckon if you groped one of their wives you'd get a smack in the mouth for your efforts.'

Andrew rolled his eyes and pushed past her to the toilet. 'You shouldn't make up stuff like that,' he said, over the sound of relieving himself. 'It's bang out of order.'

'Andrew, I think it's about time we had a frank chat.'

'Don't you mean "nag"? He shook his privates before tucking everything away. He was about to move past Chrissie, when she blocked his exit.

'Correct me if I'm wrong, but you told me you weren't aged two.'

'Eh?'

'As you're not two years old and can easily reach the flush on the toilet, how about you go back and pull the chain?'

'Oh for—'

'And wash your hands afterwards.'

'What are you? My mum?'

'Sometimes I feel like it,' Chrissie snapped. 'Do you want a cup of tea?'

'If it's not any trouble,' said Andrew sarcastically. 'Toast would be nice, too.'

Back in the kitchen, Chrissie put away her cleaning bucket and washed her hands again. They were cracked and sore in places. Even though the maisonette was as shiny as a new pin, she still felt it was dirty. She wanted to get out of this place. It was definitely time to move. She popped two slices of bread into the toaster. As an afterthought she added another for herself, even though she wasn't really hungry. There was too much anger festering away in her stomach to allow much food in there right now.

Andrew pulled out a chair and flopped down at the ancient Formica table. He rubbed the heels of his hands over his face a few times, and then regarded Chrissie with bloodshot eyes. 'I think I have a hangover.'

'Yes,' said Chrissie acidly, 'and I expect your mates have one too.' The toast popped up and she busied herself with the spreading of cheap margarine.

'Any chance of a couple of eggs? Think I need something to mop up the alcohol.'

Reaching inside a cupboard for the frying pan, Chrissie's mouth set in a thin line. She needed to stop doing that with her lips. It was becoming a habit. If she wasn't careful her facial muscles would end up permanently set in that expression, so she looked like a twenty-seven-going-on-sixty-seven-year-old battle-axe. She spoke over her shoulder to Andrew as she poured oil into the pan and cracked the eggs.

'Today I would like us to spend some quality time together.'

'Doing what?' Andrew sounded horrified. 'I have business to do.'

'What business?'

'Just...business.'

'Ah,' said Chrissie, flipping the eggs, 'you mean *dodgy* business.'

'So?' Andrew's voice was surly. 'What does it matter to you? I'm trying to make a few extra quid.'

Chrissie scooped the eggs out of the pan and set them on the almost-cold toast. 'I don't want you doing anything illegal.'

'It's not illegal.'

'Of course it is.'

'You're splitting hairs. On this estate, it goes on all the time. The police are always parked down the road. They see everything and don't even bat an eyelid. As long as Mick bungs them a few notes, they're as good as gold. They appreciate that people like us need to make a living.'

Chrissie could feel herself getting frustrated. 'What exactly are "people like us"? And are you lumping *me* into that category? Because you can think again. I'll have nothing to do with dubious drug deals, Andrew. Nor do I want you having anything to do with these people either. You've *got* a job, for heaven's sake.' She sat down on the chair opposite and bit into her toast.

'Yeah, but my job doesn't pay enough.'

'Well if you binned those shady mates, your job would more than pay enough. You'd save a fortune not buying a pub's worth of booze every week, not forgetting,' she felt her lip shift from thin line to sneer, 'your mates' *luxuries.*'

'You don't understand,' Andrew sighed.

'You're right, I don't.'

'Don't emasculate me, Chrissie. I can't live here and not join in. We'd end up being targeted. Is that what you want? A brick through the window?'

'Don't you think you're being a bit of a drama queen?'

Andrew's face darkened. 'No. You have no idea what these guys are like. It's good to keep on the right side of them.'

'Then the sooner we move from this place, the better.'

'We can't. Not yet. Apart from anything else I...er...owe them a bit of money.'

Chrissie's jaw stopped rotating. 'What for?'

'Just...well...nothing major. A couple of card games. It was a bit of fun.'

'How much?'

'Well, all right, it was a lot of fun.'

'I mean,' said Chrissie, her voice dangerously quiet, 'how much *money* do you owe?'

'Oh. Ah...give or take a tenner...about two thousand pounds.'

'Two thous–' Chrissie nearly choked on the remainder of her toast.

'Yeah. So it's important I do a few deals for them until I'm square.'

'You mean drug deals?'

Andrew pushed a loaded fork into his mouth so he didn't have to answer. Chrissie glared at him. What on earth was she doing with this man? He was rapidly turning into the biggest loser she'd ever met. Where was the sweet young lad she'd first met? It seemed like a lifetime ago.

'Andrew,' she cleared her throat, 'I don't want to know about your dodgy deals. Just promise me you're going to stop.' Andrew ignored her and carried on eating. 'I can't live with someone who is behaving not just criminally, but immorally.'

Andrew finished chewing and swallowed. He regarded her coolly. 'Perhaps it's best you don't live with me then.' Chrissie was so shocked, for a moment she couldn't speak. She stared at Andrew incredulously as he put his knife and fork together. Scraping back the chair, he reached for the jacket hanging off the back.

'W-where are you going?' Chrissie stuttered.

'I've already told you. I have things to do.'

Chrissie's eyes filled with tears. She was over-tired, overwrought and hacked off. 'What about us, Andrew?'

Andrew regarded her for a moment. When he spoke, the words were careless. 'What about us?'

Chapter Sixteen

When Monday morning rolled around, it was three very subdued young women who drooped through the old-fashioned doors of Hood, Mann & Derek.

Amber's hangover had lasted the entirety of Sunday. Although she was now headache-free, it had taken its toll on her. Under her eyes she had enormous grey circles, and her complexion was the colour of putty. She'd cried herself to sleep on Sunday night. This morning, her mouth was cast down like an upside-down crescent moon.

Dee's eyes were puffy and bloodshot from yesterday's sob fest. This morning they resembled two mini-doughnuts with jam-ring centres. She'd been astonished how much water could flow from tear ducts. She still had a pressure headache from bawling. Emotionally, Dee was feeling more fragile than her granny's prized porcelain teapot.

Chrissie was so pale she looked like a ghost with joke Halloween red eyes. To the casual onlooker, Chrissie was physically sitting at her office desk. However, her inner essence was a universe away. She looked like somebody in deep shock.

Amber was the first to speak. 'Well, girls. You both look how I feel. And I suspect *I* look how *you* both feel.'

'Words like "dog" and "pooh" come to mind,' Dee muttered.

'Chrissie?' asked Amber. 'What about you? Hello? Earth to Chrissie!'

'Hmmm?' Chrissie regarded Amber vacantly.

'Oh for goodness sake,' Amber huffed. 'Look at the state of us. We're like chuffing zombies. How can three men reduce us to *this*? I'm going to put the kettle on and make some strong coffee, and then we're going to tell each other exactly what happened yesterday.'

'Morning, girls,' said Steve Hood, sweeping through the open plan office en-route to his own.

'Morning,' Dee and Amber replied. Chrissie didn't answer. Instead she continued staring blankly at her monitor, which she had yet to switch on.

'If you're off to the kitchen, Amber,' said Steve, 'I'll have a coffee, please. And then if you could pop into my office, I need to go over some urgent files with you.' Steve gave a mischievous grin to Chrissie and Dee. 'Sorry, ladies, but your big chat about putting the world to rights with Amber will have to wait a bit.' He disappeared into his office leaving Dee with eyes threatening to brim over. Chrissie remained gazing into space.

Five minutes later, Amber returned with a tray of steaming drinks. She set a mug down first on Dee's desk, and then put the tray down on her own desk before walking over to Chrissie. 'Come on, sweetie,' she murmured, and flicked on Chrissie's monitor. 'Get that coat off and get typing.' Chrissie's boss had obviously been in bright and early. There was a stack of files on her desk with three cassettes of dictation waiting. Unlike the big law firms in London, Hood Mann & Derek had yet to up their game and switch to digital dictation. 'Let's buck up. On top of everything else, the last thing we need is getting fired. Let me take this into Steve, and then I'll give you a hand with those tapes.'

But when Amber walked into Steve's office with their coffees and her notebook, she realised it might be some time before she could help Chrissie out with her typing. Steve's briefcase was open on the long console table that ran along one wall, and his desk was already strewn with papers and files.

'Ah, coffee.' He flashed a grateful smile, then did a double take at Amber's face. 'Wow. Heavy weekend?'

'Cheers,' Amber sighed. 'I guess that's your diplomatic way of letting me know I look rough.'

'As a badger's bum,' said Steve, although his eyes were twinkling.

Amber looked at her boss. He was giving off the inner glow of someone who'd run a couple of miles before work, breakfasted on organic muesli, and then showered in mountain water. 'I'd rather talk about your weekend,' she replied, deflecting Steve's question.

'It was great, thanks,' Steve's smile widened. 'I took myself over to Trosley Country Park, and had a great hike with my mate.'

Ah, yes, thought Amber. *Spending the weekend, as usual, with his mate.* 'You're very secretive about *your mate*,' said Amber, taking a noisy slurp of coffee.

'Do you think?' asked Steve impishly. 'In what way?'

'In all the time I've worked for you, you've never even mentioned his name.'

'Who says my mate is a "him"?'

Amber arched one eyebrow. 'Is your mate a "her" then?'

'No,' Steve grinned.

'So why don't you ever mention his name?'

'He's shy.'

'You know, it's nothing to be ashamed of.'

'Is that so?'

'Not in this day and age. Anything goes.'

'Well thanks for reminding me,' said Steve. 'I'll be sure to tell him.'

'Ah, I see. He doesn't want you discussing him with me.'

'He's never actually said that.'

'Oh.' Amber frowned, and took another sip of coffee. 'So, it's *you* who would rather not discuss him with me.'

'My goodness, Amber, you have to get up early in the morning to get one past you, eh!'

Amber sniffed. 'Be like that then. It doesn't bother me either way. You know,' she leant forward and addressed Steve cosily, 'You don't need to be so buttoned-up about your private life. We've all been there.'

'Really?'

'Oh yes. It happened to me once. I was only sixteen. I got a bit...muddled.'

'I'd never have guessed.'

Amber nodded. 'At the time, I was hanging out with,' she paused and gave Steve a meaningful look, '*a mate*, but when she tried to...well, you know...I realised I wasn't that way after all.'

'Weren't you?'

'No, especially when I met Mark Stiles. He was just,' Amber put her fingers together and kissed them, 'absolute heaven.'

'I think we might be at cross-purposes you know,' said Steve. His eyes were dancing as if something was amusing. 'And what about your pals out there?' he jerked his head in the direction of Dee and Chrissie. 'What's up with them?'

'Um, they had...a heavy weekend too.'

'The three of you look like you could use an early night.'

A shadow fell across Amber's face. She didn't want to think about going home. It would mean another evening of cold war with Matthew. She wished he'd stop sleeping in the spare room. They hadn't spoken since yesterday afternoon.

'So,' Steve smiled kindly as he picked up a file, 'it was fascinating hearing about Mark Stiles and when you were sixteen, but we need to get on with some work.'

Amber drained her coffee, and selected a clean

97

page in her notebook. Steve began with instructions to telephone the Land Registry, then diarise a client meeting, followed by amendments to an eighty-page lease with more clauses than Father Christmas negotiating a loft extension with North Pole's planning department. Amber's concentration fragmented when the shriek of a familiar voice was heard outside Steve's office door.

'Dah-lings! Can you guess what Madam Rosa told me on Saturday night?'

Amber grimaced. You didn't have to be Madam Rosa to work out that Cougar Kate had come to gloat.

Chapter Seventeen

When Amber emerged from Steve's office with a stack of heavy files, it was to find Cougar Kate still holding court with Chrissie and Dee – not that either of them looked like they were listening. Dee was wearing a glazed expression, and Chrissie was transfixed by the cursor flashing away on her monitor. She didn't look like she'd moved since Amber had left her. To the side of her keyboard, dictation tapes and files remained untouched.

'*There* you are,' tutted Cougar Kate. She was perched on the edge of Amber's desk. Amber bristled with annoyance. It was *her* desk. Right now, when her home life was so uncertain and precarious, that desk was a sanctuary. The last thing she needed was this blasted woman's well-preserved derriere invading both her personal space, and her refuge.

'Hello,' said Amber curtly. 'Shift your butt, please. I need to put these down,' Amber nodded at the armful of hefty files.

'Of course,' said Cougar Kate. She jumped up, but repositioned herself at the other end of the desk.

Amber flopped down on her typing stool. 'Don't you have anything to do?' she asked meaningfully, reaching for her notebook. Just because she'd visited Cougar Kate's house and got catastrophically drunk on the woman's birthday booze, didn't mean they were now best buddies.

'No. Clive's in a meeting until mid-day. Now that you're finally here, Amber, I'll have to repeat myself all over again.'

It struck Amber that Cougar Kate had deliberately waited for her to come out of Steve's office. 'You'll have to make it very quick,' said Amber coolly. 'Some of us have a heap of work to get through.'

'Of course, I wouldn't dream of holding you up.'

'Unless you want to help?' asked Amber slyly.

'Oh no can do, dah-ling. My specialities are in probate law, not conveyancing.' She wrinkled her nose. 'I simply couldn't be bothered to wade my way through a document like this.' She picked up the eighty-page lease, held it aloft between her thumb and forefinger and regarded it as if it were dog turd. 'I mean, look at all this waffle. Why can't it be simplified? "No you cannot use the communal gardens to sunbathe in the nuddy, no you're not allowed to park your car in any space other than your own, and yes you do need to get a rota going with neighbours about cleaning shared areas." Whereas this,' she smacked the lease with her free hand, 'would likely send an insomniac to sleep.'

'It's only forty-year-old women that send me to sleep,' Amber sniped.

Cougar Kate gave a tinkle of fake laughter. 'You're so funny, Amber.'

Amber rolled her eyes. 'Seriously, I have to make some phone calls. What did you want?'

'Well, as I've not had any sense out of this one,' Cougar Kate jerked her head at Chrissie, 'I wanted to chat about your reading. Dee tells me you all had pretty rotten news.'

'Yup, but it's obvious that Madam Rosa spouted complete tosh as a marketing ploy. The three of us had almost identical readings – and not pleasant ones at that. Surely fortune tellers should have a moral code of conduct to stop them wrecking people's weekends.'

'I'm sure they have,' Cougar Kate countered, 'but nobody was told they were going to die, so whatever she said cannot be immoral.'

'That's not the point,' Amber snapped. 'Telling the three of us our relationships are in crisis wasn't–'

Too late Amber caught Dee flashing a warning look.

Cougar Kate pounced. 'Madam Rosa told you that, did she? That your relationship is in trouble?'

Was it Amber's imagination, or did Cougar Kate sound like she was purring? Amber shrugged dismissively. 'Our relationships are all fine, thank you very much.'

'If you say so,' said Cougar Kate sweetly. 'Meanwhile, let me tell you about *my* reading.' She smiled like a cat who'd been given cream bought at Harrods instead of semi-skimmed from Tesco. 'Madam Rosa was absolutely spot-on. She told me all about my love life–'

'That must have used up forty-four minutes of the forty-five-minute reading,' Amber muttered.

'–all the heartbreaks, all the disappointments. Then she gave me a message from my granny who said she was sorry she wouldn't be able to attend my wedding, but she'd be there in spirit. Granny said it's going to be a fabulous day!'

'Congratulations,' said Amber sarcastically. 'And have you met this husband-to-be yet, or is he still being sourced by supernatural forces before beaming into your life on Granny's cosmic ray?'

Cougar Kate gave another affected laugh. 'I wish I had your wit, Amber.'

'I wish I could get on with my work,' Amber grumbled, one hand hovering over the telephone. She really did need to make some calls, although her fingers itched to curl around the handset and shove it into Cougar Kate's arrogant mouth. That would shut the woman up for a bit.

'Madam Rosa indicated my future hubby has already come into my life. He just needs to, er,' Cougar Kate studied her scarlet-painted nails for a moment, 'extricate himself from his current

101

situation.'

'No surprises there, then,' said Amber, under her breath.

'What was that?'

'Nothing.'

'Anyway, I wanted to let you all know that I won't be Miss Colgan for much longer. Madam Rosa did rather spoil it by adding this man wasn't the right one for me, but I'm not going to take any notice. So, what do you think? Soon I will be getting married. Amazing, eh?'

'Thrilling,' said Amber, picking up the phone.

At that moment Steve came out of his office. 'Have you made those calls yet, Amber?'

'I'm trying,' said Amber, jerking her head at Cougar Kate.

'Ah, Katherine,' said Steve. Was it Amber's imagination or had the temperature suddenly dropped by several degrees?

'Hello, Stevie,' said Cougar Kate, fluttering her eyelashes in a coquettish manner. 'Sorry to hold Amber up. I'm just leaving.' Steve gave a cursory nod and disappeared back into his office. 'Phwoar, isn't he divine! I wouldn't say no to him taking me to task over his filing cabinet.'

'You'd be wasting your time if you did,' said Amber.

'You shouldn't say things like that,' said Cougar Kate, smirking. 'I love a challenge. I think I might have one last pre-wedding fling. It will involve me, Mr Hood, and that very snazzy tie he's wearing. Catch my drift?'

'Yes, but you're not catching mine,' said Amber. Cougar Kate obviously didn't realise Steve was gay, but it wasn't Amber's place to gossip and spill secrets about her boss.

'Well I can see you're busy.' Cougar Kate stood up, smoothing down her tailored skirt. It had a huge split up one side, revealing plenty of leg as she sashayed off. 'Catch you later, girlies,' she trilled. She blew them all a kiss, Marilyn Monroe style, and then took her leave.

'That woman is the pits,' muttered Chrissie.

'Good heavens,' said Amber, pretending to fall off her chair in shock. 'Welcome back to Planet Earth, Chrissie. We've missed you.'

'Listen, girls,' said Dee, 'we really do need to crack on. How about we go to the café around the corner for lunch? We can then properly discuss our respective Sunday sagas – away from flapping ears – and decide upon our next plan of action.'

Chrissie and Amber nodded in agreement. Feeling slightly happier, they finally settled down to work. Having a plan gave them something to focus on, even if they didn't yet know what it would be.

Chapter Eighteen

Never did a lunch hour go by so swiftly. Dee, Chrissie and Amber sat at a table in the far corner of Gravesend's answer to all-day-breakfast heaven, an upmarket greasy spoon establishment by the name of "Come Fry With Me".

'Heaven only knows what this place is doing to our cholesterol levels,' said Amber, devouring fatty bacon and fried egg running in oil.

'Listen,' said Dee, 'never mind what the cholesterol is doing to our hearts, let's concentrate on what our boyfriends are doing to them instead. Do you know, I swear I can feel mine physically hurting?' She put a hand over her left boob and massaged gently.

'I guess that's why it's called heart*ache*,' said Chrissie, 'and stop doing that, Dee. It looks like you're feeling yourself up. There's a suit two tables to the left leering at you.'

'I should be so flattered,' muttered Dee, but she dropped her hand and picked up her knife and fork again. 'I'm certainly not getting any attention in that department from Josh,' she whispered. Her mouth drooped. Her meal was all too reminiscent of the last one she'd shared with her boyfriend. 'I might as well be honest with you, girls. After Josh told me I was boring and unimaginative in bed, yesterday I pulled out all the stops for him.'

'This sounds horribly familiar,' said Amber, 'but I'll tell you my story in a minute. You go first, Dee.'

'Right. Well yesterday morning, I cooked Josh the biggest fry-up you can imagine. The subject of sex came up – or rather the lack of it – so I seized the opportunity and stripped off in the kitchen.'

'Blimey,' said Chrissie. 'Is this leading to sex food by any chance?'

'Yes,' Dee nodded. 'There I was, literally offering myself on his breakfast plate, and he told me he no longer fancied me.'

'Maybe,' Chrissie suggested, 'sex food isn't Josh's speciality?'

'Huh. In the old days, he'd have been ecstatic to see me wearing nothing but two fried eggs and a big smile.'

At the nearby table the suit dropped his newspaper, picked it up, dropped it again, and then firmly shook it out. It was obvious he wasn't reading one word.

'Perhaps you need to up your game?' suggested Chrissie. 'Swap the fried eggs for champagne, and pour it into your navel.'

'Sadly, I don't think it would make any difference,' said Dee. 'He's gone off me. Plain and simple. I no longer dong his gong.'

'The prat,' said Chrissie, stabbing at a mushroom with her fork.

Amber sighed. 'I can't remember the last time Matthew and I put our bed springs through a good workout. On Saturday night, after you dropped me home, I attempted lap dancing in an effort to get things going.'

'And did it?' asked Dee.

'Yeah. It got him going into the spare room. That's how unattractive I am to him.'

'I thought you said you were very poorly on Saturday night?' asked Chrissie.

'I was. But this was before I was unwell. Matthew makes me feel as sexually attractive as an old dog with halitosis. I mean, what man stays late at the office night after night, and works weekends without a sniff of paid overtime? When I challenged him, he said he was after promotion and doing it for us.'

'Maybe he is,' said Chrissie.

105

'Rubbish,' Amber scoffed. 'There's no affection from Matthew. No sweet words. Zilch. I might as well be a friendly housekeeper who picks up after him, puts his meals on the table and, if I'm very lucky, have him say the occasional thank you. Anyway, he's currently sleeping in the spare room and not even talking to me. In fact, I'm starting to wonder if Madam Rosa is right.'

'Whaaat?' said Dee. 'You mean–'

'Yes, that's exactly what I mean,' said Amber, suddenly watery-eyed. 'He *must* be seeing another woman. Given that he can't stay away from his office, maybe she works with him. If I find out who she is,' said Amber, viciously attacking a sausage, 'she'll be brown bread.'

'And what about you, Chrissie?' asked Dee. 'How's your love life?'

Chrissie grimaced. 'Non-existent, unless you count being groped by one of Andrew's mates.'

'No!' said Amber and Dee together. Both women were aghast.

'When I told Andrew, he called me a liar and trouble maker.'

'You have to be kidding?' said Amber, outraged.

What a jerk!' said Dee.

'Even worse, Andrew has got in with the wrong crowd on the estate.' Chrissie hesitated, suddenly unsure exactly how much to tell her friends. She felt so ashamed. Shreds of misguided loyalty to Andrew held her back from saying he was supplying drugs. She rather suspected the girls would encourage her to talk to the police, but if she did that she'd have Big Mick paying a visit.

'You can tell us,' Amber cajoled.

Chrissie dithered. 'Well,' she said, picking her words carefully, 'Andrew has played some card games. Obviously I don't mean Snap. He owes a lot of money.'

'How much?' asked Dee.

'Two grand.'

Amber puffed out her cheeks. 'It seems to me, ladies, that we're on a hiding to nothing with our men.'

'But I still love Josh,' said Dee quietly.

'I love Matthew,' said Amber miserably.

'I love the Andrew I met,' said Chrissie, 'not the Andrew that's sharing my home. I don't recognise him. But if the old Andrew wound his arms around my waist and begged forgiveness for being an idiot, I'd be putty in his hands.'

'So what's our plan of action, girls?' asked Dee.

'Isn't it obvious?' asked Amber. She put down her knife and fork and rummaged in her handbag. A second later she placed a business card on the table. There were two words printed in neat italics. *Madam Rosa.* Underneath was a telephone number.

Dee made a harrumphing noise. 'She sounds like a chuffing brothel owner.'

Amber looked from Dee to Chrissie, her expression serious. 'Do either of you believe our men might be having affairs?'

Dee bit her lip. 'Maybe.'

Chrissie shook her head. 'No. I think Andrew's too enthralled with his mates to be interested in another woman. That said, he's not bothered about me sticking around. He really doesn't give a hoot.'

'Are we all in agreement we want to fight to keep our men?' asked Amber.

Dee nodded, and Chrissie let out a laboured sigh. 'I want my old Andrew back. The sweet, caring Andrew.'

'In which case,' Amber foraged in her handbag again, this time producing her mobile phone, 'are we also in agreement we should see Madam Rosa for relationship guidance?'

107

'I still think her readings at Cougar Kate's house were marketing ploys,' said Dee, tutting.

'Well there's only one way to find out,' said Chrissie. 'I think Amber should ring the telephone number on that business card.'

'Right,' said Amber decisively. 'Let's do this.'

Chapter Nineteen

Madam Rosa picked up on the second ring.

'Hello?'

'Er, yes, hello,' said Amber, trying to be business-like but nerves got the better of her. She sounded like she'd swallowed six frogs that were now holding a tea dance in her throat. 'I'm ringing to make an appointment...ahem...for...ahem... sorry...,' she moved her mouth away from the mobile and coughed several times in a bid to speak without croaking, 'I want a reading.' She switched the phone to loudspeaker so her friends could hear the conversation.

'Okay. I can't do anything until Saturday afternoon.'

Amber gave Chrissie and Dee an enquiring look. They nodded their agreement. 'We'll take it. There are three of us, by the way.'

'That's fine.'

I'll bet it is, thought Amber sourly. *That's one-hundred-and-thirty-five quid, cash in hand, for spouting goodness knows what.*

There was the sound of pages turning. Presumably Madam Rosa was consulting a diary. 'I can do, let me see, two o'clock onwards. How does that suit?'

Chrissie and Dee nodded again.

'Perfect.'

'Let me give you my address.'

Amber took down the details. Madam Rosa lived in Vigo, a pretty village that ran alongside Trosley Country Park. Amber immediately thought of her boss. Steve had told her how he sometimes liked to visit the same park for a hike with "his mate". What a small world. After an exchange of pleasantries, Amber rang off.

109

'Well, that wasn't so awful.'

Dee blew out her cheeks. 'I guess not. All we have to do now is get through the rest of the week until Saturday rolls around. Shall we meet at yours, Amber, as you're the closest to Vigo? Then we can all go together.'

'Sure,' Amber replied. 'Actually, why don't we make a night of it? Let's go for a curry afterwards. Matthew isn't kissing me at the moment, so I might as well go berserk with the garlic. In fact, if the two of you want to bring a sleeping bag, why don't you take a sofa each and crash out at mine? We can pop the corks on some Prosecco and get horribly drunk.'

'I'd like that,' said Dee. 'Not the drunk bit,' she added hastily, 'I meant the bit about crashing at yours. It will give me and Josh some space. I'm terrified he's going to suggest we split up.'

'Why?' asked Chrissie.

'Because if he doesn't fancy me anymore, it stands to reason he won't want to keep sharing my bed – or even my life. I reckon it's only a matter of time before he demands we sell the flat and go our separate ways.' Her lip trembled, and for a moment Dee thought she might cry.

'Don't upset yourself. Everything will work out,' said Amber gently, before rolling her eyes. 'Hark at me dishing out assurances when my own boyfriend is parked in the spare room.'

'Won't Matthew mind us being there?' asked Chrissie.

'I don't give a toss if he does,' said Amber defiantly. 'It's my house. I can invite into it who I like.'

'Count me in,' said Chrissie. The thought of getting out of Saturday night with Andrew's mates in the maisonette, and not making chip butties or unblocking loos was giving Chrissie a holiday feeling.

110

'Right,' said Amber, dropping her mobile phone back into her handbag and gathering all her bits together. 'We'd better head back to the office.'

The girls had barely plonked their bottoms down on their typing chairs when Steve Hood summoned Amber.

'Can I have a quiet word, please?'

'You can have several noisy ones if you like,' she quipped. She picked up her notebook.

'You won't need that.'

'Oh, okay.' Amber discarded the pad and walked into Steve's office. 'What's up?'

Steve shut the office door and sat down opposite her. 'Is everything all right?'

'Yes, why?'

'Because this morning you looked like Morticia Addams, and Chrissie and Dee were doing a fair impression of Uncle Fester and Lurch. Meanwhile, I've had a chance to go through the lease you worked on earlier. There are quite a few mistakes.'

'Really?' said Amber in surprise.

'Yes. A landlord is usually called a "lessor". Not a "tosser".'

'What?' Amber could feel herself blushing furiously. She rarely made mistakes, and couldn't believe her mind had wandered enough to write such a word.

'And the letter to Mister Whitehead. Well, see for yourself.' Steve pushed the A4 piece of paper across the desk. She glanced at it, and her pink blush turned sunset red.

'Dear Mister Dickhead? I didn't type that,' she protested.

'And the address is wrong on this second piece of correspondence. Mister Brown lives at Pennis Close, in Fawkham. Not Penis Close in Fuckem.'

Amber's mouth dropped open. 'Someone has doctored my typing,' she gasped. But even as she

111

said it, she knew it sounded ridiculous.

'So I'll ask again. Is everything all right?'

'Yes. No. Yes. I mean–' Amber's mind darted about like a trapped butterfly as she struggled to answer the question. She didn't want to tell her boss that her personal life had disintegrated into a mess, or that she was planning on checking in with a fortune teller for guidance. Steve Hood would think his secretary had completely lost the plot.

'Is it personal?'

'No, of course not,' Amber protested. 'I really like you. You're a great boss.'

Steve gave the smallest of smiles. 'I meant are you having personal problems at home.'

'I...I...I,' Amber hung her head, studying her hands folded in her lap. Perhaps if she sat here all afternoon stuttering one word, Steve Hood would simply get bored and dismiss her with a caution to take more care over her work.

'So that's a yes,' said Steve. 'Look,' he said, gently, 'we've all been there, Amber. There's not one person on this planet that hasn't, at some point, had their life tipped upside down like a wheelie bin and suffered the contents spilling everywhere.'

Amber nodded miserably. 'Yeah. Good description.' Her eyes were suddenly very shiny. 'It's kind of you to be sympathetic. I appreciate how hard it must have been for you. At least I don't have to spring any surprises about a "mate" on my family and friends.'

Steve arched an eyebrow. 'Are you sure? So, there are no complications in that department?'

Amber's brow furrowed. That was a strange comment to make. 'I'm definitely heterosexual.'

Steve's mouth twitched. 'That's...good to know. Now then,' he pushed the lease, correspondence and files towards her, 'if you could correct this little lot that would be smashing.'

'Yes,' Amber said in a small voice. She stood up. 'I'm very sorry.'

'Don't be,' Steve smiled, 'but maybe for now don't go signing anything off in my absence, eh? I don't want Mr Whitehead ringing me up having an apoplectic fit. He's not the easiest of clients.'

'Okay.' Amber gathered everything into her arms and made for the door.

'And remember,' Steve called after her, 'if you need an ear, I'm here.'

Amber gave her boss a grateful smile, and then used the heel of her shoe to flip the door shut after her. Not for the first time she thought what a shame it was that Steve was gay. He'd make a smashing boyfriend.

***

When Amber arrived home that evening it was once again to a cold, dark house with a distinct absence of nice cooking smells. No sign of Matthew. No doubt he was working late *again*. She set about getting a dinner for herself out of the freezer. A meal for one. Stuff Matthew. If he couldn't be bothered to talk to her, why should she go to the trouble of cooking for him?

Matthew turned up as Amber was easing herself into the bath tub. From the open bathroom door, Amber watched him walk towards the spare bedroom. He totally ignored her.

'Thought you might like to know,' she called after him, 'that I'm out again this Saturday.' She saw Matthew pause as he listened to her, 'and Chrissie and Dee will be staying the night here.' Matthew's back stiffened at this piece of news, but he didn't deign to respond. Instead he disappeared into the spare room. From her vantage point in the bath tub, Amber watched the door close after him. She

113

shivered, which was nothing to do with the cooling bath water.

***

When Dee arrived home that evening it was to find Josh packing a suitcase. Her heart began to race unpleasantly as she tried not to panic, but adrenalin was already whooshing through her veins like runners responding to a starting pistol.

'J-Josh!' she stuttered. 'Whatever are you doing, darling?' She hated how she sounded. Meek and placatory. What she really wanted to do was shout, "WHAT THE BLOODY HELL ARE YOU PLAYING AT?" But she didn't.

Josh continued folding clothes. 'What does it look like?' His voice was hard.

Dee stood stock still. This wasn't happening. If she kept her attitude sunny, he'd stop what he was doing, stride over, fling his arms around her and say, "Sorry, Dee. I was having a moment of madness. It's passed now. Let me unpack. What's for tea?"

'Obviously you're packing,' she said, hating the way her voice trembled. 'What I meant was...why?'

'Questions, questions,' Josh sighed. 'Always questions.'

'One question, and surely perfectly reasonable?'

Josh tugged on the suitcase's zipper. 'I'm going away for a few days. It's no big deal.'

Dee nodded, as if this was quite normal. A part of her was relieved Josh was going for only a few days and not forever. The other part of her wanted to fire off questions and have immediate answers. She tried to bite her tongue, but she was too late applying the brake to her mouth and her lips were already forming words.

'Can I ask why you're going away, and where

you're going, and who you're going with, and–'

'There you go again,' Josh tutted, dragging the suitcase off the bed. It landed with a thud on the floor. 'I can't stand it.'

'Josh, please,' Dee implored. She could feel her eyes brimming, but it was more from frustration than anything else.

'Very well,' said Josh, extending the handle of the suitcase. He looked up. 'I'm fed up with your behaviour. I think we need some time apart to review this relationship.'

'Well I know how I feel!' said Dee indignantly. 'Are you saying you don't?'

Josh gave a thin smile. 'So now you're not only asking me question after question, but answering them on my behalf too. Don't you see how wearing it is?'

Dee looked at Josh in bewilderment. 'I-I don't understand, Josh. I just don't understand.'

'Of course you don't. You evidently have a brain the size of a pea, and are incapable of comprehending your actions. Bombarding me with questions all the time is beyond tiresome.'

'B-but I haven't!' Dee protested.

'You're blissfully unaware of it,' Josh snapped. 'The final straw was yesterday morning. You subjected me to the most unattractive striptease I've ever had the misfortune to witness. Do you know any man who likes to see a woman covered in bacon grease and egg yolk? Does it ever feature within the pages of those crap romance novels you read? Ah, I can see from your expression it doesn't. And then you have the audacity to look hurt when I say I don't fancy you. Perhaps you're not quite right in the head? Either way, we need some space to think things through. While I'm away, I suggest you make an appointment to see a psychiatrist. We'll talk when I'm back.'

115

'When will that be?'

Josh shook his head almost sorrowfully. 'Another question,' he said, his voice pained.

And Dee had no choice but to watch, dumbfounded, as Josh wheeled his suitcase out of the apartment and shut the door firmly behind him.

***

When Chrissie arrived home, it was to find Andrew gathering his keys and wallet together. Evidently, he was on his way out.

'Hi,' he gave her a smile. 'You don't need to do me any tea. I'll be with the lads. We'll grab something at the pub.'

Chrissie's first reaction was relief that Andrew had smiled at her. Seemingly a thaw had taken place since Sunday's cross words. Her second reaction was joy at the reprieve of not cooking tonight. She was still full from the massive fry-up she'd had with Amber and Dee earlier. A part of her was already thinking how nice it would be to slob out in front of the telly all by herself, maybe with a plate of warm buttery toast later. But hot on the heels of those initial thoughts was another that chased round and round in her head. Something wasn't quite right. Andrew was looking squeaky clean. It was as if he'd taken himself and his clothes through Gravesend's swankiest car wash and paid the extra quid for added sparkle and shine. His hair would have been good enough for a man's shampoo commercial, and he'd bothered to shave. His skin was sporting the sort of glow usually achieved at a posh spa, and his clothes were – Chrissie ran an eye over the immaculate shirt and smart trousers – new. As he pushed past her, she was treated to the heavenly scent of an aftershave she didn't recognise. He was certainly pulling all the stops out for the lads.

116

'You look nice,' she said.

'Thanks,' he smiled again, and plonked a big fat kiss on her cheek. 'See you later.'

Chrissie returned the smile. A part of her felt giddy with relief that things might be changing after yesterday's unkind words. She shut the door after him and felt some tension unkink in her spine. But only a little. Something wasn't right, but she couldn't put her finger on it. It was only when she was halfway through her buttery toast and the commercials were on that it came to her. Since when did a man dolly himself up to keep the company of a bunch of sink estate lads?

Chapter Twenty

The week passed slowly. Steve continued to grumble at Amber over her carelessness with typing errors, and even Chrissie and Dee weren't exempt from criticisms.

'What's the matter with you, Dee?' complained Alan Mann, the firm's matrimonial lawyer. 'My client's filing for divorce, but her husband is most definitely not called Joshua.'

Dee had gasped with horror that Josh, constantly on her mind, had somehow been typed into Affidavits and Statements.

On Tuesday, just before lunch, Cougar Kate stalked into the girls' office to see Chrissie who, as the firm's secretarial float, helped out all staff with work overflow. Kate's face bore a distinctly put-out expression. 'Really, Chrissie. This is the second time I've had to point out that Miss Penhalligan is bequeathing her estate. Not her *sink* estate. What's up with you?'

On Wednesday, as Amber pounded away at her keyboard listening to Steve droning on about car parking spaces and rights of access, she wondered where Matthew's car was parked after office hours, and whether some unknown woman was giving her boyfriend her own particular right of access.

By Thursday Dee was thoroughly upset at Josh's unknown whereabouts. Her fingers constantly itched to phone or text him. She longed to tell him how much he was missed. She'd heard nothing from him at all. She presumed Josh was staying with his parents. Dee wasn't the biggest fan of Josh's mum. Anne Coventry had more axes to grind than a medieval executioner at the Tower of London. Josh's dad, Peter, wasn't so bad, but he was more mouse than man, and totally under his wife's big fat thumb. Dee hoped Josh hadn't put her in a bad light to his parents. Maybe she would pop in at the weekend to say hi, and explain that she and Josh were having a bit of a blip at the moment. She'd reassure them both, tell them she loved their son and was looking forward to him coming home.

On Friday afternoon, Chrissie typed up another Will to help out with Cougar Kate's supposedly overflowing work tray, even though the wretched woman had been on a personal call when Chrissie had walked into the office she shared with Clive Derek. Clive had been in the boardroom with a client. Kate had been extremely busy cooing into a telephone while she twisted strands of hair around the fingers of her free hand. Chrissie wondered how much extra Kate was paid because she worked for a partner, when she appeared to do naff all most of the time. Sighing, Chrissie had set to work on the document, while her mind wandered to thoughts of Andrew. Her boyfriend was being incredibly pleasant to her at the moment. Not that she'd seen much of him. He had certainly smartened up this week, but it was always to hang out with his mates or "do some jobs". Chrissie had questioned Andrew over the latter. He'd assured her it was all private electrical work – fixing an intruder light that had been on the blink at a pensioner's bungalow, or checking a flickering transformer in somebody's kitchen. She'd sighed with relief that Andrew wasn't doing dodgy stuff for his cronies. The last thing she wanted was her boyfriend getting busted. His wallet had been full of twenties, and he'd peeled one off telling Chrissie to buy herself something nice. Shocked, she'd taken it. She would put the money towards Madam Rosa's fee. Chrissie had also been checking out a house rental website. She'd shown Andrew a decent place she was sure they could afford. Andrew had said, 'We'll see,' and she'd been filled with renewed optimism. Things were coming right again. They *had* to be.

On Saturday lunchtime, the three women met at Amber's house. As Chrissie stepped over the threshold, she felt her heart sing. Just think, another month or so and maybe she and Andrew would be renting a dear little house like this one. She couldn't wait. Andrew had even promised he wouldn't bring the lads back to the maisonette on Saturday while Chrissie was enjoying her girlie sleepover at Amber's. Chrissie had left the maisonette with more spring in her step than Skippy the kangaroo. In fact, she was privately starting to think that seeing Madam Rosa would be a waste of time and money.

Dee followed Amber and Chrissie into the small tidy kitchen. She hadn't really wanted to go inside Amber's house. Every part of her was screaming to get to Madam Rosa's as soon as possible, even if it meant they were an hour early. Dee wanted information. Was Josh at his parents' place? Why had he felt the need to pack a suitcase and leave her for a while? Was this *really* just a blip they were going through? She felt edgy, as if she'd been overdosing on energy drinks.

Amber went to the fridge and pulled out a cling-filmed plate of chicken salad sandwiches that she'd made for them earlier. 'There we are, girls,' she said, setting the plate down on her kitchen table. 'Get your choppers around that little lot. I certainly will be. I've had chuff all else to get my choppers around this week.' She also set down a huge Victoria sponge cake that she'd bought fresh that morning from the local baker's.

Dee picked a sandwich up and began toying with it. She'd not had any breakfast because she simply hadn't fancied it. Even now, hours later, she wasn't really hungry.

'What's up?' asked Amber, noticing her friend's lack of appetite.

'Just saving myself for the curry tonight,' Dee replied. Hopefully by this evening, after listening to positive news from Madam Rosa, she'd be enjoying a korma washed down with a celebratory glass of wine.

'Anyone had sex this week?' asked Amber, taking a bite from her own sandwich.

'How can I when Josh isn't around?' asked Dee.

'So what about *without* Josh then?' Amber replied, waggling her eyebrows.

'Are you kidding?' Chrissie butted in. 'Dee is waiting for a grand reunion and a wedding proposal, not a mad passionate fling while Josh is away finding himself, or whatever it is he's doing. That really would cause a rumpus if he came home early and discovered his girlfriend covered in bacon and eggs and a stranger standing over her with a six-inch sausage.'

Dee sighed. 'I'm starting to wish I'd never told either of you about my disastrous foray into the world of sex food.'

'Aww, your secret is safe with us, Dee,' said Amber. 'What about you, Chrissie? Any more blocked loos and strange men inviting you to play with their plunger?'

Chrissie swallowed her sandwich and smiled. 'No, but Andrew and I are getting along fine. He put his arm around me in his sleep last night.'

'And?' Amber prompted.

'And nothing. We spooned. It was nice. I can't remember the last time we cuddled up together.'

'Is that it?' asked Amber, astonished.

'Small steps,' Chrissie murmured. She was not going to be rattled by Amber's disgust at the lack of action between the sheets. It would happen soon enough. She knew it would.

'Well in the absence of shenanigans with our men,' Amber paused to pick some salad out of her teeth, 'have either of you made your own entertainment?'

'Eh?' said Chrissie and Dee together.

'You know,' Amber gave a saucy wink, 'as in servicing yourselves. Don't either of you have a vibrator?'

'No!' gasped Dee, as Chrissie began to choke on her sandwich. Dee leant across and thumped Chrissie on the back.

'You're missing out, girls,' said Amber smugly. 'I have one. It's upstairs in my bedside drawer.'

'Does Matthew know?' asked Dee, her eyes as round as the sandwich plate.

'Course he does,' Amber tsked. 'He bought it for me. It was a joke Valentine's present last year. We've had quite a bit of fun with it. It's bright pink with a bobbly bit on the end which never fails to find your g-spot, *and* it's eight inches long.'

'I'm crossing my legs thinking about it,' muttered Chrissie.

'You'd uncross them in a jiffy if you knew what it was capable of,' Amber giggled. 'Anyway, last night I let Matthew know that I was playing with it. I was hoping he might get turned on hearing my groans.'

'And did he?' asked Dee.

'Dunno,' Amber shrugged. 'If he was, he kept it to himself. I was pretty incensed actually. Hopefully he was annoyed when I repeatedly screamed out Harry Styles' name.'

'Harry Styles?' Dee looked astonished. 'Aren't you a bit old to be lusting after a member of One Direction?'

'Don't be cheeky,' said Amber, looking put out. 'I'm not *that* much older than him. Also, Harry Styles likes the more mature woman. When he had his fling with Caroline Flack she was practically old enough to be his mother. Anyway, upon climaxing I yelled Harry's name several times, and then I began singing "Abide With Me".'

'Abide with me?' asked Dee.

'Yes. As in the song.'

'It wasn't Harry Styles who sang that,' said Chrissie. 'It was Harry Secombe.'

'Bugger,' Amber sighed. 'Next time I'll shout out Matthew's brother's name. That will really wind him up.'

'That's dangerous territory,' Dee warned. 'You'll never get a marriage proposal if he thinks you're lusting after his brother.'

'I'm starting to feel rebellious,' Amber grumbled. 'Come on, girls. We've still got time for a slice of cake before we go.' She stood up and fished in a drawer for a slicer. 'Look at this,' she smiled, licking her lips as jam and butter icing oozed from the sponge. 'Next time I go to bed with my vibrator I might imagine this moment and yell out, "Victoria, Victoria!" Hopefully, Matthew might then come roaring back into our bed and persuade me to be straight again.'

Chrissie and Dee laughed at Amber poking fun at her situation, even though Amber's heart was heavier than a dozen boxed Victoria sponges all stacked together.

Chapter Twenty-One

The three women sat in Amber's car outside Madam Rosa's house. For a moment, they were silent. Chrissie was the first to speak.

'It's quite a normal looking house, isn't it?'

'Why shouldn't it be?' asked Amber. Her sharp tone belied the nerves playing in the pit of her stomach. 'This is Vigo Village. It's hardly Harry Potter Land. You two look petrified. Are you expecting a Dementor to open the door and suck the souls from our bodies?'

'Don't say that,' said Dee with a shiver.

Three pairs of eyes stared at Madam Rosa's house. It was a bog-standard Seventies oblong with PVC windows. A single hanging basket of winter pansies brightened up the otherwise unremarkable property. The front lawn was sprinkled with damp decaying leaves from next door's overhanging branches. A cat appeared from round one corner of the house and minced over to the front door. It sat down patiently on the outside mat, curling its tail over its paws.

'A black cat,' said Chrissie.

'Wow, there's no stopping your powers of observation this morning,' said Amber sarcastically.

'Witches have black cats,' said Dee. 'They're called *familiars*. They're meant to be demons that occupy an animal's body.'

'Stop it,' said Chrissie with a shudder.

'What are you both like?' Amber snorted. 'Right, if the two of you want to sit in the car while I go in, that's up to you. But I'm here for a reading. I want to know when Matthew is going to behave like the boyfriend I fell in love with.'

Her words had a galvanising effect on Chrissie

and Dee. Seconds later they were standing on Madam Rosa's welcome mat, with the cat giving them the once-over. It had unblinking green eyes which, privately, they each found unsettling.

'Ready?' asked Amber. Chrissie and Dee nodded, and Amber rang the doorbell. Madam Rosa opened the door almost immediately. The cat sprang in front of the three women, then nearly tripped them up by doing a full stop in front of Madam Rosa. Purring like a kettle drum, it began weaving around her jeaned legs.

'Come in,' Madam Rosa trilled. She bent down and picked up the cat. 'I'd better pop this chap away so he doesn't disturb us.'

Amber put out a hand to stroke the cat. It hissed and tried to swipe her with one paw. 'Oh!' She let out an involuntary cry. 'Doesn't he like strangers?'

'It depends what vibe they're giving off,' said Madam Rosa. 'Merlin is a very complex creature.'

Chrissie and Dee looked at each other. Their thought processes were almost telepathic.

Merlin? said Chrissie's expression.

Familiar! Dee silently replied.

Amber was ruffled. 'I have a cat,' she said defensively, 'and he loves all visitors. He's never hissed at anybody in his life. Not even the vet.' She didn't know why she felt the need to justify herself because this woman's stupid pet had taken a dislike to her.

'Ah, but your Mister Tomkin isn't subjected to a mish-mash of human energies every day,' explained Madam Rosa. Amber was about to say that Mister Tomkin wouldn't hiss even if the entire combined households of Downing Street and Buckingham Palace walked through her front door, when she realised Madam Rosa had referred to Mister Tomkin by name. How had she known that? Had Amber perhaps mentioned it during the reading at

Cougar Kate's house? But before she could ask the question, the clairvoyant was ushering them into her front room. 'Please, sit down while I shut Merlin away.'

Amber followed Chrissie and Dee into a neat lounge. She was feeling somewhat prickly after the cat having a go at her. Chrissie and Dee sat down on a long sofa, so Amber joined them. While the other two women sat back and relaxed, Amber merely perched. She presumed the lounge doubled as a waiting room and each reading would take place elsewhere.

Madam Rosa returned and sat in a nearby armchair.

'Before we start,' she said, looking at them one by one, 'I'd like to advise it's pointless having individual readings.'

Three pairs of eyebrows shot upwards like synchronised caterpillars. Amber felt exasperation wash over her. She wanted to talk to Madam Rosa privately. She had some delicate questions that she didn't want to voice in front of Chrissie and Dee.

'I'll explain,' said Madam Rosa, looking directly at Amber. 'Despite you thinking that I engage in marketing ploys, I can assure you that is not my style. I'm more than happy to take one-hundred-and-thirty-five pounds from you all,' Amber felt herself squirming, 'but that would be unethical of me.' The clairvoyant's gaze moved away from Amber, who exhaled with relief. What was it about this woman that unsettled her so?

'Why are you suggesting a shared reading?' asked Chrissie timidly.

'As soon as I opened the door, I could see the three of you have the same problem. If I do individual readings, you will make comparisons afterwards and say you've been given regurgitated codswallop.' Amber gave a little gasp and quickly

126

turned it into a cough. 'Therefore, it's better I address the three of you together. I'll charge a flat fee of forty-five pounds so nobody thinks they're being ripped off.' Her gaze strayed to Amber again, who had the grace to turn pink.

'How do you know we all have the same problem?' asked Dee.

'I know everything,' said Madam Rosa simply.

'Will Donald Trump cause World War Three?' blurted Chrissie, causing Amber to roll her eyes.

'I think we'll leave politics to the politicians,' said Madam Rosa with a wry smile, 'and stick to the immediate difficulties that need examining. I can see from your matching auras there is heartache and...not to put too fine a point on it...man trouble.'

'I *did* have man trouble,' said Chrissie, 'but things are on the up now.'

'Hmm,' said Madam Rosa, 'I'm not so sure about that.' She leant forward, reaching one hand out to the coffee table between them, and opened a tucked away drawer. She extracted a pack of tarot cards. Amber regarded them through suspicious eyes, Chrissie visibly gulped, and Dee looked like she wanted to jump on the sofa and wave a crucifix about. 'I'm going to shuffle the pack, cut them, and then you will each choose one card.' The fortune teller began quickly sliding the cards over one another. Amber scrutinised the hand shuffling like somebody trying to catch a magician out. Both Dee and Chrissie were leaning forward now, apprehension etched on their faces. The clairvoyant cut the cards, before slapping them down on the table. Like a pianist running a finger from the top to the bottom of the ivories, she swiftly spread the cards into a long line. Madam Rosa looked up at Amber. 'You first. Pick one.'

'Oh. Er, right.' Amber stood up. She wanted to choose carefully, rather than reach for the nearest card. Also, there was no way she was having Madam Rosa somehow knowing what picture card was at her end of the sofa. She walked around the coffee table and selected the very last card at the farthest end of the spread.

'Show me,' said Madam Rosa.

Amber flipped the card over so its picture was facing everyone. Like a magician's assistant she moved the card from side to side, so everybody could have a look. 'Seems like a pair of lovers to me,' she beamed.

'The two of cups,' said Madam Rosa. 'This card signifies emotional connections and bonds between two people.'

'Brilliant,' said Amber, exhaling with relief.

'However, your two of cups is reversed.'

'Eh?' Amber peered at the card. 'Oh, sorry.' She turned it upright.

'I'm afraid that won't change the significance of your reading,' said Madam Rosa quietly. 'In this case the two of cups reflects the end of a relationship.'

Amber blanched. 'Rubbish,' she snapped.

'Let's double check. Take another card.'

Amber looked from the cards to Madam Rosa, and then back to the cards. Her hand hovered, then she flicked it away like a keyboard player performing staccato notes. She stalked around the coffee table, this time selecting the very first card. Grabbing it, she had a private peek. It showed three upside-down women dancing in a circle. In their hands were golden goblets upraised in a toast of joy. She relaxed slightly and showed the card to everybody. 'It's us getting sozzled,' Amber joked to Chrissie and Dee.

'Ah,' said Madam Rosa, 'the Three of Cups reversed.' Her whole tone signified that a cold bucket of water was about to be poured over

Amber's interpretation of three friends having a boozy time. 'I always see this card where there is a love triangle, or an unfaithful partner.'

Suddenly Amber's legs felt very wobbly. She sat down abruptly. 'No!' she protested.

'Now, if this is not what you signed up for, then unfortunately it will lead to the end of your relationship. You need to tell your fella very precisely what you will and won't stand for. If you're happy to turn a blind eye, then he'll simply do what a lot of men do. That old cliché *having your cake and eating it* is never truer.'

'Who is she?' Amber croaked.

'That I cannot say.'

'Why not? You told us you knew everything.'

'It is not appropriate for me to tell you.'

'Not app–?'

'Sorry. There is an element of past life karma involved here, and karma has to take its course.'

'Stuff chuffing karma,' Amber spluttered. 'I want to know who she is. If some invisible force is whispering names in your ear, then I demand it tell me.' Amber's voice had shot up an octave. She looked very pale, and was visibly trembling. Dee and Chrissie watched the verbal exchange in stunned silence. Their eyes flicked from Amber to Madam Rosa and then back to Amber like Wimbledon spectators.

'Spirit is not telling me this woman's name. Currently, it's not permitted. However, you *will* find out in due course. And quite soon. It's important you remain calm and composed. Serenity is your weapon in this instance.'

'Are you having a laugh? When I find out who she is, she'll be lucky I don't pull her fingernails out one by one and stab her treacherous heart with the biggest kitchen knife in my drawer.'

'Quite,' murmured Madam Rosa, 'which is

partially why Spirit won't tell me her name. You need time to calm down. It's no good acting in a moment of hot-headed anger, or you'll end up cooling down for the next fifty years in a prison cell. I will examine your future shortly. For now, I need to deal with your friends.' Madam Rosa switched her attention to Dee. 'Take a card,' she invited.

'Don't Amber's cards need to be returned to the pack?' asked Dee.

'No. There are others which convey the same message, if necessary.'

'Right,' said Dee apprehensively, although she was secretly relieved the Two and Three of Cups were out of the equation. She certainly didn't want to be told anything adverse about her and Josh, or that a third person was crowding their relationship. She leant forward. From her position, the cards were all easily within reach. She put out a tentative hand and held it directly over one in front of her. She dithered. What if it was a bad card? She moved her hand slowly to the left. Five cards along. Six. Now seven. Then back again in the other direction. She paused and then started heading towards the left again. And hesitated. This was ridiculous. How long did it take to select one measly card? Like a pendulum, her arm swung to the right. Copying Amber, she headed off to the far end of the spread only to once again vacillate. *For goodness sake, pick a card*! Her hand gave an involuntary twitch, and before she could even think about it she was snatching one up. Dee straightened up and reluctantly showed it to Madam Rosa. Amber was straining forward to see, frown marks between her eyebrows. Chrissie on the other hand looked like a tense cinema goer watching a horror movie.

'That doesn't look a very happy card,' she mumbled.

'The Tower,' said Madam Rosa. 'Here we have a

lightning bolt striking a turret which has burst into flames. People are leaping from the windows. This card reflects turmoil. A major shake-up. Just when you thought you were living with your boyfriend in a safe and comfortable zone, something occurred which turned the relationship upside-down. In this case it is another woman. Regrettably you are being confronted with major change. This card signals the end of a long-term relationship.'

Dee felt physically sick. 'Are you sure?'

'Let us confirm that. Take another card.'

Dee didn't hesitate. Snatching one up, for a second she held it possessively to her chest. Slowly, she flicked it round for the clairvoyant to see. 'I'm too scared to look,' she mumbled.

'You've selected the Hermit.'

'Who?' Dee peered at the card hopefully. It was a picture of an old man, caped and holding a lantern. Perhaps he was the bearer of good news?

'Here we have a solitary figure. This card represents a time of isolation and withdrawal from others. It is indicative of being single.'

Dee gulped. 'I don't want to be single,' she whispered.

'Again, we will look at your future in a few minutes.' Madam Rosa's gaze settled upon Chrissie. 'Your turn.'

As Dee leant back to stare abjectly at the ceiling, Chrissie leant forward. Unlike Amber and Dee, she wasn't going to take cards from either end of the spread. Decisively, she selected the card right in line with her nose. As far as she was concerned, this was the logical one to pick. She showed it to Madam Rosa and Amber. Dee was still staring at the ceiling, so Chrissie laid it down on the table for her friend to look at when she'd finished communing with either God or the clairvoyant's light fitting.

'The Five of Pentacles,' said Madam Rosa. 'Two

destitute figures walk in the snow, shut out from a church even though they need a helping hand. This symbolises your relationship. You are "shut out" from your boyfriend and his circle of friends, and also experiencing financial loss. I suspect your boyfriend has borrowed a lot of money, if not from you then someone else.'

'That can't be right,' said Chrissie hastily. She was desperate to ingratiate Andrew with Madam Rosa. 'He did get into a spot of bother recently, but I think it's all sorted. He's been working really hard. There was plenty of money in his wallet earlier.'

'This card indicates failure and loss. Any monies your boyfriend has will be a matter of dispute with you.'

Chrissie thought of Andrew doing dodgy stuff behind her back. She didn't want to be reminded. Her brain instantly blocked the memory. However, there was no escaping the amount of money she'd seen earlier in Andrew's wallet. It was considerable for only a few simple electrical jobs. She swallowed nervously, hoping Madam Rosa couldn't laser beam into her mind. She would be so ashamed if Amber and Dee found out.

'Take another card,' the clairvoyant invited.

Without hesitating, Chrissie took the neighbouring card to the one she'd first picked.

'The Ten of Pentacles reversed. Your relationship is coming to an end. Again, money is key. You will be counting the pennies as you try and re-establish a place you can call home.'

'Oh,' was all Chrissie could say.

'Don't despair, girls,' said Madam Rosa. 'I *do* see bright and happy futures for the three of you. Let's select some fresh cards. First, let me put back the cards you originally chose and give the pack another shuffle.' Once again, the cards were flipped backwards and forwards under Madam Rosa's long slim fingers, then cut and spread across the coffee table. She turned to Amber. 'Back to you.'

Amber wasn't really up for continuing this fortune telling game. Predicting the future would be hearsay on Madam Rosa's part. Nobody could tell someone what was going to happen tomorrow, next week, month or year. Not unless it was very obvious. She had a sudden mental image of saying to Matthew, "I can see the future. Want to know what you're having for tea tomorrow? Pork chops. It's true. Go and check the fridge." No, there were other ways of unearthing the truth without resorting to tarot cards and auras. She could always ring up Jeremy Kyle and get his help. She'd insist Matthew be wired up to one of those lie-detector thingies, the result of which would be read out in front of a hostile audience. Everyone would turn feral the moment Jeremy proclaimed, "Matthew McCarthy, you are a liar!" And then Matthew would win Jeremy and the audience over by looking meek and saying, "But, Jeremy, hear me out. My girlfriend is a tiresome drunk." The audience would collectively suck on their teeth as Matthew publicly shamed Amber about vomiting all over him before passing out. "Is it any wonder I have allowed myself to be consoled by somebody who smells of eau de parfum, rather than puke de toilette?" And then the fickle audience would turn on Amber, booing and hissing. On the other hand, she could simply wait for Matthew to come home, point an accusing finger at him and say, "Do you remember me telling you I can predict the future, and that you would be eating lamb chops? Well, guess what! I know you're bonking another woman. And if you don't fess up, not only will you be eating chops, but you'll get a smack around them too."

'Amber?' Dee nudged her.

'Sorry.' Amber brought herself back to the here

and now. She didn't bother getting up and analysing the spread of cards from every angle. She simply leant forward and grabbed the first card her eyes fell upon. 'The Ace of Cups,' she said in a dull voice.

'Wonderful,' purred Madam Rosa. 'And now select one more to give me a little more information.' Listlessly, Amber picked another card and showed it to everybody. 'Marvellous, and as I thought,' said Madam Rosa. 'Basically, the first card heralds the beginning of a new love relationship. Your second card, the Ace of Wands, signifies this is going to be a passionate affair that takes off with speed.' And then Madam Rosa did something she hadn't done with any of them so far. She smiled. Her whole face transformed into an expression of genuine warmth and delight. 'You're going to fall head over heels in love, and will look back on this period of your life with disbelief that you put up with nonsense for so long.' She turned to Dee. 'Let's see what the cards say for you.'

Amber sank back into the sofa. Her head felt heavy with an overload of thoughts. Everything was going round and round, like an adrenalised goldfish swimming in a bowl of energy drink.

Dee shifted forward and contemplated the spread. 'Shall I pick two cards?'

'Not yet. It may be that your initial card tells me everything.'

Dee made her selection. 'The Ten of Cups.'

'Fantastic,' said Madam Rosa, beaming with delight. 'This card often appears for singletons with no apparent build-up at all. It is always quite literal – a new love relationship arrives and takes off at the rate of knots. This is usually the "sweep you off your feet" variety where love walks in unannounced and everything clicks. That's brilliant. You deserve a lucky break. This will be happening quite soon. I don't need you to pick a second card because this one has said it all.'

'Thank you,' said Dee quietly. She didn't want somebody new. She wanted Joshua Coventry. How many times had she practised writing *Dee Coventry* with a swirly flourish? Too many times. And, if this clairvoyant was right, she would never get to legitimately scribble that signature over any document – least of all a marriage certificate.

'Finally,' said Madam Rosa, turning to Chrissie, 'let's see what your future holds. Please, pick a card.'

Chrissie took a deep breath. As previously, she selected the card directly in front of her nose. 'The King of Swords.'

'Good. However, I'd like you to pick a second card.'

Chrissie selected the card directly to the left of the one she'd previously chosen. 'The Eight of Wands.'

'Wonderful,' said Madam Rosa. 'So here the King of Swords depicts an invitation for a love relationship, and the Eight of Wands signifies a very fast-moving time frame. Expect things to happen in,' Madam Rosa considered, 'two or three days.'

'Two or three *days*?' Chrissie blinked. 'Are you seriously suggesting I'll be resolving my current relationship, and starting a new one in forty-eighty to seventy-two hours?'

'Give or take a few seconds,' said Madam Rosa drily.

Chrissie shook her head. 'I don't do rebound relationships.'

'I understand. However,' Madam Rosa's gaze swept over all three women, 'I can state quite categorically that you must all put aside thoughts about rebounding. Three wonderful men are about to come into your lives. They are the real deal. Don't turn them away.' She stood up signifying their appointment was over. 'That's fifteen pounds each, ladies.'

Amber reached for her handbag and found her purse. As she counted out the notes, she wondered how she could tactfully cancel the invitation she'd extended to Chrissie and Dee. She was no longer in the mood for a girly night in with curry, Prosecco and a sleepover. What she really wanted was to go home, sit in her house with the lights off, and watch daylight turn to dusk while her head processed what her heart couldn't bear to confront. And then, when the fading light had changed to nightfall and Matthew crept in, she would flick on a lamp, shine it at his eyeballs and interrogate him relentlessly. She was determined that before the clock struck twelve and heralded a new day, she would have extracted the truth from Matthew.

Chapter Twenty-Two

The three women were very subdued on the drive back to Amber's. Dee was the first to speak.

'Girls, I don't want to throw a bucket of cold water on our planned weekend of gossip and fun but...would either of you mind if...I dropped out?'

'Of course not,' said Amber quickly. She'd been trying to find the courage to say the very same thing.

'I feel so rattled by Madam Rosa's reading, right now I'd prefer to go home and try and get hold of Josh. I have no idea where he is. He's had plenty of the flipping *space* he craved – I've not seen him all week! It's high time we discussed things properly. I'm going to phone him,' said Dee decisively, 'and if he doesn't answer, I'll drop by his parents' house and *demand* he speaks to me.'

Dee was pale apart from two pink stains to each cheek. Amber and Chrissie realised that, despite their friend being upset, there was also an angry tiger wanting to claw its way out and confront Josh.

'I agree with you,' said Chrissie. 'In fact, if you don't mind, Amber, I'd like to do the same. I want to buttonhole Andrew while Madam Rosa's words are still clear in my head. He had a wallet full of money this morning. I'm fairly sure it didn't get there from a few elec–' She suddenly clammed up.

'What's that?' asked Amber.

'Oh, er, nothing. I want to make sure he's being honest about finances with me. Madam Rosa indicated he wasn't.'

'If he's flush,' said Amber, 'you make sure he gives you some dosh. The amount of times he's left you to deal with rent and bills, he's not been fair with you.'

'Er, yes. You're right,' said Chrissie. Hell's bells, she'd nearly spilt the "dodgy" beans then. The sooner she sat Andrew down and properly cleared the air, the better.

'Well I won't lie, girls,' said Amber, 'but I, too, need to clear my head and think about what to say to Matthew. With or without Madam Rosa setting the proverbial cat amongst the pigeons, I want answers. Proper ones. Let's do a rain check.'

***

Dee's Saturday

Dee was so anxious to get home and see if Josh and his suitcase were back, she practically took the front door off its hinges when she crashed into the flat.

'Josh?' she called. 'Are you home?'

The silence let her know he wasn't. The thermostat clicked on the boiler, making her jump. Honestly, she was a bag of nerves these days. This was ridiculous. Standing in the hallway, Dee trawled through her handbag looking for her mobile. She'd refrained from contacting Josh during his *space*cation. Her boyfriend hadn't been troubled by one pleading phone call, or one beseeching text. She doubted many women would have been so patient. She'd played Josh's ridiculous waiting game and let him jack-boot around calling all the shots.

Touching the mobile's screen, Dee found Josh's number and pressed the call button. It went to voicemail. Damn. He must have it switched off. Well too bad, Josh. The time has come to invade your space. Dee nodded to herself. She was going to be a *space invader*. She gave a mad-sounding snort of laughter, and then clapped a hand over her mouth. Dear Lord, she was starting to sound like a lunatic. She really was on edge. Dee hadn't wanted to go around to Josh's parents' house, but if his phone was switched off it left her with no choice. Turning on her heel, she locked up again and went back to the car.

On the drive to Anne and Peter Coventry's place, Dee thought about what she was going to say. Josh's dad was okay, but his mum was something else. Those less polite than Dee would have referred to her as a self-opinionated battle-axe. From the very first moment of meeting Anne Coventry, Dee had sussed the woman was a drama queen and liked to be the centre of attention. Josh had taken Dee to his parents' neat ex-council house under the impression everyone was going to hit it off. Peter Coventry had greeted them pleasantly enough. He'd been wearing a frilly apron over his trousers which had conveyed his position in the household's pecking order – that of chief cook and bottle washer. He'd given Dee a vicar's handshake, her palm sandwiched between both of his. Introduction over, he'd excused himself saying he needed to get back to the kitchen and rescue his bread sauce. The smell of a roasting turkey had reached Dee's nostrils, and her stomach had rumbled appreciatively. Leading off the hallway was an open door. From within came a woman's imperious voice.

'We're in here.' It had sounded very much like the royal "we" to Dee.

Sure enough, when Josh had led the way into the lounge, Dee's eyes had widened at the sight of an enormous woman filling the only armchair in the room. It was a wing chair, and looked a bit like a throne.

'Hello, Mum,' Josh had said, leaning down to peck his mother dutifully on one cheek. Dee had felt that might not be the thing to do on a first meeting, given that Peter Coventry had not proffered his own cheek.

'How do you do?' Dee had said politely, sticking out one hand. To her amazement, Anne Coventry had ignored it, instead looking her up and down. Dee had felt like a dog from the local animal shelter that Josh had brought home for consideration – and failed inspection.

'Mum can't get up,' Josh had said, as if that somehow explained his mother's rudeness.

'Oh, I'm sorry to hear that,' Dee had said. 'Is there something wrong?'

'What isn't wrong?' Anne Coventry had sighed.

'I'll see if Dad needs a hand,' Josh had said, leaving Dee alone with this formidable woman who was issuing as much warmth as a cold radiator.

Once Josh was out of earshot, Anne Coventry's rheumy eyes had fixed upon Dee.

'What are you doing for Christmas?' she'd asked.

'Er–'

'I know it's six months away, but I like to plan in advance. You'll join us, yes?'

Dee had been astonished that Josh's mother liked to plan the festive season so early in the year. But she'd also been flattered that, in her own brash way, Anne had extended an invitation. She had no idea what her own parents would say at her not attending Christmas dinner for the first time since year dot. However, given that Josh was her new boyfriend and possibly "The One", Dee had accepted Anne Coventry's invite on the spot. She'd told herself that she and Josh would spend the following Christmas with her parents.

'Thank you,' Dee had said. 'That would be most...charming,' although she couldn't imagine Anne Coventry pulling a cracker, plonking a paper crown on her head, or clutching her sides at corny jokes. And she'd been right. When Christmas had finally rolled around it had been the most monumentally boring and depressing day of Dee's life. It was clear Anne Coventry was waited on hand, foot and finger by the loyal Peter. Nobody – including Josh – ever stood up to Anne's sharp retorts or complaints. After Christmas dinner, Josh had announced he was taking his father to the pub, and he'd leave Dee to have a girlie chat with his mother. Dee had flashed him the sort of murderous look one might give a person inflicting harm on an animal. She'd then turned to Anne with a smile that would have rivalled Melania Trump's. She hadn't the faintest idea what to talk about with Anne Coventry. The two women had nothing in common. As soon as Peter and Josh had shut the front door, Anne had pounced.

'What are your plans for Christmas?'

Dee had been momentarily nonplussed. 'Um, well I'm spending it with you, obviously.'

'Excellent,' Anne Coventry had said. 'I'm so pleased we have that sorted.'

And then Dee had realised Josh's mother had been talking about *next* Christmas. 'Ah, I've just grasped what you meant. Next time around we'll be spending it with my parents.'

'Your parents?' Anne's eyeballs had bulged, and her tone had been one of outrage. 'But you *just said* you'd spend it here.'

'Y-yes, but we were at cross purposes. My parents will be expecting to see me and Josh. It will be their turn to have us for dinner.'

'Can't you go to them the year after?'

Dee had looked baffled. 'Why would–'

'I probably won't be here by then.'

Dee had remained perplexed. 'Why? Where are you going?'

'I'm going home, young lady,' and Anne had jabbed a porky finger heavenwards, 'that's where I'm going. Up there.' She'd spent the remainder of time, until Josh and Peter returned, telling Dee all

141

about her many illnesses, the tablets she took, how the doctors had said she was a hopeless case and her days were numbered. Dee had been shell- shocked. Josh clearly had no idea his mother was ill, never mind terminally. 'This is strictly between you and me. Understand?'

'Y-yes,' Dee had stuttered.

Thus Dee had been emotionally manipulated into spending each Christmas at Anne Coventry's house because it was always meant to be her last. Dee's parents had been disappointed not to see her on the biggest family day of the year but, like her, horrified when she'd confided that even Josh didn't know how ill his mother was. Dee's own mother had shuffled family celebrations to Boxing Day instead. Even so, the fact that Anne Coventry still remained on Planet Earth, larger than life and with an appetite to rival a baby elephant's, irked Dee. She didn't wish the woman dead, but it would be so nice to spend a special day with her own family. By unfortunate coincidence, Anne's date of birth was the same day as Dee's mother's, so Anne doubly manipulated Dee to be under the Coventry roof because it was always going to be the last birthday. It was the same for Mother's Day. And Easter. On every occasion Dee would be left bored stiff when father and son cleared off to the pub, leaving Dee to hear about Anne's latest drug prescriptions and the state of her piles.

Dee would have been sympathetic to all of this if Anne Coventry had been a nice person. But she wasn't. When she wasn't privately talking about her maladies and medicines, publicly Anne would put Dee down. She'd take great delight in telling Dee she looked fat (*ha!* Dee had thought, *coming from someone who makes the back of a bus look anorexic*) or – when Dee promptly went on a diet – too thin. She told Dee her hair was awful, her fashion sense abysmal, her skin lustreless, and that she looked like a woman in her late thirties rather than one in her late twenties. Dee was too polite to ever answer back, and Josh never stood up to his mother on Dee's behalf. It was fair to say that Anne Coventry, over the last few years, had contributed in reducing Dee's self-esteem to zilch.

It was therefore with trepidation that Dee now found herself ringing the Coventry household's doorbell. As the chimes sounded, Dee's stomach twisted with a mix of fear, hope, anticipation and dread. What if Josh answered the door and told her to bog off? Or what if Anne answered the door and *she* told Dee to bog off?

Through the pane of frosted glass, Dee could see a shape approaching. Josh's dad. Peter released the catch. Caught on the hop, he failed to disguise his horror at who was standing on the doorstep.

'Ah,' he said awkwardly.

'Hello, Peter,' said Dee cheerfully. Today, Peter's apron was accessorised with a pair of yellow Marigolds. Evidently, he was washing the dishes after cooking lunch for Queen Anne – and possibly Prince Joshua.

'Ah,' said Peter again.

'I was passing and...well...I thought I'd pop in and say hello.'

'Ah.'

Dee stood awkwardly on the step. No invitation to cross the threshold was forthcoming. In fact, Peter was looking decidedly shifty. Dee held onto her bright smile. 'Is it not a good moment?'

'No.'

'Ah.'

'Yes.'

'Yes?'

'No.'

'Ah.'

143

'So...'

'Yes?'

'Ah.'

'Ah'.

Dee was starting to feel like she'd dropped into some bizarre Monty Python sketch. Any moment now John Cleese would pop out of the garden's shrubbery and say, 'And now for something different.' Fortunately, Peter was the first to snap out of the conversation rut.

'I'll get Anne.' He jabbed a rubber finger in the direction of the lounge. 'Just, um... w-wait here a moment.'

How bizarre, thought Dee. Why was Josh's dad behaving so strangely? As he bustled off, Dee's gaze fell upon the inner hallway's small console table. Set out with precision neatness was a telephone, a picture of Anne and Peter on their wedding day, a fussy vase full of clashing silk flowers and, propped against it, a postcard. The writing was clear to see, and Dee instantly recognised its familiar looping style. Josh was the author. She screwed up her eyes and was able to make out his name squashed into the bottom right-hand corner. Why was her boyfriend sending his parents a postcard? And from where? Leaning in, she snatched it up, hiding it behind her back just as Anne appeared.

'Oh, it's you,' she said, as if Dee was something rather nasty that had been trodden into the doormat.

'Hello, Anne,' Dee smiled warmly. 'I was saying to Peter, I was passing by and thought it would be nice to say hello.'

'I see. Well you've said hello. Now you can clear off.'

Dee blinked. She couldn't have heard Anne correctly. 'W-what did you say?'

'I said,' Anne enunciated, 'clear...off. We know

all about you.'

'Well of course you know all about me,' Dee attempted to lighten whatever was going on here. 'After all, you've known me a few years, ha ha!'

'Evidently we didn't know you at all.'

Dee could feel herself getting upset. 'Anne, I don't know what I've done to offend you but-'

'Are you having a laugh?'

'I've never been more serious. If you really must know, Josh packed his suitcase and left me. Temporarily,' she added.

'Permanently, if he has any sense.'

Dee gasped. 'I have no idea why he left. He simply said he needed some space. I presumed he was here. I'm missing him, Anne. I want him to come home.'

Anne's top lip peeled back like a snarling Rottweiler. 'Well he's not here.'

'Plainly,' said Dee, feeling some knee trembling coming on. Things weren't going to plan at all. 'So, where is he?'

'Away. Having a good rest from you.'

'What exactly is it that I'm meant to have done?'

'Don't you know?'

'Would I be asking if I did?' Dee was aware her voice was starting to quaver. She gave a peculiar chuggy gasp, and made a sterling effort to quell the emotion that threatened to uncork on Anne Coventry's doorstep.

'You've behaved like a harpy,' Anne waggled a finger, 'nagging my poor boy from the moment you've opened your eyes to the moment you've closed them. Josh hasn't been able to do right for wrong. He said that last Sunday morning you lost your temper and flung food everywhere. He said you even had it all over you. And then you refused to clear the mess up and stormed off.'

'I don't believe I'm hearing this.'

145

'Trust me, you are.' Anne curved her mouth into a malicious smile and ramped up her enormous bosom, Les Dawson-style. 'Josh is having a nice break without you. So go home, and stay away from my lad.' And with that Anne slammed the door in Dee's face.

Dee stood, momentarily paralysed, staring at the Coventry's high gloss wooden panels. She was tempted to stoop down to the letterbox, pull back the flap and beg and plead through its narrow gap. An inner voice sternly told her to have some pride. Dee took a deep breath as she tried to calm herself. She would not go into meltdown on Anne Coventry's doorstep. She'd done nothing wrong. And what the hell was Josh playing at making up a load of claptrap about her?

Dee slid the concealed postcard into her back pocket. Holding her head high, she retraced her steps through the front garden gate and back to her car. It was only when she was finally in the inner sanctum of her flat that she gave in to despair, and howled. She went into the bathroom and pulled off a long ribbon of toilet paper. Drying her eyes, she then trumpeted several times into the tissue. She was so distracted by the callousness of Anne Coventry's words playing on a loop in her head, that it was another ten minutes before she remembered the postcard in her back pocket. Pulling it out, she let her bloodshot eyes focus on Josh's handwriting. As she read, her emotions ran the gauntlet – from upset and incredulity, to boiling anger.

Greetings from Tenerife! Having a wonderful much-needed break from the Undomestic Dog-ess. Not looking forward to sorting things out once back, but for now enjoying fab weather, top hotel and brilliant time with Emma. She can't wait to meet you. See you soon! Love Josh x

Dee had to read the card three times to make

sure she understood exactly what it so plainly said. Who the duckery-fuckery was Emma? With shaking hands, she sought out Josh's Facebook, Twitter and Instagram accounts. This was ridiculous. She couldn't find them. They'd disappeared. The treacherous bastard had blocked her. Her hands were now fluttering faster than swallows on the wing. She found the "Secs in the City" WhatsApp chat group and jerkily stabbed out a message.

Girls. It's true. Josh is having an affair.

And then Dee sank down on her bathroom floor, tucked her legs up to her chin so she was in the foetal position, and sobbed and sobbed and sobbed.

Chapter Twenty-Three

Chrissie's Saturday

Chrissie arrived home to find the maisonette empty. She was surprised because Andrew usually spent Saturday afternoon slumped in front of the television. It was a weekend ritual. Andrew like to turn the volume up to max, until Fran thumped on the wall to make him turn it down again. Chrissie hoped Andrew was keeping himself busy with some extra electrical jobs. If so, that would prove Madam Rosa wrong about Andrew being a failure with money. Okay, he'd made a mistake with the gambling. But that had been discussed and was now out in the open. There were no secrets. He was now being sensible, and working hard to repay the money.

Slipping off her coat, Chrissie hung it on a peg in the hall. She headed off to the kitchen to make a brew, passing the bathroom en-route. She took three paces back and peered through the open door at the chaos within. The tub had a thick scummy line around it. The tide mark was three inches from the top. Andrew must have been enjoying a very deep and leisurely soak. Judging from the state of the room, he must have overrun on time and leapt out of the water in a big hurry. It looked like a whirling tornado had visited the place, sucking items into its vortex before depositing them again willy-nilly. Two sopping wet towels had been dumped at either end, discarded underpants were dangling off the flush handle of the toilet cistern, two socks were draped over the soap dispenser, and the washbasin was full of Andrew's whiskers and blobs of shaving foam. The ornate "bathroom tidy" that housed shampoo, conditioner, deodorant and

148

other toiletry paraphernalia was virtually empty. Instead bottles lay on their sides, scattered in all directions across the floor. The lid hadn't been properly replaced on the bubble bath, and a stream of blue goo had puddled across the lino. The scent of Andrew's aftershave hung faintly in the air.

Sighing to herself, Chrissie moved off to the kitchen again. She needed a good strong cuppa after Madam Rosa's earlier homily. Once fortified, she'd straighten up the bathroom, then telephone Andrew to let him know she was home. Perhaps they could share a takeaway this evening. Chrissie had been looking forward to the curry night with Amber and Dee, and her taste buds were letting her know they still wanted to savour spice, rice and all things nice.

She was just wondering why Andrew had felt the need to groom and perfume himself if he was spending his Saturday doing electrical jobs, when Madam Rosa's words came back with a vengeance. Chrissie jerked as if she'd been tasered.

Your relationship is coming to an end.

Chrissie reached for the kettle and stuck it under the tap. As she waited for it to fill with water, she chewed her lip. The reason Andrew had dressed up and taken trouble over his appearance was because...because...her shoulders relaxed...of course...he'd be meeting up with the lads afterwards and not have time to come home and change. That was the obvious answer. Wasn't it? Suddenly water cascaded everywhere as the kettle overfilled. Her concentration had been elsewhere. Chrissie tipped some of the excess water out, and plugged the kettle in. Dabbing at her damp top where water had sprayed, her mobile started to ring.

'Darling!'

'Mum, how lovely to hear from you!' Chrissie's heart gladdened at the sound of her mother's voice.

From the other end of the phone she could hear Pam Peterson taking a long drag on a cigarette. 'Are you smoking? I thought you'd given up.'

'I have – officially,' Pam added. Chrissie could hear her mother sucking in another deep lungful of smoke. 'Unofficially, I'm still smoking. But don't tell your father.'

'Won't he know? He'll smell it in the house.'

'I'm ringing you from the garden shed. I'm on my mobile.'

'At the very least Dad will smell it on your hair.'

'No he won't, because I'm going to walk around the garden afterwards.'

Chrissie smiled. Her mother made it sound as though she had an acre of landscaped grounds to wander around in, rather than a patch of grass bordered by rose bushes.

'Anyway,' said Pam, 'never mind me and my bad habit. How are you, darling? Dad and I haven't seen you for ages.'

'I know. Sorry, Mum.' Chrissie felt awful. Her parents lived in the town of Swanley, only a dozen or so miles away. 'What about you and Dad visit Andrew and me tomorrow? I'll do Sunday lunch for us all.' Chrissie did the mental maths of how much was left in her bank account until pay day, and whether it ran into buying a chicken with all the trimmings, plus a trifle and bottle of wine. Hopefully Andrew could hand over a bit of cash from his debt payment and make a small contribution. But Pam was already giving her trademark crackly laugh by way of response.

'I don't think that's wise, darling, although it's sweet of you to offer. Your father is very fond of his car. He wouldn't be happy if it went missing while we were tucking into our roast.'

'The estate isn't *that* bad,' Chrissie lied. John Peterson owned a ten-year-old Jaguar. It was his pride and joy. If by some miracle the car didn't disappear while they were eating, then at the very least the tyres would. Never a day went by on the estate without spotting a car jacked up on bricks.

'Why don't you and Andrew come to us instead?'

'That would be lovely. Andrew's at work at the moment, so I can't ask, but I'm sure it won't be a problem.'

'Excellent. Shall we say noon? You and I can have a nice glass of wine beforehand, and the boys can have their beer. It will be nice to have an overdue catch-up with my daughter.'

'Yes,' Chrissie agreed. Although she wouldn't be able to chat in confidence to her mother while Andrew was there. 'Er, Mum?'

'Yes?'

'Tell me, have you ever seen a clairvoyant?'

'I have actually. Years ago. I went with dotty June across the road. It was one of those spiritual events where you hope to get a message from a loved one.'

'Oh, no, I don't mean that sort of clairvoyant. More...the fortune teller type.'

'Ah. In that case, no. Why?'

Chrissie gave a nervous laugh. 'Well, you'll probably say I wasted my money–'

'You'll *definitely* have wasted your money,' Pam gave another crackly laugh.

'Do you think?'

'I don't need a crystal ball to guess you've visited one.'

'How–?'

'It's obvious, darling. You sound upset. Come on, tell your mother. What has the charlatan said?'

Chrissie sighed with relief. It was so good to talk to somebody sane and sensible. Her mother would never have been taken in by the likes of Madam Rosa. Chrissie had allowed herself to be swept along by a series of unfortunate coincidences fuelled by the insecurities of herself, Dee and Amber. She took a deep breath and told her mother everything…well, almost everything…from the initial brief reading at Cougar Kate's fortieth birthday, up to this morning's tarot reading in an unassuming house in Vigo Village. She glossed over the bits she hadn't like. 'So, what do you think, Mum?'

'I think,' said Pam, pausing to light up another cigarette, 'that you're not being very truthful with me, Chrissie.'

'What do you mean? I've told you everything that Madam Rosa told me.'

'This woman has played upon an insecurity. Does Andrew have financial problems?'

'No!' Chrissie protested, crossing her fingers at the same time.

'Are you sure? I mean, the pair of you have been living on that awful estate for so long now. You're both working. Why don't you rent something more decent, or even put a deposit down on something? There's a lovely little house around the corner from us that's gone on the market. I'm sure you could both afford it if you reined in extravagance.'

Chrissie managed to halt the cynical laugh that had threatened to break loose. Loyalty to her boyfriend had always stopped her from ever telling her parents about his drain on finances. Her father would be unimpressed with Andrew if he discovered that the maisonette was regularly full of beer-swilling, pot smoking, drug dealing yobs. Nor would he appreciate knowing his daughter had been despatched to the all-night supermarket at silly o'clock, and left to walk by herself through a rough estate. Chrissie had never imparted how hard up she really was, or how Andrew had exhausted her salary month after month. Instead she pretended to go along with her mother's idea of looking at a starter home.

'Yes, you're right. We've been saving hard. Andrew has been working all hours lately.'

'That's good to hear,' Pam had sounded relieved. 'I'll point out the house to you both tomorrow. And don't say I said so, but I'm quite sure Dad will agree to helping you and Andrew with a little extra for the deposit.'

'Th-that's...so kind b-but,' Chrissie could feel herself choking up at her mother's generosity. However, she wouldn't dream of taking her parents' hard-earned savings to help with a deposit on a house when Andrew had been so irresponsible – even if he was now making a belated effort to turn things around.

'That's what parents are for, darling,' said Pam, 'so don't upset yourself. Right then. If all is sunshine and roses in my daughter's relationship, you don't need me to re-iterate that this fortune-teller is simply an opportunist and a fake.'

'Y-yes,' Chrissie stammered. Right now, she was glad her mother was at the other end of a telephone and not able to see the look on her daughter's face. Pam Peterson would have known in a trice that Chrissie hadn't been entirely truthful.

'Damn, I can see your father on the patio looking for me. I'll have to dispose of this ciggie and ring off. Meanwhile, you have a lovely night in with your smashing boyfriend, darling, and we'll see you both tomorrow.'

'Okay.'

'Love you loads.'

'Love you too.'

Chrissie disconnected the call. Instead of feeling better for talking to her mother, she felt worse. She'd unloaded about Madam Rosa's readings, but skipped over the suggestion of Andrew being unfaithful, and more or less made out their joint

153

bank balance was healthier than one of the Brink's-Mat robber's. Chrissie reckoned that right now she was just as much a charlatan as Madam Rosa.

Annoyed with herself, she set the kettle to re-boil. She still hadn't made herself that brew. But Chrissie couldn't concentrate. She felt upset and jittery again, just like she had after seeing Madam Rosa this morning. Nor was she sure Andrew would even bother coming home tonight. Why should he if he thought Chrissie would be out herself? She presumed he'd tarted himself up to go straight from work to see his mates – either at the pub or one of their houses. For all she knew, he might get bevvied up and crash out on a sofa. Oh dear, and she'd foolishly agreed to Sunday lunch with her parents when she didn't even know what time her boyfriend would be home. Ignoring the boiling kettle yet again, she grabbed her mobile. She'd call Andrew right now, tell him she was home, and suggest a romantic night in complete with yummy takeaway. She dodged the sudden guilt of splurging on a curry when she'd told her mother she was never extravagant, and instead concentrated on tracking down Andrew so they could enjoy the rest of the weekend together. Chrissie started to tap out Andrew's number when, by chance, she saw his mobile sitting on the kitchen table. Oh terrific. The silly fool had been in such a hurry to leave the maisonette he'd gone off without it. How was she meant to get hold of him now?

As Chrissie stared at the phone in exasperation, it dinged with a text message. Curious, she picked up the mobile – and nearly dropped it again. Clutching it tightly, she grabbed the edge of the table with her free hand and steadied herself. Her eyes read the message for a second time. She gulped. This couldn't be right. It must have been sent to Andrew in error. On the third read-through, she could feel herself starting to hyperventilate.

Randy Mandy can't wait to play with Andy's candy xxxxxxxxxx

At that moment her own mobile let out a shrill beep. So startled was she that this time she did drop Andrew's phone. It landed with a clatter on the kitchen table. Chrissie didn't know what was making the most noise – Andrew's phone hitting Formica, her own mobile letting out another piercing dinnnnggggg, or her thudding heart which seemed to have morphed into a bass drum and relocated to her ears. With a shaking hand, she picked up the "Secs in the City" WhatsApp message from Dee.

Girls. It's true. Josh is having an affair.

Chrissie's legs started to buckle and she sank to the floor. Her breath was coming in ragged gasps as she tapped out a reply.

So is Andrew.

Chapter Twenty-Four

Amber's Saturday

After saying good-bye to Chrissie and Dee earlier, Amber hadn't gone home straightaway. Instead she'd diverted to nearby Longfield's Waitrose and picked up some shopping for the week ahead. She'd also bought some fillet steaks and peppercorn sauce. In her mind, Amber had been plotting: kitchen table laid for two; candle centrepiece lit and flickering ambient light; soft music playing in the background. She'd decided to pull out all the stops and cook Matthew something nice. She'd also trolleyed off to Wines and Spirits and purchased a bottle of her boyfriend's favourite red.

When Amber arrived home and stepped into the hallway, she knew – as was always the case these days – that Matthew wasn't in. Usually the empty house greeted her with calm silence, where even the dust motes lay sleeping and undisturbed. But this time the place felt different. It was enough to have her pausing. She stood stock still, shopping bags suspended from both arms, as an invisible antenna extended from her head. It shot up to the ceiling above her, and then grew a bit more until it was up under the eaves of the roof. Something was wrong, but she couldn't put her finger on exactly what it was. Her ears sought out clues, straining and sifting through the stillness. She frowned. She was experiencing something like...an electrical current. Whatever it was, "it" was unseen by the eye. "It" was soundless to the ear. But nonetheless "it" was being felt. Was there somebody in the house after all? A burglar? Silently, she put down the shopping and slipped off her coat and shoes.

On red alert, she moved slowly and stealthily

into the lounge. Nothing. She crept through to the kitchen. A frying pan and two cups were washed and upturned on the drainer. She paused. *Two* cups? Her eyes flitted around the room. The windows were shut. The back door locked. Her gaze returned to the two mugs. She didn't remember drinking from either one. Amber decided that Matthew must have simply had two cups of tea, and taken a second clean cup instead of re-using the first. He was a man, and men did things like that. Despite no visible signs of disturbance downstairs, Amber remained uneasy. Quietly, she removed the frying pan from the drainer and crept back to the hallway.

She paused once again, cocking an ear towards the staircase and the landing above. The electrical current seemed more vibrant here. More...*buzzy*. By the time she'd crept up the staircase, the frying pan was extended like a shield. She'd belt anybody who suddenly stepped out of thin air demanding cash, bank cards or jewellery. This house was her sanctuary. Nobody invaded it!

The bathroom door was open and so was the window, albeit ajar. It was as if somebody had opened it to let out steam and dry the condensation that might have run off the walls. The only time that was ever called for was if a very deep, boiling hot bath had been run. In the old days, she and Matthew had shared such baths. The vapour had swirled like fog over their heads, sticking to the tiles, forming droplets of moisture like rain against a window pane. Had Matthew had a long soak earlier? The towels were hanging neatly over the rail. She touched them. They were damp. *Both* of them. Her brow knitted. Why had Matthew used her towel? Amber's antenna was now swivelling left and right, left and right, assessing what she couldn't yet put into proper words: two cups on the drainer

157

but not left unwashed in the sink; two wet bath towels folded over the rail rather than dumped on the floor; the window considerately cracked open to let out condensation. Amber's female intuition began to formulate a suspicion. Had another woman been in her house?

As soon as the thought plopped into her brain, she disregarded it. It was that blasted Madam Rosa's fault! She'd upset them all with her nonsense about affairs and love triangles. Matthew wouldn't dream of bringing someone here. For goodness sake, she didn't even know for sure he *had* another woman! It was simply speculation from a stranger who happened to have a black cat called Merlin, and pretended to know the meaning of tarot cards while making an easy living hosting parties for gullible women like Chrissie, Dee and herself.

Amber tiptoed out of the bathroom. She moved towards the spare room where Matthew had currently taken up residence. Surprisingly, the bed was made and the curtains drawn. She moved slowly and carefully into the room, her nerves fraying slightly as a floorboard creaked. Her eyes fixed on the wardrobes. Both doors were firmly shut. If anybody was hiding in there, they'd need to leave the door on the crack so they could get out again. Carefully she lowered herself down to peer under the bed. Was somebody hiding underneath? Lifting the edge of the overhanging duvet, she came face to face with a pair of eyes that sent her blood pressure rocketing. Mr Tomkin blinked adoringly at her, as Amber waited for her heart rate to settle down.

There was only one room left to check. Her bedroom. Amber immediately felt a sadness, so changed that thought to *their* bedroom. Just because Matthew hadn't slept with her for the last week didn't mean it was now only Amber's bedroom. She moved cautiously into the larger of the two rooms, and the invisible antenna went berserk. She could almost mentally visualise it, like a cartoon aerial flashing on-and-off in fire-engine-red as a robotic voice screeched, "*Warning, warning, you're doomed.*"

Her eyes darted from left to right. The window was locked. Wardrobe doors closed. Bed made. Her eyes swept over the duvet. Amber was a neat and tidy person, but she hadn't made her bed like *this*. The duvet was beautifully plumped, as if it had been lifted and shaken vigorously before floating back down over the double mattress. Likewise, the pillows. All four were perfectly banked, as if hands had beaten them into the sort of shape that befitted a bed shop's showroom. Four colour co-ordinating decorative cushions had been placed with precision neatness in front of the pillows, but that wasn't how Amber had left them. She always placed the plain ones to the rear and the two florals to the front. These were reversed. Somebody had remade her bed. Correction, *their* bed. Her brain conjured up a picture of Matthew crawling between the sheets after Amber had left the house earlier, because secretly he was missing her and starting to realise the past week's ongoing silent row was simply pig-headedness on his part. Amber let her thoughts take her down the path of visualising Matthew wanting to lie where her own body had been, breathing in the faint flowery smell of Amber's body moisturiser that always clung to the bedlinen. She could see Matthew inhaling deeply and murmuring, "Amber, babe, I love you, I miss you," and then reaching out and pulling one of the decorative cushions towards him, stroking it like he used to stroke her hair. And then he would have felt rather foolish and leapt out of bed, taking extra care to pull it all back together again so that Amber wouldn't have suspected he'd been between her sheets. She allowed herself a few more rose-tinted imaginings of Matthew arranging cushions, accidentally placing them the wrong way. However, the invisible antenna above her head wasn't in agreement with this daydream.

Before she even knew what she was doing, one hand had reached out and yanked the duvet upwards sending the decorative cushions flying off the bed. Amber recoiled. Instead of the whiff of floral body lotion rising up in the air, the smell of recent sex shot up her nostrils. Amber gasped. The buzzer on the invisible antenna was now making one long endless sound. The frying pan slipped from her other hand and fell to the floor with a thud. Amber's fingers flew up to her temples, almost viciously massaging them. Swooping like an avenging bird of prey, she lunged forward and tore the fitted sheet from the mattress.

Something small and sparkly flew through the air, but Amber didn't notice. Her focus was on the sheet. Holding it at arm's length, she moved to the window so the harsh daylight could assist with a thorough inspection. The sheet was covered in stains. Eww! The linen had been fresh on the bed after her recent upchucking episode, and had certainly seen no action from her and Matthew. And then her eyes snagged on something tiny and glittery at her feet. Suddenly Amber thought she might faint, and put out a hand to steady herself. An earring. She bent down and picked it up. It was a stud, with a pretty diamond centre. It looked like the real deal too. No cubic zirconia crap for the rich bitch who'd been rolling around in *her* chuffing sheets in *her* chuffing bed with *her* chuffing boyfriend. Amber felt the start of a howl rising up through her body. It was a mixture of abject misery and red-hot fury. Dear God. Her lying boyfriend had not only cheated on her, he'd brought the tart home. He'd given her one in their bed. That chuffing Madam Rosa had been right all along – the bloody bitch. Bloody witch. Bloody cow. Bloody oracle genius.

The howl bypassed Amber's tonsils and erupted into the room making a sound like an unearthly being. She was aware of a terrified Mr Tomkin scooting across the landing and down the stairs. Tears were pouring down Amber's cheeks, running off her chin and dripping onto the stained sheet. How *dare* Matthew do this to her? Not only had he brought his mistress into Amber's house, he'd let the bitch use *her* bathtub, *her* towels, and drink from *her* mugs. The bastard. The whore. Well they could both rot in hell.

Amber dropped the sheet and, sucking in great chuggy breaths, leapt over the upside-down frying pan and pile of jumbled bed linen. She raced down the stairs. Finding her mobile phone, hands shaking like an alcoholic needing a drink, she sought out the number of a twenty-four-hour locksmith. Two minutes later she was agreeing to pay an extortionate price for a Saturday call-out.

Amber then dashed back upstairs, taking them two at a time in her hurry. She flung open the wardrobe doors in her bedroom – yes, *her* bedroom – and began divesting them of Matthew's clothes. She didn't bother packing anything, or even shoving garments into black sacks. That would have been too considerate an action for the devious scumbag. Instead, she grabbed armfuls of immaculate shirts and pristine suits before marching into the spare room. Clutching everything to her chest with one arm, she wrestled open the window with her free hand. Then, like a demented Postman Pat emptying a post box in reverse, Amber began shoving all Matthew's gear through the open window. Despite looking like a madwoman, there was a part of

Amber that was incredibly calm and knew exactly what she was doing. Once the suits and shirts were scattered across her front lawn, she started on Matthew's shoes. Boots and trainers followed. Drawers full of socks and pants were emptied and flew through the air, like strange looking birds wearing Y-fronts. Amber deigned to stuff Matthew's aftershave, toiletries, toothbrush and a pair of expensive cufflinks into a sports holdall, but then that too was flung from the bedroom window.

Old Mr Jefferies from two doors down strolled past with his ancient Springer Spaniel and stared up at the house in amazement. Amber paused and gave Mr Jefferies a manic smile.

'Afternoon. Wonderful day for a clear out, eh!'

'Are you all right, lass?' the pensioner called.

'Never better, Mr Jefferies,' said Amber, as Matthew's alarm clock landed in the flowerbed below. 'I'm having a Spring clean.'

'But it's January, lass.'

'In *this* house, Mr Jefferies,' said Amber, as Matthew's tennis racket joined everything else below, 'Spring has come early.'

'Oy!' came a shout. 'That nearly hit me.'

Amber leant out of the window and saw the locksmith had arrived. He was looking none too pleased at dodging objects.

'I'm so sorry,' she called. 'I'll be right with you.'

Mr Jefferies shook his head at the locksmith's raised eyebrows. As Amber moved away from the window, she heard Mr Jefferies say, 'I think she's having some sort of breakdown.'

Amber's feet pounded down the stairs. Shoving her discarded shopping to one side, she greeted a very apprehensive locksmith. She appreciated her tear-stained face and ravaged make-up wasn't a pretty sight. Her body was still vibrating from the adrenalin-rush of chucking Matthew's belongings from high above.

'I'm not crazy,' were her first words.

'Course you're not, love,' said the locksmith, giving an uncertain laugh. His expression said it all. *Lunatic. Humour her. Get the job done and clear off as fast as possible.*

'Please, come in,' said Amber stepping to one side. 'Would you like a cup of tea?'

'Are you making one for yourself then?'

'Don't be silly,' said Amber, smiling beatifically. 'I'm going to open several bottles of wine and get totally rat-arsed.'

'Ah ha ha ha,' chortled the locksmith uneasily, and set down his toolbox.

'I'll put the kettle on for you, and get a corkscrew for me. Meanwhile, I want the locks to both front and back doors changed super quick.' Amber lunged forward causing the locksmith to shrink back against the wall. He let out a whimper of relief as Amber ignored him and instead stuck her head through the open doorway. She looked from left to right, scanning the surrounding footpaths. She didn't want Matthew suddenly turning up. It would be the Law of Sod that he'd come home just when she didn't want him to. That must not happen. Not yet anyway. The timing had to be right on her part.

Amber was aware she'd had a meltdown, but God only knew what Matthew's reaction would be when he saw this lot strewn around the front garden. She looked heavenwards. An army of dark clouds were scurrying across a very bleak sky. A big fat blob of rain fell upon her upturned face. Then another one. Oh goodie. In a few minutes Matthew's belongings were going to get absolutely soaked. Giggling manically, Amber clocked the locksmith giving her an anxious look. At that moment, her mobile phone let out a loud *dinggggggg.*

'Do you take sugar?' Amber asked the wary locksmith.

'Nah, love. I'm sweet enough,' he said, giving a strained laugh. Flipping heck. Wait until he got home and told the wife about this bonkers dolly. He'd been changing locks on houses for thirty years and thought he'd seen it all – until this afternoon. He watched Amber stalk off with her mobile phone, and heaved a sigh of relief. The sooner he was finished here, the better.

Amber marched into the kitchen feeling strangely elated. She was calmer now, although her hands still trembled as she filled the kettle. Her body shook with post-rage adrenalin, but she felt almost euphoric at taking charge of the blow her devious boyfriend had dealt her. Amber was a firm believer in revenge – and she'd not wasted a second in taking it. As of right now, Matthew was homeless *and* clothes-less. A small high-pitched laugh escaped her lips. He was going to go doo-bloody-lally.

Her mobile phone let out a second ding reminding her of the ignored message. Amber tapped on the screen. It was a WhatsApp message under the "Secs in the City" name Dee had set up. Amber's eyes scanned the messages from her friends.

Girls. It's true. Josh is having an affair.
So is Andrew.
Her fingers moved across the screen.
And then there were three.

Chapter Twenty-Five

Dee's Sunday

Dee awoke with a heart so heavy she didn't think it would be physically possible to get out of bed. The weight in her chest was like a giant boulder pinning her to the mattress. She closed her eyes again, desperately trying to return to the safe womb of sleep. Right now, all she wanted to do was withdraw from the world. If God stepped out of the clouds and offered her one wish, she'd request He let her snooze soporifically from this world to the next one – a place where nothing hurt.

Dee felt a stab of horror at being reduced to wishing her life away. How dare Josh have done this to this! She was young and healthy, for heaven's sake. She had her whole life before her – a life she needed to get on and live. However, if Him Upstairs could throw a dollop of joy and a spoonful of love her way, then so much the better. Dee silently raged at herself. She *would* get out of bed and she *would* be happy. She swung her legs off the mattress. Hauling herself upright, she promptly burst into tears. *Small steps, Dee. Small steps. One out of two isn't bad. Just remember, you're not alone. Chrissie and Amber are feeling wretched too.*

The three young women had spent last night on Skype, shrieking and sobbing together as they exchanged sordid details about how Madam Rosa's tarot readings had unfortunately been proven true. Chrissie and Amber had been stunned to hear that Josh had swanned off to Tenerife with a mystery woman by the name of Emma. They'd also been indignant on Dee's behalf regarding Anne Coventry. How dare the woman accuse Dee of being a harpy who'd nagged her precious son into packing a

165

suitcase! Finally, the girls had gasped at Josh's manipulation of Dee's sexy morning fry-up, making out to his parents that it had been more like a scene from a *Saw* movie.

Likewise, Dee had been aghast as she'd listened to Chrissie blubbing her way through the details of discovering Andrew's sext message from the enigmatic Mandy. A movie director would have a field day turning their lives into a film for the big screen. However, of the three women, Dee thought it would be Amber who would collect all the drama awards: "Best Actress" for *The Saga of the Stained Sheets;* "Best Actress in a Supporting Role" for *Discovery of a Diamond Earring* (the winner being Mr Tomkin for portraying raw terror); and finally "Best Actress in a Leading Role" for *How to Empty Your Lover's Wardrobe in Sixty Seconds*.

Dee thanked God for small mercies. Whatever she was going through, and no matter how dreadful she felt, she had two besties who totally empathised. It didn't make her emotional pain any better, but equally it saved her depression from being a whole heap worse.

She stumbled into the bathroom, caught sight of her pale tear-stained face, and determined that, for now, her priorities had to be both realistic and simplistic – like emptying her bladder, cleaning her teeth, having a shower, and trying to make herself look more presentable. If she was looking better on the outside, perhaps she might feel a smidgen better on the inside. Stepping into the cubicle, she let the hot water blast over her body, unkinking parts of her spine that felt stiff. She wondered if the mysterious Emma was dealing with anything stiff right now.

Whimpering, Dee lathered shampoo all over her scalp. She squeezed her eyes tightly shut trying to blot out the image of an Amazonian blonde riding a panting Josh to orgasm in some swanky hotel in Tenerife.

As Dee scrubbed her skin to the colour of boiled lobster, she speculated on who had paid for this foreign holiday. Josh wasn't a man to splash cash, which rather led Dee to suspect this other woman had stumped up. In which case, was Emma a rich bitch? What did the cow do for a living? Where did she work? Where did she live? What did she look like? How old was she? How long had she been shagging Josh? Dee's head began to throb with so many unanswered questions.

Towelling herself off, Dee decided to take some care with her appearance today. It was unlikely Josh would walk in through the front door later but – if by some small miracle he did – she wanted him to be greeted by a chic and sophisticated woman, rather than the Undomestic Dog-ess he'd mentioned in his postcard to Anne and Peter Coventry. That comment had touched a nerve. Dee wanted Josh to look at her with fresh eyes, to be wowed by the attractive woman who had been by his side all the time, and for him to fall at her feet and grovel for forgiveness.

As she blasted the hair dryer over her short hair, she wondered if Emma had a long silky mane. As Dee applied moisturiser to her skin, she pondered whether Emma had tattoos. And as Dee threaded a pair of pretty hooped earrings through her ear lobes, she speculated whether Emma had piercings and, if so, where. Dee could feel herself getting obsessed by this woman. She wanted answers. And now. Suddenly an idea dropped into her brain that had her standing stock still. There *was* a way to find out the answers to most of her questions. She was amazed she hadn't thought of it before. However, it would cost money. Possibly a small fortune.

Dee instantly thought of her secret savings

account that Josh knew nothing about. Her "wedding" money. She snorted derisively. She'd been saving for an event that was never going to happen in a million years. At least, not with Josh. And then Dee experienced a moment of pure horror as another thought bounced into her brain. It rattled around like a lottery ball. What if Emma wasn't a dalliance? What if Josh considered himself to be in a serious relationship with Emma? Dee gasped. What if Josh was secretly engaged? That last question was enough to convince her that breaking into her wedding-that-never-was fund would be money well spent. She made her decision there and then.

She was going to hire a detective.

Chapter Twenty-Six

Chrissie's Sunday

Chrissie was awoken by her mobile ringing. One hand shot out of bed and snatched it up from the bedside table.

'Hello?' she mumbled. She was cross-eyed with tiredness, and had the sort of thumping headache that felt like a box of marbles had been emptied into her skull.

'Darling, where are you?' said a familiar voice.

'In bed.'

'Why? Aren't you well?'

'It's Sunday,' said Chrissie, screwing up her eyes against daylight streaming through the bedroom's thin curtains. 'I'm having a lie-in.'

'But it's nearly one o'clock,' said Pam in surprise. 'Dad and I were getting worried. You and Andrew should have been here an hour ago.'

Chrissie groaned. Of course. She'd completely overlooked her mother's invitation to Sunday lunch. She eased herself upright in bed, trying to shake off the events of last night that nobody – not even Amber and Dee – yet knew about.

'I-I'm so sorry, Mum,' Chrissie stuttered, her sluggish mind trying to come up with a plausibly quick excuse. 'Andrew had some emergency call outs. He's still not home from the last one. My sleep was so fragmented, I didn't hear my alarm.'

'You poor things,' said Pam sympathetically. 'No worries. I'll keep everything hot in the hostess trolley.' Pam Peterson had inherited the plug-in food warmer from her grandmother, and it was still going strong. 'Just get yourselves over here as soon as possible. Do you reckon you could be here by two'ish?'

169

Chrissie felt panicky. She had no idea when Andrew would be home. And even if he walked in right now, she had a feeling he wasn't going to be up for sitting around the Peterson's dining table making polite small talk. Apart from anything else, Chrissie didn't want him there. She was currently feeling like a pressure cooker. Although in her case it was rage simmering away. She wasn't quite sure what would happen if the lid flew off. She had a sudden vision of emptying the scalding contents of her mother's gravy boat over Andrew's groin and saying, 'You simply *must* have this with your meat and two veg. Is it hot enough?'

'Er, the thing is, Mum, to be with you by two I need Andrew back here with the van. If he's not home in time – and it doesn't look like he will be – I'll have to come on the bus. And you know what the buses are like on a Sunday.'

'Oh dear. Hang on a minute, darling.' Pam clamped a hand over the phone. Chrissie could hear her mother's muffled voice instructing John to pick up their daughter. Seconds later Pam was back. 'Dad's on his way. See you soon, darling. Bye-eeeee!'

Hell. The last thing Chrissie wanted was to spend the day putting on a cheerful front. She didn't know where the term "brave face" came from, but right now she didn't possess such a thing. She let out a weighty sigh just as her stomach rumbled. She was amazed her body could even register hunger after such recent events.

Stumbling off to the bathroom, Chrissie headed for the shower. She needed to be quick, so that when her father drew up outside she was completely ready. It was best if John Peterson didn't get out of his Jag to ring Chrissie's doorbell. When you lived on an estate like this one, an awful lot could happen to a car in thirty seconds.

A couple of minutes later, warm water was

170

playing over Chrissie's skin. As it trickled over her face, she prayed it might wash away the horror scenes still playing in her head. Her mind travelled back to last night when Dee, Amber and herself had Skyped each other. It had been cathartic offloading to her besties about the discovery of Mandy's sext message to Andrew. However, unburdening hadn't taken away the physical pain that was still going on in her chest. It felt like invisible hands were constantly squeezing around her heart chambers. Discovering Andrew's betrayal had left her shell-shocked. Due to her boyfriend leaving his mobile at home, Chrissie hadn't been able to contact him. He'd had no idea that Chrissie's sleepover plans at Amber's had been cancelled, or that she'd returned to the maisonette.

A part of Chrissie had harboured faint hopes that "Randy Mandy" had meant to text her sordid message to a completely different Andrew, and that somehow her contact numbers had become muddled. Chrissie had wanted Andrew to come in and say, "Oh *there's* my mobile! I wondered what I'd done with it. Good grief! Look at this obscene message. Some daft cow has sexted me, ha ha ha! Well, fancy that. It's Mrs Granger. I did an electrical job for her last week. Her old man is also called Andrew. Quite frankly, I'm stunned the pair of them still have a sex life. Mrs Granger's celebrating her ninety-ninth birthday next week." And then Andrew and Chrissie would howl with laughter on behalf of poor Mrs Granger being red-faced with embarrassment, and Andrew would fondly squeeze Chrissie's hand and say, "That'll be us one day, babe. Still bonking for Britain when we're close to receiving the Queen's telegram!"

However, Andrew had failed to put in an appearance to act out such a rose-tinted scene. Throughout Chrissie's tearful exchange with Amber and Dee, she'd had to face the awful reality that things weren't looking good between her and Andrew. After they'd all finished Skyping, Chrissie had been exhausted from so much crying.

She reached for the shampoo, working it into her scalp. Shutting her eyes, she let soap trails cascade over her sore eyelids. Her devastation was acute. It was as if a wrecking ball had ploughed through the walls of her relationship and scattered it in all directions. Her brain kept conjuring up tawdry images of Andrew's hands on this other woman's body, touching her in a way he hadn't touched Chrissie in goodness-knows-how-long. Her mind travelled back a few hours, to the point where her world had not so much as shifted on its axis but toppled right off.

The maisonette had been quiet. No rowdy, pot-bellied, dodgy men had filled the lounge demanding late-night chip butties. There had been no stink of weed seeping under the bedroom door as she'd taken herself to bed. Even Fran next door had been silent although, as soon as Chrissie had noted that observation one of the children had begun to cry. Within seconds Fran had shrieked at the offending child to put a sock in its gob because she was tired.

Chrissie had drifted off to Fran yelling, 'And if you wet the bed again, I'll make you sleep in it.' She'd felt sorry for the poor little kid. Her last conscious thought had been of her own pleasant childhood, with a mother who had never moaned at getting up in the night for her little girl. Pam Peterson had always been there for Chrissie, from holding a small hand if she'd been scared to walk to the loo in the dark, or because an eight-legged nightmare monster had caused her to scream the house down. Whatever her parents hadn't been able to give her materially, they'd more than made up for with cuddles and love.

172

Chrissie hadn't realised she'd fallen asleep until jerking awake with a start. An eerie orange glow had been filtering through the flimsy curtains, transforming the bedroom into a scene fit for a horror movie. She'd lain as still as a corpse, her heart flip-flopping in her chest. Her eyes had been the only thing that dared to move. They'd flicked to the digital clock on the bedside table. The blood-red number display had told her it was just after one in the morning. And then she'd heard a noise that had filled her with dread. The sound of somebody trying to get into the maisonette. One ear had stretched, cartoon-style, beyond the bedroom door, out into the narrow hallway, pressing up against the front door and listening for clues.

Prod, prod, prod. Stab, stab, stab.

Chrissie had presumed that whoever was on the other side of that door was trying – if such a thing was possible – to quietly crowbar it open.

In that moment she'd leapt out of bed faster than Usain Bolt over the finishing line, and stationed herself to one side of the bedroom door. Grabbing her dressing gown, she'd flattened herself against the wall and prepared to ambush the intruder. Her brain had been barking out orders like a bossy sergeant major, and her body had responded with a heightened awareness she'd never thought possible.

"Fling dressing gown over trespasser's head. Blind him with terry towelling. Push intruder forward. Shove him face down on mattress. Leap on intruder's back. Grab digital clock. Bash intruder's head repeatedly. Got it?"

"Sir! Yes sir!"

The front door had caved in, slamming so hard against the wall it had ricocheted back and hit the intruder in the face. Chrissie had caught a string of expletives as the intruder registered pain. *Good,* she'd thought, *that would teach the prat a lesson,*

173

although she'd decided the pain would be nothing to the lesson *she* was shortly going to teach him. How dare he break into her home!

But all Chrissie's gung-ho had fizzled out like a soggy firework in a thunderstorm when she'd heard a second voice – that of a woman.

'Andrew! I've told yer before. Don't bloody swear. You know I fuckin' 'ate it.'

What the–?

'I think I've broken my fuckin' nose.'

Chrissie's eyes had widened with horror. She'd certainly not anticipated a late-night housebreaker to be her boyfriend, or his accomplice to be the mysterious Mandy. Judging from the sounds of staggering about, the two of them had shipped quite a bit of booze.

As adrenalin rushed through Chrissie's veins, her brain had screamed out a contingency plan.

"Throw dressing gown over self. Curl into ball. Pretend to be dropped laundry."

And then another part of Chrissie – the one full of outrage – had poured some much-needed courage into her heart. The last thing she wanted was Andrew and Mandy barging into the bedroom and having a drunken bonk in front of her. Her skin had crawled as further sounds – slurpy ones – indicated the two of them were now snogging.

Chrissie went through the motions of rinsing her hair and combing through conditioner, but her mind was still firmly watching the re-run of last night's event.

'Yer a great kisser,' Mandy had enthused.

'Yeah,' Andrew had responded, but not very eagerly. 'Babe, I'm too drunk. I won't be able to get it up.'

'A droopy candy cane is no good to me, lover.'

'Make us a coffee,' Andrew had asked, 'and give me ten minutes. Then my candy cane will be ready

174

for a good licking.'

Chrissie had been shocked. Their sex life had never been full of innuendo – jokey or otherwise. She'd felt both revolted and insanely jealous.

'Where's yer kitchen?' Mandy had asked.

'Straight ahead. I need to use the little boy's room.'

Chrissie had remained in the bedroom, as still as a statue, listening to the bathroom door opening and closing. From the kitchen had come the sound of the kettle being filled and then switched on. Cupboard doors had opened and closed as Mandy hunted for cups. Next were the sounds of the freezer and fridge doors opening and closing as Mandy had sought out milk, but not known which door was which. Chrissie had dithered about what to do next. There had been two choices – either hide in the wardrobe until Andrew had bonked Mandy, or confront them both. Realistically, it had to be the latter.

Mind made up, Chrissie had wrapped herself in the dressing gown, and hurriedly run her fingers through her hair. She'd wanted to look presentable, even though she was swollen-eyed from her earlier tears, and grey-complexioned from shock. It would have been nice to have stepped out of the bedroom looking glamorous, so her love rival hadn't been holding all the aces. Instead, Chrissie had told herself that if she couldn't look like a bombshell she could at least behave like one. Her rival's discovery of Chrissie's presence would hopefully cause the emotional equivalent of nuclear fall-out.

Moving like a wraith, Chrissie had silently exited the bedroom and positioned herself in the kitchen doorway. The woman had been peering in the larder, oblivious that her lover's girlfriend had been studying her. Chrissie had noted the short peroxide-blonde hair, dangly earrings, and a

175

cropped sweater revealing flesh that might have recently seen a Caribbean sun. Either that or Mandy was an avid sunbed user. Chrissie's eyes had travelled up and down Mandy's body, noting the Designer label on the backside of her white jeans. She'd caught a glimpse of polished toenails peeping out of beautiful strappy gold stilettos. Those shoes had been the trigger to Chrissie feeling so incensed she'd momentarily felt insane. For a second she'd experienced the weird emotion of not knowing what she'd wanted the most – Andrew, or those gorgeous gold sandals.

All thoughts of footwear fragmented when Andrew had stumbled out of the bathroom. He'd opened his mouth to say something to Mandy, but shut it again when he'd seen Chrissie standing before him looking like an extra from *Night of the Living Dead*. A strange gurgling noise had escaped his lips. Chrissie had folded her arms across her chest, and watched her boyfriend's booze-flushed face change to the colour "Ghost" on a paint chart. When he did eventually speak it was to utter two strangled words.

'Faaaaaarkin' 'ell.'

'Stop fuckin' swearin' an' tell me where the fuckin' biscuits are kept,' Mandy had replied. When Andrew had failed to respond, she'd turned around. Unlike Andrew, the woman hadn't been in the least fazed to see Chrissie standing there. In fact, she'd been cooler than a North Pole ice floe.

"Ello, love. Do yer want ter join us for coffee?'

'Faaaaaarkin' 'ell,' Andrew had repeated.

For a moment Chrissie had thought she'd not heard correctly. What female, caught red-handed with another woman's boyfriend, casually extended an invitation for coffee *and* in the kitchen of the wronged woman? But Chrissie hadn't even got as far as attempting to answer that question, because

176

she'd been so distracted by the other woman's face. Chrissie might have looked like death warmed up, but one thing she *did* have on her side was youth. Mandy must have been in her mid-forties, and she was no Cougar Kate. Deep laughter lines were etched around her heavily made up eyes, and her conker-brown face was the texture of leather. Chrissie knew straight away that Mandy hadn't been further than Suzie's Sunbeds in Gravesend. And then she'd marvelled at how she could think about something as bizarre as Mandy's tan when the three of them were in this surreal situation. Without missing a beat, Mandy had pulled a third mug from an overhead cupboard.

'Yer look a bit shocked, love. Shall I put a couple of sugars in for yer?'

'Faaaaaarkin' 'ell,' Andrew had said, backing away from both women as if they were unexploded World War Two bombs.

Chrissie had started to feel out of her depth. She'd not known whether to lunge forward and slap Mandy's dermal-filled cheeks, or try and match her love rival's *sangfroid* with her own depleted reserves of Artic coolness. If Amber had been there it would have been a no-brainer. But Chrissie wasn't Amber. Instead, she had decided to rattle the two of them by *not* going ballistic. She had neither grabbed Mandy by the hair, nor put her knee in Andrew's privates.

'Coffee, please,' Chrissie had said.

She'd spoken in her best Kent accent. She didn't know where Mandy came from, but it definitely wasn't this side of the river. 'No sugar,' she'd added.

'Faaaaaarkin' 'ell,' Andrew had said, holding his hands out like a shield in case Chrissie went mental.

'Oh do shurrup, yer stupid tosser,' Mandy had snapped. She'd rolled her eyes. 'Go in the bloody lounge an' wait fer yer coffee.' Andrew hadn't

177

needed telling twice. He'd scarpered. Mandy had turned back to Chrissie. 'Sorry, love. Where were we? Right, so no sugar. Sweet enough, eh?' Mandy had given Chrissie a wink and friendly smile which, bizarrely, she'd found comforting. Andrew's mistress was about the same age as her mum. What the hell was her boyfriend playing at?

'Why don't yer go and sit down, love,' Mandy had invited, as if Chrissie were a guest. 'I'll bring the coffees in on this nice tray you 'ave 'ere.'

'Thank you.'

She'd walked into the lounge with her dignity wrapped around her like a blanket. Sitting in the armchair opposite Andrew, he'd averted his eyes and stared at a spot on the ceiling. Chrissie had wanted to shriek at him, but her brain had told her to behave like a lady, even if it nearly killed her.

Mandy had followed her in with the tray of coffees, and placed them down on the scruffy occasional table.

'Isn't this nice!' she'd trilled.

'Lovely,' Chrissie had replied.

'Faaaaaarkin' 'ell,' Andrew had said.

Chrissie had taken her drink, and marvelled at the stillness of her hands as they'd held the china. Not a tremble in sight. She'd glanced across at Mandy as she'd picked up her own cup. Annoyingly, Mandy's hands had also been tremor-free. She certainly was a cool customer. Perhaps she'd been in this situation before? Maybe she made it a habit of helping herself to other women's boyfriends, and creeping home with them in the early hours? Possibly this wasn't the first time she'd made a consolation drink of something sweet and comforting for the poor cow who'd been fast asleep in bed.

For one mad moment Chrissie's hands had itched to throw scalding coffee all over Mandy and her immaculate white jeans. But no sooner had the thought registered in her grey matter, another part of her brain had screamed, "No!" She'd looked briefly at Andrew to check how he was coping with the two women in his life smiling at each other over their coffee cups. Badly, it transpired. His face had been porridge-grey.

'I'm sorry yer found out about us like this,' Mandy had said cosily.

'Oh, that's all right,' Chrissie had flapped a dismissive hand. 'I've known for ages. Didn't Andrew tell you?'

Mandy had looked surprised, and she'd looked questioningly at her lover. 'Andrew? Is that right?'

'Faaaaaarkin' 'ell.'

Chrissie had taken Mandy's annoyance as her cue to make trouble. 'We have,' she'd shrugged carelessly, 'an open relationship.'

Mandy had arched an eyebrow. 'Oh?'

'Every Monday and Wednesday I see Andrew's mate, Mick—'

'Mick? Yer mean Big Mick?'

'The very one and same. And he's not called Big Mick because of the size of his beer belly,' Chrissie had grinned impishly.

'Does his wife know?'

'But of course. Andrew does his best to bonk Jane in return,' she'd glanced sympathetically at Andrew, before making a see-saw gesture with one hand, 'but unfortunately his candy cane doesn't always work, does it poppet? He's got an appointment to see the doctor. In the meantime, Andrew met you and told me he'd introduce us. You were meant to come here earlier this evening for a *ménage à trois—*'

'A what?'

'A threesome, sweetie. You were so late I presumed something had gone wrong, and took

179

myself off to bed.'

'Are yer fuckin' kidding me?' Mandy had glared at Andrew for confirmation.

'Faaaaaarkin' 'ell,' he'd replied, looking absolutely terrified.

'I don't do fuckin' threesomes,' Mandy had said, banging her mug down on the tray.

'Oh don't worry,' Chrissie had soothed, 'now that we've met, I couldn't possibly do a threesome with you.'

'What's that supposed ter mean?'

'No offence, but you're twenty years too late.'

Mandy had looked outraged. 'Right,' she'd snapped, 'I'll let yer get back ter bed. Meanwhile,' she'd hooked a finger at Andrew, 'are yer comin' with me or not?'

Andrew had rocketed upwards, nodding his head and making unintelligible noises as he'd hastened after Mandy.

'So charming to meet you at last,' Chrissie had said to Mandy's rigid back. She'd followed the hateful pair to the front door. As they'd taken their leave into the dark night, she'd pleasantly called after Andrew, 'Save a bit of that candy cane for me, darling.'

Chrissie stepped out of the shower and began towelling herself off. She knew Andrew would vehemently deny every one of the seeds she'd planted in Mandy's brain. But with a bit of luck her words would fester and gnaw. Women like that wanted to be the ones in control. They didn't like having their love affair upset by youthful girlfriends insinuating they were simply being used, especially for sordid reasons. Not that Chrissie would ever engage in a threesome. Never in a million years. But Mandy wasn't to know that. Chrissie wondered what Andrew had made of it all, listening to his girlfriend make sexual suggestions like a porn star on heat. Well he could go to hell. She was done with the prat, not that she'd let Mandy know that if their paths ever cross again. Revenge was sweet, and Chrissie had enjoyed delivering it.

As she tugged on a clean pair of jeans, through the bedroom window she saw her father's old Jag purr to a halt outside the maisonette. Moving over to the window, Chrissie flicked back the net curtain. Her father waved. She mimed for him to stay in the car, and that she'd be with him in a moment.

Picking up her handbag, mobile phone and house keys, Chrissie straightened her spine. She was going to have to do a lot of that from now on. Stand tall. No way was she letting the likes of Mandy and Andrew wear her down. All she had to do now was tell her parents the truth about her smashed-up relationship. Madam Rosa was right. There was a way out of this awful situation. Even though she didn't want to be back under her parents' roof like a big kid, unfortunately needs must. After Sunday lunch, she would ask her parents if she could come home.

Chapter Twenty-Seven

Amber's Sunday

Amber awoke on Sunday morning feeling tired but strangely elated. She stayed snuggled under the duvet for a few moments, and reflected on the events of Saturday afternoon. She'd started to gulp down a glass of wine when the locksmith had been in the house, but then poured it all down the plughole. No man was driving her to drink! She'd then spent the remainder of the afternoon and evening scrubbing her house from top to bottom to eradicate the ghost of the mystery woman. All towels and bedding to both bedrooms had been boil-washed. Afterwards, she'd cooked the fillet steaks she'd bought for Matthew and shared them with Mr Tomkin.

'From now on,' she'd told the delighted cat, 'you are going to be the only man in my life.'

Amber had munched her way through the tender meat, buttery mash and fresh vegetables resigning herself to a different existence from this point onwards. She'd be a spinster. Rather than settling down and having children one day, she'd get another cat. Maybe two. Or six. Twelve even. She'd be the Mad Cat Lady of New Ash Green. Everyone would talk about her, including Mr Jefferies, who would lament about his Springer Spaniel always trying to chase Amber's moggies.

A burgeoning bladder eventually forced her out of bed. Matthew still hadn't put in an appearance. His clothes remained festooned around the front garden. Winter shrubs had seemingly bloomed early, sporting strange flowers which, on closer inspection, were men's underpants. Amber's lawn was open-plan to the numerous footpaths that wound in and around the village. Somebody's dog had run across Matthew's scattered suits and shirts. Muddy paw prints were splodged across sleeves and lapels, and a fox had left its calling card on a pair of jeans.

Amber was trying to get enthusiastic over a piece of burnt toast, when the doorbell buzzed. Her heart began to clatter about. It must be Matthew, ready to read the Riot Act. She tiptoed to the hallway on wobbly legs, and peered through the front door's spy glass. But instead of a furious ex-boyfriend, it was Edith, Amber's immediate neighbour to the left. Edith was a retired headmistress. She had some interesting facial hair, and bore a remarkable resemblance to Del Boy's Uncle Albert. Amber had no doubt that Edith had once put the fear of God into her school pupils. From her glimpse through the spy glass, Amber could see Edith scowling at the clothes littering the lawn and flowerbeds. A pursed mouth indicated her neighbour was not happy. Amber took a deep breath and opened the door.

'Morning, Edith. How are you?'

'Hello, Amber. I'll come straight to the point.'

'I thought you might.'

'Your clothes—'

'—Matthew's clothes.'

'That *you* chucked all over the place, according to Mr Jefferies.'

Amber folded her arms across her chest. 'Ah, the New Ash Green grapevine has been busy.'

'Well it's not on, is it?'

'But they're not on,' Amber retorted. 'They're off.'

'That's my point.'

'No, it's an observation.'

'Amber, you've evidently had a domestic—'

'No, I've had a clear out.'

'This isn't normal.'

183

'What isn't normal?'

'Making this mess. The residents here have pride, you know.'

'I have pride, Edith.'

'Good, in which case you'll clear this lot up.'

'Matthew will remove it in due course. Ah, talk of the devil.' Amber's eyes hardened as Matthew appeared at the far end of the footpath that led out from a communal block of garages. He had a spring in his step and appeared to be whistling.

'He's going to go mental when he sees what you've done.'

'He is indeed,' Amber purred. 'Now if you don't mind, Edith, I need to shut my front door. You're welcome to station yourself outside if you want to watch the floor show, but if I were you I'd go indoors and stick to twitching your curtains. Good-bye.'

'Well really, there's no need to be–'

But Edith was left talking to herself.

On the other side of the door, Amber drew the bolts, turned the key, and put the safety chain on for good measure. She then scampered through to the kitchen and made sure the back door was secure, before taking the stairs two at a time. Dashing into the spare room, she flung open the window just in time to see Matthew's jaunty gait change to stalling steps. His cheerful whistling petered out, and his eyes were doing a fair impression of cartoon-like stalks.

'What the–?'

'Yoo hoo, Matthew,' Amber called from above. 'I've changed all the locks, so don't bother giving me back your house keys.'

Matthew's astonished face looked upwards. 'Have you taken leave of your senses?'

'Not at all. I've had an epiphany. Isn't it wonderful!' Amber beamed.

'Do you mind telling me what the hell's going

on?'

'Isn't it obvious? You and I are finished.'

'Finished? Well if we weren't before this, we definitely are now. You're absolutely barking. Off your rocker. Think I want a nutty girlfriend? And look at my stuff – it's ruined.' He held up his arms, then let them drop to his sides again. His expression one of dismay. Then his eyes snagged on something, and his face turned magenta. 'My *shoes*!' he shouted. 'Those are Jeffrey West. They cost me three hundred chuffing quid.' He bent down and picked them up, only to drop them again as if hot coals. 'There's *fox* crap in them,' he yelled. 'You cow! I'm going to sue you.'

'Take your compensation from the money you didn't pay me when living under my roof.'

'This is my house too, Amber,' said Matthew ominously.

'Oh no it's not,' Amber spat. 'I bought this place long before you came along. It's *my* name on the deeds.'

'And *I've* helped pay the mortgage.'

'Ha!' Amber sneered. 'Your very infrequent contributions were for food and alcohol which didn't begin to cover what you've cost me over the last few years, so don't you *dare* try and play that number on me.'

'I KNOW MY RIGHTS,' Matthew bellowed, 'and I'm entitled – ENTITLED, do you hear? – to half your house.' His face was rapidly changing from magenta to aubergine.

'You're *entitled* to ZILCH,' Amber roared. 'You never put a ring on it,' she thrust her left hand through the open window, waggling her bare fingers at Matthew, 'and thank God you didn't. Now clear off. And take your stuff with you. Go to HER,' Amber screamed, 'and let her wash and iron your clothes, and pick up after you.'

Matthew put his hands on his hips and decided to bluff it out. 'What are you on about now? Are you accusing me of having an affair? Ha, as if! There is nobody but you, Amber.' His tone switched to one of wheedling. 'Aw, come on, babe. Let me in. It's you I love.'

'Don't lie to me, you prat. Here's your tart's earring which she left in MY bed. Catch!' Amber lobbed the diamond stud. It landed with a plop in one of the shoes. 'Oh dear. Was that the one full of Mister Fox's poop?'

'You...you...you...,' Matthew tried and failed to think of an adequate name to hurl at Amber just as Mr Jefferies creaked past with his spaniel.

'Hello, lad,' he nodded at Matthew. 'Back are you? Oh dear, oh dear, oh dear. I think you've upset your lady.'

'That's no lady,' Matthew hissed.

'Now then, young man,' Mr Jefferies warned. 'Don't go insulting Amber. You've done her wrong, and she's retaliated.'

'Mind your own business, you interfering old–'

'Careful, lad. I might be nearly eighty, but I can still pack a punch.'

At that moment Edith reappeared in her slippers, brandishing a rolling pin. 'And I might be seventy, but I won't hesitate to defend Mr Jefferies. You're guilty, Matthew. Guilty of infidelity. And you know it.'

'What is this?' Matthew snapped. 'New Ash Green's kangaroo court?' Nonetheless he took a step away from Edith's rolling pin and Mr Jefferies raised walking stick.

'Good on both of you,' said Amber in delight, to the two pensioners, 'and thank you very much for standing by me. Sorry, Edith, for cheeking you earlier.'

Edith shrugged. 'You had cause.'

'Here you are, Matthew,' said Amber, lobbing a roll of black sacks at her ex-boyfriend. 'Just to prove I do have a heart, you can have these on me.'

'It's a pity you didn't have the decency to bag up my stuff in the first place,' he growled.

'Rest assured, Matthew, decency doesn't come into it. Good-bye.'

And with that she slammed the window shut, and drew the curtains for good measure.

Chapter Twenty-Eight

Dee's Sunday

Dee smiled at her reflection in the bedroom mirror. She was blessed with teeth that were straight and pearly. She was surprised to see, grinning back at her, a very attractive woman. Her glossy brunette crop was tousled to Vogue-like perfection, and thanks to Max Factor her complexion was flawless. She looked like a typical English rose. She moved her head from left to right, inspecting the newly applied make-up from every angle. How ironic that the mirror reflected such a glowing image. What it didn't capture was a heart that felt like it was permanently bleeding, and an inner churning as if an acrobat had taken up residence in her stomach. Even her legs felt like they were trembling within the jeans she'd shimmied into.

She jiggled around and glanced critically at the lower half of her body. She'd lost seven pounds in almost as many days thanks to the Misery Diet. She was now fitting into her denims like the proverbial hand in a glove. The stretchy cloth moulded her bum to perfection. If only Josh could walk in right now. She felt sure he'd drop his suitcase in astonishment and say, "Babe, you look amazing. What the hell was I playing at taking off to Tenerife with the very average-looking Emma? I'm so sorry. Please forgive me, darling." Or, even better: "Emma is a total dog. I discovered she's a hypnotist. She clicked her fingers and told me that whenever I looked at her I'd see Selina Gomez. In reality, she looks like Speedy Gonzales. You must understand that what happened wasn't my fault." And Dee would say, "Of course. Emma duped you with mind games. You were a guinea pig for little more than a

188

magic trick." And then Josh would sweep Dee up into his arms, stride into the bedroom, throw her onto the bed, and do all sorts of thrilling things to her that he'd never done with Emma.

Dee watched the smile slide from the reflection in the mirror, and the mouth settle into a downward turn. Josh's postcard was propped up on the table in the hallway. Boy would he get a shock when he came home and saw *that*. It would be the precursor for an overdue showdown from which there would be no going back. Dee's mouth drooped even further.

She spent the next hour sitting at her laptop Googling private investigators. She was astonished how many there were. Nor could she quite believe their sales spiel.

Do you need a private dick to investigate what your husband's dick is privately up to?

Good heavens, that was putting it baldly. She had a sudden vision of some cheating husband's penis surrounded by a bald pubic area. She shook her head to clear the image. She must be awfully stressed to have her brain conjuring up such things. But then again, what sort of investigator would write something so prolific? She checked his reviews.

Did the job. Five stars.

That didn't give much away. Dee sighed. The postcard proved Josh had cheated on her. She even knew the woman's name. What she wanted now was surveillance – to know where Emma lived. Dee didn't know what she'd do with such information. Pay her a visit? Beg her to leave Josh alone? Or slap her around the face? Dee didn't fancy getting arrested for assault. She wondered if she could give the private investigator a bit extra and have him do it on her behalf? Her mind played out a possible scenario.

189

Dick: Are you Emma?

Emma: Who are you?

Dick: Never mind who I am. I have it on good authority you are a total slapper.

Emma: Eh?

Dick: Let me demonstrate.

Dee imagined the satisfying sound of Emma's chops reverberating under a series of thwacks as revenge was exacted. Good heavens, not again. She rubbed her temples viciously and told her brain to pack it in.

On the other hand, perhaps she should simply give in to her dark fantasies. Why not take it one step further? What about hiring a hit man? Dee flinched. Why in God's name was she even contemplating such murderous thoughts? This wasn't her at all. Perhaps she was having some sort of breakdown. She felt a flash of anger at Josh for reducing her to playing mind games with herself. She carried on trawling through the list of investigators. Ah. What was this one? She scrolled back a bit.

Our sensitive private investigators provide a discreet and professional service.

That sounded more like it. More proficient. No smutty innuendo either. Dee read on.

A client called us because she believed her husband to be having an affair. The extra marital activity was taking place whilst our client was at work. Various options were discussed. It was decided to surveil the marital home when our client was out of the house and over a three-day period. On the first day, the husband stayed at home. On the second day, the husband left the marital home and our investigator followed him. He was trailed to an address five minutes away. It was a domestic residence and the door was opened by a female. At 2.25pm the husband left the residence. He was accompanied to the front door by the same female, this time spotted in see-through nightwear. We reported our findings to our client with supporting video evidence. The third day was cancelled because, although deeply distressed, our client was now sure of her husband's indiscretions. In this instance, the charge for the private investigator was £625 plus VAT and mileage.

Dee totted the likely total figure up and realised it would virtually swallow the entirety of her wedding-that-never-was fund. She sighed. So be it. She wanted to know who Emma was. To meet her. Until she saw this love rival with her own eyes, Dee didn't think she would rest. Even if Josh was honest and said, 'Sorry, Dee, there's absolutely no chance for either of us,' Dee still wanted to meet this woman. It was something she simply had to do. And with that thought in mind, she picked up the phone.

It answered on the second ring. Dee hadn't been expecting that. It was Sunday. She'd assumed it would be an answering machine.

'Hunter-Brown Agency,' said a man. His voice was no-nonsense, one of authority, with a deep baritone. 'Harrison Hunter-Brown speaking.'

'Hello,' Dee croaked. She cleared her throat. 'Hello,' she said again.

'How can I help you?'

'Er, my partner is having an affair.'

'I'm sorry to hear that,' said the voice, with just the right amount of sympathy. 'And you would like us to help you?'

Dee gulped. 'Yes. I hope you don't think I'm weird but I want to know who she is, and where she lives, and what colour hair she has, and whether she's pretty and,' Dee paused, aware she was gabbling, 'just...everything about her,' she finished lamely. 'I'm not sure what I'll do with this information. There's a part of me that wants to appeal to her better nature. If she has one,' she added, in a small voice.

'Understandable,' said Harrison Hunter-Brown. 'Most female customers are very inquisitive about who the other woman is.'

Dee found herself nodding in agreement at the other end of the phone. 'Exactly. Can you help me?'

'Of course. I'd like to meet you first, if that's okay?'

'Sure. When do you have availability?'

'How about in an hour?'

'Oh, as soon as that?' Dee was taken aback.

'I run a small agency, Miss..?' his voice trailed off.

'Do I have to give you my name?'

'Everything here is confidential,' Harrison Hunter-Brown assured. 'Maybe, for now, you could give me your first name?'

'It's Dee,' she said cautiously.

'Okay then, Dee. How about you pop over to the office, and we'll run through everything. If you like what you hear, we'll work out a plan. How does that sound?'

'Er, good, but...,' Dee trailed off.

'Is there a problem?'

'I'm a bit worried about fees. How much will the initial meeting cost?'

'Nothing. We only charge if you go ahead with surveillance.'

'Really?'

'Really!' He sounded amused, and his manner filled Dee with a sense of calm and purpose. She didn't know if private detectives took courses in people management, but she was already feeling confident in the person at the other end of the telephone.

'In that case,' she said, 'I'm on my way.'

'Do you have our address?'

'Yes, it's here on the website.' She peered at the screen. Seal. Ah, yes. It was a village near Knole Park in Sevenoaks. Very nice. She gave a mental sniff. Where there was muck there was brass. Or, in this case, where there were fucks there was brass. She wondered how many men – or women – Harrison Hunter-Brown and his associates rumbled on a daily basis. Enough to pay the bills in a posh area.

'I look forward to meeting you shortly, Dee.'

'Likewise.'

Dee ended the call. She suddenly felt incredibly fired up. Minutes later she was in her car, listening to the sat-nav guide her towards the A2. She took the first slip-road to Wrotham, and then meandered for several miles through an increasingly rural landscape. Twenty minutes later she was in the village of Seal, bumping along a tree-lined private road. The sat-nav told her she'd reached her destination. Dee peered through the windscreen at a smart courtyard of houses. A hundred years ago they'd been barns and stables, but some clever builder had converted them into stylish mews homes.

She locked the car and walked over to some heavy wrought-iron gates with intercom box. Seconds later Dee was buzzed into the main square. It was beautifully landscaped with huge terracotta urns full of frothing winter pansies and colourful shrubs. A rustic door opened to Number 2 and a weeping female came out.

'Thank you,' she heard the woman say in a strangled voice. 'Sorry about all the tears.'

'Truly not a problem, and please take care,' an unseen man replied.

Dee stepped aside to let the distressed woman exit – presumably a client who'd received bad news

193

– and then Dee had her first proper look at Harrison Hunter-Brown. Her body chose that precise moment to double up, as if she'd been slugged in the solar plexus by a bag of cement.

'Ooooh,' she gasped.

'Hey, are you all right?' said Harrison, leaping forward. 'Lean on me,' he instructed. 'You won't be the first person over this threshold whose knees have given way.' He gave a disarming smile as he reached out to guide Dee inside. To her embarrassment, his touch made her jerk violently, as if she'd been plugged into the National Grid and was lighting up the whole of Seal and possibly beyond.

'You must be Dee?'

She squeaked unintelligibly and resorted to nodding by way of response. She had a feeling her pupils were dilating faster than a junkie on amphetamines. The man was so good looking it was positively obscene. Obscene because her brain was doing that weird thing again and playing out scenarios – this time X-rated. In a parallel universe Harrison Hunter-Brown had already whisked her over to that sumptuous looking client sofa, and was undressing her at the speed of light. His hypnotically deep and sexy voice was saying, 'Dee, good heavens, I am *sooo* sorry, but I can't help myself. Do you believe in love at first sight? I do, and right now I want you. In fact, I've never wanted anything so much in all my life. How do you like it?'

'You decide,' she said wantonly.

'Most people like it with sugar,' said Harrison.

Sex with sugar? Dee's mind catapulted back to the present. 'Pardon?'

'How do you like your tea? My clients are usually in a state of shock when they visit, and sugar is helpful.' Harrison smiled encouragingly, the effect of which nearly had Dee passing out. 'You do look a

194

bit shaken up.'

'Y-yes,' she nodded. 'I am. A bit. Shaken.'

'Come into the lounge. As you've probably gathered, my "office" is also my home. I like to be informal with clients and try and get them to relax.' He indicated another squashy sofa, and Dee collapsed on it. 'So, Dee. Sit back. Take some deep breaths and I'll be back with the tea in a jiffy.' He gave her a thousand-watt grin complete with twinkling eyes and dimpling cheeks, before heading off to the kitchen. She slumped back, emotionally wrecked. In two minutes Harrison Hunter-Brown had unleashed a deep yearning in Dee that Josh Coventry hadn't achieved in two years. As Dee watched the private investigator's exquisitely formed bottom disappear out of sight, her only coherent thought was being glad to have made an effort with her appearance today.

Chapter Twenty-Nine

Chrissie's Sunday

'I must say, darling,' said Pam, ladling gravy over her daughter's plate, 'you look absolutely awful. I know you said Andrew had several call-outs last night and sleep was interrupted, but even so. Your face looks like a French bulldog. You know, wrinkled and screwed up. It's good Andrew is finally being diligent and earning some extra money – I won't lie to you, I've had my doubts about him before now. Even so, a bit of extra cash isn't worth wrecking your looks. Andrew can't be faring any better.'

'Yes,' said Chrissie quietly, 'you're probably right.' She had no idea how Andrew looked this morning. If it was anything like last night's expression, then words like "slapped" and "arse" would be appropriate.

'It's important to work, but not worth over doing it,' said Pam.

Chrissie pondered whether Andrew's todger was overworked. With a bit of luck it might drop off.

'You were very quiet on the drive over, love,' said John, kindly.

'That's because I'm tired, Dad.' Chrissie forked up some roast beef. It was a lovely meal. She wished she felt more enthusiastic about eating it.

'After lunch, would you like to borrow some of my make-up?' Pam offered. 'A bit of rouge on those pale cheeks wouldn't go amiss. If you look better, you might feel better.'

Chrissie knew her mother meant well, but her comments weren't helping. 'Maybe.'

'Is your food all right, love?' asked John.

'Yes thanks, Dad. Very nice.' Chrissie promptly

missed her mouth with the fork and spilt gravy all down her top. 'Bugger,' she muttered.

'I'll get a damp cloth,' said Pam, jumping up. She disappeared briefly, returning with a dripping tea towel that she sloshed over Chrissie's chest. The fabric instantly turned into a grey puddle with a tan stain. 'Oh dear. I've made it worse. Never mind, thankfully it isn't new.' She abandoned the tea towel and sat back down in her chair. 'Buy yourself another one,' Pam chirped. 'There's nothing like a bit of shopping to cheer yourself up. Your clothes look like they could do with an update. Why don't you spoil yourself, love? And when did you last go to the hairdresser? You always pull back your hair in scrunchies. It's not flattering, darling.' Pam put her knife and fork down and placed one soft, well-manicured hand over Chrissie's. 'Don't take this the wrong way, darling. After all, I know you're very tired right now, but lately you've been looking much older than your years. And look at those nails!' Pam exclaimed. She lifted Chrissie's hand up for John to inspect. 'Your skin is all cracked and sore, like a cleaning lady who works without rubber gloves. Are you doing an extra job that you've not told us about?'

Chrissie snatched her hand back. How could she explain that, yes, she was a cleaning lady – a cleaning lady for some thoroughly undesirable men who congregated in her home on a regular basis, and blocked her loo. And that she felt driven to scrub the place afterwards in order to reclaim it as her home. She knew her mother wasn't being malicious mentioning her outdated wardrobe, or suggesting a hundred-quid's worth of highlights, or splurging on half the make-up counter in Boots, but it hadn't been possible. Andrew's debts, gambling and general spending had kept her penny poor. Mind you, she didn't owe the prat anything now, not after the business with randy chuffing Mandy. The ancient cow, with her beautiful gold stiletto sandals and her Designer white jeans. Was that why Andrew had strayed? Because, unlike Chrissie, Mandy layered her face in cosmetics, dyed her hair and had clothes as stylish as Victoria Beckham?

'Are you all right, darling?' Pam's voice cut across Chrissie's reverie. 'I didn't mean to upset you. Lord, me and my big mouth. Now look what I've done. I'm so sorry. John, top up Chrissie's wine.'

'I-It's fine, Mum.' Chrissie put a hand over her glass to halt her father, who was already on his feet with the bottle poised. She caught sight of her chapped hand hovering over the crystal rim, and snatched it away. Unfortunately, her wrist caught the thin stem and sent it toppling over, flooding the table with liquid. 'O-Oh God. I'm so sorry.'

'Leave it, love,' said John. 'Pam, pass me that wet tea towel. Thanks. Now eat your dinner, Chrissie. Afterwards, perhaps you should go up to your old bedroom and take a nap – if you're in no hurry to get back to Andrew, of course.'

'N-No. I-I mean no hurry to get back. And y-yes, I'd like a nap. I-In my old bedroom.' Chrissie was desperately trying to hang on to her emotions, but everything was threatening to rush to the surface and overwhelm her. The thought of slipping off to her childhood room where everything was familiar and safe was oh so tempting. She wanted to sleep. Forever. Just so long as the images of Andrew and Mandy didn't come back to haunt her. A lone tear made a break for freedom and ran down one cheek.

'Don't, darling,' said Pam, sounding distressed, 'I didn't mean to make you cry.'

'Honestly, Pam,' huffed John, 'you and your big mouth. You've taken our girl apart. She's lovely as she is. She doesn't need make-up and fancy clothes, or a trip to the hairdresser.'

'But I didn't mean—'

'Please don't argue,' said Chrissie in a strangled voice. Another tear fell, swiftly followed by another, and then another. They splashed down her gravy-ruined top. A part of her wondered whether the salty tears might remove the stain.

'But I've upset you,' said Pam, and promptly burst into tears.

'Well this is turning into a fine Sunday lunch,' John sighed. 'I'm surrounded by weeping women.'

Chrissie began to bawl even harder. 'It's...huh huh...nobody's fault but my own...huh huh...Mum's right...huh huh...if I'd taken more care of myself...huh huh...Andrew would be here with me for Sunday lunch. Instead...huh huh...he's...he's...he's...huh huh—'

'He's what, love?' John prompted.

Chrissie sucked in a lungful of air, then spat out the hateful words like an overworked vacuum cleaner divesting its contents. 'Right now, Andrew is with a peroxide-blonde perma-tanned woman who I suspect is older than Mum.'

Pam dabbed her eyes and looked confused. 'Is this his electrical client?'

'No, although she certainly delivered a few shocks.'

'I don't understand,' said Pam.

'I think I do,' growled John, 'he's seeing another woman, yes?'

Chrissie nodded her head miserably. She picked up the paper serviette to the side of her dinner plate, unfolded it, mopped her tears and blew her nose. 'My boyfriend is having an affair.'

Pam's jaw dropped. 'And...and she's older than me?' she asked incredulously.

'Are you sure, love?'

Chrissie gave a mirthless laugh. 'Never surer. I

saw them with my own eyes. Andrew brought her back to ours, thinking I was out.'

'Oh, darling,' Pam gasped. 'Why didn't you tell us straight away?'

Chrissie shrugged. 'Shame. Embarrassment. Wanting, for some misguided reason, to protect him – despite everything.' She patted away fresh tears. 'He's changed so much.'

'Chrissie, love, I don't like telling you what to do,' said John. 'After all, you're a grown woman. But please tell me you're not going back to that maisonette to be emotionally trampled on by Andrew.'

'I have nowhere else to go.'

'Of course you do,' said John gently. 'This is still your home. Move back.'

'You don't mind?'

'As if you even need to ask,' said Pam, reaching for one of Chrissie's rough hands. She squeezed it tightly.

'Now dry those tears,' said John gruffly, 'and finish your dinner. Afterwards, I'll run you back to the maisonette and you can pick up your belongings.'

'Thanks, Dad,' said Chrissie gratefully. Right now, she felt like a seven-year-old. Her inner child was responding to her parents' concern. It was such a relief to let them guide her and tell her what to do. For now, anyway. She felt so weary, so worn out and emotionally drained. But she also felt lighter, as if a concrete cape had been shrugged off her shoulders. Suddenly her mother's Sunday lunch was full of appeal, and she polished it off with gusto.

When Chrissie returned to the estate, it was with two large suitcases that belonged to her parents. Her father remained outside in the Jag, glaring at a bunch of hoodies who were hoping he'd leave his car long enough for them to remove the alloys.

Chrissie scampered through the front door and into the bedroom, and began tipping clothes into the cases. She didn't bother to fold them neatly. She'd press them later when she was back at her parents' house. Andrew was out, and she desperately hoped he didn't turn up to see her emptying drawers and wardrobes. If he did, she had no idea whether he'd attempt apologising and beg her to stay, or whether he'd happily wave her off. But one thing was certain – she had no intention of sticking around long enough to find out.

Chapter Thirty

By late Sunday afternoon, Amber's euphoria from exacting revenge on Matthew had subsided. The initial rush of elation, fuelled by anger and adrenalin, had disappeared faster than Mr Tomkin slurping up a saucer of cream. She was left feeling as flat as a tyre that had been pierced with hundreds of nails. Reaching for her mobile, she tapped out a message on the *Secs in the City* group chat.

***

Dee drove home from Harrison Hunter-Brown's premises in a complete daze. Her meeting with Harrison ('Please, call me Harry') had passed in a blur. She hadn't so much as walked back to her car as floated. In slow motion. What the heck was the matter with her? Perhaps she was in some sort of weird aftermath of emotion. That must be it. She was glad of the distraction when her mobile dinged a message on the *Secs in the City* group chat.

***

Chrissie woke up in her old bedroom after a couple of hours' much needed snoozing. At first, she wasn't sure what had disturbed her. She was just drifting off again when the mobile dinged a message reminder. Making a long-arm, she picked it up and read a message from Amber.

Ladies, are you available this evening. I'm feeling crappier than the earring I chucked at Matthew (it landed in fox's mess).

Chrissie could see that Dee was typing. Seconds later the mobile chimed with Dee's message.

I'm feeling really weird. Possibly experiencing

the bit before a full-blown breakdown. Don't know what to do.

Chrissie sat up properly, and typed her own message.

The only nice thing about today was my mum's dinner. I've left Andrew. Back in my old bedroom at mum and dad's. Feel like a failure.

Amber began typing. *Let's meet up. Now. What about going for a drink?*

Dee instantly replied. *I passed a lovely pub when I was driving through Seal.*

Chrissie's fingers flew across the screen. *What were you doing in Seal?*

Dee's answer was almost instant. *Tell you when I see you. Want me to pick you up?*

Chrissie typed back. *Yes please.*

Amber came next. *As long as you both promise not to share updates with each other until we're all together. I don't want to miss anything! Which pub, Dee?*

Dee's reply was swift. *It's called "The Beagle and Bugle" and on the High Street. See you at seven.*

Chrissie glanced at her watch. It was a little after six. She hadn't a moment to lose. Swinging her legs off the bed, she padded downstairs to the lounge. Her father had nodded off in front of the television, and her mother was reading the Sunday supplements which were spread across the coffee table. Tortoiseshell specs were perched on her nose. Pam glanced up at Chrissie.

'Hello, darling. Feeling better?'

Chrissie gave a wan smile. 'A bit. I feel...,' she shrugged, 'empty. Like a car that's run out of petrol.'

Pam nodded. 'Hardly surprising. Can I make you a cup of tea?'

'No, don't get up,' Chrissie said quickly. 'You've been busy all afternoon, and I feel guilty that I didn't help you earlier with the washing up. Er,

203

Mum. Would you mind terribly if...' Chrissie trailed off. The downside of being back under her parents' roof was feeling like seventeen again, and having to ask permission to go out. She'd have to give assurances not to be late so they didn't worry, or feel they couldn't relax and sleep until she was home again.

'What is it, darling?'

'Um, well, Dee and Amber. You know. My two closest friends who I work with–'

'Yes, I know who Dee and Amber are. What's up?'

'They've asked if I'd like to go for a drink with them this evening. Is it okay with you if I pop out for two or three hours?'

'Of course. Do you need a lift?'

'Dee has offered to pick me up.'

'That's nice of her. And while we're on the subject of being out and about, you can borrow my car to get to work.'

'Oh,' said Chrissie, taken aback. She'd had visions of chopping and changing buses in order to travel from Swanley to Gravesend. 'How will you manage without the car?'

'Perfectly well. I'm within walking distance of the supermarket, and the exercise will do me good. I'll borrow your grandma's shopping basket on wheels. Good heavens,' Pam pulled a horrified face, 'I wasn't expecting that to happen yet! Next I'll be wearing one of those foldaway plastic hoods to keep my hair dry.' She laughed good-naturedly. 'If there is a day where I need the car, I'll simply give you a lift into Gravesend and pick you up later. It's not exactly a million miles away. We'll muddle along. Don't worry about it.'

'Thanks, Mum,' said Dee gratefully. She stooped and kissed her mother's cheek. 'I'll go and freshen up, and maybe pinch a bit of your make-up,' she said, winking at her mother.

Pam looked rueful. 'Honestly, darling, you don't need cosmetics. Truly. I'm so sorry for what I said earlier. You're beautiful as you are.'

'I'm going to give myself an overhaul,' said Chrissie, 'starting from now. And on pay day I'll be binning the scrunchies and having a restyle.'

'Good for you,' said Pam. 'It's about time my daughter spent her hard-earned money on herself.'

When Dee pulled up outside the Peterson's house, she did a double-take at Chrissie.

'Wow!' she wolf-whistled. 'I almost didn't recognise you. I can't remember when I last saw you wearing lippy and mascara.'

'Stop it,' Chrissie gave a gurgle of delighted laughter. She was surprised to hear the sound of merriment, no matter how brief, escaping from her lips. It had been so long since she'd had anything to giggle about.

***

When Dee and Chrissie arrived at The Beagle and Bugle, Amber was already there. The evening temperature had taken a sharp drop. Inside the pub a wood burning stove was gobbling up logs and emitting the occasional crackle and pop. Amber had appropriated some easy chairs around a low table by the fire.

'Ooooh,' said Dee, flopping down into a squashy chair, 'this is wonderful.' She leant forward, letting the wood burner warm her cold hands. 'All we need now is some marshmallows to stick in that fire.' She kicked off her shoes and began wiggling her toes.

'Hey,' said Amber, 'you're not at home now, madam. Put those back on!' she nodded at Dee's footwear.

Chrissie sank into the other easy chair. Leaning

back, she sighed. She felt like she was starting to relax. Was it only last night she'd been awoken by a drunken boyfriend...correction *ex*-boyfriend...with his sugar mummy? Chrissie presumed Mandy was a sugar mummy. She'd certainly been very expensively dressed. She wondered if Andrew had taken money off Mandy. And then she froze as a thought crossed her brain. Dear Lord. Surely not.

'What's up?' asked Amber. 'You look like you've seen a dead relative sit down beside you.'

'I-I'm wondering if Andrew is...is...taking payment for...you know,' Chrissie jerked her head and winked whilst miming with her hands, 'how's-your-father'.

Amber's eyes widened. 'What, you mean, like a male prostitute?'

Dee looked flabbergasted. 'Where did that idea come from?'

'Hold it right there, lady,' said Amber. 'I think you need to start at the beginning. We all do. Things have been happening to us faster than warp speed. Let's order a drink and then update each other. I know we're driving, Dee, but we can treat ourselves to one. Apart from you, Chrissie. You can get as sloshed as you like – especially if your boyfriend has been renting his willy out.'

Exactly on cue, the man behind the bar came over. 'Evening, ladies. To save you getting up and leaving the warmth of the fireside, let me take your drink orders and then I will personally bring them over to you.'

'Aren't you lovely,' cooed Amber. 'I'll have a G and T, please.'

'Make that two,' said Dee, with a smile.

Chrissie wasn't a great fan of gin and tonic, but couldn't decide what to have. As she looked up at the man to ask for Prosecco, she caught her breath. Literally. Embarrassingly, she gulped down gallons of air and began to choke. As her eyes bulged, her tear ducts spurted water, and she found herself struggling for air. Amber and Dee looked at her in faint amusement until realising their friend was in difficulty, whereupon they and the barman lunged to thump Chrissie on the back, and everybody banged heads.

'Chuffing hell,' Amber gasped.

'Flipping heck,' Dee moaned.

'I'm so sorry,' groaned the barman.

'Oh my—' Chrissie began, before being ambushed by a loud burp which had her turning pink.

'Are you okay?' asked the barman. Concerned, he placed an arm around Chrissie's shoulders. She nearly sprang off the chair like a jack-in-the-box. This guy's touch was hotter than the wood burner's glowing embers, and he was having a bizarre effect on her body. She felt as though she'd been jump-started by car leads. A dormant pulse between her legs had inexplicably roared into life. Somewhere deep inside her an invisible throttle was making *brrrrmm brrrmm* noises.

'Chrissie?' asked Dee in concern. 'Say something!'

'Make that three gin and tonics, please,' she squeaked.

For a split second everybody just stared. Chrissie had a horrible feeling she'd said, 'Take mat three tin and gonics, peas.'

'Right,' said the barman uncertainly. He gave his head a quick rub. 'Three gin and tonics coming up.'

Chapter Thirty-One

Three pairs of female eyes watched the barman walk away.

'Nice bum,' said Amber.

'Very,' Chrissie whispered.

'Not as nice as Harry's,' Dee murmured.

'Harry? *Harry*? Hellooo!' Amber yodelled. 'Your boyfriend is called Josh. Remember?'

'Yeah.' Dee leant back in her chair, eyeballs glazing with lust as she remembered the handsome face of the private investigator.

'So who's Harry?' Amber demanded.

'Harrison Hunter-Brown. He's a detective. He has his own agency – an extremely successful one if his premises are anything to go by. I've hired him to trail Josh and find out where his mistress lives.'

Amber's face cleared. 'Ah.'

'Harrison told me to call him Harry,' explained Dee, in the same awed tone a monk might say, "I've met God and He told me to call Him Fred.'

Amber leant forward in her seat. Her expression was one of concern. 'Are you doing the right thing, Dee? Listen, I know how you feel. I'd dance naked on that bar counter over there if it meant finding out more about the woman Matthew is seeing. Not because I want him back, but because I'd like to give the cheeky tart a good slap for coming into my house and leaving her diamond calling card between my sheets. That was a deliberate act on her part. She wanted me to find it.' Amber looked suitably outraged as she recalled the unhappy moment of discovering Matthew had brought another woman into her house. 'However, I'd rather do my own detective work than run up a bill paying someone else. This guy won't be cheap.'

'I can hardly trail Josh myself,' Dee protested.

'Why not?'

'Because...because,' Dee shrugged. 'One,' she ticked off her fingers, 'I don't want to be seen. Two, I'd have to take time off work, which in itself would make Josh suspicious. Three, even if I did take a couple of days' holiday to spy on Josh, there is no guarantee he'd go to Emma's in that time frame. He might simply go to work. The last thing I want to do is hide behind lamp posts, simply to watch Josh abseiling down buildings with a bucket and sponge.

'Even so,' said Amber, 'losing a couple of days' holiday is cheaper than forking out on this Harry person.'

At the mention of his name again, Dee's eyes took on a faraway look. Harrison Hunter-Brown was *the* most gorgeous man she'd ever met. He'd given her hot sweet tea and listened sympathetically. Then he'd outlined, in his sexy deep voice, a simple plan on trailing Josh and finding out Emma's address. He'd asked Dee what she planned to do with the information. She'd replied honestly that she didn't know, but she'd promised there would be no "crime of passion". Josh would live to bonk another day. Harry's eyes had twinkled with amusement and – something else, but what? It had made Dee quite flustered and possibly Harry had noticed, because he'd steered the conversation to costs – which had made Dee's heart gallop for different reasons. However, he'd assured her fees would only be incurred when she texted Harry with the thumbs up for surveillance. Dee had then shown Harry some pictures of Josh that she'd had on her mobile phone, and he'd transferred them to his computer along with details of Josh's van and registration number.

Dee yanked her mind back to the present to answer Amber's question. 'Hiring a detective is just something I need to do,' she said with a shrug.

'And what *will* you do when you discover Emma's address?'

'I'll cross that bridge when I come to it.'

'So what's he like?' Amber asked.

'Who?'

'Philip Schofield.'

'Eh?'

'I'm being flippant,' said Amber. 'Honestly, Dee. We've come out to catch up on what's been going on, but trying to get the whole picture from you is comparable to pulling weeds out of concrete. But don't worry, you're not alone.' Amber nodded at Chrissie who appeared to have gone into a trance. Their friend was staring at the wood burner with a glazed expression. 'What's going on with Dopy Dora all of a sudden?'

'She's in shock.'

'Must be delayed. She was all right earlier. So, you were saying?'

'What was I saying?'

Amber sighed. 'I want to know about Harry. What does he look like?'

Dee promptly went all pink in the face. How did you describe someone so sensational? He was the absolute cliché of tall, dark and handsome. He wouldn't look out of place on a filmset. Dee could imagine it now...Harry on the red carpet for his latest movie premiere, a camera crew filming his every move, an over-excited female presenter telling an audience of thousands...no, millions, 'Here he is! The biggest star in Hollywood, Harrison Hunter-Brown. Oh...and wait...here's his wife, Dee. He won't go anywhere without her–'

'Dee? Dee!' said Amber in frustration, as the barman returned with their tray of drinks.

'Absolutely divine,' Dee gushed, as their drinks were placed on the low table.

'I've heard gin and tonics described as many

210

things, but never "divine",' grinned the barman.

Chrissie momentarily snapped out of her trance. 'Y-yes. Quite d-divine,' she stuttered.

'Welcome back to Planet Earth,' said Amber, sarcastically. 'My friend is having a bad time,' she confided to the barman. 'Well, we're all having a bad time, but in Chrissie's case she's having a really, really, *really* bad time.'

'I'm sorry to hear that,' said the barman, his gaze resting upon Chrissie. Her eyes locked on his and she found she couldn't tear them away. Her hand patted its way forward for her drink – and promptly knocked it over.

'Oh dear,' she said, blushing furiously and flapping her hand about to dry – and sending the other two glasses flying. She stared in dismay at the three upturned tumblers and liquid puddling in all directions so it dripped off the table to the polished floorboards below. 'I'm so s-sorry,' she stammered.

'It's not a problem, really,' said the barman. 'I have some industrial-sized rolls of tissue under the counter. Let me go and grab one.'

'Better bring two,' said Amber slyly, 'she needs an entire one to mop her brow.'

Chrissie went from pink to scarlet. As soon as the barman was out of earshot, she rounded on Amber. 'Did you have to embarrass me further?'

'It was a joke!'

'At my expense.'

'What's up with you all of a sudden?' Amber frowned.

'I don't want...oh look out, he's coming back.' Chrissie stood up to take the roll from the barman but, as her hand brushed against his, she was belted with another round of thousand-watt volts and stumbled backwards – on Amber's toe. Amber yelped, and Chrissie shot forward cannoning painfully into the low table. She lost her balance, smacking down on its surface. There was a moment's silence where the entire pub went quiet. All eyes were on the young woman sprawled over an occasional table which, seconds later, collapsed because one of the legs had splintered. Everything, including Chrissie, hit the floor with an almighty crash.

'Oh my goodness,' said the barman to a mortified Chrissie. 'Are you all right?'

'Yes,' she squeaked. Dear God. Get her out of here. Sod the gin and tonic. She didn't even like the drink. She wanted to go home, get into bed, and pull the covers over her head. Mind you, she'd probably set fire to her duvet because her face was now aflame. She'd never felt so humiliated.

'Take my hand,' said the barman.

'N-no. I'm fine,' said Chrissie, struggling to get up. Her backside was soaking wet from all the spilt gin and tonic. She looked like she'd wet herself.

'I insist,' said the barman, holding his hand out.

Chrissie regarded it in terror. If she so much as touched one finger, she'd probably self-combust and the entire pub would implode.

Suddenly she was being hauled up by Amber, who was whispering discreetly in her ear.

'For heaven's sake, Chrissie. Get a grip. Go to the Ladies and dry yourself off on the hand dryer, and try not to pull it off the wall in the process.'

Chrissie didn't need telling twice. She fled.

Dee stared at the knackered table and glasses rolling across the floor. Her mouth was a perfectly formed O. 'Flaming Nora. Chrissie definitely isn't herself tonight.'

'Like I said,' Amber smiled at barman, 'my friend is having a terrible time.'

'Isn't she just,' he said, looking bemused. He snapped his fingers at two members of staff behind the bar. They hurried over.

'Want this taking away, Jack?'

'Yes, please. And fetch another tray of drinks. Three gin and tonics.'

'Our bar bill is going to be horrendous,' Amber joked. So, his name was Jack. She'd be sure to let Chrissie know. Amber wasn't daft. It was as obvious as the nose on her face that there had been chemistry arcing through the air. Unfortunately for Chrissie, it had turned her into a one-woman wrecking ball.

'All drinks tonight are on the house,' said Jack. 'After all, that table was ancient, and I don't want to get sued.'

'Oh don't worry,' joked Amber, 'we'd sue the Landlord, not you.'

'That would still be me,' said Jack. 'This is my pub. I own it.' He ripped off a long ribbon of industrial tissue and began mopping.

Amber was momentarily speechless. Good looking *and* with a sound business under his belt. Not that money should matter, of course, but it would be nice for Chrissie to have a little flirt with a guy who happened to have a few quid, rather than a penniless jerk like Andrew.

'Fortunately there's no shattered glass,' said Jack, balling up sodden paper. He looked up as Chrissie re-appeared and sat down in her chair. 'And thankfully no broken bones either, eh?'

Chrissie nodded. Best not to speak. Her face was still bright pink. She shoved her hands under her thighs. Maybe keep them out the way. She didn't want to inadvertently touch the barman again. For some bizarre reason, his effect on her had been devastating in every sense.

'This is Jack,' said Amber. 'He's going to replace both the table and our drinks. Isn't that kind of him?'

Chrissie smiled by way of acknowledgement. If

213

the wretched man could hurry up and then go away, that would be absolutely marvellous. She didn't want him anywhere near her. She averted her eyes and pretended to be fascinated by the overhead light.

Minutes later, the table had been replaced and the women had fresh drinks.

'Anything else I can get you, ladies?' asked Jack.

'Some crisps would be nice,' said Amber cheekily.

'Any particular flavour?' asked Jack, although his eyes were back on Chrissie.

'Salt and vinegar, please,' said Dee.

'Cheese and onion,' said Amber.

Chrissie risked taking her eyes off the light fitting. 'Thank you,' she said.

'You're welcome. So, is that cheese and onion for you too? Or salt and vinegar?'

'Yes,' Chrissie nodded. 'Cheese and vinegar. Perfect.'

'Get her both,' said Amber to the bemused Jack.

'Coming right up.'

As he walked away, Chrissie exhaled. Perhaps she should refrain from eating any crisps while that man was about. She didn't want to end up choking on them too.

'So,' said Amber, clapping her hands and making both Chrissie and Dee jump. 'Just look at the pair of you.'

'Why?' said Dee, looking confused.

Amber leant forward so she could speak without being overheard. 'What I'm talking about,' she said in a conspiratorial tone, 'is that before Chrissie's floor show, you couldn't say the name "Harry" without going ga-ga, and this one here,' Amber nodded at Chrissie, 'has now had exactly the same thing happen to her, thanks to the gorgeous Jack over there.' At the mention of Jack's name, Chrissie began to colour up again. 'Am I right, or am I right?' Amber smirked. 'I've just said the names "Harry" and "Jack" and two sets of eyeballs have dilated to the size of dustbin lids.'

'Don't be daft,' whispered Dee, but her reply carried no conviction.

'That's a ridiculous thing to say,' said Chrissie, but her voice had a quaver to it.

'I reckon,' said Amber, with wide-eyed innocence, 'my two besties have fallen head over heels in lust.'

Chapter Thirty-Two

Amber's words stayed with Dee throughout the remainder of their time at the pub. Dee had a horrible feeling that Amber might have been right about her falling in lust with Harry. How could she not have? After all, Dee was a heterosexual girl. Josh hadn't been interested in her for weeks, and suddenly Dee's unattended libido had responded with gusto to a man who was, quite simply, sex on legs. She had no doubt that all Harry's female clients must have the hots for him too. If they didn't, they had to be blind, or gay.

Dee realised that for the last two hours she'd hardly given Josh a thought. She was meant to be broken-hearted about her boyfriend being in Tenerife with the mysterious Emma, not sitting in a pub in Seal with a bemused expression on her face as part of her brain played, rewound and played again the bit where Harry's hand had brushed against hers as he passed her some papers. Or the way she'd admired his long, beautifully shaped fingers. Or how her mind had conjured up those same fingers burrowing under her top, unhooking her bra and—

'So what do you think?' asked Amber.

'Er,' said Dee, stalling for time. 'Maybe.'

'What about you, Chrissie?'

'Well, personally,' said Chrissie carefully, 'I'm...I'm not too sure.'

'But you were up for it yesterday,' said Amber, looking put out.

'Ah. In that case, er, yes, okay.'

Chrissie hadn't the faintest idea what Amber was talking about. Her concentration had long since fragmented, like a complicated jigsaw without a picture guide to put it all together. Her focus had

216

been on the barman, Jack. She mentally rolled the word around on her tongue. *Jack.* What a great name. So...heroic. Her eyes had been furtively seeking him out ever since she'd made a prize prat of herself. Each time her glance had strayed his way, she'd caught him looking at her. It had unsettled her, but also thrilled her to bits. She didn't, for one moment, presume he was checking her out. Not in that way, anyway. Rather, he was simply making sure she wasn't wrecking anything else in the pub. His pub. Amber had whispered to her that Jack owned The Beagle and Bugle.

It had also transpired that Jack owned two other pubs. He kept popping over between serving customers to make sure the three women were okay, and that no part of Chrissie's anatomy had since ballooned up requiring a trip to Accident and Emergency. Fortunately, it was only her pride that was injured. Jack chatted briefly each time he came over with lemonade top-ups for Dee and Amber, and fresh gin and tonics for Chrissie. She was quite drunk. It had been several hours since her mother's Sunday lunch. Jack had offered them all food on the house, over in the restaurant section, but they'd politely declined thinking it would be taking advantage of his hospitality.

Amber had nosily asked Jack if his wife oversaw the catering side of the business. He'd told them he didn't have a wife. A girlfriend then? Nope, not one of those either. Chrissie's heart had soared at this piece of information. But her joy had plunged, like a rollercoaster with no brake, as realisation dawned that there had to be a big reason why a man like Jack was single. She'd inwardly groaned. Why were all the good-looking guys gay? Chrissie suspected Amber might fancy Steve Hood if he wasn't already paired off with "his mate". Funnily enough, Chrissie had never had Steve down as being gay. Just like

Jack. She glanced over at him again to find his eyes once again on her. She blushed and looked away.

Ten minutes later he was back, this time with more crisps. Further gems of information were divulged. His three pubs were a full-on business commitment, twenty-four hours a day, seven days a week. It was rewarding, but hard graft. He didn't have time for a girlfriend – much as he'd love one. Jack had looked at Chrissie when he'd said those last words, and she'd squirmed with joy knowing he wasn't gay after all. And then Chrissie had found her mind wandering...imagining the large brass bell over the polished counter ringing as Jack called time...then Jack throwing the bolts across the door after the last customer had left. She fantasised about him giving her the sort of scorching look that would make the wood burner seem cooler than an air-conditioning unit...and then he would stride over to her and demand she set upon him in the same way she'd wrecked the tray of drinks and occasional table...and in her mind Chrissie had already placed her hands on his shoulders, trailing her fingers down to outline the shape of his muscular chest, and then in one swift movement ripped open his shirt so all the buttons pinged off and bounced across the polished floorboards as she moved down with her mouth, seeking out his nipples, her tongue starting to explore...hang on...she'd got this the wrong way round...too many gins...*he* was the one who was meant to rip all the buttons off *her* blouse and lick *her* nipples. Her brain scrambled to rearrange the scene just as Jack reappeared, this time with more drinks.

'Another two lemonades, girls, and a gin and tonic for you, Chrissie,' he smiled. He knew all their names now. 'I can tell it's your favourite tipple.'

'Yesh,' she slurred, naked images of Jack still playing vividly in her head. 'I do love a nipple.'

His lips twitched. 'I won't give you any more, otherwise you'll have a stonking hangover tomorrow morning.'

'Yes, and Dee and I have to work with her,' said Amber. 'I'd rather not be hand-feeding her paracetamol while she's staring at her computer screen, and wearing sunglasses because the monitor is too bright.'

'Tell your boss the blame is all mine, and that he must be very kind to you,' said Jack with a wink. He collected up the empties and, with a last mischievous grin at Chrissie, headed back to the bar.

'I think he likes you, Chrissie,' Dee whispered.

'Me too,' said Amber.

'Don't be ridic-less,' said Chrissie, with effort. She was feeling incredibly lethargic.

'You're pissed,' said Amber.

'I'm a tit bipsy, that's all.'

'You're certainly a tit. Fancy telling Jack you like a nipple. Here,' said Amber, passing Chrissie her lemonade. 'You have this. Dee and I will share your gin and tonic. I reckon we've eaten the equivalent of a factory's worth of crisps this evening, so a smidgen more gin between the two of us won't hurt.' She took a slug of Chrissie's drink. 'Yum. Now then, where was I? Oh yes. Madam Rosa. So that's sorted. We're all in agreement that I make another appointment.'

Chapter Thirty-Three

Dee and Chrissie were taken aback at Amber's insistence they see Madam Rosa yet again, but decided to go along with her wishes. After all, things couldn't get any worse regarding the predictions for their individual lives. They'd all hit rock bottom with their boyfriends, or rather *ex*-boyfriends. It was incredible they'd started the New Year hoping for marriage proposals, but now didn't have a man between them.

Chrissie and Dee were quiet on the drive back. Both women were mulling over their own private thoughts. In Dee's case, she was feeling strangely euphoric. It was as if an invisible magical force had visited her, waved a sparkly wand through the air and coated her in fairy dust and glitter. She couldn't wait to get into bed, pull the duvet up to her chin, and go over every moment of her earlier meeting with Harrison Hunter-Brown. She suspected that tonight her dreams might be full of heroes and heartthrobs, all by the name of Harry.

Chrissie leant against the head rest in Dee's car, and gave the sort of sigh that could have been misconstrued as contentment. She suspected the gin was responsible. After all, there was no other reason for her to feel blissed out. The last twenty-four hours had been horrific. She'd nearly caught Andrew with his trousers down, met his "amour" (that had been a huge shock in itself), then packed her bags and gone home to good old Mum and Dad. She should have been distraught. But weirdly, she wasn't. No doubt the fall-out would catch up with her tomorrow. Perhaps, when Cougar Kate summoned Chrissie for assistance with a pile of Probate documents, she would finally collapse with grief and say she couldn't type a single word because of what Andrew had done to her. She felt as though she'd been given an invisible pain-relief injection that had numbed her against all the recent blows. It had left her able to focus on other things. More pleasurable things. Like Jack. Chrissie was *so* looking forward to her bed. She was going to close her eyes and conjure up the image of Jack that she'd committed to memory. She suspected she'd have the sweetest of dreams.

Amber drove home feeling very peeved. She'd had a nice evening with her two besties, but despite the three of them all having had a weekend of emotional turmoil, somehow Amber felt like it was just her who was having the lousy time. Dee might have been sitting in The Beagle and Bugle, but her mind had taken a spaceship and launched off to a completely different planet. Amber didn't have to be a scientist to suspect the planet was called Harrison Hunter-Brown. When Dee *had* deigned to speak, it had been "Harry this" and "Harry that". Her friend had been distracted and vague, all the while glowing like a newlywed. And as for Chrissie. Amber mentally tutted. The woman hadn't so much as chuffed off to another planet as beamed off to an entirely different cosmos.

Amber sighed and put the car's gear into fourth. She wanted to get home, fall into bed and curl up in a tight ball. She wished that she, too, could be distracted by a good-looking man. Preferably one that was also kind and charming. For the briefest moment her thoughts strayed to her boss, Steve Hood, but then skittered away. He was spoken for and living happily with "his mate". Still, at least the girls had been in agreement about making another appointment to see Madam Rosa. The sensible part of Amber wondered what on earth she was thinking of wanting to waste more money on this clairvoyant who, by some sort of cosmic coincidence, had been

221

accurate about their individual dilemmas. But another part of her...the sod-it-what-have-I-got-to-lose part...thought, "Why not?" Madam Rosa had been uncannily correct so far. What if Harry turned out to be Dee's new beau? And what if Jack was the new man entering Chrissie's life? Hadn't Madam Rosa told Amber that she, too, was due a romance at any moment? In which case, where was the bugger?

Chapter Thirty-Four

On Monday morning, there was a shift in the atmosphere at Hood, Mann & Derek, one which junior partner Alan Mann likened to a sense of foreboding. He'd already heard, through the office grapevine, that Chrissie had packed her bags and left her prat of a boyfriend. Rumour had it she'd caught Andrew with a woman old enough to be his great-great-great-grandmother. There was another story circulating about Dee, who'd been spotted driving through Seal with tear-stained face, but nobody knew why.

Despite specialising in family law, Alan wasn't very good with hysterical females. He hoped he didn't find Dee sobbing over her keyboard when they exchanged their good mornings. Approximately twice a week, a female client would burst into tears and weep all over Alan's jotter pad, which he found incredibly awkward for two reasons. Firstly, in today's no-touching-or-I-will-sue-you society, he was unable to put a comforting arm around a client's shoulder. Secondly, the client's tears always made his notes, written in ink, spread out and bloom like a pH indicator test on litmus paper. Alan hoped Dee would maintain a British "stiff upper lip" over whatever had upset her. He relied heavily upon her, especially when he had the occasional female breaking down as they filed for divorce. A client always calmed down when Dee came in with a soothing cup of tea and a plate of "cheer-up" biscuits. The last thing he needed was a weeping client and a wailing secretary duetting over his jotter pad. He pulled the notebook possessively towards him as the first client of the day took a seat opposite his desk.

Cougar Kate was feeling jubilant. As she stood in

the staff kitchen pouring boiling water into two mugs for Clive Derek and herself, she was confiding in young Jessica from Accounts everything that had happened to her over a crazy but fabulous weekend. Kate was so excited because, after months of despairing it would ever happen – not to mention a warning from Madam Rosa – her much younger boyfriend had moved in. He'd *finally* been able to escape the clutches of his unstable, highly-strung, totally neurotic ex-girlfriend. He'd assured Kate his relationship had been dead for months, but he'd not been able to extricate himself before now because the wretched woman had always threatened to kill herself. But for some bizarre reason, the nutty ex-girlfriend had lost the plot and gone bonkers. Apparently, she'd emptied the entire contents of his wardrobe all over their lawn.

'Between you and me, Jessica, and this is not for repeating, I'm handing in my notice this morning. Now that my boyfriend has moved in, he can support me. I'm going to give up work and start trying for a family. I've been reading how important it is to be relaxed in order to conceive. After all, I'm now forty. Time is not on my side. So bye-bye work, and hello to getting pregnant.'

'I won't tell a soul, promise,' said Jessica, crossing her fingers behind her back.

Kate sighed happily as she stirred the two drinks. She had clouds in her coffee and love in her heart. 'The only downside to the weekend was losing a diamond earring.'

Outside, in the corridor, Steve Hood froze. He'd already overheard Amber whispering down the phone to her sister – something about chucking clothes about, and a diamond earring in her bed. Amber might have thought Steve couldn't hear her, but she didn't realise she had a voice like a fog-horn and her voice box didn't know how to talk quietly.

Steve had glanced at Amber to see if she was all right, but she'd misconstrued his expression as one of annoyance for making a personal call in company time. She'd gazed at him with watery eyes and mouthed, 'Sorry, just five minutes, please,' and he'd nodded and mimed sipping a drink, to which Amber had given the thumbs up. Steve remembered only too well how Kate had made a move on Amber's boyfriend at the last Christmas party. Now it would seem the two of them had been having it off behind Amber's back. What a despicable pair. He stepped into the kitchen, and Kate and Jessica clammed up.

'Morning, ladies,' he said, with a smile that didn't quite reach his eyes.

Jessica nodded in greeting. Grabbing her coffee, she hastily absented herself leaving Kate alone with Steve. Kate regarded Amber's boss with cool eyes.

'Hello,' she said, her lips pinching into a thin line. She'd never told a soul, but in a moment of gloominess, thinking Matthew might never leave Amber, she'd recently made a clumsy pass at Steve. He'd rejected her. Kate had felt humiliated. Her cheeks flamed at the memory. She'd heard the rumours about Steve Hood. Both conflicting. She certainly didn't believe he was gay. And he definitely wasn't a woman who'd had a sex-change operation – because that was a rumour she'd put about herself after his rejection. Revenge was sweet. She picked up the two coffees and made to leave the kitchen, only to find Steve shutting the door and barring exit. She smiled, coldly.

'If you're looking for sexual favours, you're too late,' she said nastily. 'I'm no longer interested.'

'I'm not,' said Steve bluntly.

'What do you want?'

'I want you to drink your coffee with Clive Derek and, whilst doing so, tell him that not only are you

225

handing in your resignation today, but it is with great regret you cannot work your notice. I expect you to tell Clive, truthfully, why. Your position here is not tenable.'

Kate's eyes narrowed. 'Why isn't it?'

'It won't be long before Amber finds out Matthew has moved in with you. It's bad enough that neither of you had the decency to tell her yourself, but there's no way you're rubbing her nose in it for another month while you strut around this office like the cat who's swiped the cream.'

'You bastard,' Kate spat. 'Got the hots for her, have you? I always thought you looked at her with dewy eyes when her back was turned.'

'My feelings for Amber are borne out of concern,' said Steve, 'but I'm not having my first-class secretary compromised by a second-rate typist.' He opened the kitchen door again, and stood aside for her. 'Don't let me hold you up, Kate.'

Chapter Thirty-Five

Amber ended the call to her sister and briefly massaged her temples. She felt emotionally wrecked. The events of the weekend were overtaking her faster than a jockey riding a Grand National winner. She'd have a proper catch-up with her family very soon. Maybe even spend a weekend with her parents. She needed a complete break from New Ash Green's nattering neighbours nudging each other every time she came out of her house. It was inevitable that people gossiped, but hopefully something else would distract pensioners like Edith and Mr Jefferies who had nothing better to do with their time. There hadn't been so much excitement since Derek the postman had delivered their mail wearing full make-up and a dress.

Although Amber was glad her cheating scumbag of a boyfriend had gone, it was only natural she felt miserable. Much as she loved Mr Tomkin, he was unable to sweep her into his paws and whisper that everything would be all right. Her gloom was heightened by the behaviour of Dee and Chrissie. Amber could see how distracted both women were. Dee was preoccupied with this Harry guy who didn't just have a James Bond job, but looked like him too. And Chrissie had terrible mentionitis about Jack. Amber wasn't silly. She'd seen the way Jack had looked at her friend. Amber suspected that if Chrissie stepped back over the threshold of The Beagle and Bugle, it wouldn't be only the pints getting pulled.

Both Dee and Chrissie had assured Amber they felt wretched, but Amber didn't believe them. Far from being hungover, Chrissie had bounced into the office as if her stilettoes had been pogo sticks. Instead of getting on with a pile of tapes, she'd picked up the phone to make an appointment with a hairdresser in her lunch hour. She'd then told them she was going to Bluewater, after work, as she wanted to update her wardrobe.

'Now that I don't have to stump up money for Andrew, I'm going to splash some cash on clothes. Do either of you fancy joining me?'

'I'd like to,' said Dee, trying and failing to sound sincere. 'But I'd prefer to be at home, in case I need to ring Harry.' *Or in case Harry rings me,* she'd privately thought.

'What about you, Amber?'

'Well–'

'Sorry to interrupt, ladies,' said Steve, walking into the open-plan office with two coffees, 'but I'd like you, Amber, in my office.'

Amber inwardly groaned. Ah well. She'd wanted to be distracted by work, so she might as well get on with it. She picked up her notebook and pen.

'Leave that,' said Steve, disappearing into his office.

Amber looked after him in surprise, then followed her boss into his office.

'Shut the door, Amber,' said Steve.

'Yes, sir,' she quipped. 'What's happened?'

'I think that's my line.'

'Eh?'

'I made you coffee.'

'Thanks,' she said, taking the mug and sipping gratefully.

'So, I gather you've thrown Matthew out.'

Amber nearly dropped the coffee in her lap. 'Blimey,' she said, puffing out her cheeks. 'News travels fast. Are you by any chance related to one of my nosey neighbours?'

'No,' said Steve. 'I simply want to make sure you're all right.'

Amber was so touched, she burst into tears. 'I-

I'm so s-sorry,' she stuttered, foraging up her sleeve for a tissue, but not finding one.

'Here,' said Steve, giving her his own handkerchief.

'Th-Thank you,' she hiccupped. She pressed the pristine square to her eyes, desperate to rescue her mascara. One cotton corner tickled her nose, and she caught a whiff of Steve's lovely aftershave. 'Sorry to blub. Yes, you're right. I've chucked Matthew out. It was all high drama, and rather embarrassing. You know me. Never afraid to make a fool of herself, and then stop and think about it after the event.'

'Amber,' said Steve softly. An observer would have said his tone was tender.

'Yes?' She looked up at him, eyes brimming. She was lucky to work for such a kind man. She was quite sure Steve wasn't the first boss to witness his assistant falling apart, but she was positive not many employees would be given such a long rein for their private upsets. Especially at the rate she'd been having them.

'I do know what you're going through, you know. What about, after work, I take you out to dinner? You can tell me about it over a glass of wine.'

For a moment Amber was nonplussed. 'I can't drink and drive.'

'I know,' said Steve, with a smile. One of Amber's eyelashes had worked its way loose from her lower lid, and adhered to a damp cheek. Despite being heartbroken, she looked incredibly beautiful. 'What about you go home, have a rest, and I'll pick you up around six.'

Amber stared at Steve in confusion. 'Go home? What, now?'

'Yes, now.' Steve wanted to protect Amber from the gossip fall-out that was inevitable once Katherine Colgan had left the premises. There was no way young Jessica was going to keep her mouth shut when she discovered Kate wasn't working her notice. Steve wanted to be the one to break the bad news to Amber, rather than her hearing it from someone else.

'But...but...there's no need for me to go home, surely?' Amber felt befuddled, even though a part of her was longing to do just that – back to her duvet and the peaceful world of sleep. 'How will you cope without me?'

'That's why the firm has a float secretary,' said Steve. 'I'm sure Chrissie will help.' Privately Steve knew Chrissie would have her work cut out, because Clive Derek would require secretarial cover once Kate had left.

'I think you should know,' said Amber, 'that Chrissie didn't have a good weekend either. Or Dee. We're kind of all in the same situation.'

Steve rather doubted that either Chrissie or Dee had lost their boyfriend to the office siren, but right now he wanted Amber off the premises. 'You're a sweet girl to care about Chrissie and Dee, but my concern is you.'

'Well, all right,' said Amber doubtfully, 'as long as you're sure.'

'I'm very sure.'

'And...um...what about your...you know,' she trailed off awkwardly.

Steve looked mystified. 'My what?'

'Your *mate*,' Amber whispered.

'What's he got to do with it?'

'I don't want him feeling put out because you're not home for dinner.'

'Why would he feel put out?'

'Come on, Steve. Enough of this pretence. You don't need to mollycoddle your secretary after office hours, when you could be at home with your feet up sharing a beer with your man.' Amber noticed

230

Steve's lips twitch, and his eyes twinkled mischievously.

'You're right,' Steve nodded. 'Honesty is the best policy. After I've finished here, I do like to slob around with my man.'

Ah ha, thought Amber. *I was right. There is a man.*

'But the man is a little man, and he drinks cocoa rather than beer.'

'Pardon?' said Amber. Was her boss shacked up with a dwarf who liked mugs of milk rather than pints of lager?

'Contrary to what you think, I live with my son.'

'Your son?' said Amber, looking dumbfounded. 'You have a *son*?'

'Yes. His name is Danny. He's five years old. I like to keep my private life just that. I have my reasons.'

'W-What?' Amber couldn't take it in.

'Look, let's do some straight talking – no pun intended – this evening, eh? Danny is having a sleepover with his grandparents tonight, so I don't have to rush home. There are things you need to know, Amber, and I want to be the one to tell you.'

'Right,' Amber nodded, although she hadn't a clue what Steve was talking about. She was still struggling to get her head around what he'd told her. All that chit-chat about going cycling with *his mate*, playing football with *his mate*, going up the driving range with *his mate*. She inwardly groaned. He'd been doing all those things with his *son*. 'But, hang on a minute,' she frowned, 'where's Danny's mother?'

'Later,' said Steve firmly. 'Now go home. Put your head down. I'll see you at six.'

Amber stood up. She felt quite bemused. Steve Hood wasn't gay? Oh my God, Steve Hood wasn't gay!

231

Chapter Thirty-Six

When Amber returned to her desk she was wearing the same distracted expression as Dee and Chrissie.

'What was all that about?' Chrissie asked, just as her office phone rang. 'Two ticks.' She picked up the phone. 'Hello? Morning, Clive. Yes. Oh? She's leaving? She's *left*? Are you sure? Oh dear. Of course. No, I won't say anything. Okay, I'll be with you in a couple of minutes.' As Chrissie put the phone down, she looked stunned.

'What did Clive want?' asked Dee. 'You're looking like he propositioned you, but you're too gobsmacked to even say, "ewwwwwwwww".'

'Er, nothing. He needs some secretarial cover.' Chrissie glanced over at Amber. 'Are you all right?'

'Yes,' said Amber, in a daze, 'never better.' She flopped down on her typing stool.

Dee gave Amber a curious look. 'What's happened to you?'

Amber frowned. 'What do you mean?'

'You look...elated. You went into Steve's office doing an impression of someone who'd lost a tenner, and now you look like you've found the winning lottery ticket.'

Steve suddenly appeared in his office doorway. 'Are you still here, Amber? I thought I told you to leave. Now hurry up and go home. And Chrissie and Dee, I'd like you both in my office, please.'

'Can you give me five minutes?' asked Chrissie, standing up. 'Clive Derek telephoned, and-'

'He can wait.'

'What's going on?' asked Dee, her brow furrowing.

'I have a bad vibe,' muttered Chrissie. 'Clive Derek said something about Cougar Kate and-'

'Chrissie, stop gossiping. In here now!' said

Steve, with exasperation.

'He's very masterful, isn't he,' murmured Amber. 'See you tomorrow, girls.'

'Where are *you* going?' asked Dee.

'Steve told me to go home, and this evening he's taking me out to dinner.'

'Wha–?' said Dee and Chrissie together.

Chrissie's phone rang again. 'Hello? Yes, Clive. I'm just...yes...Steve wants me to...yes, I will tell him you have a pile of typing, I'll be–'

The phone was whipped out of her hand by Steve.

'Hello, Clive. Chrissie will be with you in five minutes. I have an urgent matter to discuss with her, as I'm sure you are aware.' And with that he put the phone down on the Senior Partner. He then gave Amber a look that dared her to hang around the office for one second longer. Chrissie and Dee looked uncertainly at Amber. Her pupils were dilated and she was glowing like a chunk of radioactive Kryptonite. Gathering up her belongings she gave a cheery wave just as young Jessica from Accounts strolled in. Jessica watched Amber go with an expression of pity, which turned to glee the moment she was out of sight. She turned to Chrissie and Dee.

'You'll never guess wha–'

Jessica shut up after spotting Steve, who had a murderous look on his face.

'Er, wrong office,' she said hastily, and scampered off.

Dee and Chrissie looked at each other, then followed Steve into his office. He shut the door firmly behind him.

'Sorry, girls. This won't take long. I'm speaking to you in confidence. You're both close friends of Amber's. Are you aware she and Matthew are no longer together?'

'Yes,' they said.

'And did you know he's moved in with Katherine Colgan?'

There was a stunned silence, which answered Steve's question.

'Is this an awful joke?' asked Chrissie. She could tell from Steve's face it wasn't.

'How do you know this?' asked Dee. She had visions of Amber rushing round to Cougar Kate's house, screaming all manner of revenge through the woman's letterbox.

'I have it on good authority. Kate has resigned, and she won't be working her notice.'

'Just a minute,' said Chrissie, holding one hand up like a traffic cop. 'Does Amber know?'

'No,' said Steve, 'that's why I've sent her home. I don't want her listening to office gossip. I'll be giving her the bad news myself, this evening. I'd appreciate the two of you not mentioning anything if she phones in later, okay?'

'We give you our word,' said Dee, 'but the thing is, Steve, I think *we* should be the ones to tell her. We're her best friends. She'll need us.'

'And you can be there for her,' said Steve, 'but *after* I've spoken to her first. I'm her boss. She has to work here. Amber needs to know she can walk back into this office, when she's ready, with her head held high, and that nobody will be tittle-tattling. Otherwise they'll have me to answer to.'

'And us,' said Chrissie.

'Too right,' said Dee. 'If we hear anybody discussing it, they'll get a verbal pasting.'

Steve nodded and stood up, indicating their meeting was over. 'Thanks, girls. Oh, and sorry, Chrissie, but you're going to have your work cut out today looking after both Clive and myself.'

'Bang goes my lunchtime hair appointment,' said Chrissie, with a rueful smile.

'Don't cancel it,' said Dee. 'I'll try and help Steve too. I don't think Alan is very busy today.'

'Aw, thanks,' said Chrissie, perking up. She felt guilty that she should be worrying about a hair appointment, when Amber was going to be delivered a bombshell that wouldn't so much as rock her world as completely blow it up.

Chapter Thirty-Seven

Chrissie left the hair salon at two minutes to two, hurrying back to work as fast as her stilettoes would permit. The morning had passed in a blur. She'd typed so quickly her keyboard had practically had smoke tendrils spiralling out of it.

As her heels clicked along the pavement, her mind fragmented into a kaleidoscope of thoughts. She was so grateful to Dee for working through her own lunch hour to assist with the work overflow. It had enabled Chrissie to keep her hair appointment. She shook her head. It felt strange having silky hair billowing out behind her as she scurried along. From now on, ponytails were a thing of the past.

Chrissie caught sight of her reflection in the glass panel of a bus stop shelter. Who was that young woman with the glorious swishy mane? And striding along so confidently too! She felt empowered. Liberated. Born again. It was amazing what a hair-do did for the self-esteem. A young lad walking in the opposite direction wolf-whistled. Chrissie beamed with delight. Seconds later the grin faded as she thought about Amber, alone at home, oblivious to the treachery of Matthew. The horrible man had obviously been using Amber. Matthew and that devious witch had been carrying on together for months. And to think Cougar Kate had smiled in Amber's face when she'd invited her into her house for a reading with Madam Rosa. It all made sense now. Cougar Kate had wanted to know whether Matthew would ever leave Amber and move in with her and, even worse, whether there would be wedding bells. Chrissie sincerely hoped the two of them didn't wed, or it would add insult to injury for Amber.

Chrissie thought back to last Saturday's reading

with Madam Rosa. The clairvoyant had told Amber there was a love triangle. Boy, she'd been right about that. She hadn't revealed the other woman's name, insisting Spirit wouldn't tell her. Instead, Madam Rosa had assured Amber she'd find out soon enough. Chrissie sighed. Little was Amber to know how soon that was to be. Madam Rosa had also warned Amber to remain calm and composed. "Serenity is your weapon in this instance," she'd said. Maybe it was just as well Steve Hood was the messenger in this case. Chrissie rather thought Amber wouldn't be so quick to go berserk with Steve by her side. If Chrissie and Dee had been the bearers of bad news, Amber might have insisted they all dress in camouflage and paintball Cougar Kate's house and Matthew's testicles.

Bugger men, and bugger love. Why was it all such hard work? Her thoughts swerved to Jack. Now *that* was a man she'd *lurve* to love. Chrissie was under no illusion that the guy was completely out of her league. But she was quite happy to sit by that cosy wood burning stove again in The Beagle and Bugle, sipping her drink and discreetly watching the most beautiful man God had ever created as he went about his work.

The double doors of Hood, Man & Derek loomed. Chrissie was about to push them open when she felt herself being pulled back.

'Chrissie?'

If it were possible to identify somebody on voice alone, then Chrissie would have picked this one out in a police line-up. She found herself looking at the astonished face of Andrew.

'Bloody 'ell,' he said, gawping, 'it *is* you. What've yer done to yerself? Yer look a right babe.'

'What are you doing here?'

'I've come t'see yer.'

She glanced at her watch. It was nearly five past

two. 'I'm late.'

Andrew's expression changed to one of pleading. 'Babe, jus' give me a minute. I'm sorry. I made a terrible mistake. Please, come 'ome.'

'No way.'

'Give me another chance, babe. Take the afternoon off sick. Come 'ome with me. Let me make things up to yer. I love yer. Let me show you 'ow much, eh?' He gave her his most disarming grin. 'I've bin a fool. What d'ya say, babe?'

'No thanks.'

'C'*mon*,' Andrew cajoled. 'Remember 'ow much fun we used to 'ave?'

'Actually, no.'

'*Course* we did! Let me pick yer up later, an' take yer out for a slap up meal.'

'McDonalds with all the trimmings, eh?' Chrissie gave a thin smile.

'If yer like.'

'No.'

'Please?'

'No.'

'I'm beggin' yer.'

'I don't want to.'

'Why?'

'Because we're finished. Now please, Andrew, let me get back to work. I'm late and we're short staffed.'

'But I'm desperate, babe. I need yer.'

'You really don't.'

'I really do.' Andrew was starting to look frantic. 'I really, *really* need yer.'

Chrissie suddenly put two and two together. 'Why?'

Andrew suddenly looked shifty. 'Could you sub me five hundred quid?'

'Ah, I understand.'

'Nah, it's not jus' for the money, babe. Honest.'

'Oh that's good to know,' said Chrissie sarcastically.

'It's jus' that Big Mick and his mates are asking for an instalment on the money I owe. I really do need yer, babe.'

Chrissie stared at Andrew and was amazed she felt...nothing. How odd. And wonderful. 'The trouble is, Andrew–'

'Yes, babe?' His voice was full of hope.

'Unfortunately, I don't need you – *babe*.'

And with that Chrissie turned her back on her ex-boyfriend and disappeared through the doors of Hood, Man & Derek.

Chapter Thirty-Eight

Dee had never known a day like it. Gossip about Cougar Kate and Matthew was rife. Young Jessica had told anybody who would listen, 'Don't tell a soul but...,' until Steve Hood had summoned Jessica into his office and read the Riot Act. The next bombshell to reverberate around the office was Chrissie returning from the hairdressers. Clive Derek took one look at the slender woman with hair like a Victoria's Secret model and instantly turned into the office wolf.

'Chrissie,' he cooed, 'you look like a film star. Now about all that hard work you've done for me today. You really must let me thank you.'

'You're very welcome,' Chrissie replied, settling down at her desk and hoping nobody would comment on her being nearly fifteen minutes late. She pushed a tape into her Dictaphone and reached for her headset.

'I mean *properly* thank you,' Clive persisted, revealing a set of predatory teeth that could have landed him the body double part of Jaws the shark. 'What about I take you out after work for dinner? Those poor little fingers of yours must be exhausted.' He leant over Chrissie's desk and picked up one of her hands. For one appalling moment, she thought he was going to bring his lips down to her knuckles and kiss them. 'Tell me where you'd like to go.'

'Er, I already have arrangements for this evening, thanks.' She snatched her hand away. 'I'm going to Bluewater.'

'Wonderful, wonderful,' said Clive. 'We can have dinner there.'

'I'm going shopping,' said Chrissie irritably.

'After your shopping then. I won't take no for an

answer.'

'Ooooh, lovely,' said Dee, butting in. 'I'm sure you won't exclude me, will you, Clive? After all, I've helped you out too. My *poor little fingers* are totally knackered.' She lifted them from her keyboard and wiggled them at Clive.

'Oh,' said Clive, looking thrown. 'Well, er, of course I'm very grateful to you as well, Dee. That goes without saying.'

'Excellent. So where are you taking us?'

'Um, as you're both having girly time together, perhaps I'll retract my invitation and let the two of you enjoy your evening, eh?'

'Aw, you're so thoughtful,' said Dee, wrinkling her nose Marilyn Monroe style. 'I'll bet Mrs Derek absolutely loves being married to you, eh?'

'Ha ha,' said Clive nervously. 'I won't hold you lovely ladies up. I can see you are extremely busy.'

'Toodle-oo,' said Dee, giving Clive a dinky wave as he hastily reversed out of their office.

'Thanks,' said Chrissie gratefully. 'What the heck's got into him?'

'It's because you look amazing. The hair restyle is gorgeous. From now on you'll be fighting the admirers off.'

'Don't be daft,' said Chrissie, although she was secretly delighted at Dee's comment. That said, there was only one man she wanted to wow. Unfortunately, he didn't work at Hood, Mann & Derek. She looked at Dee hopefully. 'Are you really coming shopping with me this evening?'

'Am I heck,' said Dee. 'That was to get Clive off your back. No, I'll be heading home the minute it's half past five. After today's events, I want a long soak in the bath, then a telly dinner and chill. Apart from anything else, I need to be on standby for my detective.'

'Ah, the lovely Harry,' said Chrissie with a smirk.

241

'Got a bit of a thing about him, haven't you!'

'I'm sure I don't know what you mean,' Dee sniffed. 'It's business.'

'If you say so.'

'I do.' Dee picked up an enormous draft Will ready for its third revision. 'Good heavens, look at the size of this. There are pages and pages of bequests here. It must be nice to have a fortune to leave people.'

'That reminds me,' said Chrissie, thinking of someone who most definitely didn't have anything to leave anybody. 'On my way back to the office, I saw Andrew.'

'What did he want?' Dee frowned.

'For us to get back together. Oh, and five hundred pounds.'

'Cheeky prat. I hope you told him *his* fortune.'

'Yes. Speaking of fortunes, do you know if Amber has contacted Madam Rosa about us seeing her again?'

'I don't think so,' Dee replied. 'Let's wait until she's back in the office before we start making any more appointments with Madam Rosa.'

'Sure. Right, look sharp. There's a lot to get through this afternoon, and I don't want to be late leaving here. Bluewater, and a new wardrobe, are awaiting me.'

'Be warned. If you turn up at the office tomorrow wearing a figure-hugging power dress, Clive will be slobbering over you like a puppy.'

'Oh give over!' Chrissie made a tsking sound, and turned her attention to work. She definitely wouldn't mind a certain someone slobbering over her – and she might see if she could catch his eye.

Chapter Thirty-Nine

Once inside her apartment, Dee slipped off her coat and shoes. It had been a hectic day. In addition to her own work for Alan Mann, she'd had to help out both Steve Hood and Clive Derek.

Dee glanced at the console table in the hallway. It now held a stack of mail for Josh. The pile had steadily grown as the week progressed. On the advice of Harry, Dee had removed the postcard she'd lifted from Anne and Peter Coventry's house.

'Don't alert your boyfriend to anything,' Harry had advised. 'The element of surprise is key when catching someone out.' The postcard was now in a secret place.

Dee padded off to the kitchen and put the kettle on. Leaving it to slowly work its way to the boil, she went into the bathroom. Turning on the tub's taps, she added some luxury bubble bath her mum had given her for Christmas. The flowery scent blended with clouds of steam, and she sniffed appreciatively. Leaving the bath to fill, she went back to the kitchen and made her cup of tea. She'd have her bath, then settle down in front of the telly with a microwave dinner. Tonight she would chillax with the hunky farmer boys from Emmerdale. Dee couldn't decide who she liked most – gorgeous Ross Barton or that sexy bit of rough, Cain Dingle.

Taking the tea into the bathroom, she placed the mug carefully on the sink and then stripped off. Testing the foaming water with one foot, she decided the temperature was perfect. Picking up the tea, Dee sank down with a groan of ecstasy. She let the bubbles wash over her tummy as she slurped from the mug. Perfect. She was just taking another sip, when she froze. What was that noise? She sat up, mug of tea suspended, ears straining for clues.

243

There it was again. Someone was outside the flat's front door and jangling keys. Seconds later, Dee's worst fears were confirmed as the flat's door creaked back on its hinges. Damn. The bathroom door was wide open and here she was absolutely starkers in the bath!

'Hello?' called a familiar male voice.

Bugger. Dee hadn't known how things would play out when Josh eventually came home, but one thing she had assumed was that when it *did* happen she would be prepared – as in fully-clothed, wearing make-up, and with newly washed hair, not open-pored from steam, or sporting smudged mascara, and most definitely not naked. She sank beneath the bubbles as Josh came into the bathroom.

'Hi,' he said, as if no drama between them had ever occurred.

'Er, I'm not decent.'

'You look pretty decent to me,' he said, with a leer. His eyes flicked to the foam covering her body. She followed his gaze and was horrified to see her nipples poking out of the bubbles, like two twin satellite dishes. Dee grabbed a flannel and put it over her boobs. Why was Josh looking lustful, when only a week ago he'd said he didn't fancy her?

'I'm home,' he said, grinning.

'Nothing like stating the obvious,' Dee replied. Her tone was indifferent, as if his absence and the upset he'd caused had been nothing more than a blip on the radar of Dee's life – and a very insignificant blip at that.

'Sorry about...well...you know.' He gave a small shrug.

'No, I don't know.' What was this? An apology for flying off to Tenerife for a week's bonking with a woman called Emma?

Josh moved over to the toilet, put the lid down

244

and perched. 'The thing is I...I think I've been having...I mean *was* having...a mid-life crisis.'

'You're not yet thirty. Aren't you rather young for one of those?

'Well, better to get it over and done with, eh!' Josh's eyes locked on hers and he smiled. It was the sort of slow, sexy grin he used to give Dee in the old days. Back then it had turned her to mush. Right now, it was having zero effect. Josh noticed. He dropped the smile and moved smartly on. 'The thing is, I've missed you. I needed time out from our relationship to...well...make sure we are the real deal.'

Dee couldn't believe she was hearing this. She'd fully expected Josh to return home and demand they put the flat on the market. What was this? Sweet words of crap to pave the way for Josh sliding seamlessly back into their old life together? And how did Emma figure in all this? Dee mentally retrieved Josh's postcard from its hiding place and re-read it.

'*Having a wonderful much-needed break from the Undomestic Dog-ess...*

The cheeky sod.

Not looking forward to sorting things out once back...

In other words dumping Dee.

...blah blah... Emma. She can't wait to meet you.

Yes, the new girlfriend had been waiting to meet Josh's charmless mother and hen-pecked father. Anne and Peter Coventry must have known about this Emma woman ever since Josh had started his relationship with her – whenever that was. Dee didn't need the likes of Harrison Hunter-Brown to point out that in the last couple of days – maybe even the last few hours – something had gone wrong between the lovebirds.

'So the thing is, darling–'

'Josh, sorry to interrupt, but could you take this, please?' Dee held out the mug of tea. There was no way she could drink it lying horizontal in the bath while trying to keep her body covered by bubbles.

'Of course.' Josh sprang up and took the mug. 'Would you like me to soap your back?' he asked, a gleam in his eye.

'No.'

'Okay.' He sat back down on the loo. 'So, as I was saying, I'd like to start afresh.'

Dee looked at Josh in confusion. 'Start afresh?' Oh, hang on. Was this his way of saying, "Sorry to be the bearer of bad news, but I'm replacing you with a woman called Emma. She has bigger tits than you, a better bum, and she isn't an Undomesticated Dog-ess." Dee could feel her lip curling.

'Yes, start afresh,' Josh repeated. 'I want to put our little misunderstanding behind us, and forget it ever happened.'

'What exactly did happen?' asked Dee carefully. As far as she was concerned, she'd had a boyfriend who'd become increasingly distant with her for no fathomable reason. When she'd tried to reignite his interest, it had backfired spectacularly. So much so, Josh had packed a bag and jetted out of the country.

'Well...um...like I said...I had a bit of a mid-life crisis.'

'Define "mid-life crisis",' she said in a cold voice.

'Just...just doubting everything.'

'As in doubting us?'

'Yes,' Josh nodded, 'that's it, as in wondering if,' his brow furrowed with concentration, 'making sure we were absolutely right for each other.'

'You mean,' Dee feigned puzzlement, 'in case there might be somebody else out there who was more suited?'

Josh blanched. Dee could see the thought processes going on in his head. He was easier to read than a child's early learning book. For a moment he looked anxious, fretting that he might have showed his hand regarding Emma. 'N-no,' he stuttered, 'I always thought you were the right woman for me, Dee.'

'So why the need to disappear for a week?'

'Just to...you know...be absolutely sure you're *still* the right woman for me,' he finished lamely. 'Which you are.'

Dee glared at him. 'Your skin has a lovely colour.'

'Yeah,' said Josh, his eyes slithering away. 'Getting a tan is one of the perks of window cleaning and being outdoors.'

'It's January.'

'It's wind burn.'

'It's bollocks.'

'Pardon?'

'You heard me. Where have you *really* been, Josh?'

'At my mum and dad's.'

'Strange. You weren't there when I went round to see you.'

'I was at work.'

'Not according to your charming mother,' Dee smiled sweetly, and was pleased to note Josh's Adam's apple yo-yo nervously up and down his windpipe. 'Your mother spoke to me like a Rottweiler on amphetamines. She said you'd gone away to have a good rest from *me*, and that if you had any sense you wouldn't come back – from Tenerife,' she added. The last two words were a bluff. Anne Coventry had said no such thing, but a spiteful part of Dee wanted to drop Anne in it for the way she'd treated her.

'Ha ha ha,' Josh attempted laughing. 'Good old Mum. She does like a joke.'

'Nobody was laughing.'

'Take no notice of her, Dee. She's old. She's

probably starting dementia.'

'Must run in the family then, eh?'

'Sorry?'

'You seem to have total amnesia about how you got your sun tan.'

'Look, why don't you finish having your bath and we'll go out to dinner. I'll order a bottle of bubbly, and we'll have a proper talk. Cards on the table.'

Dee was brought up short. Cards on the table. Her mind zoomed back to last Saturday's reading with Madam Rosa, selecting tarot cards that had been strewn across the clairvoyant's occasional table. A major shake-up, Madam Rosa had said, and the ending of a long-term relationship. But right now, it sounded like Josh wanted to make major amends – which was contradictory to the card reading. In which case, had Madam Rosa got it all wrong?

Chapter Forty

Amber's Monday had been...peculiar. At her boss's insistence, she'd gone home to bed. Mr Tomkin had already claimed some of the duvet, and was curled in a tight ball.

'All you ever do is sleep,' Amber grumbled to the cat. He looked at her with half-closed eyes, his purrs punctuated by funny *brrrrrppp* noises. Amber mimicked the sound and the cat rolled on his back, paddling his paws in the air. Whatever *brrrrrppp* meant, it was obviously a good word in cat language. Amber copied him and laid back. 'Oh, to be a cat,' she murmured. 'All you have to worry about is sleeping, eating, hunting, and then repeat.' She hadn't taken her coat off, but would do so in a minute. She needed to close her eyes, only for a second or two.

Five hours later Amber awoke with a start. Sitting up, she yawned and started to stretch, but found herself confined by her winter coat. Shrugging it off, she shivered. Outside, grey winter daylight cast gloomy shadows over the bedroom walls. Struggling to her feet, she moved across to the landing and ramped up the temperature on the heating thermostat. She felt so cold. But then again, she'd been feeling cold ever since evicting Matthew. Her thoughts strayed to Chrissie and Dee. She felt dreadful that Steve had sent her home when her two besties were also having a rubbish time. Feeling guilty, Amber picked up the phone and telephoned Dee's mobile. It went to voicemail. She tried again, this time ringing Dee's personal landline at Hood, Mann & Derek.

'Alan Mann's office, can I help you?'

'Dee, it's me.' Was it Amber's imagination, or had there been a very long pause? 'Are you there?'

249

'Hi...um...can't stop, Amber. Really busy.'

'Yeah, I thought you would be. Listen, I'm so sorry you were left with all my work. I shouldn't have listened to Steve. I feel terr–'

'No worries. Must dash. Need to get the post signed.' Dee had hung up.

Undeterred, Amber then phoned Chrissie who gave her virtually the same response. Amber began to feel anxious. Were her besties furious she'd wimped off leaving them up to their eyeballs in leases? What Amber couldn't have known was that both Chrissie and Dee didn't want to talk to her until Steve had spoken to her. The last thing they wanted was being boxed into a metaphorical corner by Amber's relentless questions once she put two and two together, and realised everyone was behaving rather weirdly.

As Amber slowly put her phone down, she decided to take cakes into the office tomorrow as a "sorry" present for her friends. With that thought in mind, she turned her attention to getting ready for dinner with her boss.

***

Amber stood back from her bedroom mirror to critically study the "overall effect". Ironically, her skin was glowing like somebody who'd overdosed on happiness. In fact, the rosiness was simply down to lingering in a hot bubble bath. She'd piled her hair into a messy bun and tendrils fell in loose curls around her face. Her make-up was flawless, which was a miracle considering her hands had trembled like Mr Tomkin having his annual booster at the vet's. As she threaded some dangly earrings through her earlobes, Amber reminded herself this wasn't a date. So why was she feeling so nervous? It was basically a meeting with her boss – dinner just happened to feature. This was *Steve* for goodness sake! The man she bantered with in office hours, and who gave as good as he got in return. He'd made it quite clear there were things she needed to know, and that he wanted to be the one to tell her. For the life of her, Amber hadn't a clue what Steve had meant by that. And then she groaned as a thought occurred. Oh no. It had to be redundancy. Steve wanted to give her the heads up away from the likes of young Jessica in Accounts who made office gossip her personal business. Grrrrreat. That was all she needed. First boyfriendless, and soon jobless – not good when there was a mortgage to pay.

Mr Tomkin weaved around her ankles asking politely if his mistress could possibly stop preening in front of the mirror and sort out his tea, and if there was any more fillet steak going begging, that really would be rather splendid.

'I know exactly what you're thinking,' said Amber to the cat. 'If I get made redundant, the pair of us will be eating nothing but beans on toast until I find another job.' And then Amber chided herself for not only talking to her cat, but also imagining that her cat had been talking to her. She was losing the plot. This break-up with Matthew had literally pushed her to the edge of having a nervous breakdown. She rammed her feet into some stilettoes and grabbed her coat. 'Come on,' said Amber to Mr Tomkin. 'Let's go to the kitchen and I will feed you. But be warned. Your saucer will contain supermarket tinned meat. Not steak. And yes, I know I'm talking to you again as if you're a human being, but unfortunately your mistress isn't quite the full ticket at the moment.' Mr Tomkin meowed by way of answer and bounced ahead of Amber, his ginger tail ramrod straight as he scampered down the stairs.

Amber was forking whiffy cat food into a bowl

when the doorbell rang. As she set the dish before Mr Tomkin, she noticed her hands were shaking again. 'Steve's here,' she told the cat. 'Don't wait up for me. Well actually, *do* wait up for me. I mean, it's not like there's going to be any romance or...oh, listen to me burbling again.' She was definitely losing it. 'See you later, darling.' Stooping down to give the cat a quick rub on the head, she hastened off to answer the door.

'Hi,' said Steve. He gave her a business-like smile.

'Hi yourself,' said Amber, deliberately sounding like she did at work when Steve summoned her into the office to present a tedious pile of agreements. Amber hoped her bored attitude hid the excitement spiralling up from the pit of her stomach. *He's not gay*, sang a little voice in her head. *So what?* sneered another. *He wasn't interested in you before, so he's not going to be interested now.*

'Your house isn't the easiest to find,' said Steve, as Amber locked up. 'This place is like a maze with all these little footpaths criss-crossing everywhere. Don't you ever get lost?'

Amber laughed as she slipped the house key into her handbag. 'I did once. It was shortly after I'd moved in. I went to the next row of houses by mistake. They all look identical. I spent ages jiggling my key in the lock. Eventually the door was opened by a harassed young mum with several kids hanging off the hem of her skirt. Fortunately, she saw the funny side. She's a really nice neighbour. I know a lot of people around here. They're good sorts.'

'That's nice,' said Steve, taking her elbow and guiding her along the footpath to the road. Despite it being lit by courtesy lights, the night was inky black. Amber wasn't quite sure who was leading who to the car. Steve's touch was sending tingles up and down her spine. She didn't kid herself that it was anything more than chivalry on his part. He opened the passenger door for her, which she liked. *Mental note to self: make sure next boyfriend is chivalrous, guides you on dark nights and opens car doors.*

'The car will soon warm up,' said Steve, as the engine turned over. He indicated right, gave way to a passing vehicle, and seconds later they were cruising along the main road. 'Feeling hungry?'

'As it happens, yes. I've not eaten all day.'

'Why not?'

'I crashed out. Literally. For hours.'

'You must have needed the rest. How are you feeling now?'

'Honestly? Still ridiculously tired.'

'Break-ups are exhausting,' Steve acknowledged.

'Even so, you shouldn't have sent me home. I've behaved like a lightweight.'

'I had my reasons.'

'Which were?'

'Let's get to the restaurant first, eh?'

'I think I know what this is about,' said Amber gloomily. She gazed out of the window at the night beyond.

'You do?' Steve gave her a quick side-long glance. Amber's face was inscrutable.

'I suspect you're taking me out as a softener.'

'Sorry?'

Amber sighed. 'Is this a precursor to redundancy?'

Steve found himself exhaling with relief. Thank goodness Amber hadn't found out about Matthew and Katherine Colgan. Amber was a sweet girl and didn't deserve the way they'd treated her. Steve felt bad that he was going to be the one delivering the awful news. He was deliberately choosing a restaurant out of the locality so that if Amber broke down and wept nobody would know her.

253

'No, you're not going to be made redundant.'

Amber was both relieved and surprised. She was even more surprised when she found herself outside The Beagle and Bugle.

Chapter Forty-One

Chrissie's Monday had been fraught. It had started with the hangover from hell – entirely her fault after downing all those gin and tonics the night before at The Beagle and Bugle. She was mortified at making an idiot of herself in front of the proprietor. The phrase "sex on legs" had surely been invented just for Jack.

Chrissie had driven to work in her mother's car, confident she was no longer over the limit. Harsh January light had forced her into wearing an old pair of sunglasses. Behind the shades her eyeballs had been the same colour as the red cones cordoning off an area of roadworks. Pneumatic drills had throbbed in time to her headache.

As she'd walked into the offices of Hood, Mann & Derek the air had crackled with tension. Nobody had known why apart from young Jessica in Accounts. The girl had been visibly bursting to tell anybody who'd listen. She'd ventured into the open plan area shared with Dee and Amber, ready to spill the gossip beans but an apoplectic Steve Hood had intercepted her. Steve, normally so mild, had bristled like an angry porcupine. Jessica had paled to the colour of a McDonald's McFlurry and scarpered. Steve had then insisted a very hungover Amber leave the office and go home. This had confused Dee and Chrissie because they'd been emotionally wrecked too. Then Clive Derek had rung Chrissie on her internal line informing that Katherine Colgan had resigned with immediate effect. He'd stipulated that Chrissie must not discuss this news with anybody, and then insisted she cover Cougar Kate's workload. Chrissie had barely ended the conversation with Clive, when Steve had summoned her and Dee into his office.

He'd promptly dropped the bombshell that Amber's ex-boyfriend was with Cougar Kate.

Both Chrissie and Dee had spent the day aghast at the additional misery Amber would suffer when she found out. They'd also been terrified she'd ring in for a chinwag and accidentally find out. Predictably Amber had tried speaking to both women. They'd had to be curt to the point of rudeness to get her off the phone.

Chrissie's highpoint of the day had been skipping off to the local hair salon in her lunch hour. She'd been given a style makeover more usual for someone like Cheryl Tweedy-Cole-Fernandez-Versini-thingybob. She'd floated out of the salon like a helium balloon, until seeing Andrew outside the office. His uninspired attempts to woo her had not been appreciated, especially when he'd asked for money. She'd stalked off, outraged, only to have Clive Derek do a double-take and spend the rest of the afternoon hassling her to go out for dinner. What *was* it with some men? And why did she always end up with the prats going after her?

Chrissie had heaved a sigh of relief when the working day had drawn to a close. Dee had grabbed her arm on the way out and chatted loudly about how much fun they were going to have at Bluewater, which had sent a hovering Clive Derek back into his office. Thankfully there had been no sign of Andrew. Dee had hugged Chrissie good-bye insisting she was going home for a hot soak followed by a chillax in front of the telly.

Chrissie had then driven to Bluewater fizzing with excitement at the prospect of shopping. For one moment, she'd felt a twang of guilt at refusing Andrew financial help. A second later she'd squashed the thought. Andrew was no longer her responsibility. His dodgy dealings and debts were no longer her concern. And anyway, if she *had* agreed to help him, her plans for a big fat shopping spree would have become a big fat full stop. No way! She was single, she worked hard, and right now the money in her bank account was hers to spend.

When Chrissie arrived at Bluewater, the first thing she did was visit Boots. She bought eye drops guaranteed to put sparkle in the sorest of eyes, then browsed the cosmetic counters. Testing samples, she was like an excited child at a pick 'n' mix sweet counter. Clutching her purchases, she disappeared into the nearest Ladies. Inside the washroom she positioned herself in front of a huge mirror and began applying brown and gold-tones to her lids, mascara to her lashes, and slicked a lipstick across her mouth in fire-engine red. Finishing off with blusher to her cheekbones, she stood back and preened. She couldn't believe the transformation. What with the hair and now the make-up, she looked like she'd been dolloped with celebrity gloss. *This* Chrissie was as shiny as a new one-pound coin.

She spent the next hour impersonating a woman attempting a shopping challenge, like one of those daytime programmes on the telly where you had to try on as many outfits as possible in a time slot to win all the clothes. By half past six she was laden with carrier bags and absolutely desperate for a coffee and something to eat. She sailed out of Next looking at her watch instead of where she was going, and smacked straight into a man with such force she fell backwards, thumping down on her coccyx. Her shopping flew in all directions.

'*Ooof*,' she gasped, as hard flooring slammed into soft flesh. Chrissie had always thought her bottom well padded, but at that moment it could have done with an extra layer.

'Oh my goodness, I'm so sorry,' said the man, rushing to gather up all the scattered bags.

It occurred to Chrissie that if this person had

wanted to steal her purchases, she'd have had to let him. She was in no fit state to give chase to anyone.

'Are you okay?' he asked.

'I'll live,' she groaned, addressing the man's feet. It was a whole different world down here on the floor. A group of teenage girls walked past and sniggered.

'Here, let me help you up.' A hand appeared in front of her face. Oh, but her back hurt. 'I feel terrible,' said the man. 'I'm so sorry. I wasn't looking where I was going.'

'That makes two of us,' she said to the hand.

'Let's get you on your feet.' She found herself being hauled upwards, and her face contorted with pain. The man notice. 'We're not far from Boots. Do you want me to buy some paracetamol or...,' his voice trailed off. When he spoke again he sounded surprised. 'Chrissie?'

Chrissie attempted straightening from her bent-double posture so she could look properly at the man. Craning her neck upwards, her eyes widened in surprise as she realised it was Jack, the proprietor of The Beagle and Bugle.

'H-hello.' Hell, he was even better looking than she remembered. And here she was doing an impersonation of Quasimodo.

'You look like you're in agony. Can I fetch those painkillers?'

'I have some in my bag, thanks. I can take them without water.' She reluctantly clung on to his arm with one hand whilst rubbing her throbbing lower back with the other. 'I was finished here anyway. I'll be fine after a hot bath.'

Jack regarded her doubtfully. 'Where's your car?'

'Across the other side of the shopping mall.'

'Listen, I'm parked behind this shop. Let me take your shopping, and come with me. I'll drive you to

258

your car.'

Chrissie was going to protest but then realised this made sense. She nodded her agreement and, still hanging onto Jack's arm, the two of them made slow progress to his vehicle. By the time they'd reached her car and transferred the shopping bags across, the painkillers had kicked in and she was feeling a little better.

'Are you okay to drive?'

'I'll be fine,' Chrissie assured. 'Thanks for helping me.'

Jack smiled, the effect of which nearly had Chrissie falling to the floor again. 'Sorry again. It's my night off and I was in a tearing hurry. I only came out to buy a new pair of jeans, and then I was going to chill out in front of the footie.'

'Oh, and you haven't even bought your jeans,' said Chrissie in dismay.

'Doesn't matter. Look, have you eaten?'

Chrissie shook her head. 'Not yet. I was about to grab a coffee and a sandwich prior to–'

'–me knocking you flat,' said Jack ruefully. 'Can I make up for what happened by taking you out for some dinner?'

'Honestly, you don't need to do that,' Chrissie protested.

'I'd like to,' Jack insisted.'

'Then y-yes,' Chrissie stuttered. She suddenly felt flustered. 'I'd like that. If it's no trouble,' she added.

'It's definitely no trouble. I happen to know a very nice restaurant that does amazing food,' he said, a twinkle in his eye. 'If you're sure you can drive, follow me.'

Which was how Chrissie found herself, half an hour later, sitting at a beautifully laid table in The Beagle and Bugle.

Chapter Forty-Two

As soon as Josh had left the bathroom, Dee hauled herself out of the tub and, sploshing wet footprints across the floor tiles, hastily locked the door. Grabbing a fluffy towel off the heated radiator, she rubbed herself down, squirted deodorant into each armpit, and then wrapped the towel tightly around herself. Picking up her discarded office clothes, she unlocked the door and scampered off to the bedroom. She could hear the sound of the television. Josh was in the lounge. Hopefully he'd stay there while she sorted herself out. So much for a peaceful night in with a microwave meal. Dee slipped on a clean pair of pants, and was hooking her bra together when Josh appeared in the bedroom doorway.

'I'm not dressed,' she snapped.

'You look overdressed to me,' said Josh with a lazy grin. 'Nice undies, babe.' He came over and slid his hands around her bare waist. 'You have a fabulous body.'

'Get your hands off me.'

'That's not what you used to say,' said Josh, dropping his mouth to her bare shoulder and kissing his way down her back.

Dee shuddered, but not with desire. 'I said,' she hissed, 'get off.' The hooks on the bra met, and she quickly yanked a t-shirt over her head.

'Hey,' said Josh, putting his hands up in a gesture of surrender, 'no problem. We'll talk first, and make love later.'

Dee grabbed her jeans and stuck one leg in. The thought of being intimate with Josh after him being all over another woman made her hand involuntarily twitch. She had a sudden urge to slap him.

'Don't you want to put a nice dress on?' he asked. 'I said I'd take you out to dinner. I want us to have a champagne celebration.'

'What exactly do you want to celebrate?'

'Us, of course. Our new start.'

'I haven't yet agreed to one. And thanks for the dinner invitation, but it's a no. Right now, I couldn't eat a thing.'

'That's because you're cross with me.'

'You don't say,' said Dee sarcastically.

'C'*mon*,' Josh cajoled. 'Where do you fancy going?'

'Into the lounge. You can tell me everything in there.'

'But what about dinner?'

'I just told you. I'm not hungry. Now can you stop prevaricating?' Dee shoved past him and stalked off. She thumped herself down in an armchair, avoiding sitting next to Josh. The last thing she wanted was an octopus arm winding around her as he tried to persuade her to get undressed.

Josh sat down on the sofa and gave her a frank look. 'Okay, okay,' he sighed. 'I'll tell you the truth. As I said, cards on the table time.'

'I'm all ears.'

'Look, this isn't *all* my fault you know. It takes two to make a relationship work.'

Dee realised he was starting off by going on the defensive. She played along. 'I quite agree.'

Josh looked pleased at her acquiescence. 'Things weren't right between us.'

'In what way?'

'You were nagging me.'

Dee arched an eyebrow. 'About?'

'Everything,' Josh grimaced. 'Moving...getting a house instead of staying here in this flat...dropping hints about getting married – and you don't have to be Einstein to work out that after marriage comes a baby. There's no room for a baby in this flat. I felt pressured. Like I was being boxed into a corner.'

'I see. So why didn't you sit me down, like now, and talk about it?'

Josh shrugged. 'I panicked and ran. I spent the week thinking about us, and evaluating my feelings...like whether I wanted to spend the rest of my life with you. As the week went on, I realised I was missing you. A lot. And...and that I'd behaved foolishly.' He gave Dee a contrite look. His eyes filled with just the right amount of water to make him look both vulnerable and little-boy-lost. 'I'm so sorry.'

'I appreciate your honesty,' said Dee.

'Honesty is the best policy.'

'Absolutely.' Dee paused for a moment, allowing Josh to digest the bit about honesty. 'So where did you go?'

'To a mate's.'

'Ah.'

'Yeah.'

'That was very accommodating of...him?'

'Him?'

'The mate was male, yes?'

'Of course,' said Josh indignantly.

'Does he live far away?'

'No, no, not really.' Josh caught something in Dee's expression, and hastily corrected himself. 'Well, it depends how you look at it. Not far away in travel time but...um...quite far away in miles. If you see what I mean.'

'I think so,' said Dee. 'So, what you're trying to tell me is,' she put her head on one side and considered, 'not far away in *travel* time–'

'–absolutely!'

'–especially if you travel there by plane,' Dee finished.

'Er, w-well not exactly by plane but–'

'But you took your passport, didn't you?'

'Ah, y-yes, it was by plane,' Josh nodded.

'So *that's* how you got the suntan!' She clapped her hands together as if the whole thing was a game. 'Why didn't you say so in the first place, you big silly!'

'Ha ha ha,' Josh laughed nervously. 'Well, I wasn't sure you'd be too impressed with me taking off to Tenerife and leaving you here—'

'—in January, in good old freezing England,' said Dee, finishing Josh's sentence.

'Exactly!' Josh smiled. 'So, now that's all out the way, shall we go to dinner?' He stood up.

'Not yet. Sit back down.'

'Why?'

'Because we're still chatting.' She watched as Josh reluctantly re-parked his bottom. 'Do tell me, who's your mate in Tenerife? I don't think I've ever heard you mention a friend over there.'

Josh puffed out his cheeks. 'No, well, that's because...because he's a very private guy.'

'What's his name?'

'Emmerson.'

'Emma-son,' Dee enunciated, rolling the name over her tongue. She liked the way Josh flinched as she pronounced the "Emma" bit. She narrowed her eyes as if thinking. 'Has Emmerson, by any chance, been on your mind these past few weeks?'

'Er, why?'

'Because recently you've been sleep talking. Last time around, you woke me up shouting Emmerson's name.'

Josh blanched. 'Really?'

'Mmm. Except you called him something else. It was more like,' Dee threw her head back, closed her eyes and, in an orgasmic voice moaned, 'Emma, oh Emmaaaaa.'

'Oh dear. You've discovered Emmerson's little

secret.'

'And what would that be?'

'He's transgender. He's thinking about having the op. You know,' Josh nodded at his crotch by way of explanation. 'But he's changed his name to Emma. It's been a tough time for him. We used to clean windows together, before I met you. Happily, these days things are much easier for transgenders. I mean, it's really quite cool to say you're transgender, eh!'

'Oh absolutely,' said Dee, her tone sugar sweet.

'But a few years ago, he felt completely out of his depth. I mean, *her* depth.'

'So he-who-is-now-a-she took off to Tenerife for a new beginning, and recently you joined him-who-is-now-a-her to give moral support?'

'That's it!' Josh stood up again. 'Can we go out to dinner now? I'm famished.' He rubbed his stomach and attempted a jolly tone. 'I'm so glad we're back on track. And I might as well tell you some fabulous news. You're going to love this! I want us to get married. But I want to propose properly. This evening. While we're out. So please get changed into a posh frock, sweetheart. It's going to be lots of flickering candlelight and me down on one knee.' He grinned in delight at Dee's stunned expression. She looked like she'd been presented with six bouquets of roses and didn't know what to do with them all. Not that Josh ever gave her any flowers, but he decided that he might start doing so after tonight. Just to distract her and stop her interrogating him. Josh inwardly groaned. He'd now have to fork out for an engagement ring. Then he perked up a bit. They did some nice second-hand ones at the local jeweller's. He cleared his throat and gave Dee a dazzling smile, like a film star who'd been let loose with dentist's whitening bleach. 'So where shall we go, my angel?'

At that moment the flat's intercom buzzed.

'I'll get it,' said Dee faintly. Good heavens. Josh wanted to marry her. He'd popped the question and was prepared to propose all over again, romantically. She went out into the hallway in a daze, and picked up the intercom handset. 'Hello? Yes. I see. Yes, he's here.'

'Is it Mum?' asked Josh, appearing at her side. 'I told her I'd be back today.'

Dee gave Josh a nod, and then spoke into the handset. 'I'll buzz you in.'

She pressed the button to release the main entrance door, put the handset down, and then opened the flat's door and left it ajar. Josh didn't see her pick up her house keys. He was too busy reaching into the hall cupboard for his coat.

'I'll say a quick hello to Mum while you get changed out of those jeans and into a dress,' he said, 'and then we'll go.' There was the sound of footsteps coming across the communal landing outside. Josh patted his pockets making sure he had his wallet.

Dee looked up expectantly as the flat door opened. But instead of Anne Coventry standing there, it was a suntanned blonde – with a furious face. She stepped into the hall.

'What the–?' said Josh.

'Good evening,' said Dee sweetly. 'You must be Emmerson. I must say,' Dee stepped forward, looking the woman up and down, 'I'd never know.' She peered at the woman's crotch admiringly. 'Not a sausage in sight! And these are very authentic,' she squeezed a perky breast causing the woman to gasp in shock. 'The only giveaway is the nose.' Dee didn't feel remotely guilty as she added, 'It's absolutely enormous.'

Emma suddenly remembered that she had a tongue and a pair of tonsils, and decided to put both to use. 'Who the HELL are you?' she snarled.

265

'Didn't he tell you about me?' Dee feigned surprise. 'How remiss of him, especially when he's just this second asked me to marry him. However,' Dee turned to Josh, 'as we said earlier, honesty is the best policy. And regrettably I cannot get hitched to a liar. We're finished. I don't care whether you choose to go with *Emmerson*, or stay at your parents' place, but there's no way you're living with me until our flat is sold. I'll give you an hour to pack your stuff. Leave your keys on the hall table on your way out.'

And with that Dee turned her back on both Emma and Josh and, head held high, walked out of the flat, through the block's main entrance door, and into the night.

Chapter Forty-Three

A waitress showed Amber and Steve to a candlelit table in a discreet nook. Amber had already given the pub the onceover. There was no sign of Jack. She thanked the waitress for pulling a chair out and taking her coat, then sat down to study the huge tasselled menu that had been placed in her hands. Wow, what a selection of lip-smackingly scrumptious choices.

'Have you been here before?' Amber asked Steve.

'Now and again,' Steve replied.

'With *your mate*?' Amber teased.

'No, not with Danny,' Steve smiled. 'Little boys are too noisy and fidgety to spend an evening in a restaurant like this.'

'So who *did* you bring?'

'You are so nosy'.

'I know,' said Amber, with a little shrug.

'If you must know, the odd lady friend.'

'Why didn't you choose a lady friend who wasn't odd?' asked Amber gravely.

Steve laughed. 'What would you like to drink?'

'Prosecco, please. You previously told me you didn't have a girlfriend.'

'I don't.'

'At the moment.'

'At the moment,' Steve nodded, and turned his attention to the menu.

'What happened to the previous girlfriends?'

'They got fed up. Do you fancy a starter?'

I fancy you, Amber found herself thinking. 'I'll have the calamari, please. So why did your previous girlfriends get fed up?'

'Because I have a little boy who sometimes impacts on dates. There are times when Danny isn't well, or the sitter cries off. One girlfriend was particularly put out when we went to see Beauty and the Beast at the cinema and Danny had to come along.'

'They sound like horrible girlfriends,' said Amber indignantly. 'I love children. I want ten one day.'

'You might amend that when you've had your first one,' Steve smiled. 'Kids can be very demanding.'

'I don't care,' said Amber adamantly. 'I'd hoped that Matthew and I would one day have a brood. Anyway,' she said, not wishing to think about her ex-boyfriend, 'if you haven't brought me here to discuss redundancy, what did you want to talk about?'

The waitress appeared, for which Steve was grateful. He wasn't quite ready to deliver Amber bad news. The waitress gave Steve a full-on smile. 'Are you and your wife ready to order, Sir?'

Steve didn't correct her. 'I think we are.'

The waitress took their orders, and directed plenty of eyelash batting at Steve.

'She fancies you,' said Amber, as the woman walked away.

'I don't think so.'

'Course she does,' Amber sniffed. 'You'd have to be more myopic than Mister Magoo not to see that.' She felt a stab of jealousy.

'Then it's a good thing she thinks I'm married to you,' Steve quipped.

For the next fifteen minutes the waitress seemed to be permanently at their table, either serving their drinks, asking if they wanted more drinks, whether they were comfortable, too hot, too cold, bringing their starters, asking if the food was okay, whether they were ready for more drinks, was there anything else she could help with, absolutely sure no one wanted another drink, and all the while simpering

268

at Steve until Amber lost patience.

'Actually, there is something I'd like,' she said sweetly.

'What's that?' asked the waitress, her gaze on Steve.

'I'd like you to leave us alone so I can enjoy talking to my *husband*.'

Steve nearly choked on his drink, and the waitress turned bright red. 'Sorry,' she mumbled. 'I, er, of course.'

'Handled with your usual tact and subtlety,' Steve joked, after the waitress had gone.

'She's out of order,' said Amber moodily, 'and was really starting to annoy me. I bet she was one of the reasons your girlfriends didn't like coming here, eh?'

'Honestly, I've never had that happen to me before,' Steve replied, but his eyes were twinkling.

'I don't believe you. Did your little boy's mummy get fed up with it too?'

The sparkle in Steve's eyes died. He paused before answering. 'No,' he said. 'She left for other reasons.'

'*She* left?' Amber's eyes widened in surprise. 'When we were chatting at the office, you said you'd tell me about it. Are you still going to?'

Steve hesitated. 'I don't want to bore you.'

'You won't. I do love a good break-up story,' Amber mocked. 'It makes me feel normal.'

'Actually, I have a couple of break-up stories to tell you.'

'A *couple*, eh!' Amber raised her eyebrows. 'Excellent. I'm perking up by the second.'

The waitress returned with their mains. She practically threw the meals at Steve and Amber, such was her haste to leave them alone after Amber's complaint.

'Mm,' Amber inhaled appreciatively, and picked

up her knife and fork. 'Okay. Lonely hearts story number one, please.'

'Before I begin, can you promise to keep it to yourself? I'd rather my private life wasn't discussed with everyone at Hood, Mann & Derek.'

'That's really mean,' Amber tutted, as she cut into her steak. 'I was *soooo* looking forward to telling Jessica in Accounts.' She caught Steve's seriousness. 'I'm joking. My lips are sealed.'

'Good. Right, where to start?' Steve looked pensive as he picked up his own knife and fork.

'The beginning is good,' said Amber dryly.

'You're right. Okay. Her name was Nina. We met at uni. We moved in together and, eventually, bought a house in Stoke Newington. We always meant to get married, and started planning our wedding. But then we discovered Danny was on the way. For me, it was a happy accident. However, Nina wasn't quite so thrilled. Suddenly the wedding was on hold. She said she didn't want to be waddling down the aisle. I was happy to go along with her wishes. But after Danny was born, for some reason Nina struggled to bond with him. She always said she felt like she was looking after somebody else's baby.'

Amber took a sip of her wine and looked thoughtful. 'Was she suffering from post-natal depression?'

'It wasn't diagnosed, and she insisted she didn't feel depressed,' Steve replied. 'But she *did* change after having Danny. She said she begrudged being tied to a little human being who was totally dependent upon her. She hated being stuck in the house with a screaming baby. When Danny was six months old, Nina insisted she wanted to return to work. I said fine, whatever made her happy. Danny was thriving, it was just Nina who wasn't. I desperately wanted her to feel the way she used to, before Danny came along. So, eventually our baby went to a local nursery.'

'I don't agree with that,' said Amber, blissfully unaware of her lack of tact. 'If I have a baby one day, I want to be at home with him or her.' She couldn't imagine another person caring for her precious child, or missing out on the first word. The first step. No way.

'Try not to judge, Amber. Some parents have no choice in the matter and need two incomes.'

'But you and Nina didn't, surely? Not in your chosen professions?'

'We could have managed on my salary. It would have been tight. But Nina wasn't happy, Amber. She was miserable. And desperate. You have to understand that a huge strain is placed upon a relationship when your partner is continually in a place of despair. Nina hoped that by going back to work it might, in some perverse way, make her miss Danny...that she'd start to feel something for our child.'

'And did it help?'

Steve looked at his half-eaten dinner and paused. Amber wasn't sure but she wondered if he was composing himself before he next spoke. Eventually he looked up.

'No, it didn't make her feel any closer to Danny.'

One of Amber's quirks – and not necessarily a good one – was the ability to see things only in black or white. Right now, she was struggling to understand the shades of grey. 'Sorry, Steve, but I don't like the sound of your ex. Not one little bit.'

'I hear what you're saying, Amber, but you mustn't criticise. I can't stress enough how bad Nina felt about this... *inadequacy*. She was ashamed. Appalled that, for her, the love factor didn't effortlessly ooze towards Danny.'

'Did she get counselling?'

271

'Yes. And she also went on Prozac to see if that helped, although she insisted she wasn't depressed. She was in her element at work. It was just at home she wasn't content. And eventually she wasn't happy with me either. She said she wanted out.'

'Oh.'

'Yes. Oh.' Steve put his knife and fork together. The meal had been delicious, but it was always the same when he thought about his ex-partner and her emotional block regarding Danny. His appetite had done a bunk. He still struggled to understand how Nina and felt and, ultimately, her actions. 'One day I came home from work to find her packing clothes into suitcases. *Her* stuff, you understand. She said she was very sorry, but she couldn't do it anymore. She was leaving me and Danny. Nina stipulated she didn't want any sort of custody or regular access. And then, with a suitcase in either hand, she walked out of the front door, and out of our lives.'

'Didn't her family intervene?' asked Amber, shocked.

'I'm giving you a potted history, Amber. I can assure you that family members, on both sides, tried to talk and reason with Nina throughout the entire period. They begged her. They reminded her she was a good mother by action – she looked after Danny perfectly well. They tried to persuade her it was enough, and better than our child having no mother at all. But Nina's mind was made up. Eventually she cut herself off from her family too. Her parents were...are...lovely people. They've run the spectrum of emotions over Nina. From being stunned and appalled, to upset and angry, not to mention suffering terrible grief. They feel like they've lost a daughter, but can't mourn her. After all, Nina isn't dead.'

'So what happened next?'

'Suddenly I was Mister Mum. Both families

rallied around. I sold the house in Stoke Newington. Nina didn't want a penny of the equity. She told me to keep everything for Danny, that it was the least she could do.'

'Gosh, that was good of her,' said Amber sarcastically.

Steve ignored Amber's derision. 'To cut a long story short, I opted out of the London rat race. I moved to Culverstone Green to be near my parents. Workwise, I joined Mann & Derek Solicitors, which eventually became Hood, Mann & Derek. I take Danny to the village school every morning before driving to work. My mother picks him up at half past three. She looks after Danny until I've finished at the office. My son and I have a lovely life together, and I make sure weekends are devoted to quality time with my little mate.'

'That has to be one of the saddest break-up stories I've ever heard,' said Amber miserably. She put her knife and fork together. 'That was delicious by the way.' The waitress returned, grabbed the plates and scarpered. 'So, what is the second break-up story?'

'Ah.' Steve wiped his mouth on a napkin, playing for time. 'Well, the second break-up story doesn't essentially involve me.'

Amber's forehead creased in puzzlement. 'So...who does it involve?'

Steve took a deep breath. 'You.'

'Me?' Her brows knitted together. 'I'm not following this.'

'I'm truly sorry to be the one who has to tell you.'

'Tell me what?'

'You're a lovely girl, and deserve so much better.' Suddenly Steve was reaching across the table, taking both of Amber's hands in his. *Zinnnng.* Amber wondered if it was only her experiencing electrical currents whizzing through her hands,

273

shooting up her arms and making her spine do some very weird tingles. 'You were right about your boyfriend–'

'–ex-boyfriend,' Amber corrected.

'Yes, ex-boyfriend,' Steve nodded. 'You were right about him having an affair.'

'I know,' said Amber, none the wiser as to what Steve was trying to tell her. 'I was the one who told you he was having an affair, remember? When you called me into your office to point out my typing had gone to pot, I told you how I'd found an earring in my bed. And I also told you how I'd gone bonkers and chucked all Matthew's clothes out of the bedroom window.'

'Yes, you did,' Steve acknowledged. 'But...did you ever find out who the earring belonged to?'

Amber was now totally confused. Why would Steve be interested in who the earring belonged to? 'No. Why?'

'Because I know who she is.'

Amber paled. 'Oh no. No, no, no. You're not going to tell me this is one of those horrendous coincidences where Matthew met a woman called Nina who happens to be *your* Nina and–'

'No, nothing like that,' Steve interrupted.

'Well... what then?'

'This morning, at work, I went to the kitchen to make a coffee. Two women were in there. One of them was discussing her love life. She said her lover had finally left his girlfriend.'

'And?' Amber prompted. She still wasn't following this line of conversation.

'And the reason he'd finally left his girlfriend, was because she'd thrown him out. Including chucking all his clothes out of a bedroom window.' Steve paused, allowing his words to sink in. His grip on Amber's hands tightened as she stared at him, the thought processes visibly showing on her face.

Her eyes widened as realisation dawned.

'So...so,' she whispered, 'what you're trying to tell me is...Matthew has been having an affair with someone at our *office*?'

Steve nodded. 'That's why I sent you home. I didn't want you finding out about it via someone else. Or having the likes of Jessica gleefully telling you. Matthew has moved in with Katherine Colgan.'

'Katherine Colgan?' Amber looked blank for a moment. 'You mean Cougar Kate?'

'Yes.'

'Are you sure?'

'One hundred per cent.'

'But...but...Kate is a gold digger. She wants somebody rich. Matthew isn't rich. He carries on like he is, with his Designer wardrobe and flash talk, and he earns a fair salary, but he lives way beyond his means. The reality is,' Amber looked embarrassed, 'Matthew is a sponger.' She blew out her cheeks. 'I've never told anybody that before. Not even Dee or Chrissie.' Amber shook her head slowly from side to side. 'What a stupid woman. She's a lot older than him, and I know she did well out of her last divorce settlement. Financially speaking, Matthew will bleed her dry.'

Steve was studying Amber intently. He'd expected her face to crumple and tears to flow. Instead she was looking gobsmacked, but not particularly *upset*. 'Do you want me to signal the waitress to fetch a stiff brandy? I appreciate this is a horrible shock.'

'No. No thanks. I *am* shocked, but not in the way you think,' Amber assured. 'To be honest, it all makes sense. She made a play for Matthew at the last Christmas party, and ever since then our relationship has been slowly going down the tubes. He's probably been having a fling with her for longer than I even realised. But I'm not devastated.

275

Believe me. I've done all my crying over Matthew.'

'That's very brave talk, but it might hit you later.'

'I mean it,' Amber said vehemently. She was very aware her hands were still folded within Steve's, and how it was making her feel. And even if Steve Hood wasn't alive to the effect his touch was having on both her body and emotions, Amber most certainly was. Matthew's touch had never done this to her. Not even in the beginning. Suddenly the words of Madam Rosa's last prediction floated through Amber's mind.

The Ace of Cups heralds the beginning of a new love relationship, and the Ace of Wands signifies this is going to be a passionate affair that takes off with speed. You're going to fall head over heels in love and will look back on this period of your life with disbelief that you put up with the current nonsense for so long.

'Are you okay?' asked Steve.

His voice was full of concern and, if Amber wasn't very much mistaken, tenderness. She looked across the table at their hands linked together and had a weird moment of déjà vu. Somehow, she just *knew* these were the hands that would hold hers throughout the rest of her life. She looked up at Steve's face and smiled.

'Yes,' she said. 'I'm okay. I'm very, very okay.'

Chapter Forty-Four

When Chrissie walked into The Beagle and Bugle with Jack she was no longer bent double with pain, although her back was still aching. The drive hadn't done her any favours. Her torso felt as stiff as a sixteenth-century maiden trussed up in a whalebone corset. A smiling waitress greeted them both.

'Are you eating in, Jack?' she asked.

'Yes, with a VIP guest,' he grinned. 'Tell Chef only the best will do for this lady,' he nodded at Chrissie. The waitress regarded her curiously.

'Take no notice of him,' said Chrissie. 'The only VIP in this case is Very Idiotic Plonker. Honestly, I'm no one special.'

'To me you are,' Jack quipped. For a moment Chrissie felt nonplussed. Just for a second there, Jack had made it sound as if she was special to him. 'As far as I'm concerned, everyone who eats in my restaurant is a VIP,' he added.

Ah well, thought Chrissie wryly, *it was nice to feel like I meant something for a moment.*

The waitress placed two menus on the table, and went off to fetch her notepad. Jack pulled out a chair for Chrissie, which she thought a nice touch. Andrew had never done that for her in all their time together. Jack sat down opposite, but instead of looking at the menu, his eyes sought hers. At such close proximity, it was both off-putting and intoxicating. Feeling awkward, she looked away and studied the menu for something to do. The dishes sounded mouth-watering, but she wasn't sure she'd be able to eat a thing. A net full of butterflies had taken off in her stomach and were causing havoc. She suddenly felt anxious. The last thing she wanted was to make an idiot of herself yet again in front of this man. As it was, his nearness was causing her emotional chaos.

'So,' Jack grinned mischievously, 'will you be drinking my pub dry tonight? I seem to remember you're rather partial to gin and tonic.'

Chrissie looked up from the menu, her face reddening. 'Most definitely not,' she assured. 'I'm not even a fan of the drink.'

'You could have fooled me.'

'Honestly, it was my friends' fault.'

'Is that so?' Jack teased, raising his eyebrows.

'I'm easily led,' she said coquettishly. Oh, good heavens. Was she flirting?

'I love a woman who is easily led,' Jack bantered back. Dear Lord, now *he* was flirting.

'Do you now?' she said softly. H-e-l-p, who had given her voice box permission to speak in such a seductive tone?

There was a pause where neither of them said anything. The air around Table Twelve had begun to positively crackle. Chrissie felt like she couldn't breathe properly. Oxygen was going in and out of her lungs but at a ridiculous rate, like a bicycle tyre being over-zealously pumped up. At this rate, she'd end up hyperventilating. Either that or her lungs would burst.

The moment was broken by the waitress reappearing. 'Can I get you both some drinks?'

'Water, please,' Chrissie gasped.

'Are you sure?' asked Jack.

'Yes,' Chrissie nodded frantically, willing her heart rate to normalise. 'I'm driving later.'

'So shall we pretend it's the bubbly stuff we're drinking, but opt for mineral water?' said Jack impishly.

'That would be lovely.' *Just like you*, she found herself thinking.

'A bottle of our finest fizzy stuff,' said Jack to the

waitress, who wasn't paying attention. Her eyes kept pinging over to a couple on the far side of the restaurant. Chrissie followed the waitress's gaze, but could only see the tops of their heads. They were seated in a nook, which afforded privacy.

'Hello? Earth to Katie!' Jack flapped a menu at the distracted waitress.

'Oh, sorry,' she said distractedly. 'Right. So, where were we? Oh yes. Bubbles coming up! Are you ready to order?'

Despite staring at the menu, Chrissie hadn't taken much of it in. 'You go ahead,' she nodded to Jack, stalling for time.

'Fillet steak with all the trimmings. Chef knows how I like it.' He handed back the menu.

'I'll have the omelette,' said Chrissie. She didn't want Jack thinking she was an expensive date. Not that this was a date, but even so.

'Are you a vegetarian?' Jack asked in surprise.

'No. I adore meat and I love a good steak,' said Chrissie carelessly.

'Then why don't you have one?'

'Oh! Because...because...I'm not that hungry,' Chrissie finished lamely.

But Jack wasn't stupid. 'You don't have to penny pinch, you know. This is on me. I caused you grievous bodily harm,' he winked, 'purely accidental of course,' he added for the waitress's benefit, not that she seemed interested. Her eyes were back on the couple in the nook. Chrissie wondered why. 'Er, Katie?' Jack prompted.

'Okay, got that,' the waitress said, but even as she responded her eyes returned to the couple in the corner. It was clear the two of them – or maybe it was just one? – had her interest. 'Two fillets of fish coming up.'

'Steak,' Jack corrected.

'That's what I said.' Katie flashed a smile, took

279

the menus and disappeared.

Jack sighed theatrically. 'I don't know. Sometimes you can't get the staff.'

Chrissie giggled. 'I'm sure whatever we end up with, it will be delicious.'

The waitress returned with an ice bucket and opened bottle of champagne. 'Bubbles,' she said cheerfully.

Chrissie looked alarmed. 'It was meant to be mineral water.'

Katie raised her eyebrows. 'Jack? I could have sworn you said a bottle of our finest fizzy stuff.'

'I did,' said Jack, 'but I meant...oh, never mind.' He followed the waitress's gaze. 'Whoever he is, Katie,' Jack lowered his voice, 'he's already partnered up.'

'I don't know what you mean,' she said, flushing guiltily. 'Do you want me to pour?'

'No thanks. I can see you're having vision problems and we'd like it in our glasses. Not over the linen.' The comment was lost on Katie, who smiled vacantly and left them in peace. Jack picked up the bottle. It hovered over Chrissie's glass. 'A small one?'

'Go on then,' she smiled. 'See? I told you I'm easily led.'

'In that case I might ply you with champagne and suggest you sleep in my bed tonight,' said Jack playfully. 'I'd take the sofa, of course,' he added, but his eyes were twinkling with mischief again.

'You mean to say you'd lead me to your bed and then abandon me?' Chrissie twinkled back. *Dear God in heaven, if you are listening please control my mouth. It keeps failing to consult with my brain before speaking.* She hadn't even tasted the champagne yet, and was behaving like she was half-sloshed. This was all Andrew's fault. She'd been so well and truly under his thumb, so submissive, that now she was footloose and fancy free she was off like a dog wagging its tail at the first sight of the local stray coming over to say hello. Except Jack was no bit of rough. Jack was very debonair. And, after the bit of rough Chrissie had been shacked up with, a bit of smooth was proving seductively nice.

Jack's lips twitched. 'If you didn't want me to abandon you, you'd only have to say.' His tone was teasing, but Chrissie knew for sure he was flirting. 'I must say,' he murmured, 'I absolutely love your hair. In fact,' Jack reached across the table and tentatively took one of Chrissie's hands, 'please don't think I'm in the habit of saying this to all the ladies, but I absolutely love everything about you.'

Suddenly Chrissie had a bizarre feeling of having already experienced this situation. From nowhere she heard Madam Rosa's voice, as if the clairvoyant was whispering in her ear.

The King of Swords depicts an invitation for a love relationship, and the Eight of Wands signifies a very fast-moving time frame. Expect things to happen in two or three days – give or take a few seconds.

Flipping heck. Maybe, just maybe, Madam Rosa was right. The old Chrissie would have snatched her hand back, stammered an excuse and fled. But this was the new Chrissie. The *daring* Chrissie. And this Chrissie suddenly felt very up for seeing exactly what might come out of tonight's dinner date with the smoulderingly handsome Jack.

Chapter Forty-Five

Dee strode out of her block of flats and towards the residents' private car park. She had one arm extended like a Dalek, key fob pointing at her car. Seconds later she was lowering herself into the driver's side and firing up the engine. Her confrontation with Josh and Emma had left her with so much adrenalin zipping around her body, she felt like she was shaking faster than a wet dog getting out of the bath at a pooch parlour. Her hands clenched against the steering wheel as she screeched out of the car park, leaving tyre rubber on the tarmac.

Calm down, Dee, they're not worth it, she told herself as she hurtled along the main road. She was fizzing and popping with fury, like a firework on the verge of explosion. She roared towards a pedestrian crossing just as a group of teenagers stepped off the kerb. Dee slammed her foot against the brakes, leaving more tyre rubber on the road. At this rate there would be no tread left. The last thing she wanted was a driving licence decorated with black stars.

She cringed as a police car drew level in the adjacent traffic lane. *Oh-God-oh-God-oh-God, please don't let them have seen me driving like a lunatic. I'm sorry, God. Please forgive me. I'll never drive beyond thirty miles per hour again. I promise.*

God must have been listening because the police car cruised past her leaving Dee hyperventilating behind the steering wheel. Her legs felt so weak it was like her thigh bones had melted, leaving her jeaned legs flopping uselessly against the car seat.

Carefully, Dee pulled away from the pedestrian crossing. She accelerated slowly until she was cruising along at thirty miles per hour. From now on she would allow nobody, least of all Josh and Emma, to interfere with her concentration. In no time at all, a stream of traffic had built up behind her. Dee glanced in the rear-view mirror. A lorry was almost touching her bumper. Seconds later the driver hit his horn causing Dee to violently jump. Her nerves were fraying faster than knackered knicker elastic. She was in no mood for harassment. *I'm driving within the speed limit, dipstick*! Where were her police officer buddies when she needed them?

The lorry gave the horn again. Furious, Dee spotted a side turning and indicated. She wasn't usually given to ill manners, but right now she was madder than Donald Trump and Kim Jong-un discussing nuclear weapons. Buzzing down the window, she stuck her entire arm through the aperture. She couldn't remember whether the one-fingered-salute was with the index or middle finger. She opted for the second finger and, pointing at the sky like Superman, turned off the main road. She could hear the lorry driver shouting, 'You stupid tart. Go sit on it.'

Dee exhaled shakily. She was now driving down an unknown road, leaving behind the town and its residential roads. The scenery gave way to fields dotted with electric pylons and travellers' pinto ponies. She had no idea where she was going, and right now she didn't care. She crossed intersections that looked vaguely familiar, but stuck resolutely to the unfamiliar route she was on. After twenty minutes, her heart rate had settled down again. She spotted a sign for Sevenoaks. Hmm. She wasn't a million miles from Seal. Had her subconscious been planning this all along?

Dee drew up outside Harrison Hunter-Brown's house. Now she was here, she might as well tell him in person that she wouldn't be going ahead as a client. After all, she no longer required any information about the mysterious Emma. She'd been presented with all the proof she'd ever needed right down to what the woman looked like. And yes, Emma did have a big nose. It would be great for poking into Josh's business, if they ever properly got together. No doubt Josh would lie through his back teeth about Dee, insisting she'd made everything up about reunions and marriage proposals.

Dee walked up to the front door just as Harry opened it. As previously, the sight of him momentarily took her breath away. He was as heart-stoppingly gorgeous as ever. She had a peculiar feeling of repeating their last meeting, except this time no tearful client came out of his property.

'Hello,' said Harry smiling. For some reason, he felt ridiculously pleased to see her. 'I saw you pull up through my kitchen window.'

Hi,' said Dee, suddenly aware the time was getting on. 'I hope I'm not interrupting your evening.'

'Not at all. I'm not working tonight. In fact, I was about to stick a microwave dinner in the oven.'

Dee gave a half-smile. 'You too? I was going to do the same. But then my boyfriend returned home, swiftly became an ex-boyfriend, and I've left him packing his stuff.'

'Ah. I'm sorry to hear that,' Harry sympathised, although he found himself feeling secretly pleased at this news. How peculiar. *And not very charitable*, he sternly told himself.

'So, as I was in the area,' Dee realised her words sounded a bit ridiculous given that her address was hardly around the corner, 'I thought I'd stop by and tell you that surveillance won't be required.' She studied her feet for a moment. When she looked up again her eyes were shiny. 'Thank you for your time. It was very kind of you. Are you sure I don't owe anything for the initial consultation?'

Harry looked at the pretty young woman standing on his doorstep. She had about her an air of vulnerability. He felt an inexplicable rush of tenderness towards her. How strange. At that moment, there was the sound of a stomach growling with hunger. Hers, not his.

'Listen,' he said kindly, 'I'm absolutely ravenous, and I know you've not eaten either. Would you care to join me for dinner?'

Dee looked startled. 'That's very nice of you, but microwave dinners don't usually stretch to two people.'

Harry laughed, and Dee noticed how his whole face lit up. He really was incredibly attractive. 'Come on,' he said, picking up his house keys from the hall table and shutting the front door after him. 'There's a great little pub near here, and it does the most amazing food.'

'I don't want to put you to any trouble,' said Dee. 'Hang on,' she stalled. 'Oh no...I've come out without my handbag and purse.'

'Don't be silly,' said Harry, leading the way to his car. 'My treat.'

'B-but,' Dee stuttered, 'I feel terrible. And I look terrible too.'

'You look fabulous,' Harry assured, and he meant it. Dee seemed perfectly oblivious to how cute she looked with her short, tousled hair and sweet elfin face. Not to mention those full pink lips that looked extremely kissable. For a moment Harry's step faltered. What was going on here? Where were these thoughts and feelings coming from? He'd only ever regarded Dee as a potential client – until this evening. How very odd.

285

'Well, in that case,' said Dee, 'you must let me return the favour, and take you out to dinner next time.' The words were out of her mouth before she could stop them. Dee inwardly cringed. Oh no. She hoped he didn't think she was trying to chat him up.

'Consider it a date,' grinned Harry. As he opened his car's passenger door for Dee, he realised he truly did want to see this woman again.

'Okay,' Dee smiled shyly at him, before lowering herself into the passenger seat, 'you're on.' Suddenly Josh and Emma seemed a universe away. It was as if the events of the last hour had stretched to a decade ago. How bizarre. She buckled up and glanced across at Harry as he settled himself into the driver's seat. He caught her gaze and gave her a thousand-watt smile that set her pulse rate galloping.

'For the record,' said Harry, 'I think your ex-boyfriend is mad letting you walk away. I hope that doesn't sound like a chat-up line.' Although privately Harry wanted nothing more than to chat up Dee. She was having a very strange effect on him.

'Thanks,' Dee mumbled, half embarrassed and half delighted. A sudden draught played around the nape of her neck. As she glanced up at the passenger window to make sure it was shut, she heard Madam Rosa's voice whisper in her ear.

The Ten of Cups. This card often appears for singles with no apparent build-up at all. On these occasions, it has always been quite literal – a new love relationship that arrives and takes off at the rate of knots. This is usually of the "sweep you off your feet" variety where love walks in unannounced and everything just immediately clicks.

Dee shivered, but not because she was cold. It was more a quiver of anticipation. Of waiting for something wonderful to happen – and she had no doubt it would. She wasn't particularly surprised when Harry parked up outside The Beagle and Bugle. Nor, when she walked in, was she astonished to see Chrissie and Jack nose-to-nose on one side of the pub, and Amber and Steve holding hands over the table to her right. There was a waitress trying to catch Steve's eye, but Dee could see the only woman Steve had eyes for, was Amber.

'I think you'll like it here,' said Harry, tentatively taking her hand.

As Dee's fingers intertwined with his, lovely zingy tingles whizzed up and down her arm. 'I think you might be right,' she smiled.

Chapter Forty-Six

One year later

Dee admired the sparkling diamond on her left hand as she picked up the ringing telephone.

'Hunter-Brown Agency, how can I help you?'

'Hello?' squawked a distressed voice. 'I want to hire a detective.'

'That can be arranged,' said Dee, in a soothing tone. 'Let me take some details.' She opened a new client page on the computer. 'Who do you wish the agency to investigate?'

'My boyfriend,' sobbed the woman. 'I think he's having an affair.'

'I'm sorry to hear that,' murmured Dee. Harry had told her that engaging sympathetically with clients was extremely important. 'Would you like an initial consultation?'

'Yes,' sniffed the woman.

'Okay. Let me jot down some brief details for Mr Hunter-Brown. Let's start with your name.'

'Emma Emmerson,' said the woman.

Dee's brow puckered. Whoever had called their daughter "Emma Emmerson" must have been friends with Peter Piper who had picked all those peppers. She began to enter the name on the computer, but stopped as a jumbo-sized penny rattled through her brain. No! It couldn't be. Could it?

'And...er...the name of your boyfriend?'

'Josh,' sobbed Emma. 'Josh Coventry.'

***

Chrissie admired the sparkling diamond on her left hand as she stood behind the bar of The Beagle and

Bugle. It had been with some reluctance that she'd left Hood, Mann & Derek, but the place hadn't been the same without her besties by her side, pounding away at their respective keyboards. Apart from anything else, Jack had been desperate for a full-time manager who didn't have super sticky fingers around the cash till when his back was turned. There had been a rather nasty showdown with Katie after Jack had caught her "borrowing" two hundred pounds from the restaurant's lunchtime takings.

The job worked perfectly for Chrissie, and it meant Jack could flit between his two other pubs. It was hard work, but she loved it. And she loved Jack even more.

'There's only two conditions,' Jack had said on her first day at The Beagle and Bugle.

'What's that? Chrissie had asked.

'Firstly, you must promise not to drink all my gin and tonic.'

Jack had never let Chrissie forget her "tit bipsy" gaffe when she'd consumed enough G & T to open an off-licence. Chrissie had rolled her eyes. 'Okay, I promise. And what's the second condition?'

'The second condition,' Jack had said, dropping down on one knee, 'is you have to marry your boss.'

***

Amber admired the sparkling diamond on her left hand as she stood outside the school gates waiting for Danny. From the moment she'd met him, Amber had fallen madly in love with the little boy. She would never, even if the moon turned blue, understand how his biological mother had opted to cut herself off. Nonetheless, Amber had silently thanked Nina for giving her this beautiful little boy who looked like an angel and loved her right back. A little while ago Danny had asked, with wide hopeful eyes, if he could call Amber his own special made-up name. He'd explained it was a cross between "Amber" and "Mummy". Would she be his "Ammy"? And Amber had picked him up and hugged him tight, so he didn't see the tears in her eyes.

'Of course I'll be your Ammy,' she'd whispered.

And now, as Amber caught sight of Danny in a sea of happy children that were pouring out of the school building, she couldn't help but smile. His hair was sticking up all over the place, mini rucksack bouncing on his back, as he headed towards the school gate. A wet painting was visible in one of his small hands. He spotted her and his face split into a banana-wide grin as he rushed towards her.

'Look what I did for you, Ammy,' he beamed, thrusting the damp picture at her and flinging his arms around her hips.

As they walked home together, Amber's heart squeezed with joy. Her little boy was holding her hand, and growing inside her was another little boy. She had so much to look forward to, including her forthcoming marriage to Steve. Her fiancé loved to tease her and sing, "Here comes the bride, all fat and wide."

'And who's fault is that?' she'd quipped in mock annoyance.

'Mine,' Steve had said proudly. 'My beautiful bride-to-be is up the duff. I'm over the moon, and love you so much!' And then he'd whisked her off to their giant double bed to prove it.

Amber didn't think she'd ever been so happy.

***

Madam Rosa had a trio of women sitting in the waiting area of her hallway. None of them knew each other, but Madam Rosa knew exactly who they were.

The elegant woman sitting rigidly on the first chair had once been known as Cougar Kate. She'd married a much younger man and, in the beginning, hoped to have his babies. But no babies had been forthcoming, and the fledgling marriage was in deep trouble – as were her finances.

The blonde female slumped on the second chair was called Emma. She was living with a two-timing window-cleaner who had recently started a relationship with a customer. This had come about after the window-cleaner had sloshed soapy water all over the bathroom window of a sultry brunette. She'd been languishing in her foaming bath giving him the come-on. It had been debatable whether it had been the window or the window-cleaner who had been in the greatest lather.

A much older lady with peroxide-blonde hair was weeping silently as she sat on the third chair. Her name was Mandy. She'd stupidly fallen for a toy boy who had pushed both her credit cards and patience to the limit.

All three women wanted to know what the future held. Madam Rosa smiled mysteriously as she cuddled Merlin, her silent black cat. She would tell each of them their future, and she would do it very accurately. Because she was the woman who knew everything.

THE END

The Corner Shop of Whispers

Debbie Viggiano

Chapter One

My husband flung his arms around me. Suddenly I was being whirled round and round the kitchen. I gasped and gave a nervous giggle. There can't be many married couples who engage in a spot of Strictly Come Dancing early on a Tuesday morning in late April. But then again there aren't many married couples like us. Only yesterday my immediate neighbour, Alison, had caught Marcus and me on our doorstep. She'd been hurrying out of Number 3 about to embark on the school run just as I was waving Marcus off to work – or, rather, my husband was kissing me good-bye. Except his cursory brush against the edge of my mouth had swiftly slid to my lips and turned into a lingering kiss which almost immediately had become a full-blown hungry devouring of my mouth.

'Mmm, mmm. Oh, Florrie. Mmm, mmm. I need you. I need you so much. Mmm, mmm. I'll miss the eight oh-seven and catch the eight thirty-two. Mmm, mmm. Get back in the house, Florrie. I can't help it. Mmm, mmm. I simply have to have my wicked way with you and–'

'Oh for goodness sake, Marcus!' Alison's cut-glass accent had sliced through the air instantly putting a stop to things. 'What sort of message are you conveying to Tiffany?'

Marcus had promptly released me. We'd gazed at Alison's bespectacled daughter. Plugged into her iPod, Tiffany had been oblivious of her surroundings. The little girl had been neatly dressed in the uniform of Darwin Prep, the local private school. She was the most hot-housed child we'd ever met. The likelihood that Tiffany had been listening to iTunes was improbable, but there was every chance she'd been absorbing French vocabulary specifically downloaded for her by Alison. My neighbour had given her daughter a little prod in the back.

'Get in the car, Tiffany. Mummy will be with you in two minutes.' She'd turned back to glare at Marcus. 'It's high time you stopped this exhibitionist behaviour on your doorstep every morning. Do you really think the residents of The Cul-de-Sac want to witness borderline soft porn?'

Marcus had smiled at Alison disarmingly. 'There are only three houses in The Cul-de-Sac, Ali. It's hardly the world and his wife watching. Do I detect a touch of jealousy?'

Alison had pursed her lips and given Marcus a frosty look. 'Most certainly not. However, behaving lecherously in a public place is a big no-no. It's beyond uncouth.'

'Uncouth, eh? You don't fool me, Ali,' Marcus had playfully retorted. 'I don't think old Henry is giving you enough attention. C'mon, admit it. We've seen the sweep of your hubby's headlights along The Cul-de-Sac at midnight. What sort of time is that to be coming home from the office? Your Henry is so burnt out from City trading he's not stoking your fire.'

Alison had immediately looked like she'd swallowed a gobstopper. 'My *fire*,' she'd spluttered, 'does not need *stoking*, thank you very much. And if Henry chooses to work long hours, that's his business. At least we know Christmas will be in the Caribbean as usual.'

And with that my neighbour had stuck her nose in the air and stalked off to her brand new four by four. Any onlooker would have been forgiven for thinking Alison, a vision in full make-up and high heels, had been heading off to a smart London office instead of simply keeping up with all the other high-maintenance mothers and their spoilt offspring at the gates of Darwin Prep.

At that precise moment, Daisy, our other immediate neighbour at Number 1, had opened the door to her house. Husband Tom had stepped out, three children scampering around his legs. The kids had been wearing mismatched overcoats suitable for St Mildred's Primary, the local school where Tom was headmaster. The children had also been arguing furiously. Tom had looked both henpecked and harassed as he shepherded his clamouring brood over to the family vehicle.

'Morning, Florrie. Morning, Marcus,' he'd called over his shoulder. 'I saw you both through the window, by the way. Nice to see romance is alive and kicking, even if it is at Number 2, and not my house.'

'I heard that,' Daisy had called after her husband. She'd scowled at Tom's back. 'I'm ready, willing and available – just as long as it's before nine in the evening.' She'd shrugged and turned to Marcus and me. 'After that I'm out cold. The kids are exhausting.'

Tom had shut the car's rear door on the still noisy children. Walking back to Daisy, he'd plonked a dutiful kiss on her cheek. 'I have a pile of pastoral work to catch up on with the vicar this evening. I'll grab a sandwich while I'm out, so don't wait up.'

Daisy had given an exaggerated sigh. 'Story of my life,' she'd grumbled. 'No rumpy-pumpy for me this evening.'

'When are you ever awake for rumpy-pumpy?' Tom had countered.

'I'm awake now, aren't I?' Daisy had said belligerently. With her bed-head hair and crumpled pyjamas splattered with that morning's egg and baked beans, it was fair to say she hadn't looked her most alluring.

'You two should have a date night with each other,' I'd suggested.

'Ah, but you don't have children,' Tom had sighed. His expression had been one of long-suffering. 'They change your life. Wear you down. Pretty much wear you out too. I can't remember the last time Daisy and I managed to eat a meal peacefully together without one of the kids emitting a blood-curdling scream and all hell breaking out.'

'Take no notice of him,' Daisy had added hastily. She was fully up to date on my many attempts to get pregnant. And the many failures too.

'All I'm saying,' Tom had sighed, 'is that the days of being a loved-up couple like Florrie and Marcus here are a thing of the past for us.' He'd turned back to us with a deprecatory shrug. 'I take my hat off to you both. Honestly. I don't know any husbands and wives who have been married for five years still enjoying the honeymoon period.'

He'd given a warm smile and for a moment his whole face had transformed. He was actually a very good looking guy. Seconds later he'd morphed back into put-upon Tom complete with drooping mouth and matching posture.

'Forgive me for holding you both up. I must get the children to school and then,' he'd perked up slightly, 'have a coffee in the staff room for ten minutes. It's the one place where there is peace, quiet, and grown-up conversation.'

He'd inclined his head by way of farewell and, like a man going off to his execution, opened the driver's door. The Cul-de-Sac had briefly been filled with the din of still arguing children before Tom had pulled the door shut after him. From behind the steering wheel he'd raised a tired arm by way of farewell. Moments later he'd driven off in a cloud of exhaust.

Daisy had turned to us and suddenly given a cheerful grin. 'Hurrah! Peace until I collect the mini mob at half past three. I'm going to put the kettle on and watch a bit of Jeremy Kyle. Fancy joining me, Florrie?'

'Are you trying to persuade my perfect wife to be a lazy good-for-nothing woman?' Marcus had teased.

'Excuse me?' Daisy had instantly bristled. 'The moment Jeremy has finished telling some poor cow that the father of her unborn child is an unfaithful lying bastard, I'll be off the sofa and cleaning this house from top to bottom. I shall then tackle an overflowing laundry bin, work my way through a mountain of ironing, and finally head off to the supermarket for a mammoth shop that will leave my arms like stretched spaghetti for the rest of the week. My days are full to bursting, Marcus. Make no mistake about it.'

'I'll consider myself told off,' Marcus had said graciously.

'And *I'm* busy too,' I'd reminded Marcus.

Despite not having a litter of kids making demands upon my time, I did have a huge canvas awaiting my attention in the loft room. Whilst I'd yet to strike it big and be represented by an art gallery, nonetheless I'd recently started to make a decent living producing colourful works for a local restaurant.

But all of that had happened yesterday. Sometimes things can change dramatically in the space of just twenty-four hours, which Marcus and I discovered on this particular Tuesday morning resulting in him dancing me around our kitchen. You see, after five barren years of marriage, I was pregnant. We gazed again at the double blue lines on the pregnancy tester before my husband squashed me into another hug.

'I can't believe it,' he murmured into my hair. 'It's nothing short of a miracle.'

Suddenly I couldn't think of anything to say. Already the enormity of the situation was starting to make itself felt. My heart quickened. Anxiety? *No, Florrie*, I told myself, *just shock*. Mentally, I took a deep breath. It would be fine. Everything would be fine. To the outsider my life was perfect. Enviably so. I lived in a desirable house in The Cul-de-Sac in the popular village of Lower Amblegate. I had fab neighbours and was married to a respectable man who was earning nicely thank you very much as a property surveyor. A little baby was the icing on the marital cake. I was the luckiest woman in the world. Wasn't I?

Chapter Two

I spent the next couple of hours brushing oils onto a vast rectangular canvas. But as colour and form grew, my mind continuously wandered elsewhere. My brain was whirling. Thoughts of babies, conception, the gestation period, trying to work out exactly how pregnant I was, all kept tumbling over and over like an old-fashioned video tape stuck on a loop. This pregnancy was indeed a miracle. As soon as we'd shaken the confetti from our hair, Marcus had wanted to get down to the business of starting a family.

'I want us to have ten children,' he'd grinned. 'Five boys and five girls.'

I'd laughed and suggested we let Mother Nature take her course and that two children would be perfect. As twenty-five-year-olds we had no real qualms about money. We both did the daily commute to London. Marcus had an escalating salary, and I was a stressed PA. Together, we earned good money. Not long after becoming engaged, we'd driven through Lower Amblegate and spotted The Cul-de-Sac. Investigating, we'd noted the For Sale board outside Number 2. We'd wasted no time making an appointment to view. Walking through the front door, we'd fallen in love with the larger than average rooms and huge windows letting in streams of lemony sunbeams. We'd felt as though the house had embraced us. Even the branches of the fruit trees dotted around the paddock-like garden had seemingly wrapped their leafy boughs around our shoulders, hugging us, urging us to stay. In the misty recesses of my mind I saw a little boy hanging off a tyre that swung from one of the sturdy branches, while a little girl played tea parties with her dollies in a home-made treehouse.

Buying it was, admittedly, a bit of a push. You don't see many twenty-five-year-olds starting out in a four-bedroomed detached, but we opted for living on baked beans and toast in order to get the deposit monies together. It was more than a dream home. It was our dream *family* home. A year after moving in, the initial room we'd set aside as a nursery remained empty. Eventually I'd mentioned my pregnancy concerns to my doctor during a routine smear test.

'You're young and a busy working lady,' he'd smiled reassuringly. 'I suspect you're living life in the fast lane, skipping meals and staying late at the office.' The doctor had been more precise than Mystic Meg. 'It's time to slow down. Make some changes. Eat properly – no missing breakfast. Take your lunch hour in full and go *out* of the office. Stretch those legs. Do some walking and fill those lungs with gallons of fresh air.' The "fresh air" bit hadn't been quite so accurate. At the time I'd been working near Fleet Street. The air had always been thick with the diesel fumes of a hundred buses and honking black cabs, while a haze of exhaust belched from scores of immobile cars stuck in congested lanes. In fact, the pollution was so bad that one of my colleagues regularly used to have an asthma attack on the walk to Blackfriars Station. But I didn't tell my doctor all that. Instead I hoovered up his words of hope. 'Some women simply need to prepare their bodies for pregnancy. I would bet my stethoscope that you're simply one of them.'

After two years I went back to the same doctor, who also summoned Marcus for examination. That's when the tests began. Apparently I had lazy ovaries causing an irregular menstrual cycle. This made it tricky to plot the most fertile time of the

301

month. But, even trickier, Marcus's tests revealed a very low sperm count. There were no obvious reasons as to why. It was just one of those things.

'Try not to worry about it,' the doctor had said kindly. 'I've had many a man in my surgery with the same problem. They've all gone on to become fathers. I'm sure it will happen for both of you. One day. Meanwhile, try not to stress about it. Stress makes things much worse and, indeed, could even be the cause.'

Marcus immediately suggested I give up work. Certainly my job was full-on and incredibly demanding, but initially I'd been reluctant to walk away from my work. It wasn't simply a case of saying good-bye to the rat race; it meant saying good-bye to a lot of friends. No more gossip about who the married senior partner had secretly snogged at the Christmas party. No more jostling into the tiny rest room with the girls on a Friday night, fighting over the dingy mirror as we excitedly re-applied lipstick before setting off for an end-of-week drink at the hip local wine bar. But even more crucially, no more enjoyment of financial independence. Marcus, however, had been adamant.

'I'm earning enough now to cover the mortgage and bills. Give up the commute, Florrie. I want you to relax at home. If you're worried about being bored, take up a new hobby. Maybe knitting.' He'd looked pleased at that idea. 'Perhaps if you get those needles clicking away and churn out a few of those old-fashioned matinee jackets, it will get your body in homemaker mode. A baby is bound to follow.'

Within a month I'd gone on to fully bond with Daisy and Alison, my immediate stay-at-home neighbours. Alison, despite being a roaring snob, was a good sort with her heart in the right place.

Daisy, Alison's complete antithesis, was scruffy and scatty but equally lovely. However, even their welcome friendship couldn't stop the moments of downright monotony. My neighbours had children to keep them busy, and their social lives flourished through the school mum network. It didn't matter how many times I was invited to join their respective coffee mornings with other school mums, my face didn't fit. I didn't have the right badge you see. I wasn't a parent. The only time I felt truly able to be myself with Alison and Daisy was when there weren't any other school mums around.

As for the home-making attempts, my foray into the world of matinee jackets had produced a single garment with so many holes from dropped stitches it had looked more like a dwarf's string vest. And there is only so long one can make a house gleam before feeling utterly fed up. I'd always played with paint and charcoal, producing sketches and colourful canvases. With so much time on my hands I'd returned to my old passion, tinkering about with oils and water colours under the rafters of the loft room which had been turned into a working studio. Occasionally, through word of mouth, I'd sell a painting which would leave me glowing for weeks.

Another year went by. We had a few attempts at IVF with no success. It was at this point I realised Marcus wasn't happy. Outwardly he was the same. Jovial. Cheerful. Caring. Loving. But inwardly it was another story. Privately I suspected he was wrestling with turmoil that his inability to father a child was making him feel emasculated. This was confirmed when, about three months ago, I'd received a surprise letter in the post.

The letter had been addressed just to me in bold flowing handwriting. I'd stood in my immaculate kitchen surveying the envelope, wondering who it was from. The writing wasn't familiar. Eventually I'd tugged at the seal. And instantly recoiled in shock.

The written contents had never been discussed with anybody. Not Marcus, nor my parents, and most certainly not my dearest friends, Alison and Daisy. Nobody. I suppose my reasoning was that if I didn't discuss the letter, it didn't exist. No doubt some clever counsellor with umpteen certificates on their study walls would declare such a tactic to be a coping mechanism. And perhaps they'd be right. I still had the letter. It was hidden in a shoebox, tucked away in the depths of my wardrobe. Sometimes I'd forage within the wardrobe and withdraw the note, studying the style of writing, trying to analyse the character of the author, looking for clues as to who had put pen to paper. But then I'd hide it away again and try and forget all about it.

I put down my paintbrush, suddenly drawn to read the letter again, even though I knew what it said word for word. It was at that precise moment my mobile chirruped the arrival of a text. It was from Daisy.

Fancy a coffee?

I sighed. I was pleased her text had distracted me from digging out the letter. However, much as I loved Daisy, I knew I really should crack on with the current work in progress. The local Italian restaurant had already bought paintings off me and were after yet another. I stared at my easel, observing the riot of colour before me. It was coming together, but nonetheless not complete. I dithered. If I ignored Daisy's text, she'd take to the doorbell. If I stalled for time and asked for two hours' grace she'd only be chasing me later this afternoon. Wiping a blob of Prussian blue from my iPhone, I decided to reply. After all, I had amazing news to share. In fact, most newly pregnant women in my shoes would by now have employed a town crier to scream out an announcement. "O'yez! Gather round and know that Florence Milligan's ovaries have finally popped an egg and partied with a single exhausted sperm. God bless the fruit of Marcus Milligan's loins." I wasn't exactly behaving in a euphoric manner, was I? I began to tap the mobile screen with a paint-stained index finger.

Sounds good. As it happens, I have something wonderful to tell you!

Daisy's response was immediate.

In that case, I'll see if Alison is available too. We can't exclude her or neither of us will ever hear the end of it.

I mentally nodded. Too true.

Sure. I'll be over in a jiffy. Just give me a few moments to clean up.

I was just locking the front door when Alison emerged from Number 3. Her expensive perfume wafted on a little gust of spring air invading my senses. I sniffed appreciatively. It was a familiar smell, quite masculine with its musky overtones, although I couldn't place it, or remember where I'd smelt it before.

'Not bogged down with PTA meetings this morning then?' I grinned.

Alison shuddered dramatically, but we both knew she loved being involved with fund raising. No day was complete for Alison without sucking up to the School Governors at Darwin Prep. There wasn't a cake sale or a second-hand-uniform jamboree that Alison wasn't behind.

'There is a PTA meeting but thankfully much later this afternoon.' We stepped over the strips of grass separating the three houses she, Daisy and I lived in. 'However, I can't stay too long for coffee at

Daisy's.' She placed a perfectly manicured nail over the doorbell and gave it a couple of sharp rings. 'I have to go to Harriet Montgomery's place in an hour or so. We're finalising the arrangements for the May Ball. It's also going to provide some fund-raising for Darwin Prep. With only a week to go there's still lots to do. Harriet absolutely insisted I was involved from the start. You know Harriet, don't you?'

Alison knew perfectly well I didn't personally know Harriet, but everybody in Lower Amblegate knew who Harriet Montgomery was. A beautiful ex-movie star, she'd dominated the big screen for ten years before dramatically announcing she was getting hitched and "taking a rest". Harriet Montgomery had gone on to marry famous business tycoon Martin Murray-Wells who was old enough to be her grandfather. As Daisy had sardonically said, "It must be love." They'd managed to produce one daughter, Piper, who also went to Darwin Prep. It went without saying that Alison was very keen for little Tiffany to be Piper's bestie. Meanwhile Alison was doing sterling work cosying up to Harriet at every given opportunity.

Daisy answered the door, eyes shining. She had managed to brush her hair since I'd last seen her but was still wearing the crumpled pyjamas covered in egg yolk and baked bean sauce. Alison clocked the grubby nightwear with distaste, but arched an eyebrow at Daisy's evident happiness.

'Why are you looking so perky?'

Together we stepped over the threshold into Daisy's hallway.

'Because I've just watched the best bit of breakfast telly ever!' Daisy clapped her hands together. 'There was this gorgeous bouncer pinning down this mouthy woman who was trying to knock seven bells out of this really chavvy female, and they were arguing over this ancient bloke. I mean, *really* ancient. He had to be at least fifty.'

Alison looked affronted. 'Can I remind you, Daisy, that Henry is fifty. He is *not*, as you so eloquently put it, *ancient.*'

'Oh, yeah,' Daisy flapped a hand dismissively, 'I forgot you like oldies. Still, at least Henry isn't as ancient as your mate's hubby.' Daisy nodded at the hall window. We followed her gaze and looked into the distance at a huge mansion perched high on a hill and overlooking the North Downs. It was Harriet Montgomery's pile. Alison didn't know whether to be peeved at Daisy's insult of being attracted to old men, or flattered that Daisy thought Alison and Harriet were "mates". Alison's ego got the better of her and the latter comment won.

'Harriet's hubby is delightful,' she cooed. 'Naturally I've met Martin several times. Martin is an absolute sweetheart.'

'Good to know.' Daisy shrugged as we followed her into the lounge. 'I still wouldn't want to bonk him though.'

'I personally think Martin is extremely debonair,' Alison said defensively as we carefully negotiated the floor. It was covered in discarded toys, colouring pads and breakfast detritus.

'Someone's got mentionitis,' said Daisy. 'You've just said "Martin" three times in as many seconds.'

Alison ignored the dig and carried on talking.

'I was just telling Florrie, I'm helping Harriet put the finishing touches to the village May Ball. It's a fundraising affair obviously. I fully expect you both to attend, even if you have to drag your husbands along kicking and screaming.'

'I'm not sure I want to rub shoulders with all your toffee-nosed friends,' Daisy grumbled.

'They are perfectly normal people,' said Alison irritably as she flopped down onto a sofa, 'and

307

anyway, it's not just the Darwin Prep parents who will be there. Everyone in Lower Amblegate is invited.'

I sat down next to her, narrowly avoiding stepping on some congealed plates. Alison stared at them distastefully.

'You allow your children to eat on the floor?'

'Of course,' said Daisy. She gave Alison a strange look. 'It's near the telly.'

Alison looked appalled. 'Don't you *ever* sit up at the dining table as a family and make intelligent conversation about how to resolve world peace or debate whether Donald Trump will be a good president for America?'

'What the heck would we want to do that for?' Daisy asked in bewilderment. 'I'd miss Jeremy Kyle or Coronation Street.'

Alison's brow furrowed. 'But if you don't ever sit around a dining table, where do you entertain?'

'Entertain?' Now it was Daisy's turn to frown.

'Yes! As in hosting a soirée.'

'A what?'

Alison rolled her eyes. 'A dinner party, Daisy.'

'Ah,' Daisy looked enlightened. 'Where you're sitting, Ali. There's nothing like fish and chips out of newspaper on your lap.'

Alison looked stunned. The day she offered the likes of Harriet Montgomery a take-out whilst sitting on a sofa or floor would be the day Hugh Heffner became a monk.

Daisy cleared her throat. 'Now then, ladies, coffee or tea?'

'I'll have coffee, please,' I said to Daisy.

'Do you have any Earl Grey?' asked Alison.

Daisy placed her hands on her hips. 'Honestly, Ali, I do wish you'd drop the airs and graces. You're not at Mrs La-de-da's house now. You're at mine, complete with chaos and mess. You'll have the

308

supermarket special and love it.'

Alison looked pained. 'Well at least give me a porcelain cup and saucer rather than a cracked workman's mug.'

Daisy tutted, and stomped off. From out in the kitchen we could hear her huffing and puffing as she searched through cupboards for the elusive china. Five minutes later she returned with a tray bearing steaming drinks and a plate of biscuits.

'Have you thought about getting a cleaner?' Alison asked.

Daisy bit into a chocolate biscuit. 'Why would I want one of those?' she asked, dropping crumbs everywhere.

'To make this place ship-shape of course,' said Alison in exasperation. 'You have such a lovely house, Daisy, but inside it looks like it belongs to Mr and Mrs Slob. Doesn't Tom ever get annoyed?'

'Sure. But I just tell him I've done the housework and the kids simply messed it all up again.'

'Doesn't he ever suss that you only do the minimum?'

'Nah,' Daisy shrugged and took another bite from the biscuit. 'I just squirt a bit of furniture polish in the air before he comes home and he says, "Wow, I can tell you've been working your socks off today." That's when he's home, anyway. After school, he's catching up on pastoral chit-chat with the vicar. These days he seems to be perpetually busy.'

Alison nodded. 'Your husband too, eh?' She rattled her cup into the saucer making Daisy and I jump slightly.

'I don't mind,' Daisy said helping herself to another chocolate biscuit. 'At least it gets me off the hook in the bedroom.'

'Don't you like,' Alison paused, '*sex*?' She mouthed the last word.

'Yeah,' Daisy nodded. 'Well, I did.' She chomped away, thoughtful for a moment. 'I guess it's just all a bit predictable though. And boring. Do I really want a late-night grapple which no longer makes the earth move for me? Especially when I've just washed the sheets. It just makes another job. I guess, like housework, sex for me is a chore.' She grinned, revealing a chocolate crumb lodged between her front teeth. 'We can't all be like our Florrie here. What's it like still fancying the pants off your hubby and having mad passionate sex morning, noon and night?'

I laughed, but couldn't quite meet Daisy's gaze and took a hasty swig of coffee so I wasn't able to reply.

'Anyway,' Daisy shifted in her chair. A regrouping gesture. She looked at me expectantly. 'What's this fab news you have for us both?'

Alison straightened up, giving me her full attention. 'Fab news?' She turned two wide eyes towards me. For the first time I noticed exactly how wide Alison's eyes actually were. Surely she hadn't had a lift? After all, she was only thirty-seven. I stared at her forehead. It was as smooth as polished marble. That had to be the work of botox. And, good heavens, her mouth was looking incredibly pouty. Was that a touch of filler around the upper lip? 'What fab news?' she repeated.

I blinked and, suddenly shy, gave a tiny smile. 'I'm expecting a baby.'

Daisy immediately stood up and punched the air, slopping coffee down herself in the process. 'Fan-flaming-tastic,' she whooped.

Alison's response was more reserved. 'That's wonderful news, Florrie,' she said quietly. 'I'm very pleased for you.'

I allowed my smile to turn into a full-on grin. Inside I was still quaking somewhat. Still trying to digest it all. But now I'd told my two dearest friends, it was as if an internal light switch had been flicked on so that I immediately began to feel like I was glowing radiantly.

'To be honest, Marcus and I are shell-shocked. But happy,' I added, nodding emphatically as some butterflies took off in my stomach. Nerves. I brushed the feeling away. Surely every expectant mother felt nervous. The fact that expectant mothers were more likely to feel nervous nearer to the time of their due date as opposed to the day of finding out they were pregnant was surely neither here nor there. Everyone was different, I firmly told myself. I looked from Daisy to Alison, and my megawatt smile instantly faded. Alison seemed to be struggling with her emotions. The duck-pout was wobbling alarmingly, and the wide-apart eyes were now swimming with unshed tears. Alarmed, I leant forward and touched her arm. 'Ali? Whatever's the matter?'

'N-nothing,' Alison sniffed. 'E-everything.'

'Eh?' Daisy hunkered down in front of Alison. 'You're not fretting about this chuffing May Ball, are you?' she asked. 'Of course we'll come. Even if I'm so tired that I collapse head first into the asparagus velouté and start snoring. I absolutely promise to be there for you.'

Alison sniffed and dabbed at her eyes. She gave a watery smile. 'Sorry. I'm just a bit out of sorts.'

'Why?' I put an arm around her cashmere-clad shoulder. 'You can tell us, Ali.'

The tears were threatening again. Her face worked. She was clearly wrestling with her emotions, unsure whether to confide in Daisy and me, or not. 'It's Henry,' she eventually said, almost choking on her husband's name.

Daisy and I looked at each other and paled.

'Is something wrong with him, Ali?' Daisy asked.

'I'm sorry I said he was old. He's not old really. Well, not old enough to die anyway.'

Alison gave an imperceptible shake of the head. 'He's not ill.' Foraging up one sleeve, she removed a tissue and noisily blew her nose. 'It's nothing like that.'

'What is it then?' I urged.

She gulped a few times, still not quite sure whether to divest a secret. Taking a deep breath, the need to unburden won.

'Henry's having an affair.'

Chapter Three

For a moment, Daisy and I simply stared at our weeping neighbour. Henry was having an affair? *Henry*? Was this the same Henry who spent his Saturdays taking Tiffany to London trekking around museums or art galleries, and his Sundays dutifully manicuring the lawn and flowerbeds under Alison's watchful eye? Boring Henry? Impossible! Daisy was the first to speak. From her position on the floor at Alison's feet, she leant forward and touched Alison's arm.

'Ali,' she said gently. 'Is there any chance you might be a teensy-weensy bit wrong?'

'I don't think so,' Alison sniffed. She trumpeted into the already overworked tissue.

'So you're not one-hundred percent sure?' I asked hopefully.

'I'm ninety-nine percent sure,' Alison said flatly. There was a moment's silence while we contemplated this. Alison stared blankly at the soggy paper hanky balled up in her hands.

Daisy was the first to speak. 'Sorry, Ali, but I think you're mistaken. After all, let's not beat about the bush. Henry's fifty.'

'What's that supposed to mean?' Alison's voice was suddenly sharp.

'Well, without sounding insulting...' Daisy hesitated, 'surely he's past it.'

Alison's cheeks flushed red. 'What *are* you talking about, Daisy? Are you suggesting that at the end of Henry's forty-ninth year and on the stroke of midnight, he was suddenly struck impotent?' Alison straightened up on the sofa, indignant now. 'Is that what you think? That the moment a male embraces the Big Five-Oh all his teeth fall out, he loses his hair and bits of his body stop working?'

Daisy frowned. 'Well...yeah. I mean Henry's teeth are whiter than Simon Cowell's, so I presumed they were false.'

'Veneers,' Alison snapped. 'Cosmetic dentistry. They cost an absolute fortune.'

Daisy wasn't convinced. 'Well he lost his hair years ago. He's as bald as a snooker ball with a scalp twice as shiny.'

'He shaves his head to be trendy,' Alison hissed.

'I see,' Daisy said. She clearly didn't see at all. She rocked back on her heels and contemplated Alison. 'So are you trying to tell me his willy still works?'

Alison looked affronted. 'Yes, Daisy. It goes up and down. Mostly up. But not for me. Instead he's ga-ga about...'

'Who?' Daisy and I chorused.

'I don't know,' Alison wailed. 'A colleague maybe? He's always home so late.'

'You did say he works hard,' I soothed.

'Not hard enough to achieve full half-year bonus,' Alison's eyes flashed and her mouth disappeared into a tight line. 'Without wishing to go into how much money my husband makes, let's just say that there's always been plenty of the stuff. But suddenly I'm being told to limit my spending. Being asked to use the local hairdresser instead of popping up to Mayfair to see Nicky. Having Tiffany's education compromised with Henry refusing to pay for flute lessons.'

'Well she is already studying clarinet, violin and piano,' I patted Alison's hand.

'Whose side are you on?' she demanded.

'Nobody's!' I assured hastily. 'I'm just thinking of Tiffany trying to fit another instrument into her already busy schedule.' I did sometimes wonder what planet Alison was on when it came to her daughter's education.

314

'And do you know what he said to me this morning?' she gasped and clutched her chest dramatically.

'What?' Daisy and I chorused.

'He told me to stop shopping at Waitrose and to go to,' she gave a little shriek, 'Asda.'

'I go to Asda,' said Daisy indignantly.

'I'm sure it's perfectly all right for people like you, Daisy,' Alison said patronisingly, 'but I really don't want to shop in a store where people are still wearing their pyjamas.'

'Have you been spying on me?' Daisy narrowed her eyes.

Alison tutted. 'I have better things to do with my time than check out your shopping attire, Daisy.'

I giggled and nudged Daisy. 'You've never gone to Asda in your PJs, have you?'

'Only twice,' Daisy sighed. 'The last time I did it the security guard wouldn't let me in the store.'

'And rightly so,' Alison's chin jutted. 'Don't you ever get fed up of lounging around in your nightwear?'

'No,' Daisy shook her head. 'It's comfortable. Why on earth would I want to wear cashmere in the morning when I'm frying eggs and stirring beans?'

'Well if you slice up some fresh melon, strawberries and grapes on a side plate, and give Tom and the children homemade muesli with organic milk, there's absolutely nothing wrong with being swathed in cashmere. I don't wish to be unkind, Daisy, but how on earth do you attract Tom's attention when you always look like you've fallen into a wheelie bin?'

'Ali, I don't wish to be unkind either, but if you don't shut up insulting me in my own house I might punch your lights out.'

Alison glared at Daisy for a moment, but then visibly crumpled. 'Sorry. I'm a bit stressed.'

Daisy, never one to hold a grudge, leant forward and gave our neighbour a hug before sitting down next to her. 'So tell me and Florrie the reasons why you think Henry is having an affair.'

'Well,' Alison shifted in her seat, suddenly uncomfortable. 'We don't...' Daisy and I looked at her expectantly. 'You know.'

Daisy looked mystified. 'What?'

'You know,' Alison repeated, suddenly awkward. Clearly her prissy upbringing was well and truly coming to the fore right now. 'We don't have...*sex*.' She mouthed the last word again. 'Well, hardly ever anyway.'

'Ahh,' said Daisy, the dawn suddenly coming up. 'Because you no longer fancy Henry.'

'Sorry?' Now it was Alison's turn to look confounded.

'Well, he is fifty, isn't he?' Daisy reasoned. 'And you're only thirty-seven. It's quite an age gap. You're probably still revving up in the loins department whereas Henry probably needs Viagra.'

'I've already told you his dangly bit goes up and down. Why would he need Viagra?'

'Oh. Is it you who needs Viagra?'

'For heaven's sake, Daisy. Neither of us need Viagra. And why do you keep going on about Henry's age?' Alison was getting agitated again. 'He's a very sexy man.'

'Is he?' Daisy looked across at me for confirmation.

To be honest, Henry didn't make me swoon. Not remotely. But I couldn't say that to Alison. I nodded at Daisy. 'Mmm. Henry is very...sort of...Kojak,' I nodded.

'Kojak?' Daisy's eyebrows shot upwards. 'You mean the bald guy with the big nose?'

'The very one,' I tried to give Daisy a discreet pleading look for tact. 'Absolute pin-up in his heyday.'

'Exactly,' said Alison smugly. 'Henry is extremely sexy to lots of women. But somebody out there isn't just finding him sexy, they are getting the full works.'

'The works?' Daisy looked blank.

'Yes!' Alison said impatiently. 'Some woman is availing her services to him.'

'Services!' Daisy scoffed. 'Why can't you just talk like me and Florrie and say that some two-faced tart is bonking him.'

'Daisy,' said Alison in a pained voice. 'We've known each other for a few years now. When have you ever heard me use the word...' she paused before mouthing, '*bonk*?'

'Oh stop being so uptight, Ali,' Daisy pooh-poohed our neighbour's rigid desire to behave like a lady at all times. 'It's high time you loosened up and said things how they are – Henry's todger still works and he's waving it around at some female and rogering her senseless.'

Alison gave a little gasp at such frankness, but Daisy ploughed on regardless.

'If you really think this is the case, then you must confront Henry. Preferably when armed with a rolling pin. But not when you have PMT,' Daisy added hastily. 'You don't want to make a mess over the carpet.'

'Daisy, you really aren't helping,' Alison cried in exasperation.

'So to get back on topic,' I prompted. 'Do you have evidence of this suspected affair?'

Alison took a deep breath. 'I think so. Yes.' She closed her eyes for a moment, as if trying to blot out an awful memory. When she opened them again they were far away, clearly recalling something unpleasant. 'I went through Henry's last few credit card statements looking for clues.' She paused,

317

struggling for composure. 'Last Christmas he spent thousands of pounds at a Hatton Garden jeweller. He bought two bracelets. I received one of them.'

'Perhaps he's saving the other bracelet for your birthday,' I suggested.

Alison shook her head. 'No. You see, I rang the jeweller in question. Both bracelets were identical.'

Daisy frowned. 'Why would Henry buy two identical bracelets?'

'I'm coming to that,' Alison's lip wobbled slightly. 'My bracelet had an inscription on the inside. It said, "To dear Alison with love from Henry." I asked the jeweller if the other bracelet had been inscribed with a message. The jeweller confirmed this to be the case. I asked him what the engraving was.' Alison's voice cracked slightly. 'The jeweller went off to check the paperwork.'

Suddenly Daisy and I were holding our breath.

'And?' Daisy prompted. She looked both fascinated and horrified. There had never been a situation like this on the Jeremy Kyle show.

When Alison next spoke her voice was little more than a whimper. 'The inscription on the second bracelet had said, "To the most beautiful woman in the world with all my love."'

The breath whooshed out of Daisy and I in one big chuggy gasp.

'Oh,' we chorused.

'I don't know what to do,' Alison wailed.

We contemplated for a moment. What to do indeed.

'Do you still love Henry?' Daisy asked.

'Of course!' she said looking shocked. 'I have a beautiful house, my daughter is in the best school for miles, and I'm accepted into the homes of people like Harriet Montgomery.'

'That's not love,' I said gently. 'That's a lifestyle.'

'Same thing,' Alison snapped. 'I love my lifestyle.

And I'm not about to have it jeopardised by some little hussy with a nose piercing and a skirt hem up round her ear lobes.'

'Do you know who she is then?' I asked.

'I've a good idea,' Alison's eyes narrowed. 'One of the secretaries was all over him at the Christmas 'do'. A typical cliché of a woman. Peroxide blonde hair. Cheap red lipstick. I could almost see a flashing neon sign over her head saying "I want you to be my Sugar Daddy."'

'I see,' Daisy puffed out her cheeks. 'So do you actually want to stay married to Henry?'

'Of course I want to stay married to Henry,' Alison snapped.

'Well in that case,' Daisy said conspiratorially, 'we're going to have to catch Henry out.' She looked from Alison to me, her eyes shining like they did when she first opened the door to us an hour ago. 'We're going to set a trap.'

To continue reading
The Corner Shop of Whispers
please buy a copy from:
Amazon.co.uk
Amazon.com

ALSO BY DEBBIE VIGGIANO
Stockings and Cellulite

As the clock strikes midnight on New Year's Eve, Cassandra Cherry's life takes a turn for the worse when she stumbles upon husband Stevie lying naked, except for his socks, on a coat-strewn bed with a 45-year-old divorcee called Cynthia. Suddenly single, Cass throws herself into the business of getting over Stevie with gusto. Her main problems now are making her nine-year-old twins happy, juggling a new social life with a return to work and avoiding being arrested by an infuriating policeman who always seems to turn up at the most inopportune moments. Then, just when Cass is least prepared, and much to Stevie's chagrin, she crashes head over heels in love with the last person she'd ever expected.

AVAILABLE NOW AS E-BOOK AND PAPERBACK

ALSO BY DEBBIE VIGGIANO
Flings and Arrows

Steph Garvey has been married to husband Si for twenty-four years. Steph thought they were soulmates. Until recently. Surely one's soulmate shouldn't put Chelsea FC before her? Or boycott caressing her to fondle the remote control? Fed up, Steph uses her Tesco staff discount to buy a laptop. Her friends all talk about Facebook. It's time to get networking.

Si is worried about middle-age spread and money. Being a self-employed plumber isn't easy in recession. He's also aware things aren't right with Steph. But Si has forgotten the art of romance. Although these days Steph prefers cuddling her laptop to him. Then Si's luck changes work wise. A mate invites Si to partner up on a pub refurbishment contract.

Son Tom has finished Sixth Form. Tom knows where he's going regarding a career. He's not quite so sure where he's going regarding women and lurches from one frantic love affair to the next.

Widowed neighbour June adores the Garveys as if her own kin. And although 70, she's still up for romance. June thinks she's struck gold when she meets salsa squeeze Harry. He has a big house and bigger pension – key factors when you've survived a winter using your dog as a hot water bottle. June is vaguely aware that she's attracted the attention of fellow dog walker Arnold, but her eyes are firmly on Harry as "the catch".

But then Cupid's arrow misfires causing madness and mayhem. Steph rekindles a childhood crush with Barry Hastings; Si unwittingly finds himself being seduced by barmaid Dawn; June discovers Harry is more than hot to trot; and Tom's latest strumpet impacts on all of them. Will Cupid's arrow strike again and, more importantly, strike correctly? There's only one way to find out....

AVAILABLE NOW AS E-BOOK AND PAPERBACK

ALSO BY DEBBIE VIGGIANO
Lipstick and Lies

41-year old Cassandra Mackerel is loved up and happily re-married to new husband Jamie. Together they have a ready-made family and a six month old baby boy. Juggling her own children with step-children and an infant is both hectic and stressful, especially with a mother-in-law who seems to have taken up permanent residence.

Cass has a strong support system in good friend and new mum Morag – who is the fourth Mrs Harding with more step-children she can keep up with – and also old neighbour and great pal Nell who has a baby girl.

Rising to the challenge of a second marriage and the emotional baggage that comes with it is tough. The last thing Cass needs is the reappearance of husband Jamie's ex-girlfriend Selina. Gorgeous and glamorous but utterly unstable, Selina once stalked Cass and contrived to split her and Jamie up. And now Selina is engaged to Jamie's business partner, Ethan Fareham. Seemingly it is appalling coincidence.

Cass can't shake the feeling that Selina is up to her old tricks. And she's right to be worried. For if Selina has her way, she'll split Cass and Jamie up permanently. Because this time it's murder...

AVAILABLE NOW AS EBOOK AND PAPERBACK

ALSO BY DEBBIE VIGGIANO
Mixed Emotions

Life is a funny old thing. There are times when we love it, relish every moment and can't get enough of it. Equally there are other times when life is jail sentence. Something comes along that knocks us right off our feet. The sun ceases to shine and our smiles vanish.

As we walk through life we fall in love, out of love, and in love again - sometimes many times over. We forge long and rewarding friendships - but sometimes are betrayed. We deal with tricky ex partners, and picky neighbours. We get pregnant, give birth and some of us experience stillbirth. And just when we think we can't take any more, something happens to cause our hearts to expand with love. We are left feeling warm and fuzzy inside.

Life is full of mixed emotions. And that's what this little book is about.

AVAILABLE NOW AS AN EBOOK AND PAPERBACK.

**WARNING – CHANGE OF GENRE.
DIVORCE DRAMA. CONTAINS SWEARING
AND UPSET.**

Sam Worthington is married to Annie. He's also a loving, hands-on dad to daughter Ruby. Then Sam discovers Annie is having an affair. Even worse, she wants a divorce. Devastated, Sam has to cope not just with the dismantling of a marriage, but being parted from the daughter he adores.

When Annie's new relationship breaks down, she wants Sam back. But Sam has now met teaching student Josie, and re-discovered love. Annie hatches a plan to seduce Sam and win him back, but her plan fails. Sam hadn't counted on his rejection of Annie backfiring on him so spectacularly – for Annie vows to use Ruby to destroy her ex-husband.

Hell hath no fury like a woman scorned. And for Sam Worthington, his journey to hell is just beginning...

**AVAILABLE NOW AS AN EBOOK AND
PAPERBACK.**

ALSO BY DEBBIE VIGGIANO
The Perfect Marriage

Rosie Perfect is trapped in a loveless marriage to feckless husband Dave. Unlike her surname, the marriage is far from perfect but, as she's also mum to baby Luke, leaving isn't an easy option. When best friend Lucy announces she's getting married and having a hen night, Rosie relishes a night off from drudgery. Waking up the following morning in businessman Matt Palmer's bed wasn't on the agenda. But Matt is no marriage wrecker. Or is he?

Suddenly Rosie's life is turned upside down...from not recalling what took place between Matt Palmer's silk sheets to discovering her drunken husband is also a gambling addict...from having her home wagered away in a poker game to being pursued by a murderous loan shark. As Rosie lurches from one crisis to another, life is far from perfect. Indeed, will Rosie Perfect ever get her perfect happy-ever-after?

AVAILABLE NOW AS AN EBOOK AND PAPERBACK.

ALSO BY DEBBIE VIGGIANO
Secrets

Janey Richardson thought she had it all – the perfect job, a drop-dead gorgeous boyfriend, a cutesy cottage love nest, and a socking great diamond on her left hand. But things aren't always as they seem, as Janey is about to discover when an unexpected stranger turns up exposing a secret that shatters her world. There's only one thing for it. She's going to have to disappear.

Garth Davis thought he had it all too, until a secret is revealed that turns his world upside down. He is left with one burning question, but he's going to have to take a five-thousand-mile journey to find the answer.

When Janey's and Garth's worlds collide, a thaw takes place in Janey's heart. But is Garth 'The One'? Making the right decision isn't easy, especially when Janey's own past rushes back to meet her.

AVAILABLE NOW AS AN EBOOK AND PAPERBACK.

ABOUT THE AUTHOR

Prior to turning her attention to writing, Debbie Viggiano was, for more years than she cares to remember, a legal secretary. She lives with her Italian husband, a rescued puppy from Crete, and a very disgruntled cat. Occasionally her children return home from uni bringing her much joy - apart from their gifts of dirty laundry.

Tweet @DebbieViggiano or look her up on Facebook

www.debbieviggiano.com
http://debbieviggiano.blogspot.com/

\###

Printed in Great Britain
by Amazon

58219902R00190